Praise for the novels of *New York Times* bestselling author Heather Graham

"Murder, intrigue, and some hot-and-heavy magnetism between Quinn and Cafferty make for a fast-paced read. You may never know in advance what harrowing situations Graham will place her characters in, but...rest assured that the end result will be satisfying."
—*Suspense* magazine on *Let the Dead Sleep*

"Graham does an amazing job of bringing real-life elements into her fiction worlds... [The] messages are subtle, expertly woven through a story that focuses on solving mysterious crimes using the Krewe members' unique talents. Graham also brings the surrounding areas of Nashville alive, with vivid details and lush descriptions— so authentic you can practically see history happening."
—*RT Book Reviews* on *The Night Is Forever* (Top Pick)

"Bestseller Graham launches the third arc in her paranormal romantic suspense Krewe of Hunters series (*The Unseen,* etc.) with a rousing tale of the intriguing haunted town of Lily, Arizona.... Readers will enjoy Sloan and Jane's interactions as romantic partners and competent professionals, aided by Lily's ghosts."
—*Publishers Weekly* on *The Night Is Watching*

"Graham deftly weaves elements of mystery, the paranormal and romance into a tight plot that will keep the reader guessing at the true nature of the killer's evil."
—*Publishers Weekly* on *The Unseen*

"I've long admired Heather Graham's storytelling ability and this book hit the mark. I couldn't put *The Unholy* down."
—*Fresh Fiction*

"The very prolific and best-selling Graham has crafted a fine paranormal romance with a strong mystery plot and a vibrant setting."
—*Booklist* on *Haunted*

"The paranormal elements are integral to the unrelentingly suspenseful plot, the characters are likable, the romance convincing."
—*Booklist* on *Ghost Walk*

Also by Heather Graham

Look for Heather Graham's next novel

AND THE DEAD PLAY ON

available soon from Harlequin MIRA

HEATHER GRAHAM

THE
BETRAYED

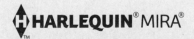
HARLEQUIN® MIRA®

ISBN-13: 978-1-62953-174-8

THE BETRAYED

Printed in U.S.A.

For Washington Irving

I wish I could have known him!

And to the beautiful state of New York.

To Al, Mystery Mike and all those at

Bouchercon, 2013.

To Connie Perry and Shayne Pozzessere

for a wonderful trip into the shadows

and forests of the Hollow and the mind—Irving's cottage,

the church, the cemetery...and

all those places where wonder

exists and the imagination can fly.

Prologue

"They got me, my old friend. They got me."

Aidan Mahoney woke with a start.

His room was dark; instinct made him reach for the Glock at his bedside and then remain dead still.

Listening.

He'd heard the words as clearly as if they'd been spoken directly in front of him. And when he'd first opened his eyes, he could have sworn that there'd been a form—the form of a man. A man beseeching him—for help. Tall, nicely dressed in a suit, leaning toward him.

But he'd blinked.

And now...

Now there was no one.

He tensed, searching the darkness, listening carefully. He heard the hum of the heater, the noise of a car in the street below and, distantly, the blaring of a horn.

Nothing else. The usual sounds of New York City at night.

But something teased at the back of his mind. Something he should have realized, something he should have recognized about that whisper. His eyes adjusted to the shadows. No, there was nothing in his room. No one stood by his bed. He glanced to the side, but he knew he'd slept alone the night before. He occasionally brought a woman home, but there hadn't been anyone regular in his life since his crush on Tina Hastings in high school and his passionate college romance with Kathy Flanders.

The passion had lasted until college ended—and cooled almost overnight when their career choices clashed and Kathy had gone on to study anthropology in Cambodia.

Even then, he'd been the one to keep his distance. Sometimes it was just best to be alone and to fight your own demons.

And right now he was definitely alone.

But hc'd heard the voice.

He'd seen *something*.

Cautiously, he crawled out of bed. He kept the light off and made a quick but thorough search of his immediate space, checking next to the dresser, quietly opening the closet.

From there, he left his room just as quietly. Nothing in the hallway. He kept moving, wearing only his boxers, inspecting the apartment's second bedroom—his office—the kitchen, living room and dining area. No sign of anyone. Anywhere. He'd dreamed the words. He must have.

From down below, he heard the angry squeal of a cat; a garbage can was knocked over. A lot of street noise came into the apartment, since he was on the third floor of an old brownstone in the Village. But the voice he'd heard hadn't come from the street.

He groaned aloud, setting his Glock on the kitchen counter and opening the refrigerator door, letting the cool air wash over him. He was always wary; training in various military and law enforcement branches had caused that. But he wasn't paranoid. There was no one in his apartment and he was sure of that now.

But, to his mind, the alternative was almost worse. He'd *known* the voice. But he couldn't quite place it. *They got me, my old friend. They got me.*

Aidan glanced at the clock over the fireplace. The time was creeping toward 5:30 a.m. What the hell? He might as well stay awake, shower, get dressed, then head on in to work.

He put coffee on to brew while he got ready, but checked the locks on his door before he went to shower. By 5:35 he was dressed and pouring a cup of coffee. With his gun in its small holster he went to the door to get his newspaper. He still liked reading the *Times* in its old-fashioned form.

When he picked up the rolled bundle, he saw the headline: Highsmith Missing!

It suddenly seemed that his blood really did run cold—a physical impossibility, of course, but for a moment he felt frozen in place. He felt a distinct chill coursing through his body.

Then his phone rang.

And, of course, he knew that call presaged a hell of a day. Just as he now realized that the voice he'd heard had been that of Richard Highsmith.

"Mahoney," he answered, aware of how terse he sounded.

From the caller ID he'd seen that it was his new unit chief, Jackson Crow. He liked Crow, all right, and working for him wasn't going to be a problem. But...

He'd known Richard since they were kids. Once,

they'd been great friends. But time went by, people got older. Life and work intruded. Obligations kept old friends from being together, kicking a ball around or playing video games, but that didn't change the fact that a few hours grabbed for a football game or a quick dinner wasn't damned good. And yet even those occasions became less and less frequent.

Richard was missing.

This was going to be about Richard.

A phone call from Crow was new for Aidan. He'd been working as an FBI field agent out of the largest office in the country, the New York City office—for the past ten years. He'd worked briefly with Crow on a case that had included the D.C. offices. Then they'd gone in different directions. Now, Crow was heading up a special unit—and that unit was opening new offices in NYC.

Aidan hadn't asked to transfer to the new unit. He hadn't *wanted* it. And when he'd received a call from the director of the bureau, he'd known he could refuse the transfer. If he did, however, his career with the agency might well be at stake.

But this call? He was almost certain it would be about Richard. He wanted to work Richard's case; he desperately wanted to find his old friend. And find him *alive.*

He was afraid he wouldn't.

And he still wasn't sure about the new coworkers he'd wind up with on the case.

Aidan reassured himself that they'd be fine. He'd been afraid they'd be a bunch of freaks bearing crystal balls. The truth couldn't have been more different. The new offices in a small Federal building just down the street—closer to St. Paul's and Trinity—was state-of-the-art. Five seasoned Krewe members had been sent to help with the setup.

They certainly *seemed* normal. They'd read all the books, gone through all the rigors of training. They'd passed the academy classes. Everyone he'd met seemed bright, efficient, competent. *Nice.* He'd liked them all.

But they had a reputation for being called in on the weird cases. And *weird* was an area he'd rather avoid.

The new base for the NYC Krewe unit had only recently come into existence. Before Aidan had seen the paper today—*heard the voice!*—he hadn't expected to be in the field anytime soon. He'd been told by his old superior that Jackson Crow had been watching him, noting his methods and his work, and had specifically asked that Aidan be brought in when the Krewe's New York office was formed.

Aidan was still getting to know his new unit, accepting that he was part of it.

"We've got some serious trouble," Crow said.

Yeah, Aidan thought. *Richard's dead.* But he didn't speak.

"The New York office got a call from the sheriff up in Westchester County," Crow said. "The director called me—since you're part of the Krewe now. You're the man he wants. I understand you're from the area. Plus, he'd like to cover all the bases—the usual aspects of an investigation into a disappearance like this...and, shall we say, the *unusual* ones." There was a brief silence. "This one could be described as unusual in that Richard Highsmith apparently disappeared into thin air. He was in Tarrytown for a fund-raiser yesterday. He disappeared around dusk. He was there—at the center where he was scheduled to speak—and then he wasn't. He still hasn't made an appearance and his staff is worried sick."

"The locals are on it?"

"They've been on it. They did a lockdown at the center for several hours. They questioned everyone there before letting anyone go. His car was in the lot, and there was security all around." Crow was quiet for a moment. "If he was your average Joe, they wouldn't even have a Missing Persons report on him yet, but..."

"But it's Richard," Aidan said quietly. He probably should have told Crow right then that Richard Highsmith was more than a rising politician to him. The reason he didn't was that he wanted the assignment.

He chose not to mention that he knew Richard well. He wasn't a hundred percent sure about his new position with the agency, but he knew one thing. He was *not* going to be pulled off this case, and while he didn't want to be dishonest, he wasn't going to tell his new supervisor about his friendship with the missing man—yet.

"Yes. And it's hitting the news this morning," Crow said. "Tarrytown's about an hour away from here—"

"Less," Aidan told him. At this time of morning? Hell, yeah, he could get there fast.

"Then go. I'll call your cell with any particulars we have. By this evening, I'll have a few more agents assigned."

"Consider me gone." Aidan hung up, drained his coffee and started for the door.

They got me, my old friend. They got me.

He was going to find Richard Highsmith.
And the saddest thing of all...
Aidan knew he was going to find him dead.

1

It was a horrific sight.

And, bizarrely enough, one that might be missed, at least in Sleepy Hollow. Here, and in the surrounding villages and towns, images and effigies of headless horsemen were common.

A pole had been stuck into a man's likeness created from wood and stuffing and plaster and cotton— a likeness that ended at the neckline. Right where the Revolutionary-era jacket and shirt left off.

And Richard Highsmith's severed head had been stuck onto the pole.

It was bloody, and the midlength, salt-and-pepper hair was matted and dark. The face might once have held character and dignity.

Maureen Deauville stood with her enormous wolfhound, Rollo, and stared at it. For a moment, she felt as if she'd been teleported back to medieval times. The breeze rustled through the trees and the sounds of traffic from the road seemed to fade. She might have been standing in distant woods, viewing the results of a gruesome execution carried out by some long-ago government.

In reality, she was on the street that bordered a cemetery to the west. There were houses here—some very old, some not so old—and a few businesses, including Tommy Jensen's Headless Horseman Hideaway Restaurant and Bar. His effigy of the headless horseman, a good seven or so feet high, lurked on the roadside to attract clientele.

And it had been used to display the head.

The parking lot was filled with cars, mainly cop cars. It was barely 7:00 a.m. At least seven uniformed officers were there, ready to handle crowd control and keep the few cars on the street moving along. A crime scene unit van had just arrived and jerked to a halt, followed seconds later by the ambulance from the morgue.

They'd begun the search for the missing man that morning, just half an hour earlier.

"You've done it. You and Rollo have done your jobs," Lieutenant Purbeck said with a sigh. "Not what we expected to find, or hoped to find, but…" He paused. "But that's *part* of Richard Highsmith, anyway."

The blood was congealing. It had dripped over the crisp collar and seeped onto the shoulders of the white cotton shirt and blue jacket on the should-have-been-headless mannequin. The eyes were open in death, and crows and blackbirds lurked, waiting to attack. Even as Maureen stared up at the atrocity before her, a crow zeroed in, aiming for the soft tissue.

"We've got to get that down!" One of the cops, a young man, new to the force—Bobby Magill, Maureen thought—groaned, sounding ill.

"Anyone who's going to puke, get the hell away from the crime scene! Let's get it covered!" Lieutenant Purbeck shouted.

At Maureen's side, Rollo gave one of his deep, bone-jarring barks. Maureen quickly soothed the large wolfhound. "Good job, Rollo," she murmured. Men scrambled, as Lieutenant Purbeck said, "I want a step…a block…something. We need an investigator up there. And crowd control! Someone arrange detours until we've got all this out of here. And I sure as hell don't want anyone around gaping and snapping shots for Twitter and Facebook!"

Gina Mason, head of the forensics unit, stepped forward and yelled at them. "Get the birds away! And then get some kind of screening set up. We have to preserve the scene! Can we get rigging and tarps around the— the— Around it! Everyone will be breathing down my neck for trace evidence and I'll have to say we were defeated by a crow!"

Dr. Aaron Mortenson from the coroner's office had arrived, as well. He got out of his car and walked over to Gina.

"Let the photographer up there first, and then I'll take a quick look. I won't disturb anything until you've had a chance to get what you need," he told her.

Mortenson was middle-aged, trim in appearance and always reserved. He saw Mo and Rollo. To her surprise, he nodded to her with something that was almost a smile. A silent acknowledgment that said, *Work well done.* He sighed loudly. "Since it's so early, thankfully no four-year-old saw this and realized the head was real. God knows— Halloween. It might well have taken hours even in broad daylight before anyone saw that it wasn't just part of some grisly display."

She nodded solemnly back at him.

Lieutenant Purbeck came to stand near Mo, allowing the technicians and the medical examiner the space they needed.

He set a hand on her shoulder.

"I'm okay," she assured him.

Then she turned away, grasping Rollo's collar and taking him with her. He'd done his job well. Too well. This was one search she wished she could've sat out. Sooner or later, someone would have really looked at the headless horseman that stood outside the entrance to Tommy's place. The police hadn't really needed her services. She actually wished that they hadn't called her; this one was a little too close to home.

"Why *my* horseman?" Mo heard. She turned.

Tommy Jensen, an old friend—and owner of the Headless Horseman Hideaway Restaurant and Bar—had been allowed through. The restaurant didn't open until eleven; his staff didn't even arrive until nine or nine-thirty. But, she realized, looking at his grim face as he stared at the scene, it was *his* horseman and his parking lot. She figured he'd been called in.

He looked at her bleakly and tried to smile. "Of all the horsemen in all the world…"

Mo touched his arm. He was her senior by a few years; she'd known him since she was ten or so. She recalled that the older girls had often teased him because he'd been a big, awkward kid. He still liked to moan about his dating life. But now that they were all older and presumably more mature, the group she'd hung out with growing up now frequented his restaurant. It was her favorite hangout when friends met up at night for dinner, coffee or drinks. He always took care of them.

He'd been born and bred in the area and was a true lover of the Hudson Valley. He'd owned the restaurant for about two years and it was charming, offering pool tables, dart boards and an "enchanted forest" for young children when their families came for lunch.

Purbeck turned to him. "What time did you leave last night, Tommy?"

Tommy was startled—as if he'd just realized he might be a suspect. "About 2:30 a.m. And I didn't leave alone. I left with Abby Cole. We cleaned up, locked the place and were together the whole time. I drove her home."

"And you didn't see anything? Anything at all unusual?" Purbeck demanded.

Tommy shook his head. "Sir, I'm telling you, we were worn-out. Halloween's coming, you know? We're busy. We had to announce last call and practically shove people out of their chairs. When we finally took off, my car was the only one in the lot and…"

"And?"

"I didn't even glance at the horseman, to be honest. But, like I said, we'd been busy. We had a lot of visitors and people were talking at their cars before leaving. They'd been to the attractions, the haunted houses, the storytelling, all that. So…I'm not a cop, but I don't see how this could have been done until the wee hours of the morning."

Purbeck released a sigh. "Call your people. We're going to have this area closed off for the next five hours or so."

"The poor guy! I feel really bad about this." Tommy frowned. "But why did it have to be in front of *my* place? Oh, Lord, will anyone ever come here again?" he asked, his tone dismayed.

"They'll flock in—to see where the head of Richard

Highsmith was found," Purbeck said dryly. "You can open, but not until dinner." He paused, glancing at the scene. "I'm giving my crime scene techs a good five hours. Until then, the crime scene tape stays up. Oh, and, make sure I can get hold of you."

Tommy looked at Mo. "Don't leave town, huh?" he said. Then he looked back at Purbeck. "I don't leave town often, sir, so no worries there. Can I go home?"

"For now. Tell Abby we'll be talking to her and the staff," Purbeck added.

Tommy waved as he turned to leave. Then he stopped. "Mo, can you come by later? He could be right about business being okay—or people could be so creeped out, they won't come anymore."

"I'll come by, Tommy," Mo promised. "I'm sure you'll be okay."

She wished she believed her own words. But talking to him, encouraging him, was at least keeping him from seeing the head spiked on *his* effigy of the headless horseman.

Lieutenant Robert Purbeck walked over to her. "Mo, you can go, if you like. We'll take it from here." He sounded gruff and uncomfortable. "You and Rollo were dead-on, as usual." He paused, rolling his eyes at his unfortunate choice of words. "That came out wrong, but this whole thing is just…bad. Very bad. Are you all right?"

Was she *all right?*

No one there was all right. But she wasn't a cop or a forensic expert; she was Rollo's owner. She was an "expert consultant." And, sadly, she'd seen the very bad before.

Sometimes, more often than not, she and Rollo found

those who were still living. She could proudly say that many a time they had helped save lives.

Not today.

"Yes, I'm fine," she assured Purbeck. "But it's not a picture I'll forget."

"None of us will," he murmured.

She squared her shoulders and patted Rollo's massive head. "We've found terrible and tragic things before, Lieutenant. And we've survived them."

Purbeck was a tall, muscled man in his late fifties. He could be a tough cop, but he was also a sort of father figure to her, and his expression was one of parental concern. "We just discovered a head on a pole, Maureen. Here. In Sleepy Hollow. That's damned… scary and disturbing."

All she could do was agree. "I'm worried about you," he said next. "You live alone."

"I have Rollo."

Rollo was huge. Standing on his hind legs, he was nearly six feet tall and dwarfed most men. He was one of the largest of his breed she had ever seen.

"Rollo, yes. He might well scare the common car thief," Purbeck said. "And, yeah, he's great at what he does. He's not a bloodhound, not even a scent hound, he's a sight hound, but he's always right on the money. I guess dogs have it over us." He shrugged. "And he's one hell of a companion. But, Mo, whoever did this is sick. *Really* sick. I'm no expert on nutcases—and I don't think I have to be. This is—" He paused, searching for a better word. Apparently, he didn't find one. "Sick," he repeated.

Maureen nodded again. "I…I would hope that someone suffering from a serious mental problem, an illness, would be the only person who could do something so horrible," she said. She gestured around her. "Most people come here because of Washington Irving and his short story 'The Legend of Sleepy Hollow.' They're intrigued by it, they love history—and, well, they just want to see the place. But with this... Someone's turning it into an obscene joke."

"Yeah. Some whacked bastard out there has taken the work of the first American man of letters and twisted it into something tragic. I'm going to stop it. I refuse to let any more of this happen in our town. I'm going to track down whoever committed such a...such a dreadful crime, such a travesty—" Purbeck broke off. "I will get this bastard!" he vowed.

Maureen placed one hand on his arm. People here were extremely proud of Washington Irving, and of course the tourist trade that sustained many businesses in the village of Sleepy Hollow and in Tarrytown was due to Irving's time-tested stories. She knew that herself. Like many who found their way to Sleepy Hollow, her parents were Irish New Yorkers who had fallen in love with the Hudson Valley. They hadn't purchased property in the area, though. Instead, they'd rented every time they'd come for the summer or other holidays. She'd been the one to set down permanent roots here, buying a cottage down the Hudson from Irving's Sunnyside. It had belonged to an older couple, friends of her parents, who'd gone to Arizona because of the husband's severe asthma; they and Maureen had made a deal that was amenable to both parties, and she'd become a full-time resident. Her parents, too, had decided to retire to Scottsdale, joking that they'd never again have to shovel snow.

While she still loved the city—there was, truly, nothing like New York in the world—she'd needed to get away from the nonstop energy, the frequent chaos. And while she loved many places around the country, she'd never seen anything quite as beautiful as the Hudson Valley. Yes, areas off a few of the main roads seemed remote and very dark. But she'd bought what she considered the perfect home in Sleepy Hollow.

"And Richard Highsmith," Purbeck said. "Lord, why?"

Neither of them had an answer for that.

Mo was hardly an expert on politics, but she'd admired Highsmith. He was that rare politician willing to stand and fight alone. He hadn't adhered to any political party; he was an independent. He seemed to have taken the best policies and beliefs from everyone else out there. People loved him. He had plans for fiscal responsibility and he also had plans that focused on making equality part of the fabric of America.

Yes, he was loved.

But he was also hated.

And yet…

Hated this much?

"Was someone after Mr. Highsmith specifically?" Mo murmured. "Or…"

As she'd told Lieutenant Purbeck, she *had* to hope that only someone truly ill could have done this. Even worse—if such a thing was possible—was the chance that Richard's murder had been random, that he'd just been taken and that…

If that were true, there could be more heads on top of horsemen who should have remained headless.

She knew Purbeck was thinking along the same lines.

"While this is going on, you might want to stay with a friend or move into a hotel," Purbeck said to her.

"Lieutenant, we have no idea what's going on yet," Mo reminded him. "Highsmith was a politician. He was very likely to be voted in as New York's next mayor. He was an independent, which means that most people loved him but that he also had enemies in the major political camps. I know—I followed him and his politics. He also had plans to run for governor at some point in the future, and a lot of people here still have homes in the city and use the Valley for escape. So…it makes sense that he was speaking here."

Purbeck nodded. "Yep. He was special and he was different. But getting back to you… You're in a remote area. I don't know if Rollo, big as he is, can protect you from this kind of insanity."

"His size scares people all the time," Mo commented.

"Normal people," Purbeck agreed. He stood awkwardly for a moment, watching his officers and the crime scene technicians working. "But if you actually *know* the dog, he's one friendly guy."

"Don't kid yourself, Lieutenant—Rollo can be fierce!" Maureen bent down to hug the dog. He didn't exactly prove her point when he rewarded her with a sloppy kiss. One of her mom's best friends had bred Irish wolfhounds; the dogs had been special to her from the first time she'd seen them. She and Rollo were family.

"And Richard Highsmith—" She started to turn back to the head on the mannequin but stopped herself. "He was a politician, in from the city. I do have to wonder whether someone decided to kill him and to use the legend to get away with it. Let's face it, no one can look at this without thinking that a maniac is at work. That could throw an investigation in the wrong direction."

"I almost hope you're right." Purbeck glanced at the effigy and the head—now covered with blue canvas in case the gawkers arrived. And in case media cameras showed up. Given media presence at the convention center last night, Mo was surprised that no members of the press were here this morning—and equally relieved. That was obviously because not many people knew there was a severed head here or that it had belonged to Richard Highsmith. They would soon enough. Police were trying to protect the scene of the crime and, she felt, Richard Highsmith's dignity. No one wanted the grotesque and heartbreaking image of Highsmith's severed head appearing on TV or the internet or the papers. "I hope this *is* a political thing. Because if it's not…"

"You think there really might be someone here… who's crazy and going after heads?" Maureen asked. "But we have the head."

Purbeck nodded grimly. "What we don't have is the rest of the body, and that's the next order of business. But you—"

Detective Lee Van Camp, a lean man with a thin face and a haggard appearance, stepped over to them, interrupting whatever the lieutenant was about to say. Mo knew he'd be lead man on the case. He worked with Jimmy Voorhaven, a younger detective, and they were probably the two best men in the county. Purbeck was a good commander and usually directed his detectives from his office. Purbeck was here himself because Richard Highsmith's disappearance—and now confirmed murder—was about as high-profile as it got.

He would remain involved. The media had already gone crazy but news people were being kept at a distance.

She'd worked with Detective Van Camp before. In fact, of all the local cops, she'd worked with him the most. They'd met when she was just a teenager. She hadn't had Rollo then; she'd had his mom, Heidi. Working with the wolfhounds had been a godsend for her. When she was in her teens, her parents had discovered how effective she and Heidi were at search and rescue, and she remembered hearing them argue about whether they should allow her to continue. They'd decided that yes, if she *could* help, they were morally bound to let her do so.

She'd never really known what Van Camp thought about her and her almost foolproof ability to find the missing. He simply watched her with his dark, unblinking eyes. And he was always courteous.

"Well?" Purbeck asked softly.

"Political execution taken to a dramatic extreme?" Van Camp asked Purbeck. "Or mental case?" He turned to Mo. "What do you think?"

Maureen wasn't taken aback by the question. And it wasn't because she and Van Camp knew each other or that they'd worked together before. He'd told her once that he just listened and tested everything he heard; he listened to everyone, taking in what worked for him and ignoring what didn't. But he didn't brush off anyone or discount any opinion. Mo liked him a lot. He was an exceptional detective for that very reason.

She took a deep breath. "It's certainly dramatic. But

in the legend, the headless horseman is looking for heads. He takes the heads and leaves the bodies behind."

"Yeah, that's what I was thinking," Van Camp said.

Purbeck narrowed his eyes. "People say there are really no new stories, just new ways to tell them. The headless horseman was an old legend in the area—Washington Irving just wrote it up with literary talent. Whoever this is, they're putting a new twist on it."

"If you go by the legend, the horseman is searching for a head," Van Camp continued. "And he killed old Ichabod Crane with a pumpkin head he'd been carting around. But if you read between the lines, either Bram Bones did in his rival or Ichabod went off to live happily ever after somewhere else. But if you think this is a political assassination, the drama's an attempt to throw off suspicion. Hard to be sure at this point." He cleared his throat. "We'll know more, I'm sure, after autopsy. I mean— Well, we'll need to know how the head was removed from the body."

"Whatever the answer may be, I really don't think we're looking for a long-dead Hessian soldier still fighting the Revolution!" Purbeck said.

"No, but these days, politics can be close to war," Van Camp said with distaste. "Poor guy. He sure as hell didn't deserve anything like this. I hope, I *really* hope that—" He paused again. "I hope it was quick."

"I want to send Mo and Rollo home. No reason they have to watch all this," Purbeck said.

Van Camp shook his head. "Mo can't go yet. We still need her and Rollo."

"Oh?" Purbeck asked.

"Boss man, hey," Van Camp said. "We've got...part of Mr. Highsmith. We need to find the rest of him."

"Yeah, but I was hoping to give Mo a break. She and Rollo have already found Richard— Well, his head. I thought we'd search for the rest of the remains ourselves....but, Mo, it probably does make more sense if you and Rollo do your thing, get a head start." He winced. "Sorry. You okay with doing that?"

"Of course," Mo said, crouching down by Rollo. "Good job, my friend. But we need more. Are you ready?"

The question was just as much for her. She studied the site. Van Camp had left them. He was speaking with Voorhaven, requesting help to get up on a make-shift hoist for a better look at the head in situ. Gina Mason was beside him, accepting a camera from one of her assistants.

"Mo?" Purbeck asked. "Are you sure you can handle this?"

She nodded, closing her eyes. She envisioned the man in the picture she'd been given hours before.

When she opened her eyes, she looked across the road to the cemetery.

Most people thought the old burying grounds were part of Sleepy Hollow Cemetery, which included hills and covered a lot of space. The Old Winchester Burying Grounds was actually a separate entity. At one time, St. Andrew's Episcopal Church had stood somewhere in the center, although it had burned down during the Revolution. So, officially, this had been a burying ground rather than a cemetery. Traditionally, unlike a cemetery, a burying ground was attached to a church, although over the years the terms had become interchangeable.

Now—be it cemetery or burying ground—the place beckoned to her.

"Rollo," she said to the dog. "We're on."

Aidan knew this area very well.

Nestled in the Hudson Valley, surrounded by mountains and bordered by the Hudson River, Sleepy Hollow was simply charming. Carved out of Tarrytown and once known geographically and locally by the unimaginative name of North Tarrytown, the village had become Sleepy Hollow in 1996 in honor of its most famous resident, Washington Irving. The entire area was ripe with Revolutionary history, along with tales of the Old Dutch community and legends from the Native Americans who'd once called it home.

The Woman in White appeared now and then, and Major Andre's ghost was said to roam the area. The dashing gentleman had been hanged as a spy by the patriots. Of course, he *was* a spy, but he'd been handsome and charismatic, and many had lamented his death.

The woods were dense. Creeks and streams danced over rocks and down slopes. At night, when fog wandered in these woods, it was easy to imagine how frightening it might be to roam what would've been an eerie landscape in the dark, with only the light of the moon filtering through the trees.

The Old Dutch Burying Grounds by the Old Dutch Church were filled with worn old stones and vaults that had been dug into the cliffs, and it was spooky by moonlight.

Of course, there was also much that was warm and welcoming in Sleepy Hollow and Tarrytown.

There were hotels and motels, bed-and-breakfasts

and inns, as well as shops that offered the usual T-shirts, souvenirs, handmade arts and crafts, and one-of-a-kind clothing.

And there were headless horsemen.

There were headless horsemen everywhere.

They were on signs that advertised stores and restaurants.

They were on village welcome posts along the roadside—some made of wrought iron and some of wood etchings, and others were done using a variety of other artistic media and techniques.

As a child, Aidan had scrambled up and down the hills and leaped over the many lilting brooks and streams. He and his friends had created their own stories about the patriots and redcoats and traitors, the Indians who had once claimed the land and, needless to say, Irving's headless horseman.

It had been a great place to grow up. The entire Hudson Valley was, in his opinion, one of the most beautiful places on earth. And, for a boy, it had been filled with adventure. Hiking, fishing, boating, walking with his friends...learning their world and its history.

Richard Highsmith had been one of those friends.

Aidan hadn't gone to the local station yet. Neither had he headed over to the center where Richard would be speaking. Jackson Crow had called Aidan with specifics about the last time Richard had been seen. In fact, Highsmith's assistant, Taylor Branch, had feared that he'd just walked out—that he'd suddenly had an epiphany regarding politics and its negative, nasty side. Branch was sure that Richard would realize he was a different kind of politician, one who could bring about change, and that he'd come back. So he'd waited, entertaining the crowd with musicians hired for the event.

Richard had been missing for three hours before Branch had called the police. Then there'd been confusion. Next the place had been shut down and those who'd come to see him speak had been held and questioned, but finally they'd all been allowed to leave.

A search had actually begun last night around midnight. From Jackson Crow's last call, Aidan knew that more people had been called out at the crack of dawn.

The police had searched through the night. Many of the tourist attractions in Tarrytown and Sleepy Hollow—like Washington Irving's Sunnyside and the old Philips Manor—had acres of farmland, surrounded by forest.

The police had called in all kinds of assistance. Officers from the county and state. Bloodhounds and other canine search-and-rescue units, including an Irish wolfhound and his keeper who seemed to have an extraordinary rate of success. Anything and everyone was out there—and now the information had hit the airwaves.

Aidan had decided to go on instinct. On the voices he heard in his head. He hated when that happened, loathed it. But the voices still came now and then. And today…

He'd heard Richard. Heard him when it was too late. *They got me, my old friend. They got me.*

He wished he'd heard something different. Like, *I'm in danger, old friend.*

Cursing, he began to walk. First he climbed uphill, by the Old Dutch Church. But somehow he knew that was wrong, so he changed course, got back in his car and drove beside the Sleepy Hollow Cemetery. Finally, he reached the end and parked again.

It was fall; mid-October had just arrived. The day had been beautiful when he'd started driving and even when he'd first parked. The leaves were turning, offering brilliant touches of color here and there. The temperature was cool but not cold.

Suddenly a chilly breeze was whipping around him, and when he looked up he saw that the sky was gray and ominous.

A brook trickled between the boundaries of the Sleepy Hollow Cemetery and Saint Andrew's burying ground. He hopped over the brook, studying the expanse of trees that flourished everywhere—the plan when the Sleepy Hollow Cemetery was designed had been to make it a serene and beautiful place, a place where families might come to picnic and find peace while they honored their lost loved ones. And it *was* beautiful here. The dead rested between the graceful trees and gurgling water. Nature at its best.

The one land of the dead blended into the next. There hadn't been a burial at the old grounds for a century while Sleepy Hollow Cemetery still accepted new denizens. But the old burying ground was just as beautiful, though not actually planned that way. Nature, on her own, had stepped in. The grounds were somewhat overgrown, yet that made them more forlorn and more poignant. Crosses rose in high grass; cherubs appeared by tombstones.

Angels wept.

There were vaults dug into the hill where the church had once stood, surrounded by trees and bushes. Tombs had been built above the ground, and these old mausoleums endured within a fairy-tale land where the dead rested and the living might contemplate the beauty of life—and the inevitability of death.

He passed one of the old vaults and crawled high atop it to survey the area. A stone angel knelt in prayer to his left, an obelisk rose to his right. He hurried by them and clambered down an overgrown path to the rise of a second hill. For a moment, he paused. He could hear the tinkle of water and saw where a tree had broken several stones.

The day was darkening; it was going to rain.

The breeze quickened and Aidan felt an urge to hurry. He walked across the hill, looking around. So many graves. So many years of men living in this region—and dying here.

He noticed that a new flag marked the grave of a Revolutionary soldier. He passed a general on horseback—a tribute to the men of the valley who had fought in the Civil War.

He walked over graves and by monuments, past mausoleums and vaults, and then he peered into the distance.

And saw a man. Or the shape of a man. The area suddenly seemed very dark, even though it was almost seven-thirty and the sun had surely risen. The breeze was now a wind; the sky roiled.

"Hey!" he called. There was no answer.

Was he imagining the man? The figure leaned against a free-standing vault with great pillars before it.

The wind seemed to be against him as he hurried over. He was fighting to get there.

The man didn't disappear.

As he struggled forward, he paused at the sound of a dog barking. He turned.

A massive animal was racing toward the other figure, straining at his leash, which was held by a young woman in a black trench coat. He had the rather irrelevant thought that she resembled Cousin Itt from *The Addams Family*, since the wind had covered her face with her long brown hair. She and the dog—the wolfhound, obviously—were threading their way through crooked tombstones and monuments listing at different angles.

He heard voices. The dog and the woman were being followed.

He ran forward, too. The dog was in a rush—not after him, but intent on something else. Or someone else.

The figure leaning by the vault. The young woman tripped on a broken headstone but found her footing.

He continued forward himself, realizing that dog and woman were headed for the man—and at the rate the dog was going, they might well knock him over.

"Rollo! Slow down!" the young woman commanded.

Rollo passed Aidan and skidded to a halt within ten feet of the figure.

Running, Aidan barely managed to stop himself from toppling over onto the woman.

Then she came to a standstill so quickly that she lost her balance and fell back.

Into Aidan's arms.

She gasped and he righted her.

She turned to apologize, pulling strands of hair away from her eyes. They were like crystals, gray-green and shimmering with flecks of both colors.

She didn't speak but her beautiful eyes widened, as

if wondering what she'd seen just before she'd fallen backward—into his arms.

Their eyes met briefly in that confusion.

Rollo, the giant wolfhound, kept barking.

And as they both turned to look at the man—the figure by the tomb—a horde of people came panting up behind them.

They were mostly men in uniform.

Aidan ignored them. So did the young woman and the dog.

They were still staring at the man who'd been propped against the vault. He wore a long billowing coat and black boots, and might have been casually waiting there.

He just didn't have a head.

But something else about the scene didn't seem right.

"Oh, my God!" someone shrieked behind him.

Aidan noticed that the headless man stood as if he were about to enter the vault—or perhaps ask someone to join him.

It was staged. It was *staged* to be horrific.

One of the newcomers stopped about three feet from the young woman.

"Well, I believe you've found the rest of Mr. Highsmith, Mo." He stopped speaking. Perhaps, under the circumstances, all their minds were working a little slowly. The man frowned, then gave Aidan a thorough look and said, "This is a crime scene, sir." He paused, his expression grim. "But..."

Aidan was in a suit and trench coat, certainly not clothing worn by any of the others here. He guessed—hoped—that he wore it with a certain authority.

"You're with the federal government?"

Aidan nodded and presented his credentials. The older man studied him again. "Took them long enough to get you here," he said. "I called last night."

"Sir, I got the word about an hour and a half ago," Aidan said.

The older man didn't offer his hand; he seemed to be an old-time lawman. "Lieutenant Robert Purbeck, Agent Mahoney," he said. "Glad you made it. Things like this don't happen in Tarrytown. Except in stories, of course."

Someone next to him was on a radio, telling someone else to get the M.E. and crime scene techs up the hill.

The wolfhound barked.

"Shh, Rollo," the young woman said.

"Agent Mahoney, meet my lead men on the case— Detectives Lee Van Camp and Jimmy Voorhaven. And—" he gestured to the young woman and the dog "—Maureen Deauville. Mo…we have a Fed here. Agent Mahoney of the FBI. Oh, and that's our wonder dog, Rollo."

Aidan nodded in acknowledgment. The other cops, a weary-looking lean guy and his younger partner, watched him curiously as they shook hands but they didn't appear to resent his presence.

"God help me," Purbeck muttered. "I hope that's the rest of Richard Highsmith. If not…"

He didn't finish his sentence.

But Aidan knew what he meant.

They'd found Richard's head.

And if this *wasn't* the body that went with the head…

Well, there might be headless bodies and bodiless heads all over the Hudson Valley.

But, as he stood there, staring at the form, Aidan saw that the loose coat had fluttered open—and he understood what was wrong with the scene.

And he knew their worst fears were realized.

"I'm sorry to say this," Aidan announced, "but that's not Richard Highsmith."

"What?" Purbeck demanded. "How the hell do you know that?"

"Take a closer look," Aidan said. "That's not a man's body. It's a woman's."

"What?" Purbeck demanded again. "Rollo found a body, a *woman's* body? But…he was on Richard Highsmith's scent!"

"He sure as hell found something," Aidan said.

The young woman, Maureen Deauville, spoke quietly then.

"Rollo is— Well, he's really a sight hound, but—" She paused, glancing around. "He's never wrong. Richard Highsmith is nearby," she said. "The, um, rest of him."

Aidan looked at her, then at the headless body by the tomb. Ms. Deauville seemed very certain. In a second, he'd pulled on a pair of neoprene gloves.

Then he stepped forward.

There was an iron gate that guarded the tomb. Beyond that was some kind of heavy metal door.

Aidan pulled at the gate; it creaked, but gave.

He pushed at the iron door. It groaned on its hinges but opened.

Taking a penlight from his pocket, he flashed it over

the inside of the vault. He saw a stone sarcophagus or tomb in the center.

And on the stone tomb, a body. In a suit.

"This, I think," Aidan said, rigidly controlling the emotion that ripped through him, "is Richard Highsmith."

2

Purbeck looked in and sighed. "Back out, everyone but Mahoney, Van Camp and Voorhaven. I don't want evidence compromised. Get the M.E. and the crime scene people here," he ordered.

Aidan followed him, then carefully stepped through.

He threw the beam of his flashlight over the stone floor. No hope of prints, since the stone was bare of dust. He walked carefully toward the body, touching nothing, keeping his light trained on the corpse.

Aidan wasn't an M.E., but it seemed to him that the head had been cleanly severed with great strength and probably a single blow. Highsmith hadn't been killed in the tomb; there wasn't much blood. And, of course, Aidan couldn't know if he'd been killed and then decapitated—or killed *by* decapitation. He found himself reminded of a history lesson: Queen Anne Boleyn asking Henry VIII for a headsman from France so her execution would be swift and clean.

Purbeck had come in behind him. He, too, touched nothing and studied the body.

As the two detectives—Van Camp and Voorhaven—also walked into the tomb, Aidan put down his flashlight and checked for Highsmith's wallet with gloved hands. He found it in his pocket, just as he'd expected to.

"Anything in there?" Van Camp asked him.

"Wallet, keys…"

Carefully, Aidan checked Highsmith's other pocket. Lint—and a matchbook. He held it up to Voorhaven's flashlight glare.

"From some place called Mystic Magic," he said.

"Whoa," Van Camp muttered.

"It's a new strip club down close to Irving," Voorhaven explained.

"Doesn't sound like Richard Highsmith," Purbeck said.

Voorhaven produced an evidence bag, but Aidan briefly held on to the matchbook, flipping it open. He wasn't surprised to see that Highsmith had scribbled something in it. "'Lizzie grave,'" he read aloud.

"Odd name for a stripper," Van Camp commented.

"I doubt it's a stripper's name," Aidan told the others.

"Then what?" Van Camp asked.

"Maybe it has to do with a dead woman named Lizzie. Lizzie's grave," Aidan said impatiently, dropping the matchbook in the evidence bag.

Voorhaven snorted. "Ah, hell! Do you know how many Lizzies have died and been buried here over the last several hundred years?"

Purbeck shook his head. "Let the M.E. and the crime scene techs in now," he said, turning to leave the vault. He paused at the door. "We have another victim out there—and another head to find."

Aidan stayed behind for a minute, his gloved hand resting lightly on Richard's arm. Rigor had come and gone; he'd been dead awhile. He'd probably been killed soon after he disappeared.

"Old friend," he murmured. "I'll get whoever did this to you."

The young woman, Maureen—or Mo— Deauville, had not come in. She stood with her dog just outside the gates and Aidan felt her eyes on him, even though he was darkness and shadow.

He exited the tomb and approached Maureen just as Purbeck came up beside her. The place was now crawling with people. Voorhaven and Van Camp were by the corpse that had been so strategically arranged to look like a host—welcoming them, inviting them to enter the tomb. They had to discover the identity of this woman. Her death was as great a crime, as great a tragedy, as Highsmith's.

"I know Van Camp already mentioned this, but are we *sure* it's not a name? Lizzie Grave?" Purbeck asked Aidan. "Not necessarily a stripper's name. Maybe someone he met?"

Aidan shook his head. "I'm almost certain it's not," he said. "I think he grabbed that matchbook wherever he was—could've been anywhere—and jotted down a note. I agree with you that it's highly unlikely he was ever in that strip club—not when he was here on an important speaking engagement. I think he just saw the matchbook somewhere. In a dressing room or at a lunch counter, maybe. Or someone gave it to him. And I think *Lizzie grave* means…Lizzie's grave. But the first thing we need to do is discover the identity of our other victim."

"God help us," Purbeck said. "We started out looking

for a body. Now...now, we've got to find another head."
He turned to Mo Deauville. "You and Rollo ready?"

Aidan believed she was fighting her own mental
battle, but she nodded. "Yes, of course," she said. She
brought the wolfhound to where the headless corpse
leaned. The cops made way for her. The dog stood at a
distance, but lifted his nose high—almost as if he were
weighing the merits of a perfume.

Mo Deauville commanded the dog to sit, then approached the corpse and rested her hand gently on the
woman's shoulder.

As if she could...somehow feel *something. A com-
munication—from the corpse!*

She lowered her head, then looked at Purbeck.

"We're ready," she said.

She touched the dog's head. Aidan couldn't be sure,
but he thought she was giving Rollo some kind of sig-
nal.

Well, of course she was. She was asking him to
find...the rest of the woman.

No, it seemed to be more than that.

But she quickly set off, tightly clutching the dog's
leash.

With the exception of the crime scene personnel
and a few cops left standing guard, everyone trailed
after her. They went up and down hills as they walked
through one cemetery to get to the other, and eventually wound up on the street again.

"Oh, no. Oh, God, no," Purbeck said.

Yes.

Across the street, at yet another headless horseman
effigy, this one in front of a dry cleaning business, a
crowd was gathering.

People weren't alarmed; they seemed to be in awe.

There were pictures being taken.

The crowd wasn't even being particularly ghoulish. The horseman stood in the midst of a Halloween display of pumpkins, bats, black cats and flying witches.

"Get the people away," Purbeck said quietly.

Rollo woofed.

Voorhaven and Van Camp went running across the street, along with half-a-dozen men in uniform.

Aidan glanced at Mo. She stood there, holding Rollo's leash. She didn't turn away, although he could tell she wasn't going any closer. There was a stoic expression on her face, but sadness in her eyes.

"Thank you," Aidan murmured to her. He crossed the street and hurried over to the display. The area was now being cleared of people.

He knew the crowd hadn't understood that the horseman with its witch's head wasn't part of this gruesome display. The head...was *real*.

Purbeck followed him. As Aidan stepped up onto a bale of hay beside a wire-and-plastic assembly, he heard the lieutenant mutter.

"God, I pray this means both our bodies are complete!"

Aidan thought they were. It was difficult to be sure, but he had to believe this was what they were looking for. The "witch's" wealth of long dark hair had been adorned with a black pointed hat. Van Camp stood on a second bale near him, silently inspecting the scene. He motioned to one of the photographers to capture the image from a number of different angles. When the photographer finished the initial shots, Aidan turned to Van Camp, who nodded. He removed the hat and passed it down to Jimmy Voorhaven. Jimmy bagged it, then he carefully brushed aside the tangle of dark hair.

"Mid-thirties?" Van Camp murmured. "Attractive, good bone structure. It doesn't appear that any of the bones in the face were broken or disturbed."

"No bruises or contusions. Naturally, the skin is somewhat…"

"Yeah," Van Camp said.

"You recognize her, by any chance?" Aidan asked him.

Van Camp shook his head. "No. And I guess we can't be a hundred percent sure if this head goes with the body by the vault until…until the M.E. puts her together."

The two men scrambled down; the police photographer got into position to take more pictures. Members of the crime scene unit assembled to search for trace evidence.

Aidan rejoined Purbeck. The man just stared at the display. He shook his head. "You know what our murder rate is around here? Practically zero."

"Doesn't help that we're close to Halloween," Voorhaven said.

That was probably true. There were few places in the country to rival the Sleepy Hollow area for Halloween. It came complete with the rolling hills, brooks, fog and spooky woods that first gave rise to legends and then to the stories written by the first American recognized as a great writer by the European community. So there were a zillion "haunted" venues: haunted houses, haunted hayrides, haunted happenings. Usually, it was an entertaining and commercially successful time—and the merchants were in a frenzy of happiness.

And the headless horseman reigned supreme.

"Whoever did this has to be stopped. Fast," Van Camp said.

"Van Camp, I need you and Voorhaven to go to the station with Special Agent Mahoney. Get him up to speed on everything. Mahoney, you're alone on this?" Purbeck asked him, apparently puzzled.

Aidan hesitated. It wasn't that he couldn't be a team player; he usually enjoyed working with others. True, he wasn't completely familiar or completely comfortable with his new team yet. But he trusted that would happen in time.

Everyone wanted a trusted coworker at his back.

Still, he was well aware that he didn't work like most agents. Sometimes his methods of investigation were...different.

Just as he'd heard that the agents in the Krewe had what might be considered different methods of investigation.

His methods worked—and that was why, he assumed, his superiors had decided to make use of him in a way that brought about results.

"We'll bring in more people, I'm sure," Aidan said. "When necessary."

"Nice. Seems they give the locals some respect," Voorhaven muttered sarcastically.

Aidan looked squarely at the man. "Detective, I'm here because Lieutenant Purbeck called my office. Because, thank God, there aren't many murders in this area. I was sent because I grew up here. More than that, I grew up here with friends—one of whom was Richard Highsmith. I know how the man thought. I know his habits, his virtues and his weaknesses. I'm not here to step on toes. But I'm going to get whoever murdered my friend." He realized that, without really thinking about it, he'd made the decision to disclose his relationship with Richard to these policemen, even though he hadn't yet told Jackson Crow.

Voorhaven stared at him awkwardly. "I, uh, I'm sorry. By all accounts, Highsmith was a really good man."

Aidan nodded. "Yeah." He looked at the headless horseman effigy—with its head. "And now we have a Jane Doe and she might have been a good person, too, and if not…well, she's still entitled to the very best law enforcement can give her. So, I'm willing to do anything it takes to get to the bottom of this."

"Of course," Voorhaven said.

"The kid just got his shield a year ago," Van Camp told Aidan. "He'll learn. When you've been around long enough and you see something like this, you're happy to accept whatever assistance you can get."

Aidan nodded.

"So, now we've kissed and made up," Purbeck said. "Good. You two, give the nice Fed anything he needs or wants, okay?"

"You got it, yeah, sure, of course," Voorhaven said.

Aidan looked across the street.

Mo Deauville was still there, Rollo at her side. She was watching them.

Purbeck raised a hand in a gesture of thanks or farewell or both.

She waved in return. For a moment, the wind caught her hair and lifted it around her. The Cousin Itt comparison no longer seemed the least bit apt and he wondered why it had ever occurred to him. She might have been wearing a trench coat, but she suddenly created an image in his mind. He pictured her as an ancient warrior princess. A Viking goddess, maybe.

A moment later, she was gone, but the image lingered.

Mo moved through the different cemeteries until she reached her point of arrival that morning—street parking by the Old Dutch Church.

Rollo trotted obediently along. She thought she should've put on his service-dog vest, since dogs weren't really allowed in some of the places she walked through to get where she was going. But it was a Thursday morning, and although there were a few people in the various historical cemeteries and burying grounds, she remained at a distance and no one bothered her. Still, she did hear a few people exclaim what a beautiful dog Rollo was and, one girl squeaked that there was a woman walking around with a *pony.*

She pretended not to hear any of it as she made her way back to the car. Everything she'd seen that morning seemed to be imprinted on her mind.

The scenes she'd witnessed weren't easy to forget.

"Remember, Rollo? We figured it would be such a lark, living here!" Mo said aloud.

Rollo let out a deep, rich *woof,* as if he understood.

She'd worked with the police for a long time. First in New York City and then—when she moved out here—with the county.

Fortunately, she could live wherever she wanted. She had a freelance career and was lucky enough to have a nice contract with a greeting card company. Many of her cards were e-cards, but many were also constructed of paper. Her company was actually based not too far away, in Connecticut, and she drove over for meetings once a month. Other than that, she worked on the internet and with graphic programs. She produced her paper creations by hand and on her own time, which allowed for her sideline of finding the lost and missing with Purbeck and Rollo.

Purbeck called her whenever a child went missing in the woods, and she and Rollo would find that child. It wasn't always children. The last time she'd been called out, Mr. Husseldorf—one hundred and two, and looking forward to his next birthday—had wandered out of his nursing home. She'd found him down by one of the brooks, fishing without a pole. But the expression on his face and his every movement showed her that in his mind he was fishing.

Shc'd left the city because she preferred to find the living. In the city, it seemed, she too often found the dead.

But then, that was her real talent, wasn't it?

Arriving at her car, Mo opened the door for Rollo to hop into the front, then walked around and slid into the driver's seat. Technically, she was in Tarrytown and not Sleepy Hollow. There were signs that announced when you actually reached Sleepy Hollow.

She loved her home. It was right on a little twist on the river. She could stand in her backyard and see Sunnyside, the home where Washington Irving had lived for many years, and where he'd died. And sometimes, looking across the river, she could see *him*. He was older; he walked with a cane. But he was tall and lean, an extremely attractive older man. Sometimes, when a train went by, he lifted his cane as if cursing it.

Everyone in the area knew how much he'd hated it

when the tracks had gone in. The trains blocked his view of the river when they went by, creating a nuisance with their horns and whistles and noise, day and night. After all, the writer had purchased Sunnyside because he loved peace and quiet. He'd added rocks to his stream so he could better hear the rush of the water and he'd built up a mound in front of his cottage so it wasn't easily seen when visitors—or the curious—arrived via the road.

"Well, Rollo," she murmured, "why do you think you and I live in a cottage and not a house? It means I'm going to have to look that up, the difference between a cottage and a house."

Rollo had no answer, other than a wriggle in the passenger seat. She assumed he was trying to wag his tail, but he barely fit in the car.

Her home was surrounded by trees and stood about a quarter of a mile off the road.

It had always astonished her that you could leave New York City and less than an hour later, you'd reach a countryside of hills and vales and streams and trees. The wonder of it had been with her from the time she was a child.

She parked beneath the porte cochere at the side of her cottage. Once, the parking spot had been a carriage drop. She hadn't closed it in, although sometimes, in the dead of winter, she ended up scraping a lot of ice off her windshield. She just couldn't bring herself to add clunky garage doors to a spot that was so lovely.

Rollo went bounding out of the car, ready to find a tree of his own choosing.

Mo walked down to the river and gazed out toward Sunnyside. She shielded her eyes against the late-

October sun that had risen through the clouds and the mist. And there he was.

Repair work was going on at Sunnyside, with scaffolding up by the porch where Washington Irving had often sat, enjoying the peace of the river—when the trains weren't rattling by. There was no train at the moment.

Irving wasn't sitting. He was walking, as if taking a midday constitutional. Shoulders high and squared, he moved slowly but with dignity, handsome in a jacket, vest and cravat. She watched him for a few minutes— and she saw him look down the slight bend in the river to where she stood. She wasn't anywhere near close enough to see his face clearly, but she knew he was watching her, too. He waved at her, and she waved back.

She doubted he knew yet that his beloved Tarrytown–Sleepy Hollow area had been visited by a flesh-and-blood demon who was killing people—and taking heads.

During his life, people had often asked Irving whether he believed ghosts existed. Irving always said that if they did, and if he came back as one, he'd certainly haunt a place he'd loved. Sunnyside.

And, of course, there were frequent sightings of "the ghost." He was often caught in "orbs" and "patterns" on film and digital cameras

This amused Irving no end. He'd told Mo once that he derived great pleasure from studying people as they walked around Sunnyside gaping at their photos—and swearing they'd captured his image in a slew of dust motes when he'd actually been standing right behind them as they'd taken the pictures.

She didn't have the opportunity to speak with him

often. It only happened on days when she went back to Sunnyside to walk the grounds and revel in the peace and beauty of the place.

And to shop in the gift store. She loved going in at this time of year; they always had delightfully spooky things for sale. Sometimes, the "essence" of Irving—as he liked to refer to himself—followed her into the store and teased her as she did her shopping. He was quite a prankster and particularly liked making her look as if she were talking to herself—ostensibly driven crazy by the ghosts of Sleepy Hollow.

"Rollo! Let's go in," she called to the dog.

He came loping over to her from the woods, where he'd no doubt had a number of good sniffs and marked several trees—an Irish wolfhound was capable of a lot of "marking." She stooped to give him a massive hug. She'd taught him long ago not to jump on people, since he'd knock most of them to the ground if he did.

In the early 1800s, her home had been a one-room wooden farmhouse. Sometime before the Civil War, the Ahern family had come from Boston and purchased the house. They'd added a wing as well as a second story. During the war years, Sean Ahern had built another wing. He'd had a son killed at Shiloh and had turned his pain into a passion for helping wounded soldiers. He'd taken in many who had been displaced.

The ivied entrance with its small pillars led to a long hallway. The dining room was to the left of the kitchen, which came complete with modern conveniences. A door from the dining room led out to what was still called the "hospital porch." To the right was the staircase and the parlor, and beyond the parlor was an office/library. Behind that, she had a large family room. The house was filled with marvelous little features—a recessed area in the office for a daybed, a bay window at the front of the parlor and built-in shelving for bric-a-brac and plates and books. The family room had French doors that opened onto the back porch with its view of the river. There were the trains, of course. That was okay. For her beautiful little piece of the world, she could deal with the trains.

She set her keys on the eighteenth-century occasional table by the door and pulled off her jacket, hanging it on a hook. Then she started a pot of coffee in the kitchen, and after that, went to the office to sit at her computer—and stare at it. While Halloween might be approaching, she was working on designs for Valentine's Day.

His nails clicking on the hardwood floors, Rollo came down the hall and settled in her office, next to her desk. She tried to focus on the screen. She'd been working on a verse for a pop-up card she'd designed that revealed a cherubic cupid pulsing with sun rays when the card was opened. He was aiming an arrow with a heart for a tip, and so far she'd written, "Roses are red, violets are blue, my world is brilliant, since I have you."

Mo loved what she did. She'd been a visual arts major, and while still in college she became fascinated with pop-up cards. She'd worked for a number of card companies, but eventually she'd started working at home. She did the artwork and the "paper engineering" on the cards before they were sent off to be replicated in large numbers.

She made a decent living from her art. She and Rollo never accepted money for working with the police; to her, it wouldn't have seemed right.

"What do you think of my latest card, Rollo? Simple and sweet. Gotta tell ya, this isn't easy when…"

She could still see that first horseman—with the head of Richard Highsmith on it.

Mo heard the slight creak of old floorboards and turned around. Rollo was already at her feet so she knew it wasn't the dog moving.

Her heart quickened for a moment. She had just seen two people who'd been decapitated. Noises in the house didn't usually bother her. It was old; it was constantly settling. And, of course, she had several resident ghosts—some better than others in their abilities to make floorboards creak and cause solid objects to move.

This time it was Candy Lewiston who had come to see her.

Even as a ghost, Candy was rivetingly beautiful. She'd come to the house through the Underground Railroad during the Civil War. Her heritage was mixed—African-American, European and Native American. She had large, dark eyes, her cheekbones were perfectly sculpted and she moved with effortless grace. Ghosts could appear to float, yes, but Candy moved as if she were still flesh and blood, graceful and lithe beyond measure.

She knew the good and the bad of history. As a child, she'd had a gentle master who'd been happy to spend time with his slaves, attend baptisms of their children and be as generous as a father. At his death she'd found herself the property of a new master; she said he was the cruelest man to ever walk the earth. The daughter of her first owner—who'd been forced to sell the slaves—had actually helped Candy escape, and in their friendship, they'd both realized how wrong it was for any man or woman to own any other.

They'd ended up living at the cottage down from Irving's Sunnyside, and while Sarah Jane—Candy's friend—had gone on after death, Candy had lingered. But that was because she'd fallen in love with one of the few Confederate soldiers who'd died here, brought north to be cared for by his brother, who had chosen to fight for the Union.

Colonel Daniel Parker remained in the house, as well. He and Candy were together in death as they'd never been in life.

Candy paused long enough to give Rollo a spectral pat. Rollo knew she was there. His tail thumped on the floor. Smiling, Candy perched on the desk and looked at Mo. "What happened? What did you and Rollo find?"

Mo sighed and gave up on work, leaning back in her chair. "A man's head without a body, a woman's body without a head, the man's body—and the woman's head."

Candy stared at her in dismay. "How awful! Do they know, was it the politician from New York they were looking for?"

Mo nodded gravely. "And it's not...it's not just that he was dead. He was murdered. Horribly." She went on to tell Candy about the morning—about everything they'd discovered.

Candy shuddered. "And with the village and all of Tarrytown bustling with our October visitors...that makes it even worse. I hope they find the murderer quickly."

"Lieutenant Purbeck is running the investigation. At least, I think he is. An FBI man showed up, too," Mo said.

"Federal Bureau of Investigation," Candy said. She might be a ghost, but she loved watching as time went by, even though—as she'd often told Mo—time didn't always go by so well. Wars went on; people just didn't seem to learn. Candy and her beloved Daniel Parker liked walking the grounds along the river—and keeping up with history as it passed.

"Well, Mr. Highsmith was an important man," Candy said knowingly.

"Yes, very," Mo agreed.

"And this FBI man, he seems to be capable and good?" Candy asked.

Mo thought about her answer. Then she nodded. "He was serious and seemed to understand that...that Rollo knew what he was after when we found a body that wasn't the right body," she said. Actually, she'd liked the man immediately. She wondered if she'd been influenced by the fact he was very good-looking. Tall, dark, blue eyed, altogether striking. If he walked into a room, anyone—male or female—would notice, even if he was in a typical dark suit. He wore the suit damned well. She remembered feeling stunned when she'd fallen into his arms. Just for a split second, of course, but he *had* given her pause.

"He looks capable," she said. *He looks like he belongs on the cover of GQ,* she thought.

Candy nodded. "So, the police are investigating and the federal government is involved. What happened is devastating—unimaginable!—but you have done what they asked you to do. Now let them handle it. I understand that you can't forget it. To suggest such a thing would be ridiculous. But let them do their work, and you concentrate on yours. Maybe you should take a vacation, leave this place until they find the killer."

"I don't think I can."

"And why not?"

"What if...?"

"What if what?" Candy asked.

"What if the killer isn't finished?" Mo wondered aloud. The very possibility chilled her. "What if it wasn't a political assassination? I—I can't leave now. Rollo and I might be needed again and if we are, there's always the hope that we'll find the next victim still alive. Before he kills him—or her."

"Here's what I have to tell you," Dr. Mortenson said, leaning against one of the gurneys at the morgue. "The two bodies, when put back together, are definitely two people. Not more, in other words. Thank God. We still haven't ascertained the identity of the woman, but we're running fingerprints and searching out dental records."

"How did they die?" Aidan asked.

Mortenson frowned at him for a minute, as though to say, *They were decapitated. Wasn't that perfectly clear?*

But he quickly understood. He sighed. "I wish I could tell you it was the clean sweep of a sword or one blow from a big ax. A quick death."

Aidan's heart sank. He suddenly knew exactly what that expression meant. "But it wasn't that way?" he asked.

Behind him, Voorhaven sucked in his breath.

"A hatchet job?" Van Camp asked. His tone was rigid. Aidan liked Van Camp; he seemed to be a by-the-book detective, calm, collected, doing his job with dedication and competence. But he had retained empathy for victims.

He was probably better suited for this job than Aidan. Because, like it or not, Aidan knew *he* wasn't really calm, collected and by the book. He wasn't just empathetic—he was *involved*.

"Yes, but...thankfully, the victims were dead before their heads were removed."

"How were they killed?" Aidan asked bluntly.

"Strangulation. Manual strangulation. That should help you. Of course, with the chop job—sorry about that—it's difficult to get a complete picture. But I couldn't find ligature marks and there was heavy bruising around the neck. Now, the trauma could've come from the, er, removal of the heads."

He paused. "I worked in the city for years and saw just about every form of murder out there, although some sick bastard will always find a new twist. In my opinion, however, they were manually strangled, something that takes a significant amount of strength, especially considering the size of a man like Highsmith. The heads were removed afterward, probably for effect, for theatricality—but that kind of theorizing belongs to you investigators. I'm merely stating the obvious here."

"Or what appears to be obvious," Aidan murmured.

Mortenson hiked up two bushy white brows. "Yes, well, as I said, I leave theorizing to you gentlemen." He walked to one of the gurneys in the room. Both bodies had, mercifully, been covered with sheets.

Now Mortenson rolled back the first.

Aidan winced inwardly. He didn't want to see what was revealed. He had to.

Mortenson started with the female victim.

"Female, between the ages of twenty-eight and thirty-five. Approximately five foot seven in life, 135 pounds. In excellent shape and health, judging by the state of her heart and organs, muscles and bones. She was a blue-eyed blonde, no contacts, highlights in her hair. We've done a computer mock-up of what she looked like before the tissue and muscle damage to the face. We're turning that over to the police now."

Mortenson glanced at his clipboard and his notes, then pulled out several sheets, handing them to Aidan, Van Camp and Voorhaven.

Aidan studied the woman's face. She had nice bone structure, large eyes, a small nose and a pert chin. But there was no life in the image; he wasn't sure he would have recognized her even if he'd known her.

"What about her clothing?" Van Camp asked.

"Her personal effects are boxed and ready for you and the lab," Mortenson said. "But due to the blood on the outfit and various fluids stiffening the fabric, I believe she was killed and then beheaded in the suit you saw on the body, under that big coat. I've rushed everything, and the lab has, too."

"Thanks," Aidan said.

"Now, as to Mr. Highsmith…" Mortenson began.

Aidan felt his muscles tighten. He steeled himself not to flinch, not to show emotion. He didn't want to be hauled off the case.

Mortenson rolled the sheet back.

And there was Richard, the head placed where it should have been but showing not just the trauma of death, but of autopsy, too. He was almost unrecognizable.

Mortenson was all business, his gloved hands showing what his medical eye saw as he pointed out the bruising caused by the strangulation that had ended Highsmith's life.

Aidan stared at the corpse on the gurney. Richard Highsmith looked like something created by a master of bizarre special effects.

Mortenson's voice droned on and on, until finally the sheet was drawn back over Richard.

"I'll keep you posted," Dr. Mortenson said. "But I'm not sure what else I'll be able to tell you."

"Toxicology reports," Aidan said. He was quiet for a minute. "The timing here seems to be virtually impossible. Richard was seen, then he disappeared—but he wasn't put on the headless horseman until the very early hours of the morning. Whoever killed him must have gotten him out of the convention center and held him somewhere—dead or alive."

"Well, we need to find the crime scenes, too," Mortenson responded. "Both victims were dead when they were beheaded, but you're still going to have blood somewhere."

Aidan nodded, then indicated the bags of clothing and personal effects. "Wallet, cash, ID?" He already knew they were there; he'd checked before the medical examiner had taken Richard's body from the vault.

"Yes. Of course, I'm not a detective, but...no robbery. He had about a hundred in cash on him, several credit cards and his New York State driver's license."

"No cell phone?" Aidan asked. "It didn't show up in a secret pocket or anything?"

Mortenson shook his head. "No cell phone."

"Purbeck was going to get a fix on its last location," Van Camp murmured.

"It'll be the convention center," Aidan said. "If this killer is a psychopath, he's a smart one."

"Call us," Voorhaven said, "if you get anything, anything at all."

"We need an ID on Jane Doe as soon as possible," Van Camp pointed out.

"I'm on it. Like I said, I've done dental impressions and taken her fingerprints. Swabbed her for DNA, but of course, we have to have something for comparison," Mortenson said.

"Has the image of the young woman you showed us been made public?" Aidan asked.

"Definitely," Mortenson said. "It's been shown on the media. Uniforms are putting pictures up all over the city now."

Aidan left, followed by Voorhaven and Van Camp. "On to the strip club?" Voorhaven guessed.

"I want to head over to the convention center to meet the assistant first," Aidan said.

"You never met him?"

"No, I never had reason to, and it's been a while since I've seen Richard."

Van Camp shrugged. "We questioned everyone. We had police in there from the county helping out. We searched. We asked the assistant and Highsmith's people if they'd stay around another few days, and they were agreeable."

"The Fed doesn't seem to think we did it right," Voorhaven said in a low, sarcastic voice.

Aidan didn't have to answer; Van Camp did it for him. "Don't start with that crap, Jimmy. We have dead people here. We'll give Mahoney our total cooperation. Maybe he'll learn something more. He's a pair of fresh eyes and we have new info, as in bodies," he said, turning to Aidan. "Forgive the kid. He's a good cop, but like I said, new to having a detective's badge."

"Sure." Aidan shrugged "We don't know what we have yet. I'd still like to talk to Highsmith's assistant."

"Sorry, yeah," Voorhaven muttered. "We have dead people. I guess I think we're *supposed* to resent federal intervention. And Lee is right. We need to stop this, whatever it takes."

"We could split up, but I wouldn't mind an introduction to Mr. Branch, the assistant," Aidan said.

"Of course," Voorhaven agreed.

"I'll follow you," Aidan told them.

Van Camp nodded and led the way to the cars.

Aidan paused, looking back at the morgue.

Most of his life, he'd hated it when he saw—or imagined he saw—what others didn't. He hated whatever it was that made him see the dead walking.

He often denied it, even to himself.

But right now…

His thoughts were different.

Talk to me again, my friend. Talk to me, please. Talk to me again.

3

Somehow, Mo managed to get work done during the day, although she did keep the television on and listened as the news repeated the morning's findings over and over again.

A police spokeswoman was shown frequently, assuring the public that all local resources, the state police and the FBI had been called in, and a task force was investigating. The killer would be pursued until caught. The public was warned, of course, to be careful when out; people should travel in groups and make sure they were carefully locked in at their homes or hotels.

Naturally, the press questioned the young woman about the possibility of a serial killer on the loose.

News media and the police constantly reinforced the fact that all investigative paths were being followed.

Mo jumped when Rollo began to bark excitedly. There was a knock at her door and she froze. But Rollo was wagging his tail, so he knew her visitor.

"Who is it, boy?" she asked.

At the same time, her cell phone rang.

She picked it up. "Hello?"

"Mo, where are you? Let me in!"

It was Grace Van Mullen, a close friend. Grace had grown up here, and throughout the years, the two of them had stayed friends, meeting whenever Mo and her family came in from the city. As an only child, Mo had always valued her friends, none more than Grace.

These days Grace was often her sounding board. She worked for a tourist company and during the Halloween season that included taking on the role of a character at the Haunted Mausoleum. There was actually more than one mausoleum at this particular tourist attraction, as well as a scattering of graves. They were situated on a property that had long been forgotten and lay in the middle of what was once a farm. The farm and the old graveyard both belonged to Grace's employer now.

When the season wasn't going on, there were still tours of the place, but they were more historical and factual in nature. From the end of September through the first days of November, however, it was a popular attraction. Like everything else in town, the burial ground on the property was decorated with the usual— spiderwebs, fake rats, skeletons and, of course, a headless horseman. At Grace's main place of employment, though, live actors took on the roles of historic personages, legendary beings and all kinds of ghastly and ghoulish creatures.

"I'm on my way to the door."

When Mo opened it, Grace burst in. She was full of fiery energy, a young woman with a generous mouth and a nose that was almost as generous. None of her features were exactly pretty, yet Grace was one of the most attractive people Mo knew. It was that energy of hers, Mo thought, or her simple love of life and her willingness to look for the best in everyone.

"Oh, my God, thank you! Even at your place, I don't like waiting outside!" Grace gave an exaggerated shudder. "Not while all these terrible things are going on."

Grace locked the door behind her. Rollo woofed and she greeted him appropriately.

"This is so awful. Can you believe it? You were probably there. You and Rollo... And such a good man dead. Oh," she added. "I'm out of work. For tonight, at least."

"What? Really?" Mo checked her watch. It was now going on five, and she was happy, *relieved,* to have Grace's companionship for the evening.

"We just got word. They'll announce all the closings on the media soon," Grace told her. "I just wonder what they're going to do. The cops, I mean. How soon do they think they'll catch this guy? Maybe... Well, you'd have to be crazy or a monster to commit these crimes. So a crazy monster is running around here. And you'd notice a crazy monster, wouldn't you?"

"Monsters can live right next door," Mo said, and immediately regretted her words. Grace's look of horror was absolute. Her mouth formed a silent *oh.*

"Of course, whoever this is...it *could* be political," Mo said.

"If it was just Highsmith. But two people were killed."

"She might have been in the way," Mo said quickly.

"A government conspiracy!"

"Oh, Grace, I really don't think so. I don't believe that's the case at all. But...I guess we should be vigilant for a while."

"We'll all go broke if we have to be vigilant for too long," Grace said. "I don't want to die! But I need to be able to pay my mortgage. I should have gone your route, Mo. As in having a real career. You have your art *and* you volunteer, especially with Rollo! But you have a gift for working with animals. I wish I had a gift."

"You do have a gift! You know this area backward and forward. People love you. You've been given nothing but high ratings on the internet travel sites. And don't worry, the police will handle this situation," Mo said. "We'll be okay."

"Moneywise, yeah, I should be okay. I'm good at my job. The problem is I'm a shoe hog. Jeez, I'd have some financial backup if I didn't go crazy buying shoes. It's from all those years of watching *Sex and the City*. I should've been watching *The A-Team* or something."

"Hey, we can always put some shoes up on eBay!" Mo laughed. "Anyway, I do have some savings."

"Yeah…but that's *your* money."

"The police are being cautious, that's all. I'm sure this will be over soon."

"I'm feeling…trapped!"

Mo rolled her eyes. "You've only been in the house fifteen minutes!"

"Yeah, I know. You got any movies? Oh, wait, you're working. Okay, you keep working. But I'd love to see a movie. Nothing scary or creepy, though."

Mo went to her computer and saved her work. "We'll find a comedy we feel like watching. The remote's on the table by the TV. Pick out something on Netflix. I've done enough work for the day."

"Really? I don't want to mess you up, too. One of us needs an income!"

"It's fine. I finished the Valentine's card I was working on."

"Great! I locked the door, didn't I?"

"I'll check," Mo promised.

Grace headed to the family room in back, where the TV was, while Mo walked through the house to the front door, Rollo trotting behind her. She opened the door and carefully peered out.

Her house really was isolated.

Usually that seemed like a good thing, something she valued and enjoyed. But now...

The sky was overcast today. There was a breeze, and she could see the trees moving in the strange gray light. From her doorway, it was easy to imagine the past, the eerie land where darkness fell quickly over the groves of trees, and shadows chased each other beneath the moon.

There could be anything out there in those trees, she thought.

She closed and locked the door. It was late afternoon, and darkness would come soon.

Aidan knew that the convention center had been searched from top to bottom. Each of the thousands of attendees had been interviewed, a process that went on through the night, after which they were finally allowed to leave.

Taylor Branch, Richard Highsmith's right-hand man, was staying at an elegant new hotel recently built by one of the major chains. A police officer was on duty outside his room when Aidan and the detectives arrived. The officer had a chair for his vigil but had been standing near the elevator. He recognized Van Camp and Voorhaven and nodded as he was introduced to Aidan, then indicated that they could move on down the hall.

Taylor Branch greeted them in his suite's sitting room, wearing a long white robe. His hair was damp and he appeared to have showered. He was a young man—maybe thirty-five—although he looked older at the moment.

Lee Van Camp performed the introductions. Branch didn't protest their arrival; he glanced at Aidan with red-rimmed eyes and asked, "How? We were backstage. Richard and I were in the greenroom together. I left when Ms. Macaby, the convention hall manager, came to see what he'd like to eat. When I returned, there was a cup of tea and a plate of cheese and crackers on the table in front of the sofa—but no Richard."

"Why did you leave?" Aidan asked.

"I had to consult with security. There's a laugh for you," Branch said bitterly. "Well, sit down, please. I'm so tired and I've gone over it all so many times, in my own mind, as well as for others, I can envision practically every minute."

They took seats. "There's coffee on the counter there. And a bottle of whiskey," he told them.

"Thanks," Voorhaven said. "I'll have some coffee. Anyone else?"

Aidan looked over at him and nodded. "Thanks. Coffee would be good." The newbie detective was making himself comfortable and therefore making Taylor Branch comfortable. Which was smart.

"Let's start at the beginning," Aidan said. "When did you leave New York?"

"Let's see…we left the city at around five in the morning yesterday. We checked in here. They were ready for our early arrival. Everyone loved Richard, even when they opposed him politically. Well, almost everyone," he added glumly. "When I heard he'd been found—and how…"

His voice trailed off.

"So, you checked in here around seven or eight?" Aidan asked.

"I guess it was around nine when we got into our rooms." Branch cleared his throat. "Richard was next door to me. His things are still there. Connecting door between these suites," he noted, pointing.

"We'll take a look before we leave," Aidan assured him. "You have a key to the hallway door?"

"Ah, yeah. On the wet bar," Branch said.

Van Camp procured the key.

"Go on, please," Aidan encouraged Branch.

"You know, I've gone through all this so many times."

"Yes, and I'm grateful you're going through it again for me," Aidan said.

Branch took a deep breath and then resumed. "We'd stopped for coffee. That always makes me nervous, but we were traveling with private security. Richard hired a team himself. He said too many people use public money for things like that. And, of course, he isn't official yet, so…"

"So you stopped for coffee. How many in the security detail?" Aidan asked.

"Three men. The company is called Shields," Branch told him. "And, of course, the men are still here. Richard called them Muscles, Mischief and Magic. Muscles is Cory Stile and you'll see why they call him that. Mischief is the youngest of the guys and a flirt—real name Rob Little. And Magic is Ben Wilkes. He's a retired SEAL. Knows his stuff and can get you in and out of anywhere in the blink of an eye. They're good. They've been with us about a year—ever since the polls started saying Richard would win the mayoral race."

"They're in the hotel?" Aidan asked.

"Across the hall," Branch replied.

"So, you left this hotel when?" Aidan nodded a thanks to Voorhaven as he handed him a cup of coffee. It was hot and black, and not bad for hotel-room coffee.

But then, in this kind of suite, Aidan figured it was probably gourmet coffee.

"We had lunch at a restaurant in Tarrytown. Richard was wonderful, as usual, meeting people, speaking with them, shaking hands. Then we went on to the center. Cops were already there. The place had been thoroughly searched and everything seemed fine. We met with the audio-visual people, then headed back to the greenroom so Richard could get in some downtime before speaking. He and I were in there, and Jilli had just left. She works on schedules and that kind of thing.

"A center employee, Bari Macaby, the manager I mentioned earlier, came to ask if we wanted anything. She went to order Richard's snacks, and I went out to speak with Muscles, Mischief and Magic as well as the local cops. We were checking the metal detectors. When I came back in…Richard was gone. I hunted down Jilli first. She was onstage working with the AV people. She hadn't seen Richard. I found Bari Macaby in the auditorium, where she'd been watching Jilli doing a sound check for the night. I panicked. I let everyone know I couldn't find Richard. Then we tore the place apart."

"You called his cell first thing, I assume?" Voorhaven asked.

"Of course. He didn't answer."

"Did the cell phone show up?" Aidan asked next.

"Not that I know of," Branch replied. He looked at Van Camp, who shook his head.

"We're going to need your help. We'll need you to hang around for a few days," Aidan told him.

Branch smiled grimly. "I wasn't going anywhere. Helping Richard was my life. I swear, he was the best thing since Lincoln, to me, anyway. He had integrity and vision—he was an independent who was going to make it." He sighed. "I'll be here. I have to decide what to do with my life now. I figure I'm a suspect. But I was at the center when he disappeared. You can ask the security guys, Jilli, Bari… I didn't leave until this morning, when I heard that Richard had been found."

He sounded sincere. But Aidan had known some good actors in his day.

"What about Mr. Highsmith's enemies? Anyone in the political arena—or any other—stand out for you? You're his campaign manager, his chief aide, right? So, you'd be the man who'd know," Aidan said.

Branch thought. "Every politician has enemies. Mark Jacobs from the far left, and Harvey Applebaum from the right. Lots of people just couldn't believe that a moderate who looked logically at all the issues could actually get in! But Jacobs was speaking in Central Park at the time, and Applebaum's wife is in the hospital with a heart condition. He was with her all day yesterday."

"What about strip clubs?" Aidan asked. "Did Richard ever visit one?"

"What?" Branch was incredulous. "Richard didn't have time for a strip club—or any other kind of club."

"Come on, the guy was unmarried and you told us

this morning that he wasn't with anyone," Voorhaven put in.

"I didn't say he'd never dated or had a relationship!" Branch protested.

"What about a jilted lover?" Van Camp asked.

"His last long relationship was with Julia Underwood. They split up last year. She's a kindergarten teacher and the political scene was too much for her. It was an amicable breakup," Branch said. He opened his hands, staring down at them. "I'd give you a name if I had one, trust me on that." He shook his head. "I can't see anyone doing something like this! Not to Richard."

"No. But they might pay other people to do it," Aidan said quietly.

Branch shook his head again. He didn't want to believe it. No one did.

"Did he have a close friend named Elizabeth or Lizzie?" Aidan asked. "Does the name mean anything to you?"

"There are a lot of Elizabeths out there," Branch said. "No one who was special in Richard's life, that I was aware of, anyway. He was an open man, but I didn't pry. I admired him. He was my friend. That doesn't mean I knew everything about his life."

Aidan rose, setting down his cup on the table beside his chair. "Thank you. We may need to ask you more questions later."

"Like I said, I'll be here," Branch told them, rising, as well. "I'm about to hit the whiskey—and try to sleep."

At the door, Aidan paused. "Where will we find the security guys, Bari Macaby and Jilli—"

"Jillian Durfey. Jillian is down the hall on the other

side of Richard's room. The security men are across from us," Branch said, pointing at the doors. "Muscles, Magic, Mischief. Did you want to go through Richard's room? It's locked because of the investigation, of course, but..."

"We'll have a chat with one or two of the others first, Mr. Branch," Aidan said.

"Sure. Whenever you need me, I'm available."

"Oh, by the way, you know a woman was murdered, too?" Aidan asked.

Branch nodded dully.

"Any idea who she might have been? Was Richard seeing someone recently? Even casually? Did any aides or groupies or anyone like that disappear?"

"No. Richard was a straight shooter. He wasn't seeing anyone right now. He was focused on the campaign. We traveled here with just the security men, Jilli, me and Richard. We're not that far from the city, you know. This should have been a speech and some hand-shaking. But..."

His voice faded, but then he suddenly stared at Aidan, eyes narrowing. "Aidan Mahoney."

"Yes."

"Your name was on one of his lists. You were going to be invited to a dinner. You...knew Richard?" he asked.

"Yes," Aidan said. "Thank you for your help. We'll be in touch."

Taylor Branch closed the door.

Aiden turned to see Lee Van Camp studying him. "You knew Richard well, didn't you?" he asked.

Aidan nodded. "I hadn't seen him in a while. I

watched his career, though, with pleasure. He was always a good kid. A good guy."

He waited for one of them to ask if he should be on the case.

Neither did.

"Let's start our interviews with Jilli," Aidan said.

They walked down the hall to her room and tapped on the door. It opened almost immediately.

Jilli was definitely affected by what had happened. Like Branch, it looked as though she'd taken a shower. Aidan wondered if it was a subliminal way to attempt to wash away the shock and horror of Richard's death.

"You're back," she said, looking at Van Camp. "Do you know anything? Have you found out who did this? My God, I still can't believe it!"

She had a glass in her hand, half full of some amber liquid—Scotch, he figured, or bourbon. Aidan had a feeling she'd already knocked back a few. Her eyes were red and swollen. She'd obviously been crying and crying hard for a long time. Even as she looked at them, a trickle of tears started down her cheeks.

Van Camp introduced Aidan. "So we've got locals and Feds," she murmured. "Well, we may need magic police in on this one, because it was, like, *poof!* Richard just…disappeared."

"Tell me about your day—and the last time you saw Richard," Aidan said.

She didn't offer them anything to drink and didn't suggest they sit. Her room wasn't small, although it was a junior suite. Nothing like Branch's. But she had a desk, sofa, coffee table and small kitchenette.

Voorhaven leaned against the wall. Van Camp didn't

wait for an invitation; he walked across the room and took a seat on the sofa.

Jilli turned, her fingers curled around her drink, and sat on the bed.

"It was a good day. A good travel day that became a good campaign day," Jilli said.

"Why was he campaigning up here?" Voorhaven asked. "He was a mayoral candidate in the city."

Jilli smiled. "This is the Hudson Valley! It's beautiful and it's about two hours out of the city. People come here for respite. New York City residents buy property up here—time-shares, little cottages, condos—you name it. It's an escape zone. Richard was from this area and he loved it."

Yes, he had. He'd loved roaming the forests. His parents might have moved to Florida, but he still felt a strong connection to the place. He'd loved a campfire at night and all the haunted happenings that went on around Halloween. He'd loved Washington Irving and tales of the Revolution and the hardy Dutch settlers who had first farmed the land.

"Okay, so you arrived here with your security detail."

She nodded, studying her glass. "Richard was good about his security, knew he needed it for practical reasons. But he truly loved people. It wasn't fake or part of the game with him. He'd shake hands or talk with anyone who wanted a word with him. So, we'd seen people at lunch, and when we came here we were high on the enthusiasm he received. We were in the convention center. There were cops everywhere, plus the center itself had its own security, and we had Muscles, Mischief and Magic. They were just checking the scanners—metal scanners, you know—when Richard disappeared. At first, we thought he'd wandered somewhere to practice his speech. Or gone outside for a breath of fresh air. But…I'm telling you, it was as if he disappeared into thin air."

"You were testing the audio when that happened?"

"Yes. If they get a level with one person, then they just have to tweak it when Richard comes out," she said. "That was the idea."

"But you and Taylor Branch and the convention manager—Bari Macaby—were the last people to see him, correct?" Van Camp said.

Jilli nodded.

"Did Richard ever say anything to you about a strip club?" Aidan asked.

There was shock in her eyes. "A strip club?"

Aidan smiled. "Most men I know—and women, too, for that matter—have been in one at some point. Bachelorette parties, bachelor parties, birthdays."

"Yeah, but *Richard? In the middle of a campaign?*"

"Did he have a friend named Lizzie? Or Elizabeth?" Aidan asked.

She shrugged. "He might have. I didn't know all his friends. Lizzie…or Elizabeth. Not an unusual name. I know several."

"Thank you," Aidan said. "I hope you get some sleep."

She still looked confused by the strip club question. She hadn't moved when they reached the door. "Come and lock this," Aidan told her gently.

She rose like a sleepwalker. When they were out in the hallway, Aidan heard the bolt slide home.

"Muscles, Mischief and Magic next?" Van Camp asked.

"No, let's do Richard's room," Aidan said.

Van Camp opened the door to the suite.

It was larger than Branch's with a huge living area, a conference table that would seat twelve, a good-size kitchenette and a bedroom. Richard had been almost OCD neat; the outer rooms could be described as Spartan. Aidan headed into the bedroom. "See what you find out here," Aidan told Van Camp and Voorhaven.

Richard's clothing had been neatly hung and his shoes were lined up in the closet. His computer was gone. Aidan knew it was at the police lab so they could search for anything that might give them a clue.

There was a notepad by the phone. It was blank.

But Aidan picked it up and held it to the light. He could see where a pen had pressed into the paper.

He didn't have a pencil to run over the slight indentations on the page. But he studied it for a minute, trying to make out the words.

They said *Lizzie grave.*

Aidan had the strange feeling that Richard had idly written the same words over and over again.

Because they were always at the back of his mind?

4

Mo was curled on the sofa with Rollo's massive body taking up the second half, and Grace was in the rocker. They were just reaching the end of *Elf* when Mo's phone rang.

"Hello?"

It was Tommy Jensen.

"They've finished up here," he said. "They've let me open!" he told her. "My God, Mo, you should've seen it. They went through the parking lot inch by inch. They collected more garbage than I ever knew existed. My headless horseman is gone, of course—I almost feel I should change the name of the place. Then, after they were finished with the outside, they came in. They sprayed stuff all over—fingerprint stuff. Jeez! There were hundreds of people here last night. But I guess the cops are dotting their i's and crossing their t's. Anyway, they're letting me open. Will you come out to the bar tonight? Please?"

It occurred to her that the police had warned people about going out. But she wasn't alone; she was with Grace. And she had Rollo. She looked at her wolfhound, who was watching her as if trying to discern her conversation.

"Grace is here. I'm sure she'll want to come, too."

Grace nodded enthusiastically.

"Have you heard anything else?" Tommy asked.

"Only what they're saying on TV."

"They closed down all the headless horseman attractions today. It's going to be a killer for the merchants. Oh, bad wording!" Tommy said.

"That's why Grace is here. They closed the Mausoleum tonight."

"Yes, of course. Well, come out here and commiserate with me. My staff's heading in. I'll miss the dinner hour...but maybe if people see your car, they'll come."

"I can bring Rollo?"

"Sure, but you know the law—put on his service-dog jacket."

"Yeah."

When she hung up, Grace was ecstatic. "Yes! We're out of here."

"Hey, you didn't *have* to be here."

"What? You think I wanted to be at my house? Uh-uh! But I'm ready for a bunch of people, society...and good food. Tommy has the best cheese steaks around."

"Want me to drive?" Mo asked.

"I guess we should take both cars. I can just go home from there."

Mo agreed, and they were ready to leave within minutes. Darkness had fallen, and she paused after opening her car door. The breeze moving through the trees created a distinct rustling sound that was almost like a strange whisper. She could see movement in the shadows cast by foliage in the moonlight. The air was crisp and cool, and the night seemed to have its own sense of expectation.

Of waiting.

Then the late train went chugging by; it screamed of the everyday and the mundane, and the odd spell that had taken hold was lifted.

As it turned out, Tommy had been wrong to worry about business. While traveling to his restaurant had seemed like a voyage through a land that was asleep, his parking lot was so crowded that Grace called her cell and suggested they park on the street by the Old Dutch Church.

They did. Mo wasn't afraid. Rollo was with her and wagging his tail.

But she found herself pausing again. Seeing the old graves up the hill at the Old Dutch Church and then beyond at Sleepy Hollow Cemetery, she felt there was no place where the past seemed more alive. She could hear the water trickling under the new bridge, and she could easily imagine Irving's Ichabod Crane as he rode home on a broken-down nag through the trees, their skeletal branches dipping and swaying in the moonlight.

"Hey!" Grace had parked near her. "We going in or what?"

"Yep. If we can get in. Look how busy it is! And it's only a little after nine. Early for the bar to be hopping like this."

"Go figure!" Grace said. "Gruesome murder draws a crowd!"

"Hey, people love haunted houses," Mo reminded her. "*You* should know that."

"Yeah," Grace admitted. "True enough."

"I like old mysteries," Mo said thoughtfully. "I don't

like to think about the families left behind when something terrible happens, though. If it's far in the past, everyone's at rest and there's no one still alive to be hurt by this kind of fascination with blood and guts."

"Yes, well…heads showing up in headless horseman territory…that is, I don't know, scary, so we need to band together."

While the streets had been quiet, it seemed that everyone in the village of Sleepy Hollow as well as Tarrytown and Irving had descended on the Headless Horseman Hideaway Restaurant and Bar.

"Nice! I love it. All these people! Tonight it feels good," Grace said.

Mo looked back at the Old Dutch Church. White wraiths seemed to slip between the graves and mausoleums up on the hill. It was just the moon playing tricks, she knew. Because tonight an autumn mist was actually forming.

When they walked in, the crowd at the bar was three-deep; all the tables were taken. But Tommy, working behind the bar, saw them arrive.

"I saved a table for you!" he called to them.

Hurrying out, he caught hold of Mo's arm and smiled over at Grace. He was beaming. "I should feel bad, right? I *do* feel bad. I feel terrible. But…I didn't know Richard Highsmith. And the crowds at Halloween and during the fall and at Christmas keep us going through the rest of the year."

"It's okay, Tommy," Mo said. She was glad they'd come, and he was obviously pleased that she and Grace were there.

As they moved through the crowd, people kept turning to look at Rollo. Some patted him; some asked first.

Luckily, Rollo would never hurt anyone. Mo caught bits and pieces of conversation as they walked. Most people were talking about what had happened. Speculation ran high as to whether it was a political assassination or a maniac on the loose.

"But then, why the murdered woman?" someone asked. "Was she killed just for effect? Or maybe she walked in on the first murder!"

"Your table's back here," Tommy said, escorting them through the restaurant, apparently oblivious to the stream of words around them.

"Hey, don't worry about us. Take care of your customers," Mo said.

"No, I'm good. You're the first friends who promised to show up and actually have!" Tommy said happily. He led them to a booth near the back, one Mo particularly loved because it was private.

The whole restaurant had been designed to resemble a wooden cottage deep in the woods. The walls were decorated with framed pages from Washington Irving's work and various prints of the illustrations done for his stories throughout the years. Fabricated trees and vines separated booths and areas of the bar, and the overall impression was decidedly charming. But Tommy had also seen to it that from every section of the bar you could see one of the large-screen TVs he had high on the walls.

The menu was attuned to the story, as well. Brom Bones was a rib dish. Ye Olde Dutch Churchyard was a house specialty—a stew with carrots, potatoes, onions and roast beef so tender it melted in the mouth.

"I'm having the Katrina Van Tassel!" Grace announced. She was ordering the chicken potpie, each one baked with a picture of the lovely fictional lass impressed into the crust.

"I'll put your order in myself," Tommy told them. "Mo?"

"Uh, the same. Great."

"And I'll have a chardonnay," Grace said. "What about you, Mo?"

"Going to stick with water tonight," she replied.

"Suit yourself. I'd be downing a bottle of Jack if I dared!" Tommy said with a laugh.

Grace's eyes were on one of the television screens. She looked over at Mo. "I can hardly hear, but we're major national news," she said.

"Highsmith might have been mayor, then governor or senator—and possibly a presidential candidate. Not to mention the state of the bodies when they were found," Mo said. "It's big news, yes."

Mo stared at the closest screen as Rollo settled beneath the table at her feet.

She could see two of the screens. On the second one she saw quick images of Sleepy Hollow and Tarrytown. The numerous headless horsemen set up for the Halloween season were spotlighted. Fortunately, no one had caught the murder scene on a cell phone. Although she couldn't hear well, she was pretty sure a reporter was saying that nothing had shown up on YouTube, and that his station would never sensationalize such a tragic situation.

Abby Cole, a tall, attractive redhead and Tommy's lead bartender, came sweeping by their table with their drinks. Both Mo and Grace greeted her warmly.

"You doing okay?" Mo asked her.

"I'm going to make a fortune—if I survive to spend

it," Abby said. "We have two new girls on the floor. That's why I ran over with your drinks. You should have food in a few minutes. If you get bored, you can always hop behind the bar!" This was something Mo had done on a few occasions, as a favor to Tommy—her part-time college job as a bartender coming in handy.

In a whirl Abby was gone. Five minutes later, a smiling young girl hurried over with their food. "One Cemetery Salad and one Brom Bones!" She set the plates down, then dashed off.

Mo and Grace looked at each other and burst out laughing.

"The salad or the ribs?" Mo asked Grace.

"Ah, the ribs. Okay?"

"Absolutely. I think when we're finished, I may go help at the bar. Can you watch Rollo?"

"You bet. And I'll watch for anything good-looking and unattached that walks in. Okay, forget good-looking. I'll keep an eye out for semi-reputable and bathed."

Mo smiled at that and ate the salad, which was really very good. It had strips of tuna, fruit, nuts and all kinds of great flavors. It wasn't, however, a chicken potpie.

"Okay, I'm heading to the bar," Mo said.

"Is it all right if I give Rollo a piece of meat?" Grace asked.

"No, he has his own treats."

Grace just smiled at her; she was already passing Rollo a tidbit of her food.

Mo slipped behind the bar, and Abby cast her a look of gratitude. They weren't alone. Josh Whitby was there, too, but the place was so busy, she figured she could be helpful by making drinks at the service station for the floor servers.

She was creating a house specialty—a Head of the Horseman, a strange concoction of beer, liquor and a touch of soda—when she saw that Grace wasn't alone.

Mo almost dropped the glass.

The tall, dark and handsome FBI agent was at the table with her. He was still wearing his suit—but his tie was gone and his top shirt buttons were loosened. He was patting Rollo and smiling at something Grace was saying.

"Mo?"

She caught herself just in time to keep from spilling the specialty brew and turned to Abby.

"Thanks, Mo. You were a lifesaver tonight. It's wound down now. I'll cut you in when I divvy up—"

"Abby, don't be ridiculous. I don't want anyone's tips." Mo shook her head, distracted.

"Grace got herself a hot one, huh?" Abby said. "Nice! But right now, she shouldn't be going home with strange men. I don't think I've seen him before."

"He's FBI," Mo told her. "I met him this morning."

"Oh. Ohhh! Cool. I imagine an FBI man would be safe—and good to have around."

"Yeah, one would imagine."

"Seems Rollo likes him, so he must be okay."

Rollo did choose his people, and Rollo liked the agent. He was greeting him with tail thumps and licks that should have gone to a long-lost relative.

Mo returned to the table, watching the man. She was disturbed to realize that she felt as if she *needed* to be there. She found the man fascinating. She'd met him under the most disturbing circumstances possible, and yet...

She'd simply stared at him when they'd met. When she'd pitched right into him. He had the kind of physique that made a suit look good. He wasn't overly muscular, yet he was obviously strong and solidly built. Then there were his eyes. Blue. Intensely blue. In a ruggedly handsome face.

Great. In the middle of a dreadful situation, she was falling into...a crush? Infatuation, maybe. Or maybe he'd mesmerized her. But then...

She hadn't dated in a long time. Not quite true— she'd had one dinner with a friend of a friend. Nothing had sparked. She'd claimed a headache while he was droning on about his brilliance at the stock market. The guy had driven her home, and thanks to Rollo she'd been able to escape inside before the good-night kiss. Rollo had barked on cue; he was very good at getting rid of anyone she didn't want to ask in.

Before that, there'd been Kyle.

She still went to see him sometimes when he and his group were playing in Albany. They were friends— they just weren't meant to be the great loves in each other's lives.

"Ah, here she is!" Grace said, as Mo reached the table.

Agent Aidan Mahoney stood and smiled at her.

"Hello." She smiled back.

"I'm sorry, I don't mean to interrupt. I saw the dog and I guess he just drew me over."

"I told him he wasn't interrupting," Grace said, looking a little starry-eyed.

"Not at all," Mo agreed politely.

"Then, please, sit," Agent Mahoney insisted. "Let me get out of your way. I should—"

"Don't leave!" Grace broke in.

"I'm just surprised to see you. How did you end up here tonight?" Mo asked him. "Have you learned anything? Did you get the guy? Sorry, I'm bombarding you with questions."

"I'm here for a few reasons. This is one of the few places in the area where you can still get food at—" he glanced at his watch "—almost eleven. It's also where we found Richard's head and I thought I should get the lay of the land and figure out how and when someone might have come here to, uh, place the head on the effigy." He spoke easily and his manner was relaxed. He was a man who exuded confidence. Why wouldn't he be? Yet, oddly, she recognized a tension in him. Maybe that made him even more attractive; he seemed aware of everything around him, even as he paid attention to the two of them. She thought that if danger did arrive, he'd be up and prepared to confront it in a flash.

"So, nothing new?" she asked.

He shook his head. "What we do is very methodical. Very routine. Check and recheck stories and find the discrepancies, follow every little thing."

"He was telling me how good you and Rollo are," Grace said, sipping a cup of coffee now. "I told him you two are like a wonder team, finding people all the time. Luckily, most of them alive. She *used* to find lots of dead people in the city—that's why she moved here. Fortunately, our murder rate is extremely low. We like to be spooky, not lethal."

"This crime is unusual," Aidan Mahoney said. But he was staring at Mo. And she suddenly felt uncomfortable, as if he'd seen something in her. Something she kept hidden. Secret.

Did he somehow sense her ability to see the dead? How could he? How could he even suspect such a thing?

And if he *had* guessed, he didn't like it. He seemed to wince and turned away from her.

Mo was surprised. She almost felt as if he'd slapped her. Up until now, he'd been courteous, and he and Rollo still seemed to be on extremely friendly terms.

His food arrived. Apparently, he'd ordered the chicken potpie and actually gotten it.

The noise level in the place had gone down—to a dull roar, as Tommy said when he came by their table. He shook Mahoney's hand and thanked him for allowing the bar to open.

"I wish I could take credit," the agent said. "That call was made by the local police."

"I haven't heard yet if they're opening any of the attractions tomorrow," Grace said.

"The sheriff's office will be handling that decision," Mahoney said. "This is like having a suspect list of thousands. And, of course, it's a delicate balance. You have two people who've been decapitated. And you're in an area where tourism thrives because of a great American author's tale about a headless man. I'm glad I'm not making the decisions."

"I thought the FBI always took over when they came in," Tommy said.

"We come in to work together, to pool resources. When you have an area that seldom deals with murder, it's good to bring in the teams that are most experienced." Mahoney stood up, evidently preparing to leave.

"I'll go settle up at the bar," he said.

"The house will be happy to comp your meal," Tommy told him.

"Thank you, but I can't accept. Besides, it's slowed down, so I can ask Abby a few questions." Mahoney turned to Grace. "Ms. Van Mullen, a pleasure." He turned to look at Mo again. She thought he was going to speak, but he just nodded. He still had that strange look about him. As if he was afraid to get too close.

"Good night," Mo said.

Rollo woofed.

Mahoney paused to pet the dog. There was a different expression on his face; he obviously liked Rollo.

Then he was gone, a tall, solid figure heading toward the bar—and drawing every eye in the place, male and female.

"Whoa!" Grace let out a long breath. For a moment, the three of them watched as he spoke with Abby. Abby seemed enchanted as she stared at him, answering questions when he prompted her—and just staring when he didn't.

Eventually, he left.

"Wish he would have stayed around awhile longer," Tommy said. "A guy like that makes you feel safe."

"You don't feel safe?" Mo asked him.

"Mo, there was a *head*. In my parking lot. So, no, I don't. And how can *you* not want to feel safe? You and Rollo found the head—and then the body. Bodies. And *another* head!"

She swallowed uncomfortably. "I have Rollo," she said.

"Wish I did," Grace murmured.

"Rollo and I will follow you home."

"But then you have to go home alone," Grace said. "Rollo isn't a person."

Mo smiled. "He's better than a person. He has the best instincts and nose in the world. If anyone threatens me in any way—or if there's something that even hints at danger—Rollo lets me know."

"I wish he had a brother!" Grace said, and laughed. "That's what I'd say if you had a hot guy. In fact, I wonder if your hot FBI guy has a brother."

"He's definitely not *my* FBI guy," Mo said.

Grace seemed surprised by her response. "He spoke very highly of you when he came to the table. And Rollo knew him right away. I kind of had the impression you two had bonded."

"I don't think so," Mo said. Both Tommy and Grace gaped at her. She made a point of yawning. "I've got to call it a night. Ready?" she asked Grace. "Tommy, may we have the check?"

"Uh, no. You rescued Abby at the bar. I should have been paying you. And, Grace, if you can hang around a little longer, I'll follow you home, since your house is just down the street from mine," Tommy said. "That way, Mo, you and Rollo can head straight home."

"Okay." She looked at Grace uncertainly. "Are you sure?"

"I'm not tired yet. I'm wired. Remember, I've been working nights," Grace said.

Mo wished them both good-night and picked up Rollo's leash. She wondered if Grace was staying behind in hopes that the FBI man would return.

But he'd already left the bar.

Mo went out to the parking lot and started across the pavement to the street. The Old Dutch Church sat high on its little hill in the moonlight and shadows seemed to dance around the gravestones.

Rollo suddenly stopped and sniffed the air. He turned, wagging his tail.

Mo felt unease creeping along her spine.

She didn't know what she expected to see. Irving's horseman, thundering silently toward her on a giant black steed?

No. Rollo would be barking, she was sure of that!

It wasn't the horseman.

It was Aidan Mahoney. He was leaning against one of the pillars by the entry, watching her.

Waiting? Watching?

Rollo barked and, before she was prepared, hopped into a running start to reach the man. He nearly pulled her off her feet.

"Rollo!" she said in dismay.

But he'd already hurried over to his new friend. Mahoney hunched down to pat the dog as Rollo rushed toward him.

She followed. Rollo rarely disobeyed but she didn't want to reprimand him. Not in front of Mahoney.

Mahoney stood up. "Pretty impressive dog," he said.

"Yes, he is."

"How long have you had him?"

"He's six. I've had him since he was a puppy."

He nodded, looking down at the dog then back at her. "And how long have you been out there searching for corpses?"

"I don't usually search for corpses. I search for the living."

"You're not originally from here. Your friend said so."

She shrugged. "I'm from the city. But I came here for years with my parents. Every year."

"Why did you leave New York?" he asked. "What Grace told me—is that right?" These weren't casual questions. It was as if he was daring her to say something.

Such as…admit she had special abilities? To connect with the living when they'd disappeared, gone missing—and to connect with the dead?

If that was what he wanted to know, she wasn't going to oblige.

"I don't have to live in the city. I'm a greeting card designer and writer. I happen to love the Hudson Valley." She couldn't help herself. "If Grace hadn't said anything, I have a feeling you would've figured out I wasn't from here, anyway."

"The reason I suspected you weren't really a local is because I am," he said quietly. "And I would've remembered you."

"But…"

"We wouldn't have met, but I was thinking I would've noticed you somewhere along the line." He looked her up and down, and she knew he was estimating her age. She didn't think he was *that* much older— five to seven years, maybe. "I probably headed off to college when you were in high school. But from the way you're so familiar with the valley and its history, I realized you must've been around here a fair bit." He apparently felt he'd talked enough. "Where's your car?"

"Down on the street."

"I'll walk you."

"I have Rollo."

"It's all right."

An argument would have somehow been more dis-
quieting than just giving in. "Come on, boy," she said to
Rollo, tugging at the leash. Walking briskly, she started
down the street again, aware that he was close behind
her. She didn't stop, and she didn't turn around until
she'd reached her car. When she opened the passenger
door to let Rollo in, she finally looked back.

In the light thrown by nearby street lamps, she could
see that he was staring up at the Old Dutch Church.

"From now on, let Rollo in by the driver's side," he
said. "That gives him the ability to jump out and help
you if someone comes from behind while you're getting in the car."

"Sure. Thanks."

She shut the door and hurried around to slide into
the driver's seat. Starting the ignition, she saw that he
was staring at the church again.

She didn't wave; she turned the car around and drove
home.

The roads were dark and quiet as she left the village
of Sleepy Hollow. She came to the quiet road that led
through foliage and trees to her cottage in the woods.
Parking, she realized she'd done the same thing many
times before, even at this hour, and never felt the slightest fear.

Until tonight. Now, the woods seemed to breathe.
The night air seemed to dance. Malevolence might well
have whispered in the breeze.

She quickly opened the door and let Rollo and herself into the house. The dog whined, and she thought he
felt it, too, whatever was in the air. But he didn't bark;
there was no one out there.

Her ghosts were quiet when she entered. Rollo accompanied her as she went from window to window, making sure they were locked.

When she finally climbed up the stairs to bed, she paused, looking around. "I need a weapon, Rollo. Just so I'll be able to get to sleep."

She settled on the fireplace poker and went upstairs. When she lay down at last—Rollo taking up the foot of the bed—she was convinced she'd never sleep.

If she did, she feared, she'd have horrible nightmares.

But she did sleep. It was a matter of the human body giving out, needing rest.

And she didn't have nightmares.

She dreamed of walking in the woods, clad in nothing but a white mist that swept around her like a beautiful satin gown. As she walked, she saw a tall, dark figure coming toward her. She wasn't afraid. His face emerged from the shadows. It was Aidan Mahoney. He smiled, the way he smiled when he looked at others. She ran to him, the mist magical as it swept around her.

He was naked when she reached him.

She threw herself into his arms and he brought her down with him to the soft, verdant earth where they were embraced by a sweet-smelling bed of leaves....

Then she woke, bathed in sweat and embarrassed beyond all measure, despite the fact that she was entirely alone. Except for Rollo, of course.

And Rollo didn't know that she'd been having an erotic dream about a man she barely knew. A man who didn't seem to like her.

She groaned and glanced at the bedside clock. It was three in the morning. Punching her pillow, she lay back down.

The moon was full, and its light drifted into her

room. Since that morning, when she'd left the house with Rollo to search for Richard Highsmith, it seemed that even the earth and sky had changed.

At 3:00 a.m. Aidan was still up.

He sat in a front row at Mystic Magic, the place advertised on the matchbook found in Richard's pocket.

In front of him, a very busty blonde gyrated around a silver pole.

The club appeared to be straight up—there were warnings all over to look and not touch. The dancers were beautiful girls, mostly enhanced for their chosen profession, but it wasn't a last stand for down-and-out prostitutes.

He'd spoken to a few of the women, and he'd shown them a picture and asked if they'd ever seen Richard Highsmith before. None had. He was a good judge of liars. He'd studied all the physical tics and nuances that were typically signs of lying. But lots of liars had studied the signs, too. Still, he was pretty certain that he was getting the truth. Richard had been given the matchbook or picked it up somewhere, and he'd used it for the note he seemed compelled to write. Twice, at least.

The blonde was the last of Mystic Magic's lineup. Her name—or her stage name—was Starlight. Her G-string was crystal studded; the same crystals had adorned the cape, bra and skirt she'd started out with, along with her bountiful blond hair. She was extremely popular, with a magnanimous smile for each horny bastard who leaned forward to slip money into the studded belt.

She slithered around the pole, posed and gyrated.

Her audience went wild. She simulated sex with a gusto he was sure most men had never seen in a bedroom.

Then she rose and bowed to thunderous applause, blew the audience a kiss and hurried offstage.

For the most part, the crowd began to leave. There were still some private lap dances to be had, but most of the men—and the few women—in the establishment were paying service tabs and heading out.

Aidan waited.

In a few minutes, the bubbly blonde came out from the rooms behind the stage and walked toward him, smiling.

"Hi!" she said. She didn't posture. At that moment, she might have been the girl next door, scrubbed clean of makeup and wearing a T-shirt and jeans. "I understand you wanted to ask all of us some questions. You're really an FBI agent?"

He smiled back. "Yes." He pulled Richard's picture from his pocket and held it out. "Do you know this man? Have you ever seen him here?"

She gazed up at him with huge blue eyes. "Of course I know him! He's Richard Highsmith. He was a wonderful speaker. And the poor man died *here*. In our town. A really awful death. I've been watching the news all day."

Aidan nodded. "Yes, he's on the news. But was he ever in this club? Did you run into him anywhere? Did you ever meet him?"

"He shook my hand," she said proudly.

"Where?"

"At the Coffee Spot, just off the highway. He was even better in real life—he had the best smile. He was so sincere."

"Did you actually meet him?"

"We spoke and he asked me for my name. It's Debbie. Debbie Howell," she said.

"Thank you." Aidan presented a second picture, the computer rendering of their Jane Doe.

"What about her?"

"What about her?" Debbie repeated.

"Have you ever seen her?"

"I'm not trying to be rude or anything, but how would I know? She just looks like...like tons of people," Debbie said. "She could be anyone. I'm sorry, but...it's not a very good picture."

"No," he admitted. "It's not."

He pocketed both pictures again.

"I'm so sorry. I wish I could have helped," Debbie said. "But what made you think that Richard Highsmith would have, um, been in a place like this? I mean we're perfectly legal—and we're really dancers, not whores."

"No, of course you're dancers. Listen, Richard was found with a matchbook from this place in his pocket," Aidan said. "You didn't happen to give him a matchbook when you saw him, did you?"

She shook her head. "I don't smoke. But people leave matchbooks all over. He might have picked it up anywhere."

"True." He'd already concluded that himself. "Except that Richard didn't smoke, either," he pointed out.

"Oh," she said thoughtfully. She brightened. "Maybe he needed matches to light candles on a birthday cake—or for some other reason!"

"Maybe," he agreed. But he doubted that Richard had planned on celebrating any birthdays in the middle of a campaign trip. Back to his original conclusion—

Richard had probably picked it up just to scribble on it. Or someone had given it to him for that purpose.

"Well, thank you, Debbie. I appreciate your time."

"Oh, no. It's my pleasure. I'd love to help!"

He handed her one of his cards. "Call me, please, if you think of anything."

"Oh, I will, I promise. And if you need me for any other information, you can call me." She grabbed a cocktail napkin and wrote her name and number. Her handwriting was clear and careful. "Did Maureen Deauville and Rollo help you find Mr. Highsmith?" she asked.

He was startled by the question.

"Why do you ask?"

"Oh, they never put Mo's info out there anywhere. That's her choice. When we were kids—she used to come here for summers and a lot of the girls our age were friends then—she had another dog, a big wolfhound like Rollo. Mo was just sixteen when Robbie Anderson went missing. Everyone was going nuts. She went out with her dog, and she found Robbie. He'd fallen into a sinkhole at the cemetery. Went right through the ground into one of the mausoleums. Poor kid had to go to a shrink for months, but... No one heard him down there and they might *never* have heard him. It was way over from the far side of the church. Anyway, I heard from Tommy Jensen that he saw her there, so I assumed she had something to do with finding the...head. I'm just hoping she's okay. That had to be hard. And Mo...she's not like other people. When I see her, she's still as friendly and nice as ever. And, well, there are people here who don't associate with me anymore and pretend they don't know me when they see me in the grocery store."

"I'm sorry about that. Some people aren't very open-minded," Aidan told her. He hesitated, not telling her in so many words that her assumption about Mo was right. "Maureen Deauville is fine. I saw her a few hours ago. She was having dinner with a friend."

"Tell her hi for me."

"If I see her again, I most certainly will," Aidan said. "Can I walk you out?"

"No, that's okay. Denise, the bartender, and I will go together. We're roommates. And Danny, the doorman, will get us safely to the car. He does that every night," she said. She raised one shoulder in a half shrug. "Freaks. They're an occupational hazard."

"Well, I'm glad Danny's such a good guy," he said. He left, and Danny, whom he'd met earlier, bade him good-night. The door was locked firmly behind him.

Mo didn't have any more wild and wicked dreams.

But she still found herself suddenly awake and alert...and listening.

The bedside clock showed that the time had crept up to 4:00 a.m.

She had no idea what had awakened her.

Then she realized there was something like a dark shadow in the room.

Rollo was awake, but not alarmed. He seemed to be staring at the shadow, too.

She was ready to reach for the fire poker at her bedside, despite Rollo's calm, when the shadow became clearer in the moonlight.

It was Candy. Who never came into her bedroom at night.

"Candy?" Mo's voice sounded like a croak. Yes, she was afraid.

Candy turned to her. She'd been trying to look out the window but the drapes were closed and her efforts were ruffling them but not moving them enough so she could see out.

"Mo! I'm sorry. I didn't mean to wake you. Forgive me. This is so rude. I never enter a bedroom without being invited," Candy said.

Mo waved a hand in the air. "It's all right. Is something wrong?"

"No. No. Ah, I mean…maybe. Yes. Perhaps."

"Candy!"

Candy came and perched by Rollo on the foot of the bed. "I don't think it's anything…dangerous."

"Candy, talk to me! You're scaring me out of about a decade of life, so just spit out what you're trying to say."

"I think there was someone out there," Candy said.

Mo sat bolt upright and started to fumble for the phone on the bedside table.

"No, no! He's gone now."

"Yes, but still, if someone *was* there—"

"Calling the police won't do any good now—or with this."

"Candy, there might be something he left behind."

"No."

"No?"

"Not that the police can find."

"Why not?"

"Because whoever it was, well…he's not alive. It's not someone living," Candy said.

5

Aidan sat studying the notes he'd taken the previous day, and every report he'd received from the police and the medical examiner thus far.

He was still waiting for toxicology reports, and he believed they'd be important. If Richard had been drugged before he was taken, the list of suspects might be narrowed down to those who'd had access to the food he'd eaten or anything he might have had to drink.

If he hadn't been drugged, then he'd somehow been tricked into bringing about his own disappearance.

Sitting back in his chair, he thought about the Headless Horseman Hideaway Restaurant and Bar. As far as Aidan could tell, there was only one way up the road and into the parking lot and one way out. As Tommy Jensen had suggested, whoever had come and placed the bloody head on the effigy had probably waited until the wee hours of the morning.

It wouldn't have taken long. But it would've been planned beforehand. Which meant that the execution of the crime had been the work of an Organized Killer—someone of above-average intelligence, who'd meticulously planned every aspect of the murder.

That still brought him back to the locked room concept. Richard Highsmith had disappeared from a well-patrolled facility. One that his own security force had checked out, along with the police.

Aidan had kept in touch with Jackson Crow by phone and email throughout the day, providing reports on whatever he learned—and didn't learn. He'd been able to assure Crow that the local police were more than congenial and that they'd been diligent with the countless interviews and reports they'd written up so far. He'd also mentioned that Detectives Van Camp and Voorhaven were basically letting him take the lead.

It was during one of his afternoon conversations with Jackson the day before that he discovered he'd been booked into the same hotel where Taylor Branch, Jillian Durfey and the private security guys were staying. Throughout the long day he hadn't given much thought to his sleeping arrangements. But, of course, at the brand-new offices of what was being called the "Yankee" Krewe, such details had been handled. His hotel had been chosen specifically because it had been Richard Highsmith's—and because all of Richard's on-the-road staff were there.

"Keep your friends close and your enemies closer," Jackson had told him dryly. "Classic advice."

"I'll bet the friends are mortified—and sincerely saddened, as well. The three security men were together when Richard disappeared, and Branch was with them. They were also in easy sight of a convention center employee. And they're in no hurry to leave town," Aidan had informed Jackson.

Aidan had spent some time with the security trio after leaving Richard's room earlier that afternoon.

They fit their nicknames. Muscles was indeed huge, Mischief was a striking young guy, and Magic was serious and dedicated and gave the impression that he could do just about anything—except, of course, answer the question. But then, none of them had expected Richard to put himself in harm's way. Somehow, he'd left the convention center, presumably following an agenda of his own. Or he'd been coerced to leave. His security staff had been blindsided—expecting their client to have regard for his own safety.

"We were accustomed to him shaking hands in a restaurant, going from the car to an establishment—that kind of thing," Muscles had told him. "But we never thought he'd wander out of the convention center!"

Muscles was defensive and obviously felt bad—as well as ineffectual and guilty. He and his crew had been Richard's personal security detail.

Richard had ended up dead, his body violated.

Now, Aidan had a room one floor below Richard's aides and guards. It was a suite with a large work area, but he understood from Jackson Crow that they'd be using his room as their local base when he was joined by fellow agents.

Late today, his floor would be hosting more of his new coworkers, who'd be booked into adjacent rooms. He'd specifically asked for a forensic artist—Jane Everett—because he didn't like the computer-generated image of the dead woman that was going around; he wanted a new one. Once they learned who she was, they would at least know if she'd been killed because of whatever relationship she might have had with Richard—or if she'd somehow been caught up in the situation.

Knowing her identity could be a major key to solving the murders. Unless she'd been a random bystander, but all the indications suggested the opposite.

He stood. He hadn't had many hours of sleep, and what he'd managed to get had been restless. But it was now eight o'clock, and he wasn't due at the task force meeting for another two hours.

Leaving his hotel room, he headed for the elevator. He started out the main door, paused, went back to get a quick coffee from the hotel's complimentary station, then hurried out. He wasn't even sure where he was going at first. After a few minutes, he realized he was driving to the cemetery.

When he got there, he parked and walked past gravestones and monuments, cherubs and angels, until he reached the yellow crime scene tape that still marked off the tomb. The place where they'd discovered Richard's body—and that of the unknown woman.

An autumn breeze moved through the trees. The day wasn't blue and wasn't gray, but somewhere in between. He stood there, staring at the tape, at the flattened grass where police, the medical examiner and a dozen crime scene techs had walked. He was certain they'd found all that could be found.

"Lizzie grave?" he asked aloud.

His voice was carried softly on the breeze. But if he'd hoped for an answer, he didn't get one.

He shook his head. "Richard, you old bastard! You haunted my dreams, and now..."

Now what?

He'd denied a thousand times over that he saw or heard anyone who wasn't there, wasn't *alive.* He often told himself that something in his mind had led him to find victims. It wasn't *images* he saw moving before him. Or voices he heard from the shadows. He'd been uncomfortable with his transfer to the Krewe of Hunters, afraid that it revealed and made all too evident a truth he'd rather deny. But he loved his job too much to turn it down. He didn't want to get stuck behind a desk for the next thirty years.

And now...

He remembered the day before. Remembered it almost as if he were seeing it again.

Maureen Deauville, running after the giant wolf-hound...literally falling into his arms as they discovered the body. Uncanny. He remembered the pretty brunette with crystal gray-green eyes staring up into his. He remembered feeling that the moment was charged, that she had an elusive quality that had instantly seemed compelling. Yes, she was very attractive, well-spoken, and she had a certain grim courage about her, a strength that drew him. But then, later, as he'd seen her, as he'd befriended the dog, he'd known.

There was something else about her, too. It wasn't just the dog; it was her.

He curled his fingers into his palms until the nails cut his flesh.

One great thing about his position now was that he could call a tech at the office and get anything he needed, ASAP. In less than a minute, he had her address.

He checked his watch as he walked down the hill to his car. There was still time before his meeting. Driving to her home, he passed the road to Sunnyside, Washington Irving's beloved home in the valley, and soon came to another small, barely paved road. He took it toward the river and saw a charming cottage, smaller than Sunnyside and architecturally different. It had two floors with several gables but was also graced with stonework and detailed molding.

He heard a trickling brook as he stepped out of his car and saw that the land sloped toward a forest. To his left, he could see the river. As he paused, he thought that the air itself felt electric, shivering with a strange sense of expectation.

He heard Rollo barking as he neared the door. Just 8:30 a.m. now. She might still be asleep.

No matter.

He knocked on the door.

It seemed she wasn't much of a sleeper, either. She opened the door, apparently aware that it was him. She was already dressed for the day in jeans and a soft blue sweater. She looked at him with a frown, not alarmed that he was there, but surprised and wary.

"Agent Mahoney."

"I need you to come with me," he said.

She flinched. "Is someone else missing?"

"No. I need you to…to see whatever the hell it is you see."

Some expression he couldn't readily identify passed over her face. Her eyes didn't meet his. "I don't know what you're talking about."

"Yes, you do."

"I don't. If you think I can help in any way, I'll come with you. But I don't know what you're expecting and I don't know what you think I can do."

"Yeah?" He was surprised by the hostility in his own voice. Great way to get someone to do what he wanted. "All right, fine. Just come."

She seemed to dislike the very sight of him. For a moment, he thought she'd refuse. The word *please* formed in his mind but didn't make it to his lips.

"Rollo's coming, too," she said flatly.

"That's fine. I like the dog."

"Yes, I've noticed."

Neither of them said anything else, but the inference was there.

Yeah, he liked the dog—not her.

It was irrelevant; they didn't have to like each other.

"Let me get his leash," she said.

She stepped back inside. The door closed, and he wasn't asked in.

For a moment he wondered if she'd locked him out and was calling her friend Lieutenant Purbeck to tell him the FBI man was crazy and that he was harassing her.

But the door opened again. She appeared with Rollo, who wagged his massive tail madly and nudged Aidan for attention. Aidan gave it to him briefly.

"Thank you," he said formally.

She didn't respond but strode to his car, letting Rollo hop into the backseat.

"Where are we going?"

"The cemetery."

She didn't ask why but remained silent as they drove. He was keenly aware of her beside him. Her head was high, the angle emphasizing the fine lines of her features. He inhaled her scent and for some reason, the fact that she was beautiful and poised and possessing such a demeanor of strength began to irritate him.

When they reached the site and parked, she led the

way up the hill, weaving through the stones and memorials with the dog and coming to a halt before the tomb.

She turned to look at him. "Why are we here?"

He answered her question with another. "Why did you come here yesterday?" he asked.

"You saw. Rollo was on the scent!"

"Yes, I saw. But how did you get to the head? Richard's head," he added, as if there was any risk she might misunderstand.

She flushed. "I'm…not sure," she said.

"I think you are."

"Really? And what are you? Psychic?"

"No. I don't read minds, and neither do you. But you have…something."

"What makes you say that?"

"Tarrytown, Irving, Sleepy Hollow—there's a fair amount of territory. Miles of woods, streams, water and, hell, there's a damned big river. But you immediately homed in on the right area. You found a head. Kind of like finding a needle in a haystack."

"Someone would have found it soon enough."

"Yes, but *someone* didn't have to. Because you did."

She waved one hand airily.

"You see the dead," he told her.

"Yes, *we* saw the dead!" she snapped. "Two heads— and two bodies!"

He struggled to keep his distance from her. He wanted to grasp her shoulders at that moment and shake her.

He wouldn't, of course. He still had that much control.

He almost smiled; if he made a move toward her, the

wolfhound, friendly to him or not, would be on him in a flash, ready to tear him to pieces.

She inhaled deeply, then released her breath. He didn't have to say more, and he wondered what he must have looked like, standing there, because she suddenly gave up.

"There's nothing here," she said softly. "No one."

"You can't see him, feel him?" he whispered.

She shook her head. Her response seemed odd to him, though. "I don't know why you think that...that a dead man would hang around in the cemetery where his body was dumped. I mean, if such things were real—as in revenants, ghosts, what have you—they'd be here for a reason. And how productive would it be to hang around *here?*"

He glanced at his watch yet again. Maybe this had been a foolish idea. He had to be at the task force meeting.

"I'll take you home," he told her. Then he managed a stiff, "Thank you for obliging my whim."

She nodded. "Rollo always enjoys an excursion," she said.

He was quiet as he drove. When they reached the cottage he stepped out of the car to open the door for her, but she'd exited the passenger side before he could come around.

He let Rollo out.

"You might want to go inside while I'm still here," he said.

"It's daylight. I have to be able to walk into and out of my own house in broad daylight." She gestured around her. "And if anyone was here, Rollo would tell me."

"Yeah. Well, be careful."

"Of course." She started to walk toward her front door but paused, turning back. He still stood by the car, watching her.

"If you think I have *something,*" she told him, "it has to be because you have *something.*"

"If I ever did, it's long gone," he said.

"You just want it to be gone. But that doesn't make any difference. It's not something you get rid of. Because you can't get rid of what you are—tall, short, dark, light, hearing, deaf, sighted or blind—and you can't get rid of this. All you can do is lie to yourself. Deny it all—and mess yourself up pretty good."

She met his eyes, but obviously wasn't expecting an answer. Then she went into her house with Rollo and closed and locked the door.

Mo leaned against the door, shaking. It took her a minute to catch her breath and calm her heart.

She wasn't sure why she'd gotten so angry. Yes, she was. Aidan Mahoney was a jerk who was dishonest with himself and others, trying to protect himself from a reality he feared.

Most of the world didn't see the dead—the *majority* of the world didn't see them. To all those people, that meant they weren't there and if they *were* there, it was imagination. Or fantasy. Or, worse, lunacy.

Apparently, he didn't remember that once upon a time the so-called sane world believed the Earth was flat.

Rollo barked at her and wagged his tail expectantly.

"Sorry, boy! Want a treat? My dog food and dog treat bill is probably as high as someone else's rent!"

She headed to the kitchen and the large ceramic con-

tainer that held Rollo's extra-large dog biscuits. She
loved the sound of his toenails clattering on the hardwood floors as he trotted behind her.

"You know what, Rollo?" she said. "Men! Why
do they only seem to come in three forms? Known-
you-forever-and-I-love-you-like-a-brother. Total jerk-
off slime. Or to-die-for-but-what-an-ass? Huh, Rollo?
Dogs aren't like that, are they? Nah. Although I hate
to admit it, kid, but you guys is where that expression
came from—*you dog, you!*"

Rollo just wagged his tail.

"Really, I must beg your pardon."

Mo raised her eyes to the kitchen door. Colonel Daniel Parker stood there, handsome and casual in his field
uniform.

*I should have said that they came in four differ-
ent types,* Mo thought. *The first three and totally-
charming-but-taken-and-dead.*

"Sorry, Daniel. The world's changed a lot since you
had to deal with things," Mo said.

Candy swept in behind him, setting her spectral
arms around his shoulders and peeking around him
to speak with Mo. "It's changed in a lot of good ways!
When Daniel and I fell in love, we would've been os-
tracized if we left this house. Slavery, remember? I was
a runaway slave. But Daniel loved me, anyway. He was
ahead of the rest of the world."

Mo nodded and poured herself more coffee. "True,
but there are still people out there who are—" She
paused, trying to think of the right word. In greeting
cards, the writing had to be brief, succinct, effective.
She knew there was a better word for what she was
trying to say.

She couldn't think of it.

"Jerks!" she exploded.

"Eloquent," Candy said to Daniel.

"Oh, very," Daniel agreed.

"I mean, thank God, yes, we have laws that protect people now, and our constitution declares that we are all equal, regardless of color, religion, et cetera. But *people* are still jerks!"

Candy smiled. "And now you believe the 'sane' world discriminates against those with a sixth sense?"

"No. Yes. I—"

"But you accept it—and you hide it," Daniel said softly.

"Yes. Which is what people with a sixth sense do." It was information that could only be shared with a select few. And it wasn't as if you could grab your cell phone and *call* the dead. Some knew why they stayed behind. Some weren't really sure.

"He's so…intense," Mo said. "I've been with cops at murder scenes before—although I admit this has been the worst. When I was living in the city, it wasn't that they were jaded or cold or didn't care, but they dealt with murder quite often and they weren't so involved. I don't mean they were cold or that they weren't a hundred percent dedicated to solving the crime. But I've seen them talk about their lives, ask about each other's kids, make off-duty plans. With this guy, it's…different."

"Maybe he was a fervent believer in the dead man, in Richard," Daniel said. "I felt that way about the general—Robert E. Lee. He was a man of principle. He felt as if he bled himself, watching men die. I didn't know him personally, but I would've followed him to hell and back."

"Or maybe he knew Mr. Highsmith personally," Candy suggested.

Mo nodded. "He did."

"And maybe he had a bad experience somewhere along the line," Daniel said. He hesitated, drawing Candy close. "I've seen people who I'm sure have seen me—and I've seen them panic and run away as if they were being chased by fire."

"He doesn't look like the kind who'd panic," Mo said. "And yet…" She'd already seen that he was deceiving himself about his unusual ability.

"No, he looks like the kind who would fight it," Daniel said. "And fighting it might mean that he's determined to deny it. So much so, he's managed to create a block he can't break through."

Mo turned and poured herself a cup of coffee from the pot she kept on during the day. "Okay, thank you both. I'm off to work now."

Neither of them moved. She, could, of course, have walked through them, but she felt uncomfortable doing that.

It also seemed incredibly rude.

"What?" she asked.

"I think he's out there," Daniel said.

"He?"

"Richard Highsmith. He might have been at one of the crime scenes—watching. Sadly, it's something the dead are sometimes compelled to do," Candy said.

"Or he might have heard about you before… Politicians usually know the police. You worked with the police in the city as well as here," Daniel reminded her.

"Perhaps he feels he can't really reach Agent Mahoney, so he's coming to you," Candy said. "I know there was someone out there last night."

"If he wants to reach me, I'm here," Mo told her.

"We should take a constitutional." Daniel bowed slightly toward Candy.

"He means a walk," Candy said, grinning up at him.

"I know that," Mo said. "And thanks again for telling me about Richard. If he comes back, maybe he'll be willing to make contact."

They left. She took her coffee and headed for the computer. She looked at the array of Halloween cards she'd created, which now decorated her desk. A friendly pop-up ghost opened its arms to say, "Boo." Witches at a cauldron worked up a spell for good times and happiness. A vampire offered a kiss on another card. Her most popular creation for the season had been a headless horseman; he held a grinning pumpkin filled with candy. When the card was opened, a mirror showed the recipient's face atop the headless horseman.

She picked up the card, closed it and slid it into a drawer.

Think Valentine's Day!

Keying Agent Mahoney's name into her laptop, she discovered that it wasn't easy to find anything on the man. But then, FBI field agents probably didn't post any of their personal information on Facebook—or tweet about their cases. He didn't have any LinkedIn or Wikipedia pages, and the Aidan Mahoney she did find was an attorney in Scottsdale, Arizona.

She began advanced searches, adding *New York, paranormal activity* and *Sleepy Hollow* to his name. Nothing.

Finally something did pop up on the screen.

She found the picture of a boy of about fifteen along with the headline Los Angeles Police Clear Young Tarrytown Suspect of Murder. The boy was clearly Aidan Mahoney. Handsome, with dark hair and a striking face that hadn't matured, did not yet display the hard angles and lines that now completed his face.

She read eagerly.

The police today offered an official apology to Aidan Michael Mahoney and his parents. Mahoney, on vacation in the area with his family, had been a suspect in the murder of a homeless man found under a bridge. Police admit that, desperate for a suspect, they had questioned the young Mahoney—who discovered the body of the dead man—in an attempt to bring charges. Yesterday, Maynard Griffin, another drifter, was arrested at the site of a second murder of a homeless man. His arraignment is pending. In an effort to put an end to various rumors, the lawyer speaking on behalf of the Mahoney family agreed to the release of Aidan's name.

Mo sat back.

So that was it. Aidan Mahoney had used his gift—and nearly been arrested for it.

She studied the picture of the boy Aidan Mahoney had been.

He'd had a smile and a look of eager anticipation, excitement about the world.

That boy had changed and become the man he was now.

* * *

Walking into the station for the task force meeting, Aidan was impressed with the number of officers who were waiting to be briefed by Lieutenant Purbeck and him. He was also surprised to see that two of his colleagues had arrived, sooner than he'd expected—Jane Everett and Sloan Trent.

He'd met them in New York, but just briefly. They were officially part of the new office but there'd been no companionable nights out at a local bar yet; no life stories had been spilled. The two were a couple, he knew, but since the female agents in the Krewe tended to retain their maiden names, he wasn't sure if they were married. Somewhere along the line, he'd ask them. Or Jackson.

Trent was a big, rugged guy, tall and trim but heavily muscled. He'd come from the West and still looked the part, even in a dark navy suit. The ghost of a cowboy hat seemed to linger on his head.

Jane was a very pretty woman who seemed to tone down her natural assets for the workplace—her dark hair was swept into a bun and she, too, was dressed in a business suit and wearing flat, serviceable shoes.

"We tried to reach you to let you know we were here," Sloan told him. "We got to the hotel at nine, but you'd left and you weren't answering your cell."

"I'm sorry." Aidan wondered if his introspection and his curiosity about Mo Deauville had distracted him to the point that he'd paid no attention to his phone.

Their phones were a lifeline for all of them; he had to shake off whatever mood he was in and play his part competently.

"Jackson said you wanted an artist. The police have done a computer rendering of the Jane Doe, right?" Jane asked.

"Yes, but no pun intended, there's no life to it. I showed it around last night. When I asked someone if she recognized the woman in the picture, she said it could have been anyone."

"I'll get on it as soon as we're done here," Jane said.

They were in the back of the room, sipping bad coffee. Purbeck announced that they'd begin.

He started by giving a report on the case from beginning to end, starting with the disappearance of Richard Highsmith, and bringing them to where they were now.

An officer raised his hand. "Are we looking at this as a nut on the loose or a possible political assassination?"

"Both. Either. We don't know yet. We still have no identity for the woman found with Mr. Highsmith. Hopefully, when we've discovered who she was, we'll learn more."

"Well, they're not officially serial killings, are they? Two dead, found together. At least three need to be dead with a similar M.O. for it to be classified as so, right?" another officer asked.

Purbeck gestured at Aidan, who set his coffee down and walked to the front of the room. Purbeck introduced him, although he'd met many of the officers already.

"As Lieutenant Purbeck said, we don't know what we're looking for yet and we can't rule anything out. You're aware that we categorize killers as organized or disorganized when we're seeing a potential serial situation. Whoever did this is extremely organized. He or she—most likely a he, since the victims were strangled before they were beheaded and that takes considerable strength—managed to whisk away a well-known political figure from a conference center crawling with security.

"Perhaps our Jane Doe saw something and was killed to silence her. Perhaps, in an attempt to confuse us, the killer liked the idea of us discovering the head of a man and the body of a woman first. Who knows if he suspected we'd take it further and search the vault? We certainly have enough vaults and mausoleums around here.

"The thing is, right now, we need to find where the victims were beheaded. We need the tool used for the beheadings. We have to be vigilant regarding everyone and everything we see. Thanks to you and your fellow officers, the convention quarters have been thoroughly searched and anyone with access to the facility or to Mr. Highsmith has been questioned.

"We're still sifting through information here and at our main offices in Virginia. We're also searching records for enemies Mr. Highsmith might have had. When the toxicology reports are in, we'll know if Mr. Highsmith was drugged before he disappeared.

"It definitely wasn't a case of robbery. Highsmith was found with all his belongings, except his cell, and we don't know yet if that was significant. He was also found with a matchbook from a strip bar called Mystic Magic. The employees I was able to interview are positive that they never saw him in the place. There was a note on the matchbook—*Lizzie grave*. Does that mean anything to anyone here?"

Aidan waited. No one spoke. They all glanced around with puzzled expressions.

"Strange name for a hooker," one officer said.

Aidan sighed inwardly. "I don't believe it's the name of a hooker. I believe it's something Richard Highsmith was looking for."

"We have a lot of graves around here," another officer muttered.

"And hundreds of people named Lizzie have lived and died in the area over the centuries," said a third.

"If anyone does think of anything, however wild or improbable your theory might be—please come to Lieutenant Purbeck, Detectives Voorhaven and Van Camp or me. Pooling all available information and suspicions is going to be of the utmost importance," Aidan told them.

"Two of my coworkers are there in the back—Jane Everett and Sloan Trent—and you can seek them out, as well. Jane is one of our country's foremost forensic artists, so if you have a witness who can provide any description of a suspicious person, she's here," Aidan advised them. "Thank you for working with us, and thank you for your diligence in so quickly shutting down the convention center the other night, conducting such thorough interviews and simply doing such exceptional police work."

"That's it," Purbeck said. "Oh, one more thing. We closed our attractions yesterday, and the city, village, town and county offices have asked that we let them reopen. This is going to be a nightmare for us, of course. As we've already experienced, it's not always easy to tell the difference between what's real and what's fabricated for Halloween."

The meeting broke up. Jane and Sloan joined Aidan and Purbeck at the front, followed by Voorhaven and Van Camp.

"I've done this for years," Purbeck said. "And I'm not even sure where to go from here."

"Jane will head to the morgue now and try to get us a better image. I'm really hoping that will help," Aidan said.

"Our computer renderings are pretty good," Purbeck told him, a bit defensively.

"They're excellent," Jane agreed.

"Not to be obvious, but they lack a sense of life," Aidan said. "Hey, let's try everything we can, okay?"

"Yes, absolutely. Any murder is obscene, an affront to all of humanity, but the pressure on us in a case like this, when we're looking at the death of such a high-profile man, is staggering," Purbeck said. Van Camp nodded. "We're going back over everything at the convention center."

"Good," Aidan said. "There's no such thing as a locked-room case. Somehow, a door is always opened. Or a window."

"I'll get Jane to the morgue," Sloan said. "And where should I go from there?"

"I think you should visit Mystic Magic. Spend a few hours hanging around, just watching."

"All right. I'd also thought about interviewing the employees of the restaurant where you found the head," Sloan told him.

"Great idea. But we need to know more about Mystic Magic."

"Keep me posted. I'll be in the office filtering through reports," Purbeck said. "So far, we've been called out to inspect three pumpkins, a hanging skeleton—and, yes, a cloth rendition of the headless horseman wearing a *Jason* mask"

"We'll keep in touch." Voorhaven and Van Camp left.
Jane asked Aidan, "What's your plan?"
"I'm going to find *Lizzie grave*."

6

Mo wasn't surprised when she heard a car on the gravel drive outside her house around noon.

She knew it was a friend, since Rollo gave a happy woof and wagged his lethal tail.

She salvaged a cup of pens and markers just before he could send it flying to the floor.

She'd managed to work for a while—with half her mind. Doodling, and letting her subconscious take over, often resulted in some of her best pieces.

Going to the door, she glanced out the small window; as she'd expected, it was Mahoney returning.

The day had become bright and beautiful, a fall afternoon when the sun was shining as a golden orb and the colors of the leaves were stunningly beautiful.

She opened the door and waited for him.

"May I come in?" he asked when he reached her.

"In here? You don't want to go to another graveyard? This is the Hudson Valley. We have *plenty* of churchyards and cemeteries and even family plots."

His look told her that he didn't appreciate her sarcasm.

"Sorry," she said. "Please, come in."

He moved past her. She watched the broad contours of his shoulders and the straight line of his back. Just her luck. She'd always thought that real attraction was much more than the physical. That it was easy to admire someone who was beautiful or handsome or striking—but you didn't necessarily really *want* that person.

Well, Mahoney made a lie out of that. He was simply compelling, from his stature to his long fingers and the bronzed breadth of his hands. His blue eyes were direct, searing at times.

As Grace would say, *I'd do him in a heartbeat!*

Mo quelled her thoughts and followed him through her house. He usually looked at her as if she were a root vegetable. It wasn't too smart to get a crush—even purely physical—on a man like that.

He paused, surveying what he could see of the house, then he hunkered down to greet Rollo.

"Great place," he told her

"Thank you. I love it. And I love that I'm so close to Sunnyside."

"You're a Washington Irving fan," he said.

"I am. I love his stories and I love the stories about him, too. He was a fascinating man, good to others, smart, filled with humor," Mo said. "But then, you know all that. You're from here."

"Yes."

"And you didn't come to my house to talk about Washington Irving."

"No."

He straightened and continued to stand there.

"Has anything new happened?" she asked at last.

"A couple of my coworkers are here. One's a fantastic artist."

"Great." He still hadn't explained what he wanted. "Can I get you a drink? Soda, water—cup of coffee?"

"Yes, thank you. I'd love a cup of coffee."

"How do you take it?"

"Black."

She walked into the kitchen and poured him coffee, then handed it to him. He leaned against the counter. "It's good. Nice and strong. I don't know what it is, but I haven't found a police station yet that brews anything but mud."

"Well, I'm happy to offer you coffee anytime you like," she said. She quickly turned to pour herself another cup and asked, "So, why are you here?"

"Lizzie's grave," he said. "I'm assuming it's a grave, but I'm trying to figure out who Lizzie might have been, and why her grave was significant to Richard."

"Want to come and have a seat?" she asked.

They went back to her office, where she took the chair behind the desk, allowing him the one across from her.

He sat, picking up her "witch's cauldron" Halloween card from the edge of the desk.

He smiled. "You made this?"

"The art, the words and the paper engineering," Mo said as he worked the pop-up angle of the card. "Well?" she couldn't help asking.

He put it back down. "I'd buy it," he told her.

"Thanks. So, Lizzie's grave?"

"I found the words *Lizzie grave* scribbled on a matchbook Richard had in his pocket. They were also impressed on a notepad in his hotel room. Not the page he actually wrote on—he must have taken that with him, although it wasn't found on him or among his things."

"Did he have a relative who died here?" she asked.

"I thought about that, but—"

"You knew his family."

He stared at her. "Yes." She could sense another rise of hostility in him; she felt certain he was wondering, *Has this woman been looking me up? Checking out my credentials or my past?*

"You said you were from here," she said. "Logical assumption."

Of course, she *had* been looking him up.

She didn't blink. Liars, she believed from television, moved their eyes downward or to the left or right.

She kept her eyes on his.

He nodded.

"So, you were friends with Richard Highsmith?"

He looked away for a moment and then met her gaze again. "Yes. We spent a lot of time here together. We used to walk through the woods, making up our own stories. We told ghostly tales in the old cemeteries and graveyards, had campfires…ate pizza and played ball. All the things kids do. Then we grew up and went our separate ways. We became the kind of friends who follow each other's careers, and call or write once in a while. Still friends, always friends, but leading separate lives."

"I'm sorry for your loss."

He nodded again. "I hadn't seen him for a while. But I gather I would have soon. His campaign manager told me I was going to be invited to a political dinner."

They were both silent for a minute.

"Maybe Lizzie was a long-ago ancestor," Mo suggested.

"Yeah, I thought about that, too. I can get people started on tracing his ancestry," Mahoney said. "But I have a feeling it didn't have anything to do with his family. What I was hoping is that you might know about some legend or local story that has to do with a Lizzie or a Beth or Elizabeth." He offered her a wry smile. "Grace was telling me that you know local history and legend like very few others do."

Mo shrugged off the compliment, but took a minute to think.

"We have headless horsemen, women in white, Native American spirits and all kinds of legends," she began. "You're probably familiar with them all," Mo said. "And historically, we have the tragic story of Major Andre, hanged as a spy. He *was* a spy—against the Americans—but even those who brought about his execution were sickened by it. He was just so charming that everyone loved him. Supposedly—"

She broke off, and he leaned forward. "Yes?"

"Well, supposedly, he fell in love with a local girl while he made his way through the area," Mo said. "His captors liked him so much that while he was imprisoned, they let her in to see him. There's a copy of a drawing done at his hanging that's alleged to have his mystery woman in it. Hang on, I'll find it. She's usually called Andre's secret love—he'd fallen for the woman who eventually married Benedict Arnold—but this was later and I think the relationship was more... real. Sometimes she was referred to as his Kat or his Molly—or his *Lizzie*."

She hopped up and went to one of her bookcases,

searching through her historical reference material until she located the book on Andre. Flipping through the pages, she found the picture and passed the book to Mahoney. "This was written in 1820, but it's not public domain. The author was a man named Caleb Van der Haas. His family has kept up a copyright on it—adding forewords, extra chapters, info on the area with every new edition. My copy actually belonged to my mom and it was her mom's, printed about 1920. But you'll notice, Agent Mahoney, that in this rendition of the Andre hanging, the caption says 'Andre's *Lizzie* weeps as her beloved Major Andre swings to the hanged man's dance.'"

He studied the picture, then looked up at her. She thought he'd continue with the subject they'd been discussing.

"Aidan," he said instead. "Please just call me Aidan."

She nodded. For a moment their eyes met, but she glanced away quickly. She wasn't sure she liked him being so courteous and engaging. She could feel herself blushing, afraid that he could sense the effect he had on her.

Mo took a step back, leaving the book with him, and nearly tripped over Rollo. The dog seemed to need to be close to both of them.

"Where do you think this Lizzie—if that was her name—might be buried?" he asked.

His attention was all on the book. He hadn't noticed her reaction or her embarrassment, and didn't, apparently, feel any of that sweet and blazing chemistry himself.

For a minute she went blank.

Then she saw that he was staring at her again, waiting for an answer.

Her tongue didn't want to work.

She pretended to weigh the question. "Well, not in Sleepy Hollow Cemetery," she said. "It wasn't built until 1849. And we're assuming a lot. She might have died and been buried elsewhere. But if she really did exist, and her name was Lizzie and she did die here, she might be buried at the Old Dutch Church or the old graveyard that belonged to St. Andrew's."

"Where we found the woman's body leaning against the pillar of the vault—and Richard's body inside," he said.

She nodded again. "This area is so rich in Revolutionary War history. And I've always had a keen interest in all the characters involved with the Revolution. While Andre was instrumental in causing Benedict Arnold to turn traitor, he's still a beloved character—even now and even as the enemy.

"The man spoke at least five languages, and George Washington was said to have admired him. The truth has been obscured by legend. He supposedly joined the British army because of a broken heart. He didn't have the name or the money to buy any kind of real rank, so he worked his way up. He was captured once and exchanged—and then caught with papers on him that proved him to be a spy.

"They say that he haunts much of the Hudson Valley, and that his specter is seen in Philadelphia, where he was the rage of Tory society during the British occupation. He was hanged in 1780, and he was only thirty-one at the time. From that day onward, stories about him ran rampant because he was such a romantic figure. But if it's true that he had a young woman in this area willing to risk all for him, I'd say she must have been born sometime between 1750 and 1760. Even if she lived a long life, she probably died when burials were still occurring at the Old Dutch Church—or one of the other churches or family graveyards. Like St. Andrew's."

"Why would Richard have been looking for her grave?" Aidan mused aloud.

She didn't have an answer for that.

His phone rang as they both sat in thoughtful silence. He answered it. "Mahoney."

Mo watched his face. She couldn't hear the person on the other end.

"Thanks," was all he said.

He smiled at her and rose. "Thanks for humoring my obsession. I appreciate all your help."

"I wish I could do more." She rose, as well. "Did... did they find something?" she asked.

"Yes," he murmured. "But we're keeping certain information out of the press for now."

"I know. I've often helped the police. I've never shared anything that's come up when Rollo and I've been working with them."

"Well, that was the M.E. The toxicology reports came back. Both of the victims had traces of chloroform in their systems. They were knocked out before they were taken."

"Hopefully they were unconscious when they were killed."

"We did learn that they were strangled before they were beheaded."

"I guess that's a small mercy."

"Yes."

They walked to the front door, Rollo trotting beside them.

When Aidan opened the door, he told her, "I'll keep you abreast of the situation. We owe you that, and I know I can trust you to maintain strict confidentiality. In the meantime...be careful."

"I'm always careful," she said. "I always know when anyone's near this house."

He grinned at that, resting his hand on Rollo's head. "Don't let him accept any candy from strangers," he teased, then shook his head. "Seriously, people have been known to throw out poisoned meat or treats to take down a dog. Just watch out for him, too."

"Of course. Thank you."

Then he was gone; she stood at the door while he got into his car, watching until it disappeared down the drive.

Rollo let out a pathetic cry of loss.

"Hey! I'm your owner, the love of your life!" she admonished the dog. "Come on, we'll get another dog treat." She locked the door and walked back through the house to the kitchen and dug a treat out of the bowl. When she gave it to him, she thought about Aidan's words.

Don't let him accept candy from strangers.

"Aidan said we should look out for strangers," she told Rollo.

She winced as she heard herself. They were now on a first-name basis. That didn't make her any more comfortable. It was as if the man's essence lingered, along with the scent of his aftershave or cologne.

"Back to work!" she said.

But she didn't go back to work. She went into her

office and began to skim through the various history books she had on the area, especially those that dealt with Major Andre—and all the legends that had arisen around him.

"Old-fashioned method of knocking someone out. Pretty simple, I guess," Dr. Mortenson told Aidan and Sloan Trent. "You soak a rag, you put it over your victim's face and he or she is out in a matter of seconds. The victim can struggle, of course, but any struggle is brief. Must've been *very* brief in the case of our two victims. They didn't get their nails on their attacker. I found no skin, no fibers, nothing to indicate that either of them even touched him."

"It might well indicate that Richard—and the young woman—wcre tricked into being someplace that would give their attacker a chance to knock them out," Aidan said.

"Well, yes, it's not something you could do in front of someone else without being noticed," Dr. Mortenson said.

Sloan looked at Aidan. "That would most likely mean that Richard Highsmith was knocked out in the greenroom—or tricked into leaving the convention center and then taken in the parking lot."

"There was security in the parking lot," Aidan said. "But there were also dozens of trucks granted entry to service the food and drink concessions at the center."

"Which probably brings us back to someone Richard knew. He either went out to see a person or persons he trusted—or he was taken in the greenroom, using the same scenario," Sloan said.

Aidan pulled out his phone and called Van Camp.

The detective was already at the convention center and had been advised about the chloroform.

"We may be too late, but we need to search the rooms of the security guys, plus Jillian Durfey and Taylor Branch," Aidan said.

"Warrants are on the way, and Voorhaven and I are headed over to the hotel now," Van Camp told him. "We may not need the warrants. If all of them are innocent, they won't care whether we have warrants."

"Or if they've already gotten rid of anything that might indicate they ever had a drug," Aidan said. "But we'll meet you there."

He and Sloan stopped by the office at the morgue where Jane Everett was working.

"How's it going?" Sloan asked.

"I'm ready to send this out," Jane said. "Do you want to see?" She showed them the computer screen. While the face she presented wasn't different in its shape, its lines or symmetry from the computer-generated version, it was somehow a totally new image. There was *life* to the woman. Her eyes were bright, her lips slightly curved. She'd been a lovely young blonde, and in Jane's rendering, she was vivacious and *real*.

"Beautiful work." Sloan placed a hand on her shoulder.

She flashed a smile at him. These two were intimate, Aidan thought. Emotionally connected. They weren't overt, both of them too dedicated to the job to indulge in any but the briefest of private moments. Jane turned to him. "Is this more like what you wanted?"

"Definitely," he said. Jane was really good. He wasn't an artist himself, but he could see that she'd created an image that was far superior to what they'd had.

Looking at it, he felt that he'd remember this woman, even if he'd just seen her walking down the street.

"I'll distribute it right away so we can get the media helping us," she said.

Aidan and Sloan went back to the hotel. When they arrived, they found police and crime scene investigators there. The security crew, aka Muscles, Mischief and Magic, as well as Jillian and Taylor, were standing in the hallway—out of their rooms while they were being searched.

It had to be one of the most courteous examples of a search he'd ever seen. Courteous on both sides, the police and those whose rooms were under inspection.

Taylor Branch immediately approached Aidan. "They didn't need warrants," he said. "We would've willingly stepped out. I guess you have to go with us as your first suspects because it was Richard, but you only had to ask."

"I figured as much," Aidan acknowledged, and introduced Sloan all around. "You realize, Mr. Branch, that once you're eliminated, we'll be able to concentrate elsewhere."

"Yes, that's always the line, isn't it?" Branch asked, a dry smile twitching his lips.

"Always—because it's the truth," Sloan said.

One of the crime scene techs emerged from Jillian's room. "Detectives? Agents?" she called.

Aidan walked over to her with Sloan, Van Camp and Voorhaven joining them.

The crime scene tech wore a shirt with a name tag that identified her as Garcia. She held a green container in one of her gloved hands.

"Could be chloroform," Sloan guessed, frowning as he looked at Aidan. "We'll test it."

"I believe so," Garcia said.

They all turned to Jillian Durfey, who stood close enough to hear. She stared at them in astonishment. "That's *not mine!*" she protested.

"It was in the bottom dresser drawer, under what appears to be your clothing," Garcia informed her.

"No, no, no!" Jillian backed away, hands raised. "Oh, no, no. You planted that! *Someone* planted that! I loved Richard. I adored him. I wouldn't have hurt him for the world."

"We have to take you in for questioning," Van Camp told her.

"I didn't put it there! I've never seen it before, I swear!" Jillian said passionately.

"We have to take you in. I'm sorry." Aidan studied the young woman. Her eyes were huge and filled with horror as she looked at Taylor Branch. He was staring back at her in shock and growing anger, but managed to control his response. "I'll get our attorneys on this. Don't say anything until you've been advised."

"But I didn't do anything. I'm telling you—" Jillian began.

Voorhaven had come up behind her. "Will you come with us voluntarily or do I need cuffs?"

"Cuffs!" she repeated, spinning to face him.

"Jillian, just go with them. I'll take care of it," Taylor Branch promised her.

Van Camp came to stand by Aidan. "You want the interview, I imagine?" he asked in a low voice.

"Yes, thanks," Aidan said. "I'll follow you in about fifteen minutes."

Van Camp and Voorhaven left with Jillian. She kept looking back, her eyes wide, tears streaming down her cheeks.

"That's absolutely impossible," Muscles—or Cory Stile—insisted.

"The chloroform was in her drawer," Garcia said flatly and dispassionately.

Muscles shook his head. "She's…she's far too sweet and what she said was true. Jillian hero-worshipped Richard Highsmith. And I saw her—we all saw her!—testing the sound equipment."

"She's not under arrest," Aidan explained. "We just need her to answer some questions. She's right that the chloroform could have been planted. This is a hotel. There are passkeys. Maids and other staff come into the rooms. As I said, we'll need to talk to her and, actually, Mr. Branch, an attorney isn't going to help much at this point, because we're going to try to find out if the chloroform *was* planted in her room."

Branch scowled. "That's what you say when you want to bully and trick people into confessions. You just want to ask questions," he added sarcastically.

"I'm sorry you believe that," Aidan said.

Branch started toward his room. "They're not done in there," Aidan told him.

Irritated, Branch stopped. "Fine. I'll wait." He pulled out his cell phone. "I need to get in touch with a lawyer right now. I can do that here as well as anywhere."

Mischief—Rob Little—walked over to Aidan. "Muscles told you the truth. We've all come to care about Jillian. She's a good kid. Idealistic. That's why she loved her job, working for Richard. I'm telling you, you're wrong."

"Who in this group had access to her room?" Aidan asked.

The three "Shields" and Taylor Branch looked at one another.

"All of us," Mischief replied.

"Then we'll all have to talk, won't we?" Aidan said quietly.

"Please? Pretty please?" Grace asked Mo over the phone.

"Oh, I don't know," Mo said.

The local attractions were reopening. Grace was on duty that night—and now she wanted Mo to play a part at the Haunted Mausoleum.

Sleepy Hollow and Tarrytown always put on a spectacular Halloween season. Like Salem, New Orleans and various other places of historic interest, Sleepy Hollow had the reputation and the buildings, graveyards and other locations to create a spooky atmosphere and attract visitors.

Philipsburg Manor put on Horseman's Hollow, there were readings at the Old Dutch Church and a wonderful Haunted Hayride. Grace's venue, the Haunted Mausoleum, was both effective and successful. There wasn't really a main mausoleum; instead, there were several family tombs and graves on the property. The largest building was an old mortuary, originally built and opened just before the Civil War. It had done a booming business as the death toll during the fighting increased, and it had survived as a working mortuary well into the twentieth century. Finally, it was purchased by Grace's employers in the late 1980s.

These days, visitors were taken on a tour through the

main building and then out to the graveyard. At Halloween, the mortuary offered grim reapers, the dead trying to rise out of coffins and "the gauntlet," a hallway filled with character actors portraying historical personages from all over the world known for their heinous acts, including Vlad Dracul, Countess Bathory, Jack the Ripper and more.

The cemetery itself concentrated on specters from local lore. Among them were Major Andre, the Woman in White, a Native American maiden who had killed herself over her lover, and the Bronze Lady—a large statue from the cemetery said to cry real tears. The infamous historical-murderer actors made appearances now and then, too.

While the haunted house was pure fun, visitors also went away with a booklet that gave real histories of the characters, and information on the other ghost stories of Sleepy Hollow.

There was usually a Headless Horseman of Sleepy Hollow who rode around the property, too.

He was not going to appear that night.

"Mo, if you don't take Alicia's part, they'll hire someone else—someone I don't know. Or trust. Come on, please?"

"What's wrong with Alicia?" Mo asked worriedly.

"She's in the hospital with an emergency appendectomy."

"Oh, I'm sorry!" But the last thing Mo wanted to do that night was play the Woman in White.

"If the Horseman isn't being used—"

"The Horseman is Robbie Anderson. He's becoming H. H. Holmes for the night in the Gauntlet—and he's not a woman."

Robbie Anderson was a historian, but he was also big in local theater.

"I've seen Robbie play a woman," Mo said.

"Please?" Grace continued, as if Mo hadn't spoken. "My bosses know you and love you, and they said I could ask you first!" she told her. "And you know Sondra, who's in charge of the horror nights? She loves you. She's said you're our best backup possibility."

Mo sighed. "Okay, okay. Just until Alicia can come back!"

"Pick you up in an hour." Grace abruptly ended the conversation.

"Fine."

She hung up. Rollo was by her side, looking at her reproachfully. He must have sensed that she was going out—and that he wasn't going with her.

"You'll be okay. Candy and Daniel are here. And you need to watch the house," Mo said.

As she spoke, Candy came sweeping into the room. "Mo!"

"What?"

"Come! Come quickly."

Mo followed Candy to the front of the house. When Candy tried to pull back the drapes, they just fluttered, so Mo took over.

"I will move them one day!" Candy insisted.

Mo nodded. "Sure, but what is it, Candy?" she asked.

"Look. Look there."

Mo did. And then she saw him, a dark figure near the trees. He grew more distinct as she blinked.

It was man, a dead man.

It was Richard Highsmith.

Forgetting safety, Mo rushed to the door and threw

it open. She slipped out of the house and called softly, "Hello! I'm here. Come and speak with me!"

The figure seemed to vanish instantly.

There was nothing there now but the trees.

"Told you! Told you he was lurking around," Candy said.

"Tell me when you see him again, okay? I can't do anything if he vanishes as soon as I speak. I have to get ready. Thank you, Candy. Maybe…maybe he'll come closer to the house next time. Maybe you and Daniel can try to reach him."

"We can try," Candy promised her. "We can try."

Aidan sat across from Jillian Durfey. She'd been given a soda and he was trying to make the interview easy on her.

She was still crying when he'd arrived.

She'd finally stopped. Now she just sat there dully, repeatedly denying that she'd ever had the chloroform.

There were no prints on the bottle; it had been wiped clean.

An attorney had yet to turn up.

"What do you think could have happened—if you never had the chloroform?" Aidan asked her.

She shook her head, threading her fingers through her hair.

"I…I don't know. Someone came and put it in my room. I know that much. I've never seen that bottle or vial or whatever before. I swear it," she said. Her voice wasn't passionate anymore. It was flat and tired.

"Who do you think would have done such a thing?" he asked.

"Someone else."

"Maybe Muscles? Or Mischief or Magic? Or...Taylor Branch?"

"That would be crazy! We all worked for Richard. We depended on him. We're all being used and framed."

He leaned toward her. "Jillian, we've pulled the security tapes from your hallway. If anyone went to your room, we'll find out who it was." That wasn't the truth. The hotel manager had been apologetic and mortified to tell them that at the moment, the security cameras were for show. Their first company hadn't worked out. The camera systems had failed and they were in process of redesigning the system.

But Jillian didn't know that.

She lifted her head and looked at him. "All I can tell you is it wasn't me."

He leaned back in his chair, watching her.

"I loved him. It wasn't me," she said again.

Sloan was with Taylor Branch in another interrogation room. Voorhaven and Van Camp were working with Muscles, Mischief and Magic, leaving one man alone and observed by Purbeck while he waited his turn. Separating them—giving them time to sweat and wonder what the others were saying—was one way of getting at the truth.

"I don't *know* what's going on. But look at me! I'm barely a hundred pounds!" she said in confusion. "How on earth could I have done this? Knocked out a big man, dragged him to some other place and cut off his head, then found a woman and attacked her, too—all while doing the sound check." She hesitated and seemed to brighten. "Bari!" she said. "You have to talk to Bari, the woman from the convention center. She'll tell you. She saw me all the time. Well, almost all the time. Oh!

That's who else you need to check out—the convention center people! They were in charge of the trucks and vendors bringing people into the parking lot. Someone—"

There was a tap at the door, and Aidan rose and went to open it. Purbeck was standing there. "Sorry, but there's a woman who got through to me. She said it's urgent and that you weren't answering your cell phone."

He hadn't been; he always had it on vibrate when he was in interrogation. He hadn't felt the vibration, because the phone was in his jacket and it had been thrown over his chair.

"Who is it?"

"Said her name is Debbie and that she really needs to talk to you. She sounds desperate." Purbeck shrugged. "There was a lot of music in the background and whooping and hollering. I told her I'm the lieutenant leading the case, but she wants to speak with you."

"Thanks."

"You know who she is?"

"Yes. She's a stripper at Mystic Magic."

"Ah," Purbeck said. "Come on, you can take it in my office. I hope she's still on the line."

Aidan followed Purbeck to his office. Purbeck watched as he picked up the phone.

"Aidan Mahoney," he said. "Debbie?"

"Agent Mahoney, it's really you, right?"

"Yes, it's really me."

"Can you get here? Fast?"

"Yes, of course. What's wrong?"

"No one else has seen it yet…not here, I don't think." She paused. "But I'm sure they will soon."

"Seen what?"

"The picture, the picture on the news. It's up on the web, too."

"The picture—"

"Of the missing woman. Agent Mahoney, I do know her. She works here. She worked here, I mean. She wasn't due in yesterday and today is her day off—but it's her! It's Wendy Appleby. She was— I'm not sure how I didn't see it before, but... Oh, Agent Mahoney! She's a friend of mine. She *was* a friend of mine. And she's dead—and I'm scared! Please get out here!"

"I'm on my way, Debbie. Is there any reason you fear for your safety right now?"

The line went dead.

7

Mo sat patiently in the makeup chair while piles of white foundation were applied to her face, neck, hands and arms. Ron Cary was good at what he did; when he wasn't working at the Haunted Mausoleum—his favorite place in the world, he'd told her—he worked for a special effects company in Hollywood.

"You're a great subject!" Ron stepped back. "Beautiful!"

"And done?"

"And done." He grimaced comically. "I'm onto Vlad the Impaler."

The dressing room for the twenty characters at the mansion was in the old carriage house. Originally, they'd used the embalming room in the basement—but that had been such a marvelously atmospheric spot that it had been turned into a Mad Doctor's Experimental Lab and fitted with all kinds of plastic "bloodied" body parts. Guests would travel among them and, of course, scream as the mad doctor and his deranged nurse popped out and one "victim" came to life.

"Coffee and cookies are on the table," Ron said. "Help yourself."

Mo walked over to pour a cup of coffee. The mad doctor himself and Jack the Ripper were there, munching away as they discussed the football season. "Hey, Mo," Jack the Ripper greeted her. She peered at him more closely and greeted him in return. It was Phil Ainsley, one of Mo's old friends.

"Hello, Phil."

"So, you got dragged in."

"I did."

"It'll be fun."

Mo nodded. "Yeah, I know."

Grace—painted in bronze—came up and said hello to everyone.

"I was just telling her she'd have fun," Phil said.

"Hey, I've done this before. You guys are all so good, I'll probably wind up scaring myself to death," Mo said.

"It *is* a little creepy tonight," Phil agreed. "I mean, we're opening after real body parts were discovered. But we're all about entertainment, and the only body parts here are plastic."

"Except that we're working in a real graveyard," Grace noted.

"No one's been interred here since the Civil War," Phil said. "The mortuary kept working, but the cemetery closed after the war." He shuddered dramatically. "It got crowded fast!"

"Who keeps up the graveyard?" Mo asked Grace. "Your company, right?"

"Of course." Grace said. "They'll do another clean-up after Halloween when we're all out of here. Oh, there's Jerry Martin, our stage manager. He's sent the plainclothes guides on in. We're about to open. Come on, I'll show you the Woman in White's walk. You'll probably remember. It's so easy. You just glide around one of the little family mausoleums. There's a nook in back where you hide before you step out to scare people."

"I guess I'm on. Great to see you, Phil."

"You, too. Hey, some of us meet up at the all-night café up on the highway for a bite afterward. It's the only place other than Tommy's that's still open by the time we're out of here," Phil said. "Join us, huh?"

"If I'm still half-awake," Mo promised.

Red-and-blue lighting had been designed to cast eerie shadows over the graveyard that stretched to the side and the rear of the mausoleum.

Music began to play, macabre funeral music. It drifted around the tombstones and decaying mausoleums of the dead. The late-October breeze, shifting the fallen leaves, only added to the effect. "That's your stage set," Grace said cheerfully. "So to speak. When you see one of the guides directing a group, you just take a walk around the tomb. Don't crack any smiles. And don't touch anyone and don't let anyone touch you."

"Got it," Mo assured her.

She took her position leaning against the tomb. She could hear screams from inside the mortuary, so she knew it had all begun. As she waited, she looked across the burial ground.

A man sat atop one of the tombstones, casual and smiling. He was dressed in Revolutionary garb and resembled Major Andre. He appeared to be amused by the evening as he watched the other ghosts take their places.

She'd thought the Andre character was supposed to be in the mortuary, in the historic ghost area.

And then she understood that she wasn't seeing an actor; the *ghost* of Major Andre was sitting on the tomb.

A sound left her throat, and she started forward, ready to speak to him.

He turned and the amusement fled his face as he stared at her. He whispered something, lifting one hand.

There was a strange expression on his face.

As if he'd realized she was alive, just as she had realized he was dead.

His lips seemed to form a single word. She couldn't hear him across the distance, but she thought the word was a name.

Lizzie.

A light waved across the path that wound through the small burial ground. People were coming, laughing, jumping and shrieking as they passed another of her coworkers.

Major Andre was gone.

The crowd came closer. In her long white gown and veil she eased around the corner of the mausoleum and began her slow walk.

A startled scream told her she'd been seen. And appreciated.

The night wore on, and periodically she continued her ghostly walks.

She kept looking for what seemed to be the fun-loving specter of Major Andre.

He did not reappear.

When the cell abruptly cut out, Aidan asked Purbeck to send the closest patrol car, afraid something was happening that needed immediate action. When he and Sloan arrived at the club, the two patrol officers were at the back of the room—enjoying the show. They were obviously embarrassed, stumbling a little in their speech, but told Aidan that they'd found the manager and all the girls, and everyone was fine. They'd explained to the employees that they'd come in response to an anonymous call and that they were there to make sure everyone was all right.

"Nothing's going on, Agent Mahoney," one officer said.

"We checked everyone who was supposed to be working today, from the girls to the waitstaff and the bouncers," the other uniformed officer told him. "All accounted for."

While Aidan was getting info from the officers, Sloan had gone off to meet with the manager. Timothy Bolton was a man of about forty who'd clearly been in the business too long. He didn't so much as blink when topless girls went by, didn't even seem to notice.

Grinning inwardly, Aidan realized he didn't quite feel the same. Many of the showgirls here were stunning.

He could appreciate their beauty objectively, but he felt a little...numb. These women were definitely attractive and sexy, yet he wasn't particularly stirred by any of them. The face that appeared before him, in his mind, was that of Maureen Deauville. He remembered the wariness she had often shown toward him—his own fault—and he remembered her as she stood on the hill, looking down when they'd found the woman's head on another effigy. She had seemed like an ancient goddess standing there, or a long-ago queen saddened by the depravity of the people in her kingdom.

Mo Deauville was different. The kind of different he didn't need. He'd already been transferred into a unit that dealt with the unusual, and that was enough. More than enough.

"You're welcome here, Agent Mahoney. The second crew told me you were in the other night, too. I'd really like to help you. This is terrible. Not only that, it's going to hurt every business out there—especially the 'haunted' venues, you know." Aidan could see that Debbie had gone onstage. She was evidently fine.

He turned to Bolton, pulling his smartphone from his pocket and bringing up the newest likeness Jane Everett had created—the one that was being shown on the news.

"We're still looking for our Jane Doe," Aidan said.

"A John Doe I could probably help you with more," Bolton responded dryly.

"But what about this woman?"

He handed his phone with Jane's image of the dead woman on the screen to Bolton. The man's face immediately paled. "Wendy," he managed. As Aidan had assumed, Debbie hadn't told anyone at the club, certainly not her bosses.

"You do know her."

"She's…she's one of ours. Is she—"

"Yes, I'm sorry. She's dead. She's our Jane Doe," Aidan said.

Music soared to a crescendo. Across the expanse of tables and men, Aidan saw Debbie finishing her act.

Her eyes went directly to his.

He nodded, trying to tell her she was safe; the police were here.

She nodded in return before she took several bows, smiling that great smile of hers for a cheering audience.

Bolton was still staring at the picture. He glanced up at Aidan. "I saw what they put on TV yesterday, but I never thought... Lord. She was supposed to be in the city for a few days, visiting friends. We didn't even know she was missing. We didn't know...."

His voice broke, and there were tears in his eyes.

He wasn't that jaded, after all.

"I'm very sorry," Aidan said quietly.

Bolton looked at him. "You probably think this place is filled with immoral, disgusting people. Strip club—criminals, prostitutes and drug addicts. Half of my employees are in the middle of getting degrees and the other half are single mothers doing what they can do to support their children. We're not a drugged-out has-been place at a strip mall. Believe it or not, we have some class. There are no perks to be had here—when we say no touch, we mean no touch. So, you go ahead and judge. Everyone loved Wendy. The girls are as close as sisters and...well, all the world will think is, hey, another stripper dead. There you go. The wrath of God."

"I'd be the last one to pass judgment, Mr. Bolton," Aidan told him. "And I promise you this—I'll be looking to put away Wendy's killer with the same dedication and determination as if she were a kindergarten teacher—or a politician."

Bolton shook his head.

"That's the truth, I swear it," Aidan said.

"I believe you. Here's the irony, Agent Mahoney. Wendy *was* a kindergarten teacher. Until budget cuts.

She'd been a dancer in Broadway musicals. Then she got married, had a little boy, and went back to school. Her husband died a few years ago, all very tragic. She began teaching, and then her position was cut...." He shook his head again. "She was a good person."

"If she was the Virgin Mary or the devil's mistress makes no difference. We will catch her killer. What *does* make a difference is what we can learn about a victim—because that helps us find the killer," Aidan explained. He filed away the information about Wendy's child; this was urgent, and he'd look into it as soon as he could. He figured Debbie was more likely to know about it.

Bolton nodded. "Is there anything else I can tell you?"

"Was she at all political?" Aidan asked.

"Political?" Bolton seemed to find the question confusing. "No, I never heard her talk about politics. We don't usually talk politics here, especially not with our clients. Men actually look down on these girls. What they don't know is how the girls talk about them—and how they make fun of these guys who think they're the studs of the world. We're friendly here, more like a family. Maybe we purposely avoid politics and religion. That's kind of a get-along rule, isn't it?"

"Probably best to avoid both," Aidan said.

"If you want to know more, talk to the girls. They were close."

Aidan thanked him, adding, "I'll do that."

"Debbie Howell knew her best, although Wendy hadn't been here long. I'll call the dressing room from the hostess stand. She'll be right out." He gestured at the bar. "Wait for her there, okay?"

Aidan walked toward the bar area. The young woman working there offered him a drink. He accepted a cup of coffee and asked her about Wendy, saying he was sorry, but that she was dead. The girl was horrified, and tears sprang from her eyes. But as for being helpful, she was afraid she wouldn't be able to tell him anything. She'd only known Wendy vaguely. "Bartenders have it easy in a way. We change at home. When I've cleaned up after last call, I'm out of here. Takes our dancers a bit longer. It's not that we ostracize one another, it's just how it is. But Wendy was always so nice. So pleasant. I'm really sorry about this."

Aidan noticed that Sloan was across the room, speaking with one of the bouncers. Sloan nodded toward the rear by the stage; Debbie Howell was coming around to join him.

She was now dressed in jeans and a T-shirt, her hair in a ponytail.

"Thank you for coming so quickly!" she said. "I wasn't the only person to see the news when the picture went out earlier today." She glanced at the woman tending bar. "Not that *everyone* knows yet."

"Your boss didn't."

"A couple of the other girls were talking. They're afraid, too. They also thought the woman in the picture—the new picture, I mean—was Wendy. The other picture was really generic, and like I said the other day, it could've been anyone. Besides, I had no reason to think Wendy was even in town." Her eyes filled with tears. "It's so sad! We thought she was in New York taking a few days' break and having a wonderful time. Wendy...wasn't like the rest of us. She was a really good person."

"You're just making a living here—not stealing, cheating or hurting people. There's no reason not to think you're a good person yourself," Aidan told her.

She smiled. "So far, I think I'm okay. But...well, the life. It *can* lead to drug use and sometimes addiction, and then...whatever it takes to feed the addiction. I've seen it before. But Wendy—Wendy just worked and smiled and was nice to everyone. She didn't even drink."

"Debbie, did someone here threaten you? Why were you so frightened when I talked to you on the phone?"

"I don't even really know. Although I didn't mean to hang up on you—and scare you. Forgive me. I'm sure the officers you sent out had better things to do. What happened is that my cell battery died. I'm sorry. I guess I panicked and that's why I called. It was horrible, what was done to her! And I suddenly looked around and wondered who might have done such a thing. Could it be someone *here?*" She looked nothing like the wicked vamp who had graced the stage moments ago.

"I have another question for you. I learned that Wendy has...had a son. Do you—"

"Oh, Lord!" Debbie broke in. "Her little boy! I wonder where her little boy could be!"

"A friend? A parent?" Aidan asked urgently.

Debbie shook her head. "Wendy's husband died in a car accident and her parents were older and they're gone and she had no sisters or brothers. She had distant cousins in Great Britain, and that's it! If she needed to go out, she usually asked me to watch J.J.—John Jacob—for her. He's a darling, eight years old. Agent Mahoney, that little boy is out there somewhere! Oh, my God! You don't think he's dead, too?"

The possibility was a horrible one. Aidan tried to reassure her. "We'll find him. Write down Wendy's address for me. I'll start at her house. We'll check with the neighbors, and—"

Debbie shook he head, even more wildly this time. "He won't be there! He was supposed to go to New York with her! She would've had me watch him if he hadn't gone with her. You have to find him!"

"What about the school? Wouldn't the school have called?"

"She told the school they were going out of town!"

She took the paper he handed her and wrote down an address. Aidan stood and summoned Sloan, who left the man he'd been questioning and strode over. Aidan introduced him to Debbie and tersely explained that they had the identity of their second victim—and that she had a child. "We need an APB immediately, an Amber Alert—everything we can blast out. Agent Everett needs to question the Highsmith party again. We have a missing child on our hands. I'm going to go straight to the Appleby house. Can you grab one of the officers and a cruiser, and get more information from Ms. Howell here? See that she gets home safely tonight, and call me once you've dropped her off."

"Sure."

"I haven't come up with a connection between Richard and Wendy Appleby yet," Aidan said in a low voice. "Also…there's another venue here for finding a missing child. Mo Deauville and her dog."

Sloan smiled encouragingly at Debbie Howell, who was sitting with a blank stare and misty eyes. "Where the hell would she even start? There's a lot of territory here."

"I don't know how she does what she does, she just does it," Aidan responded. "And I think, with her record of success, she's the person we need."

Sloan wasn't a man prone to waste a lot of time—or ask too many questions. He nodded and turned to Debbie.

"Ms. Howell, my pleasure," he said. He had taken out his cell phone and was calling Purbeck to get the notices going. Then he nodded at Aidan.

As Aidan left, he heard Sloan ask, "Debbie, do you have a picture of J.J. on your phone? We need to get that to the media. And tell me anything else you can about him."

Aidan was already out the door. He felt his stomach churning.

Didn't matter how long he'd done this, how many times.

There was a little kid out there. Dead or alive.

It wasn't much of a challenge playing the Woman in White. If not for the current situation in Sleepy Hollow, she would actually have had fun. She wasn't one of the terrifying characters, so she wasn't expected to elicit terror. She was merely creepy.

But half the scare tactics at such a venue came from the art of surprise. All she did was walk—but when she appeared on the path unexpectedly, people screamed. She never broke character, never cracked a smile.

Yes, it could have been fun.

Except that she spent most of her time waiting to see if the ghost of Major Andre would appear again.

Andre made no more appearances.

When they were called in for the night and she went

to scrub her face, she paused. Her makeup was really good. She looked both ethereal and very real.

"Hey, are we going to go out with the others?" Grace asked her.

Mo was tired; she should go home. But she didn't think she'd sleep, anyway. "Sure."

She and Grace headed out, followed by Ron, the makeup man, her old friend Phil and two young women who played historical characters, Greta Sanders and Mindy Cheswick. Phil extolled the blueberry pancakes at the diner, and Mo decided she was actually hungry. They ordered, and she was in the middle of learning how Mindy and Greta were costume designers in from the city for the season—they had begged for jobs as actors for the event after they'd been hired to design the costumes—when she heard the little bell at the door. When she turned casually to look, she was startled to see Aidan Mahoney entering the café.

Initially she thought he'd come in for coffee and food after work, just as she and her group had done— She couldn't imagine why he'd be looking for her at 2:00 a.m.

But he walked straight to her table.

Aidan reached them and excused himself to the others. "Sorry to bother you. Mo, we need you. Now. There's a missing child."

She stared at him for a few seconds, stunned—and slightly ill. She'd been hungry. She wasn't hungry anymore.

Child.

The word seemed to echo in her ears.

Finding a missing child. It was something she and Rollo often did. Families visited the local museums and parks, and parents lost track of their kids. Little kids could move like bats out of hell. They could easily go missing in the myriad historic venues in the area.

She was always optimistic; she'd been called out at least ten times in the past few years.

In all of those cases they'd found the missing children, alive and mostly well. One ten-year-old had broken his arm playing in a tree. One little girl had fallen down into a hollow in the woods and sprained an ankle.

They'd been dirty, frightened and crying—but alive.

But there hadn't been a known murderer in the area at the time— beheading his victims.

"A child?" she said weakly.

"Please," Aidan said quietly.

The others at her table were silent—just watching. Listening.

"Of course. Excuse me," she told them. As she rose, she told Aidan, "I'll need Rollo."

"I'll take you to get him right now."

"I have several articles of clothing that belonged to the boy," Aidan said. "I got them at his house."

"Good. Rollo will need a scent," Mo said.

As they left the restaurant, Mo was aware that Ron and the others were plying Grace with questions and Grace was explaining that Mo had a search-and-rescue dog named Rollo.

"A kid. Damn, that sucks," she heard Ron say.

Outside, she found Van Camp and Voorhaven standing by their car; two patrol cars were parked next to them, the officers awaiting their next order.

"Hey, Mo," Van Camp called to her. He walked over and pressed something into her hands. "We went to the Appleby house to see if the boy was there—he wasn't.

Here," he said, and she realized he'd brought her the boy's clothing in a plastic bag. She could see the shirt he must have worn for his Little League games and a small polo shirt with a school logo on it. "The boy's name is John Jacob Appleby. Goes by J.J. He's eight years old," Van Camp said.

"You found his mother yesterday morning," Aidan told her.

"Oh, no," Mo murmured. Her heart sank. "So...you learned the identity of Jane Doe?" she asked in a whisper.

Aidan nodded. "Wendy Appleby. Her son, J.J., is just...gone. You can help, right?"

"Rollo can help," she said. "Except that we need somewhere to start."

"His house? I don't really know what else to suggest. They would've been there recently. And they might have been kidnapped from there." He paused. "Wendy Appleby and her son were supposed to be going on a trip to New York. That's why they weren't missed."

"I guess the house makes sense. But..."

Her voice trailed off. The mother had been dead for almost forty-eight hours. That didn't bode well for the child.

"We have to find him," Aidan said firmly. "And we will."

Within ten minutes they were at Mo's house. As they drove, Aidan filled her in on the situation regarding Wendy and her son. It took less than five minutes at her cottage to pick up Rollo. Ten minutes after that, they were at the Appleby home. It was a newer house for the area, a ranch style that was about sixty years old. It was spotless; Wendy Appleby had obviously been a

meticulous housekeeper. The house was also charm-
ingly decorated for Halloween. There were drawings
that J.J. had done proudly displayed on the refrigerator,
and scattered around the house were pictures of the boy
and his mother at various places.

She'd had a beautiful smile.

Mo let Rollo free in the house. "You're sure they
were taken from here?" she asked Aidan. "There's no
sign of a struggle."

"I'm not sure of anything," Aidan said.

Rollo went to the front door and began to bark.

She followed the dog—and tried to open her own
mind, tried to watch and listen with every instinct,
every power she had.

It wasn't difficult to find the dead. They seemed
to call out to her. She heard their voices in her mind.

Oddly enough, it was usually harder with the living. And always, she used logic together with whatever
sense it was that helped her.

Rollo sniffed around in a frenzy and then stood in
the drive barking.

"The boy's scent ends there," Mo said. "The boy was
put into a vehicle of some kind, I imagine."

"That's it?" Aidan asked. His disappointment was
evident.

For a moment, she wanted to snap at him. This
wasn't easy. It involved creating a mental map of the
area in her head and making an attempt to touch the
mind of a killer or kidnapper. Or a child who'd wandered off.

She closed her eyes.

Wendy Appleby had been murdered. They didn't
know if she'd been home or somewhere else when she'd

been kidnapped and then killed. There was no car in the yard; Wendy could have left the house with her son. Maybe they'd even set off on their trip and been intercepted. Sleepy Hollow's earth had been accepting the dead for hundreds of years. Many of the old vaults led deep into the hills.

Where things could happen and remain unheard.

Where the dead might be beheaded and prepared for a macabre display.

And where a child, not part of the design, might be kept prisoner.

Or just left to die.

"The cemetery," she said with certainty.

"Which cemetery?" Aidan asked.

"The one where we found his mother's body," Mo told him.

He looked at her, eyes narrowed. "You're sure?" he asked.

She repeated his earlier words. "I'm not sure of anything."

"Are you saying you believe he's been killed and displayed somewhere, too?"

"No," Mo said. "No." She couldn't tell if she was denying that possibility for Aidan or herself. "I don't think he fit the plan. I think we may find him there. Injured, perhaps. Terrified, certainly."

He nodded, studying her. She felt he was watching her again, that he knew about her again—that he looked into her mind or soul and saw that there was something different about her.

You have it, too! she wanted to scream.

She refrained.

Van Camp walked over to them. Aidan said, "Mo

has a good suggestion. We have Rollo, who can find the scent so we'll have something to go on, but since the two bodies were found in the cemetery, it's possible the boy wound up there, too."

"Sweet Jesus!" Voorhaven murmured.

"We don't know where the murderer brought the victims to behead them. And Mo's suggestion gives us a place to start looking," Aidan said.

"No, wait." Mo raised one hand. Van Camp turned to her and waited for her to speak.

"One of the vaults," Mo began. "They're deep in the earth. Some are very big—when we were kids, we used to play in the old Stewart vault. Time destroyed that one. The gate was gone, the seal was broken, and who knows what happened over the years. It was just a big empty space with a lot of coffin shelves when I was growing up. I'm assuming the authorities took care of the bodies. When I was a teenager, it was filled in. But we know there are dozens more."

"Let's go," Aidan said. "Time has passed—but time may still be everything."

Van Camp nodded and gave directions to the other officers present. Mo opened the door of Aidan's car for Rollo to hop in and then slipped into the driver's seat.

Aidan was on the phone. She watched him as he spoke.

"Anything? Anything at all?" she asked as he ended the call.

He hung up. "As I mentioned earlier, we discovered today that the victims had been knocked out with chloroform. We found some in the room of Richard's assistant. Two of my colleagues have arrived, and they've been questioning the assistant, Richard's campaign manager and his security detail."

"And they haven't told you anything?" she asked.

"We have them all at the station. We can actually charge Richard's assistant, a woman named Jillian Durfey, but we haven't got anything on the others. She swears the chloroform was planted in her room, which we haven't been able to prove one way or the other. The rest of them continue to deny they know anything about it." He was quiet a minute. "I haven't been with my unit for very long, but I know that the members are exceptionally good. If anyone could get something out of this group—even a shred of information—they're the people. But right now we have to find the child, Mo. That's our immediate focus."

She looked at him. "You just said 'we.' I hope you mean that because I'm going to need your help. This isn't flat land. There are hills everywhere and who knows how many forgotten dead. Nature has taken over in a lot of these areas."

"Obviously, I'm here with you," he said stiffly.

She didn't respond.

They drove to the cemetery and he parked on the rise, just steps away from the point where she and Rollo had run up the hill yesterday, when they'd found the bodies of Richard Highsmith and Wendy Appleby.

Mo got out of the car and went to open the back door. She showed Rollo the shirts again, letting him get a good whiff. She didn't put him on a lead.

Barking, he jumped out of the car. She raced after him with Aidan Mahoney close behind.

There was no real path. There'd been burials here for so long that the ground had shifted; stones stuck out at odd angles. She nearly tripped but grabbed one of the stones, righted herself and hurried after Rollo.

She reached the top of the hill and looked around. She could see the vault they'd come upon during the early hours of the previous morning—where the body of Wendy Appleby had reclined, as if asking them in.

And where they'd found the rest of Highsmith.

The moon was high that night, only partially cloaked in clouds. It cast an almost sinister glow as shadows appeared and then fell around the praying angels, cherubs and monuments.

There were more vaults built into the rise of the next hillock. Mo assumed Rollo would race straight toward them, that the scent of the shirt would lead him there.

She could be wrong, of course. They were working on her theory right now. And even though it was a plausible theory, she might be wrong.

There were dozens of plausible theories.

She felt Aidan close behind her. He didn't speak.

They both watched Rollo.

She could hear Van Camp shouting, ordering his officers to search for anything that looked as though it didn't belong.

A team of medics was with them, too.

At least they'd sent medics and an ambulance. Everyone was hopeful.

False hope?

Rollo dashed toward the vaults. They weren't neatly aligned—they were as haphazard as the hillside itself. He ran from one to another.

And then he disappeared.

Mo ran after him, careful as she traveled the uneven, stony ground.

Rollo reappeared. He was still searching.

"This may not be right," she heard Van Camp murmur.

"Give him time," Aidan said.

Rollo now ran toward the edge of the hillside that led to what was officially Sleepy Hollow Cemetery. He galloped back and forth, back and forth, barking.

"What the hell is he doing now?" Van Camp asked.

Mo simply watched her dog, who sat, looked at her, thumped his tail—and barked again.

"This is useless," Van Camp muttered. "And we've got a kid out there somewhere."

"No, no, I don't think it's useless at all," Voorhaven said. He walked toward Mo. "He means something by that, doesn't he?"

Mo nodded. "That posture means he's found him."

"There's nothing there," Van Camp said. "Mo, you're the best, I know that, but he's just sitting on a grave, barking."

Mo didn't answer right away. She stood unmoving among the graves as the moonlight played over her in the misty night.

Because she heard a sound. Like a muffled sob.

She turned slightly. There was an angel of stone, hands folded in prayer, head bowed in sorrow. Her beauty was decaying and yet somehow shimmering in the unearthly light.

She might have been crying.

Mo looked at Aidan, who was studying her. He asked quietly, "Mo? You have something, don't you?" He gave her a nod of encouragement.

"Rollo isn't wrong and he hasn't lost his touch," she said slowly. "We're close to the boy. I believe we're standing right on top of him."

8

The police spread out. Flashlights swept across graves and the edifices of dozens of mausoleums and vaults.

At some point during the night, Aidan's fellow agents Jane Everett and Sloan Trent arrived to help, and Mo was pleased to meet them. Jane was eager to hear about Rollo and his gift for finding the missing, but Mo had the feeling that she was asking her much more.

When they were briefly alone while the men searched the cliff sides, seeking vaults and entries, Jane asked her quietly, "You haven't seen anyone here who could help, have you?"

"Seen anyone?" Mo repeated carefully.

Jane smiled. "In the cemetery. Any spirits who might help?"

Mo inhaled, looking at Jane. The woman was an artist, she knew. Her ability to put life into the two-dimensional image of a face had led them to their second victim. Jane was sophisticated in a casual way, attractive—and confident. And she was talking about ghosts.

"No," Mo said. "But…I wasn't looking. And I seldom see—"

"The dead in cemeteries," Jane finished for her. She smiled again. "Your dog is fantastic. And I'm sure he's found the boy. We just have to get to him."

"I know he's here somewhere," Mo said. "And," she added softly, "I believe he's alive."

Rollo came trotting over to Mo. He whined and slipped his head beneath her hand, obviously impatient. He wanted her working with him.

"Well, we're not going to get into a vault by standing here," Jane said.

"You're right. Rollo, let's go."

Jane went ahead. Rollo ran down the hill, seemingly without effort. It wasn't quite as easy for human beings on two legs. But, like Jane, Mo made her way to the bottom.

There were officers in front of them and behind them. On Aidan's orders, they were meticulously searching the hillside—not for clearly visible vaults seen with rusted iron gates that couldn't be opened, but for entries time had hidden, with vines and foliage that completely obscured any opening there might be. It was slow going, especially in the dark. The sun would come up soon enough, but no one wanted to wait.

With Rollo at her side, no longer barking, Mo took a hands-on approach, hoping she didn't disturb a stinging insect or awaken a snake or some other creature. She had her hands flat on the earth when she paused.

She could hear the crying again.

For a moment, she went still. It seemed that she was standing before an area on the face of the hill that was nothing but dirt. Vines grew profusely here. But when she stuck her fingers through them, she touched metal. Hard, cold metal.

She didn't cry out for the others at first. She tore at the vines, and as she did, she realized that someone could have just slipped between them.

There was a door. Iron? It had a massive brass ring for an opener, and she pulled on it. By her side, Rollo barked.

Then she heard it again—the sound of a sob.

Is it in my head? she wondered. *A remnant of something that once was?*

Rollo barked excitedly.

The sound came again.

It wasn't real—or at least it wasn't now.

But it *had* been real…she was hearing an echo in time. Did that mean the child was dead—or merely unconscious? The door gave.

It should have creaked. It should have groaned and been almost impossible to open. Time should have created a seal stronger than any made by man.

But the door slid open and before she could stop him, Rollo rushed in.

Mo followed her dog, crying out for the others to come.

Aidan was cracking open a lock on a vault when he heard Mo scream. He hurried along the overgrown path to the source of the sound. Jane was just reaching the door. He hurried past her, pushing his way through, aiming his flashlight into the tomb.

Coffin shelving lined the walls, the old seals mostly intact, but there were cracks here and there. A broken altar featuring a pair of praying angels stood toward the center of the front area. The vault itself stretched deep into the hillside.

"Mo!" he called.

"Here!" Her voice echoed and he could hear Rollo barking.

Aidan went farther inside. Before he could reach Mo, he paused.

There was another old stone, set like an altar in the center of the long aisle of tombs. The stone was broken and it looked muddy—but it wasn't mud that marred the altar. It was blood. A hatchet and a knife leaned against the makeshift altar.

"Aidan, come quickly!"

He moved past the broken and bloodied altar. Mo was just beyond it, hunkered down, trying to lift a bundle from the floor.

"Mo?"

"It's him! It's the boy, Aidan. And he's alive!" Jane hurried in behind Aidan.

"Get the medics," he said tersely.

She ran out, and Aidan rushed to Mo's side. "Let me," he told her.

It was easy for him to pick up the eight-year-old boy. The child was unconscious, but he seemed to be breathing without any problems. Although he was covered in dirt and spiderwebs, he appeared to be unhurt.

He looked at Mo, and she looked back at him with relief. She was shaking.

"Thank you," he said simply.

He turned and walked out of the tomb. There would be a lot to do that night. He felt her behind him. She followed him out, obviously concerned about the boy.

The EMTs were waiting outside and they sprang into action with a speed and competence that was reassuring. Aidan listened as they called off vital statistics. The boy's pulse was low but acceptable.

"How's it look?" he asked, aware that Mo was silent but right behind him.

"Well, I'm not a doctor," the young man in charge told him. "But I'm seeing dehydration, minor cuts and bruises. Not much more than that. The kid obviously hasn't had anything to eat or drink in two days, but he'll probably come out of this none the worse for wear—physically, anyway. Mentally? I don't know. I've got to admit being locked in there would've done me in as a kid!" He indicated the vault. "Gotta take him now, okay?"

Mo suddenly spoke up. "May I ride with him?" she asked.

"That's obviously a great dog, but he can't come. And it's usually one of the police—" he started to tell her.

Aidan was surprised when he found himself saying, "The dog will come with me. I don't think the boy's going to regain consciousness for a while. It may be unorthodox, but hey, this lady rescued him. She'll ride with you. Mo, I'll meet you at the hospital."

Mo nodded with obvious gratitude.

"Rollo *will* go with me, won't he?" Aidan asked.

"Yes." She rolled her eyes. "That traitor might like you even better than me," she said.

The EMT helped her into the back of the ambulance.

Jane and Sloan were behind Aidan, and so were Van Camp and Voorhaven.

Van Camp said, "Go ahead and follow. I've put the call through to the crime scene department, and we'll keep a vigil here."

"If they can just find *something* in that tomb…then we might have some answers—and something to compare with our suspect's DNA."

Jane smiled. "That boy has to be tough, a survivor. Maybe he'll be able to give us some more information."

"Let's pray he does," Aidan murmured. "All right, I'll take the dog in my car. We can switch off shifts at the hospital until I convince Ms. Deauville that she can leave. Rollo?"

Rollo barked.

"That's one impressive dog," Voorhaven said.

"And one impressive woman," Aidan added quietly.

Van Camp smiled and slapped his partner's back. "Yes! Hell, it's a good night. We found the kid—and we found him *alive*."

J. J. Appleby was one cute kid. He had wavy dark hair that fell to his neck, and a tuft in front hung naturally over his forehead. His cheeks were still cherubic. He was ashen, but with an IV started, he seemed to be getting back a little color. Mo held his hand. She felt him squeeze hers in return, just slightly, once.

The EMT—Stan—was a pleasant and solid man of about forty. He was quiet most of the time in the ambulance, watching his patient. His partner, the driver, was in contact with the hospital during the ride.

"Looks like he's going to be fine," Stan assured her.

"Why is he unconscious?" she asked. "I mean, if he isn't hurt."

"No food, no water and pure terror. Could you imagine being locked up in there?" Stan asked.

With the sirens blaring, and at this hour of the night, they were at the hospital in no time. Mo stayed in the

E.R. waiting area until the boy was taken to a room and she was told she could go see him. She'd barely gotten there before Aidan arrived. He sat on the other side of the bed and assured her that Rollo was fine. He was with Jane at the hotel.

They hadn't been there long when J.J. woke. For a moment, his eyes were wide-open and unseeing. Then he bolted straight up and let out a bloodcurdling cry.

Mo quickly reached for him. "J.J., J.J., it's okay. You're in the hospital now."

He stared at her as if she were some kind of monster, recoiling from her touch.

"You're all right, you're all right," she murmured. "You're in the hospital."

He relaxed in her arms, and then began to sob. The sound was heartbreaking.

It was the sound she'd heard in her mind when he'd been in the vault below her.

He allowed her to hold him. She let instinct take over and just sat there, rocking him. Over his head, she looked at Aidan. She knew he wanted—*needed*—information from the boy, but he was also aware of J.J.'s fragility and the agent had, she realized, tremendous compassion.

Finally, the boy's cries subsided. "My mom?" he whispered. The hope in his voice tore at her soul. She realized that he knew his mother was dead.

"I'm so sorry, J.J.," Mo whispered.

Aidan sat forward. "I'm Aidan Mahoney, J.J. I'm with the FBI. And this is Mo. We're going to find whoever did this and make sure they're locked up forever—I promise. But you can help us."

J.J. was shaking again. He pulled back a little. "I can?" he asked, his voice weak.

"Can you tell us what happened?" Aidan asked.

He stared blankly at Aidan for a minute.

"How did you wind up in the vault at the cemetery?" Mo asked.

The boy frowned with the effort to remember. "We were going to New York City," he said dully. "We were going to visit some of Mom's friends. She was going to take me to a play. And we were going to see the Statue of Liberty."

"But what happened? Had you left your house?"

J.J. nodded. "Then what?" Mo asked softly.

"We were going to hear a man speak at the convention center. After the speech, Mom said, the traffic would be better and it would be an easy drive. If we were tired, we'd just stop outside the city and stay in a motel for the night. We were s'posed to have a great adventure!"

"Did you make it to the convention center?" Aidan asked.

"Yes…"

"And then?"

J.J. began to cry silently, with tears streaming down his face.

"Take your time, J.J.," Mo said.

"We got there. We got out of the car. We started walking over to the building."

"What happened after that?" Mo pressed gently.

"Mom started to turn around. Someone was behind us. I started to turn around, too. But it went dark. There was something over my head. And…I smelled something that was sort of sweet. And then…"

"What?" Aidan asked.

"Then I woke up in that horrible place. And I couldn't see anything, and I screamed and screamed and screamed but no one could hear me. I tried to move around in the dark and I...I touched dead people! There were dead people on slabs and I screamed again and... and there was blood. I touched blood, and there was a hatchet and a knife and..."

He started crying once more. Mo kept on holding him.

A nurse was standing at the door. "No more right now," she said urgently.

Mo and Aidan nodded. "I'm expecting one of his mother's friends," Aidan explained. "Can you let her stay with him, please?"

"Yes, of course." Mo glanced across the boy's bed at Aidan. A moment later, there was a tap at the door and she turned to look.

To her surprise, she knew the woman standing there. She hadn't seen her in a few weeks, but when they were all young, the two of them had gone to many of the same parties. Her name was Debbie Howell. She was dancing at a strip club now. She'd always been nice to Mo, and Mo liked her. Debbie was still a beautiful woman. There was a sense of joy about her, something in her face that said she expected the best from people and from life. Debbie reminded her of Grace. Even without a bit of makeup on—or maybe because of that—she looked young and innocent.

"Debbie!" she said, hoping her shock wasn't evident.

Aidan rose quickly.

Debbie cast her a grateful smile but then made a

beeline for the boy. J.J. dropped his hold on Mo and immediately reached for Debbie.

"Oh, J.J., J.J., you're safe and sound and alive and… Oh, J.J.!"

She hugged the boy, tears in her eyes. When she pulled away, she threw herself at Aidan, hugging him.

She startled him as no armed enemy could, Mo thought. He could hardly keep himself from stepping away, and he looked decidedly awkward as he patted her on the back.

"It's okay, Debbie! J.J. is okay."

"Thanks to you," Debbie told him.

"No. Thanks to you. And thanks to Mo—and Rollo."

Debbie turned to Mo, who was prepared for the hug that came her way.

"Of course, you and Rollo. I should've known that!" Debbie said. "Thank you."

"Nothing could have made me happier," Mo murmured.

"What will happen to me, Debbie?" J.J. asked. "They won't say it—but my mom is dead. Like my dad. What'll happen to me? Debbie, my mom…she was the best mom."

He cried again, this time clutching Debbie Howell like a koala. She reassured him. "I can't be her. You're right, she was the best mom ever. But you'll have me, J.J. You'll have me forever and ever, I promise. Your mom and I talked about this. She had a will and made it clear that you'd be with me."

The nurse was back at the door. "He needs to get some rest," she said sternly. "If the doctor comes by, you'll be out in the hallway. *She* can stay—" the nurse pointed at Debbie "—but no more talking."

Mo noted that J.J. hugged Debbie even more tightly.

"J.J., I need to leave," Mo said. "I'll see you later, okay?"

He pulled away from Debbie's embrace for a minute. "Thank you," he whispered. "And thank…Rollo. Rollo is a dog, right? I wish I could see him."

"Actually, he's a certified service dog so, legally, I can bring him in here. He'll come to see you tomorrow, J.J. You can thank him yourself."

She wasn't sure if a dog coming in thrilled the nurse, but it seemed to brighten the world for J.J.

If she could do that at this moment, she just didn't care what others thought.

Aidan, too, stepped around the bed to leave. "J.J., we'll be back to see you when you've had some time to rest," he told the boy.

When they left the room, Mo saw a police officer in the hallway.

She glanced at Aidan.

"They'll keep an eye on him. We'll let J.J. get some sleep, and then Voorhaven and Van Camp will talk with him. We'll talk with him again, too."

"It doesn't seem like he can help much. He didn't see anything," Mo said.

"But he might have heard something. He told us he smelled something sweet—obviously the chloroform. There might be other memories he hasn't brought forward yet."

Aidan didn't stop to talk to the officer on duty; they just nodded to each other.

Heading out to the parking lot, Mo saw that the sun was up, strong and bright on a beautiful fall morning.

It *was* a beautiful morning. They'd found J.J. alive.

Jane and Sloan were waiting in the parking lot with the dog. Rollo rushed to greet her—and Aidan.

Mo realized that Aidan's coworkers were waiting for a report, but they didn't ask questions. They knew he'd fill them in.

"We're going back to the convention center," Aidan said. "J.J. told us they'd arrived there, gotten out of the car and then they were taken. He didn't see anything. Whoever grabbed them slipped something, probably a cloth saturated with chloroform, over their heads."

"That would suggest two people. Even when it's a woman and a child, how do you take them by surprise?" Jane said. It was a statement more than a question.

"What's the story at the station?" Aidan asked.

"They're going to arraign Jillian Durfey this morning. As for the others," Sloan said, "we've got nothing else to hold them on. They've been released. But we'll be watching them now. Logan Raintree is heading up here with one of our best men as far as video, film and what-have-you goes. Will Chan can set up cameras where you'd never suspect them. And Logan…Logan can track anything. Oh, yeah, we'll keep our eyes on Taylor Branch and those three security guys."

Mo was quiet. She looked at Aidan and noticed for the first time that they were both covered in soot, grime and grass stains. They were still bearing traces of spiderwebs, too.

She figured they were probably lucky the hospital had let them in at all.

"We should catch a few hours' sleep," Jane suggested.

"When Logan gets here with Will."

"The cops are on this, too, Aidan," Sloan reminded him.

"I know. I just don't think I'll sleep well until we've got some reinforcements. Mo, I'll take you and Rollo home."

She said good-night—or good morning—to Jane and Sloan, and took Rollo's leash from Jane. He hopped into the backseat of Aidan's car as if he belonged there. She slid into the passenger seat, and in a few minutes they were on their way to her place.

"You think you might have it solved?" she asked him. "So J.J.'s explanation helped you?"

"Yes," he said. "Although someone went for the bizarre in displaying the bodies, I believe that it was someone close to Richard. He was taken from the convention center with the use of chloroform, and chloroform was found in Jillian Durfey's room. She still claims it was planted. If it was, that definitely points to an inside job."

"So you believe Highsmith was targeted," Mo said. "Possibly by his own people."

"Yeah. But what I can't understand is this—why J.J.'s mother, Wendy Appleby? And she was killed, but the boy—thank God—was not."

"What will happen to J.J. now? Debbie is a good person. Is she going to be allowed to adopt him? She says Wendy stipulated that in her will. "

"It's complicated. The state will have to make that decision. It depends, too, on the exact provisions in Wendy's will. At any rate, he appears to care deeply for Debbie, and vice versa, so I hope it works out for them," Aidan said.

"Poor kid. His dad dead and now his mother," Mo said. "Thank God she left a will."

Aidan nodded.

"You knew Debbie…before?"

"I met her at the club where she works, Mystic Magic. I was following a lead—the matchbook in Richard's pocket. I still can't help wondering what *Lizzie grave* meant." He flashed her a quick smile. "Lizzie might have been Major Andre's love, but even if she was, what did she have to do with Richard?"

"I don't know. We don't know where her grave is, either," Mo said. "What I do know is that I'm so tired I can hardly keep my eyes open."

She hadn't been aware that they'd driven the length of the road and reached her cottage until he stopped the car. Rollo barked from the backseat.

"Uh, would you like to come in? Would you like coffee or something?"

"You just told me how tired you are," he said.

"Yes, but I have to shower, I'm hungry and I'll still be up for a while."

"All right," he agreed. "I could use some coffee."

Once inside, Mo started the coffee and dug through the refrigerator and cabinets. "Omelets, grilled cheese or peanut butter and jelly?" He was standing by the end of the counter, watching her, a smile on his face.

"What?"

"I feel like I've been invited to breakfast by the Spider Queen," he said.

She flushed and then laughed. "I'm wearing a lot of webs, am I? You do realize you're not much better? I'll run and clean up before I contaminate our food. There's another bathroom in the hall. Washcloths and towels and soap are in the little wicker cabinet."

"Thank you. I suppose that was rude. As you pointed out, I probably don't look any better than you."

He turned to head for the downstairs bathroom and Mo went scampering up the stairs.

When she saw herself in the mirror, she shuddered at how ghoulish she looked. She took a three-minute shower and washed her hair. Within another three minutes she was dressed and hurrying downstairs.

He saw her shiny-clean wet hair and grimaced. "Cheater," he said.

She smiled. "You look like you cleaned up okay."

"Ah, but it's not as good as clean clothes and clean hair." He sighed. "The coffee's ready. I poured you a cup. I would've whipped up the omelets, but it would have felt rude rifling through your kitchen."

"A cook, too?" she asked.

"I live alone. And I don't like processed, microwaved food. It's all about necessity, not talent." She took out the ingredients and cracked eggs into a bowl, then added milk. She stirred the mixture and tipped it into butter sizzling in the frying pan.

"What can I do?" he asked.

"Plates, I guess. They're in the cabinets. And silverware—"

"In the silverware drawer."

"Quick learner! No wonder you're an investigator," she said, shaking grated cheese onto the eggs.

It was nice, preparing breakfast with him moving around in her kitchen. Despite the deaths that had occurred, their last night had been a victory. They hadn't had any sleep and surely needed some, but this felt like a strange and even *light* moment between them.

"Oh, and juice is—" she began.

"In the refrigerator. As you've already discovered, I'm not an investigator for nothing," he finished.

A few minutes later, the table had been set and everything was on it—omelets, toast and fresh coffee.

"You must be really hungry," he said. "I interrupted your late dinner."

"How did you find me?" she asked.

"It wasn't that hard. I knew they'd reopened the attractions. I assumed you'd be with Grace. I got the info on where Grace worked, checked that out and learned from one of her bosses that some of the crew hit the café at night."

"Sounds like a lot of effort."

"Took about five minutes." He hesitated, his fork halfway to his mouth. "I also *wanted* to find you," he told her.

She hesitated, too, staring down at her omelet.

"How do you do it?" he asked quietly. "How did you determine where the bodies were? Where J.J. was? Good as Rollo is, I know it's not *just* him."

"I explained my reasoning to you," she said. "It's unlikely that someone could hack up bodies like that in one place and then move them to another, a hotel room or public location."

"There are warehouses around, other venues."

"But the bodies were found at the cemetery, and that's the other part of my rationale. We—most people—don't disturb the dead."

"What does that mean?"

"It means that unless someone's just died and is

being entombed, no one has any real reason to go into the old vaults."

"That's it?" he asked. "That's all there is to it?"

"Logic," she said with a shrug. "The likelihood of being found in a long-forgotten vault while cutting up bodies is pretty much nil."

"So, you worked out that the actual murders—certainly the mutilations—took place in a vault, in a cemetery. Because that's where the bodies were found."

She frowned. "Whoever did this had to know the area well. I knew about the old vaults—and that some of them were long decayed and forgotten—but you have to be really familiar with this area to know that."

"And this morning," he asked. "How did you find J.J.?"

"I...I didn't. Rollo did."

"Rollo was spectacular. But *you* found the vault."

"I was in the right place at the right time."

He stared at her for a moment, clearly skeptical. She leaned forward, irritated. "We found him alive. What else matters? And it had nothing to do with speaking to the dead."

"So you *do* speak with the dead."

"The only way people ever recognize that possibility is if *they* speak with the dead," she said.

"Whatever I had," he told her, "I don't have now."

"We were lucky, and timing is definitely part of it. We found J.J. alive."

"And he might not have lasted much longer. You have something more than logic and a smart dog," Aidan said. "Even more than good instincts or intuition or whatever you want to call it. You have more than I ever had." She felt again as if he were observing the behavior of an exotic animal or studying a new species.

"I have excellent hearing," she said.

"He was unconscious when we recovered him."

"I don't know, Aidan. I thought I heard him. Rollo showed us the way. If I hadn't come across the entry, someone else would have."

She saw that he'd consumed all the food on his plate.

"Can I get you anything else?" she asked, taking the last few bites of her toast.

"No, thank you. That was excellent." He lingered at the table, watching her.

"I'm good with dishes. Actually, I'm a better dishwasher than a cook."

"I just rinse them and put them in the machine."

"I'll help."

When they were done, he said, "Well, I guess I'll get back. I should have a few more coworkers coming in. Once they're here, I'll sleep for a while. I promise I'll keep you filled in on whatever's going on. And if you need anything—" He paused, as if not sure what she might need from him. "Call me," he finally said.

She nodded and walked him to the front door. Rollo trotted beside her, his toenails making the little *tap-tap-tap* sound that was so reassuring.

At the door he turned to her. "Thank you again. For your work—and for coffee and breakfast."

"Finding J.J. is the kind of thing that…that makes everything worthwhile," Mo told him. "As for breakfast, that was certainly easy enough."

"I owe you a meal."

"Hmm. A lovely lobster with an exceptional bottle of wine," she teased.

But he didn't laugh or demur.

"You choose the time and the place," he said.

When he left, she closed and locked the door. As she turned, she would have collided with Candy had Candy been flesh and blood.

"I like him!" her resident ghost announced. "And you found a lost boy— Oh, that's so wonderful! You and Rollo found the boy! I'm so proud of you, Mo. Now, I really do think you need to be friendly to this agent. He's a delightful man. Reminds me of my dear colonel. Granted, he was a Confederate officer, and he fell in love with me! This man is like Daniel, yes. Ready to fight, longing for peace. A man of his time, yet so far ahead. And he likes you, Mo."

"He looks at me like I'm alien spawn, Candy. He's grateful to me, that's it."

"I personally think you're showing a bit of coward-ice there, my dear," Candy chastised her.

"Candy—"

"You want him, but you're afraid of rejection."

"I can't be afraid of rejection when I've already been rejected."

Candy shook her head. "No, give him time. Oh, and lead him to the truth. Gently."

"You heard him— Whatever he had he lost."

Candy laughed. "What was lost can be found again. Oh, and speaking of which…"

She crooked her finger, leading Mo to the window again. "The curtains, please. It's exhausting for me to move them."

Intrigued, Mo pulled back the curtains.

He was there again.

The ghost of Richard Highsmith stood at the edge of the woods.

He moved toward the house. Suddenly he stopped.

He seemed to shimmer in the sunlight for a moment. Then he was gone.

Mo started for the front door.

She felt the brush of Candy's hand on her shoulder.

"No," Candy said. "Don't chase him. He's gaining his strength. He will come to you."

Mo nodded slowly. "I hope so," she murmured.

"I'm glad you're listening to me. What are you going to do now?"

"Sleep!" Mo told her. And smiling, she raced up the stairs, Rollo at her heels.

9

The sound of Aidan's alarm was pitiless.

He'd actually fallen into a deep sleep for the few hours he'd allowed himself.

Logan Raintree, one of the unit heads, had shown up with Will Chan soon after he'd returned from Mo's house. While Aidan was still new to this unit—and he'd feared that being part of it labeled him *odd,* to say the least—he liked the Krewe members and had an instinctive trust in the men and women who were now part of his team.

Before joining the FBI, Logan, like Sloan Trent, had worked in Texas; he'd been a Ranger, while Sloan was a Houston cop who went on to become an Arizona sheriff. Will Chan—a tall striking man with family roots in Trinidad—had actually come to the FBI via a different path. He was a self-termed "master of weird trades." He'd been a professional magician among other things. But he was an expert with film and computers.

Once Will and Logan had arrived, they all met briefly in Aidan's suite. Directly afterward, Will got to work, setting up cameras in the hallway and the elevators. Taylor Branch, Muscles, Mischief and Magic wouldn't be going out or coming in without the Krewe's knowing it.

Before Sloan, Jane and Aidan had dropped into bed for their few hours, they'd discussed the current situation. Jillian would probably be out on bail, despite the fact that the chloroform meant she'd be arraigned. Still, a good lawyer could point out plenty to suggest that there was reasonable doubt as to her guilt.

"Not to mention," Jane observed, "that Jillian Durfey is a tiny little thing. Even with the assistance of chloroform, was she big enough to have done this? Or strong enough, I should say."

"There had to be two people involved," Aidan said. "According to J.J., he and his mother had parked and gotten out of the car—and they were *both* attacked from behind. Based on what he said, they were knocked out almost instantly and it sounded like some kind of bag or hood or even just a cloth was thrown over his head."

"If that's the case, you think it was one of the others?" Logan had asked Aidan.

"It's certainly possible," was Aidan's reply. "They were all here—and they all alibi one another. By the way, there's someone who should be interviewed again, although I know the police already questioned her, and that's the woman who works for the convention center—Bari Macaby.

"She, Jillian and Taylor Branch were the last people to admit they saw Richard alive. I have a timetable in my notes, and there's a gap when Richard was supposedly in the greenroom alone. That's when he disappeared.

"I think we can safely say he was targeted. I don't believe that we're looking for a psychopath who's choosing victims at random, no matter how sensationally and bizarrely the corpses were displayed. Wendy Appleby was targeted, too. Whoever took her didn't want to murder a child—but didn't mind leaving him locked in a vault to die."

Still thinking about that conversation, Aidan quickly showered and dressed, then headed down the hall to the room Logan Raintree had taken. Will was there on his own; he'd set up a complex set of computer screens that showed the entry to the hotel, the delivery area, the parking lot, hallways and elevators.

"Impressive," Aidan said.

"We're lucky. We have first-class equipment," Will told him.

"You got it set up so fast."

"It's like anything," Will said with a shrug. "You do it often enough, you get good at it. Anyway, we've got this covered. We've also got everyone assigned. Logan follows Taylor Branch, Jane's got Muscles, Sloan follows Mischief and I wind up with Magic. We always keep in contact if we're out. Logan's already down at the courthouse, doing surveillance on Taylor Branch. I assume Taylor's working on bail for Jillian. That means she'll be out, but you and Logan have established solid connections with the detectives here. We'll have an officer on call if for some reason the five of them all go in different directions at the same time. That leaves you free to be where you feel you need to be when you feel you need to be there."

"I don't think they'll stay in the area, and we can't legally hold them here," Aidan said.

Will shook his head. "I bet they'll stay awhile. Branch is still claiming that he'll find the real killer and clear them all." He smiled. "The media has been carrying the news about Jillian Durfey's being charged and arraigned—and about J. J. Appleby being found alive.

"At our request, they've given out as little information as possible, but people around here know that Maureen Deauville and her dog, Rollo, are often called in on such cases. So right now there's not much talk about anything else. Naturally, the public is doing the same thing we are—wondering if a small woman like Jillian Durfey could have carried out these acts. Is she innocent or, if not, does she have an accomplice?"

Aidan thanked Will for the update and told him he was on his way to the convention center for an interview with Bari Macaby. "I've got you on speed dial," he added.

At the center, Aidan walked around the parking lot for a while. The problem with a convention center was that it had dozens of entrances and exits. There'd been guards on every door the day Richard was scheduled to speak; they'd all been interviewed and they'd all sworn they hadn't seen Richard leave the building.

The delivery trucks for food service came around the back. If Richard had been snatched from the greenroom, he'd likely been spirited out through the back doors. There, with the trucks' frequent arrivals and departures, it was possible the guards had grown lazy and not noticed that the man of the hour had been coerced or persuaded to leave through a delivery door. Or he'd been dragged out...

But that left the problem of two different places, if Richard had been taken out via the back entrance and Wendy and J. J. Appleby had been kidnapped from the parking lot. Timing could be an issue there, as well. He made a mental note to ask Van Camp and Voorhaven to check all the delivery vehicles that had arrived on the day planned for Richard's speech.

Inside, he was directed to an office, where Bari Macaby was waiting for him.

"Agent Mahoney, I wish I could help!" she said, standing to shake his hand and indicating a chair in front of her desk. "That this happened here— Well, we're just horrified. I've spent hours with the police. I don't know if there's anything else I can possibly say.

"I did get Mr. Highsmith a snack. I manage the place, and I'm not usually involved with service situations related to our clients, but...I was a fan," she told him, blushing slightly. "I don't even live in New York City, but I was convinced that Richard Highsmith would've been elected—and his next step would've been the governor's mansion or the senate, and then, who knows? He might have gone all the way to the top." She sighed. "As you can tell, I was a *huge* fan."

"I'm sure Richard appreciated your feelings, Ms. Macaby," Aidan said. She sounded very sincere. Dressed for efficiency in a pantsuit, she was a slender woman and appeared to be in her mid-fifties. Her hair was iron-gray and neatly tied back. She looked very natural, proud of her age and wearing it beautifully.

He had a feeling she spent much of her free time hiking or perhaps at a gym.

"Richard," she repeated. "The way you say that, you knew him, Agent Mahoney?"

"Richard and I grew up in the area. Yes, I knew him."

"Oh, you grew up here! Lucky man. I escaped the city to come here about ten years ago, once my children had moved on and my husband…well, he moved on, too. The city's exciting but it's filled with crime—nightly muggings, murder, rape. Here, bad things just don't happen at an hourly rate. In fact, they seldom happen at all." Tears welled up in her eye. "And now…this."

He nodded sympathetically. "Ms. Macaby, the last time you saw Richard, he was in the greenroom, right?"

"Oh, yes, he was a man who asked for so little! He wanted tea, and cheese and crackers. I was happy to get them for him."

"When you went to the greenroom to inquire about what he wanted, he was with Taylor Branch?"

"Yes. Mr. Branch and Ms. Durfey. They were going over some last-minute notes on the speech. Jillian had her clipboard and she was about to do the initial sound check." She sat back, sighing. "That little girl! They say she was charged with the murders!"

"Evidence was found that indicated she might have been at least involved," Aidan said carefully.

"According to the press, chloroform was found in the bodies. And there was chloroform in her room."

"That's right."

"If you have her, I'm a bit confused. What else can I give you?"

"She swears she was framed. And, admittedly, the chloroform is circumstantial evidence," Aidan said. He steered the conversation back to the greenroom. "So, Taylor Branch and Jillian Durfey were in the room when you went in there. You found out what Richard wanted—and you brought it to him?"

"Yes. Well, I brought it to the greenroom. There was no one present when I came in with the tray. I called out to him, assuming he was in the restroom. Then I was sure of it because I heard him answer me. I left the food and went back to my office."

"You heard him answer you. Are you *certain* it was Richard?"

"Oh, yes."

"Absolutely certain?"

She stared at him, unblinking.

"It had to be him. Mr. Branch and Ms. Durfey had gone. They were checking the sound system."

"You knew that because?"

"That's where they said they were going. And I'm sure— Yes, I saw them there when I went out to the stage."

"Yes, but was that right afterward?"

She hesitated.

"You told the police it was right after you'd dropped off the tray in the greenroom, Ms. Macaby. Is that accurate? Or could there have been a few minutes in there?" Aidan asked.

"Agent Mahoney, I'm not a liar!" she said.

"I didn't suggest that. But, trust me, it's easy to forget that we might have been distracted—checked on something else, slipped outside for a cigarette."

She turned a million shades of purple. "I...I don't smoke!" It had just been a suggestion. He could as easily have said that she'd gone for a soda or a cup of coffee for herself.

But he hadn't—and she'd given herself away.

"That's it, isn't it? You stepped out for a cigarette?"

She seemed to explode. "Oh, but I don't smoke! I really don't. I'd quit. But there was so much pressure, what with the size of the audience and the fact that he might've been a future president and I...I was gone less than five minutes. I really did quit. I just needed a few puffs to calm my nerves, you know?"

"Can you show me where you went?" he asked her.

"What?"

"Where's the hideaway? You didn't go out where others go out, did you? You wouldn't have wanted them to see you."

She stood up, looking a little ill. "Did I mess up the investigation? Could you have saved them?"

"No, Ms. Macaby. The fact that you slipped out that night wouldn't have changed the course of events. It was all set in motion so that everyone would be looking for Richard while he was being killed. What you did or didn't do wouldn't have changed anything. But you can help now."

She nodded. "This way. And God forgive me!" she muttered.

She escorted him around the convention center main stage and past the side entrances. The greenroom was at the far end. Aidan asked Bari Macaby to wait for a moment as he searched it.

The room was set up with three mirrored stations, a counter, refrigerator and microwave. A sofa grouping was arranged around a coffee table that held all kinds of magazines. There was a workstation with computer access. Toward the rear was a small hallway. One side offered a men's room and the other side a ladies'.

He went into the men's room. There was one stall as well as two urinals and a counter with sinks and a mirror. He wasn't sure why he paused there, but he decided that he'd come back with a Krewe member and try to figure out what it was about the greenroom that disturbed him.

There was only one entrance, which led out to the hall.

He rejoined Bari and she took him to the stage door. There was easy access to the stage just outside it. She pointed out that when an event was going on, velvet ropes prevented visitors or attendees from reaching this area; the doors to the actual auditorium, the seating for the performances or events, were closer to the main entrance.

"And here…well, just out here…is my little escape hatch," Bari said.

It was another ten feet down from the entrance to the greenroom. A short hallway brought them to a door marked Emergency Exit Only.

"I key in the code so the alarm doesn't go off," Bari explained.

She did that and opened the door. They stepped outside.

Her smoking niche was dark, despite the brightness of the autumn sun. It was well hidden from the rear—where the deliveries were made—and the parking lot, which extended to the far left of the property. It was almost like a private foyer.

A person standing here could see what was going on at the back—and in the parking area.

Had Richard left this way? With or without someone else? Or had he been drugged inside the building—and then pulled or carried out? *Possibly—and was this woman suspect? She definitely knew about this more-or-less hidden exit.*

"Thank you, Ms. Macaby. Is there an event scheduled for tonight?"

"We'd had a rock star who was supposed to do a show tonight, but the police asked that we hold off for at least another three days. Of course, our employees and the venue are being hit hard, but, under the circumstances..."

"Thank you. I need to make arrangements to get in here later. I do that with you?"

"I'll see that you have every access you need," she promised him.

She took him back through the convention center and to her office, where she gave him keys and codes so that he and the Krewe could come in at night.

"Oh, Agent Mahoney?"

"Yes?"

"You won't tell anyone, will you?"

"Tell them what?" he asked.

She flushed again. "That I was smoking. I mean, it's on my insurance forms that I don't now, and..."

"I won't say a word." When he left, he observed the parking lot again. Suddenly anxious, he put through a call to Will, who told him the Krewe were assembled at the hotel. Taylor Branch and Jillian Durfey, now released on bail, had returned to their rooms. Taylor had assured the police—voluntarily—that they didn't plan on leaving the city until the real murderer of Richard Highsmith was discovered. Richard's death, he'd stated in a press interview, was more than just a murder, it was a crime against the people of the United States.

"It's a regular love-fest here," Will said dryly. "Logan's gone up to speak with Branch. Logan is good at getting people to talk because he makes them feel he's on their side. So, it looks like we're hunkered down here for a while."

"We'll need some extra help tonight," Aidan told

him. "Keeping track of everything. I'd really like to get our Krewe to the convention center."

"Van Camp and Voorhaven are at the vault, trying to put together what went on there. I'm sure they'll arrange all the police help we need."

"I'm on my way to see them," Aidan said.

He ended the call and keyed the ignition of his car. He hesitated before driving off; instead, he dialed Mo Deauville's number.

Her phone just rang. He felt a surge of unease.

But then, on the seventh ring, she picked up.

"Just checking in," he said.

"I'm fine, thanks."

"Did you get some sleep?" he asked.

"Several hours, actually. You?"

"Ah, yeah, thanks." He cleared his throat. "I'm heading out to join Detectives Voorhaven and Van Camp at the vault," he said. "And, at some point, I'm going to go see J.J. at the hospital."

"I was planning on going to see him, too," she said. "I told him I'd bring Rollo."

"Yeah, I remember. Wait for me. I'll pick you up and we'll go together."

"I have to be back here for about five. I'm working the Haunted Mausoleum again," she said. "Wow. Does it ever seem strange to say that today?"

"Give me a couple of hours." He glanced at his watch. It was 1:00 p.m. "I'll come by around three."

"Okay."

It was important that he keep her in on this. As he'd seen, and as he'd told her, she had *something*. She might well have the ability to get to Richard—even if he didn't.

His Krewe was here. While he hadn't wanted to be part of it, he knew that the group he was working with was reputed to be special. They might be referred to as ghostbusters, but they solved cases where others failed.

Maybe they were a lot like Mo.

And him.

He needed to stop lying to himself.

He should just sit down with the group and tell them he knew what they had, what made them different—and that he understood why they'd thought he'd be a good fit for them. And yet he believed he just didn't have it anymore himself. He needed one of them to try and discover the truth of the situation—through the dead.

Then he could leave Mo Deauville alone.

The problem was, he realized, he didn't *want* to leave her alone.

Mo had barely hung up the phone when Candy came running to her. "Mo, come quick!"

Candy was on her way to the front door, and Mo ran after her. Candy went right through the door.

Mo shook her head and opened it to follow her out, the dog at her heels. He woofed and pushed through ahead of her.

Just outside, Mo paused.

Her Confederate colonel, Daniel Parker, was on the lawn. He seemed pale and ethereal in the bright light of day, but she could still see him clearly.

And she could see the man he was standing with!

Richard Highsmith.

Daniel pointed at the house—and at Mo. The other man nodded. Daniel made a motion that Richard should join him.

He did.

He walked toward Mo, and he seemed to marvel as he realized she could see him. He came forward offering his hand, then let it fall.

"Ms. Deauville." His voice was raspy and yet faint. Like a ripple on the wind. He was still learning how to make himself heard—to those who could hear him.

"Mo," she said, "Mr. Highsmith, I do see you. Please don't be afraid to come to me. I'm trying to help. Your friend Aidan is up here, hunting for your killer. If I can be a go-between, that's wonderful. If I can tell him anything—"

"I don't know what happened," he broke in. "One minute I was standing, the next I was not. And then it seemed that I was removed from my body and I was in darkness. And I…"

He was fading. "I can't!" he whispered. "I need to… I'll come back," he told her in dismay.

He was gone.

"He's having a very difficult time adjusting, learning," Candy said, compassion in her voice.

Daniel was back by her side. "You forget, my love, we've had many years to gather strength and to learn."

"He sucks as a ghost," Candy muttered.

"Candy, my dear—such a manner of speech!" Daniel shook his head disapprovingly.

"My love, we must keep up with the decades!" she said.

Daniel let out a sigh. "My belief is that we should retain what is best in each decade and allow what is not fine or eloquent to slip away. I'm sorry, Mo. I thought I had breached the gap, that I had gotten him to come forward for you."

"You did, Daniel," she assured him. "He'll come back. And I won't waste any time when he does. I'll be ready with the right questions."

She called Rollo, who had decided to roll in the leaves for a while. He was coated in autumn's colors when he ran up to her.

"Rollo!" she chastised softly, dusting the leaves from his coat. "I'm going to give you a good brushing and dress you up in your best service-dog coat. You have a little boy who's lost his mother to visit today."

Rollo wagged his tail happily.

She looked around, feeling oddly uncomfortable. The wind had picked up, creating an eerie whistle in the trees. Mo and Rollo went inside and closed the door, then carefully locked it.

There was no danger out there; Rollo would have let her know. But she was anxious for Agent Mahoney to come and get her.

Strange, she reflected. She wasn't afraid of being painted up as a ghost to walk around an old mausoleum all night—and yet she was unnerved in her own cottage, a place she loved.

Yes, that was it. She was nervous about everything that was going on, all the unexplained events, so she wanted to see him.

No, that wasn't it at all.

She just wanted to see him.

The vines had been pulled away from the old vault entrance and the heavy brass and lichen-covered door had been fully opened. Rigging had been set up for lights to flood the interior of the vault.

When Aidan arrived, crime scene workers were still

taking out whatever small specks or fibers could prove to be evidence.

Van Camp and Voorhaven stood in front of the tomb, watching the proceedings.

Voorhaven greeted Aidan with a friendly handshake. "Hey, glad you're here. I sketched a diagram of what the vault looked like before they took out the hatchet and the knife, scraped off the blood and collected any hair and fiber they could find. Naturally, Van Camp and I went through first in booties to try to reconstruct what happened. I've also included the outside environs. Can I show you what I've done?"

"Of course." As he spoke, the head of the forensics unit, introduced to Aidan as Gina Mason, stopped by to tell him and the detectives that her people had finished.

"They'll send someone to clean up the blood. Not that anyone should be in this old place, anyway, but we don't want to create a possible health hazard," she told them. "But, Detectives, Agent, you're free to try out more theories."

"Did you get anything promising? A cigarette butt, a thread, a hair?" Aidan asked her.

"Hair. Plenty of it on the altar. Where the heads were hacked off. I believe, however, that we'll discover that the murderer was aware of what we'd be looking for, since he wore gloves. Maybe even a snood to protect his own hair—or, hell, maybe he shaved himself bald. Not a button, a cigarette butt or even old beer cans. College kids didn't get in here for frat night or anything— so there's no unrelated evidence. That should make it a little easier for us. The killer left the hatchet and the knife. That's it. I'll report on them as soon as I can."

Aidan nodded. "Thank you."

"I hope we can help!" she said. "I *really* hope we can help."

She waved goodbye and walked to her truck.

Van Camp turned to Aidan. "I think the kid here has done a good job with that sketch," he said.

Voorhaven looked at Van Camp and then at Aidan. "The *kid?* Lee just has to refer to me as 'the kid'? Old man, I'm thirty-three," he said. The "old man" was said teasingly. Aidan could see that the two partners cared about each other and despite Jimmy Voorhaven's initial hostility to the FBI's moving in, he wanted to be a good cop.

"Hey." Aidan grinned at Van Camp. "It's okay. I wouldn't mind being a kid again. And when a job's done right, doesn't matter how old someone is."

Van Camp shook his head wearily. "Let's just do this," he said.

"All right," Jimmy said, holding out his sketch and pointing at two parallel lines he'd drawn. "Here's the way in. We might have gotten tire tracks if we'd found this place early enough. Not many people use this road, since it's almost more of a trail and it goes through a line of forgotten vaults in a hill. Access is through one of the cemetery roads. But our killer knows this. He has his victims in a car—I'm thinking a van or SUV. He stops. Moves the vines and cracks open the door."

He indicated the opening to the vault on his sketch. "We had to use crowbars to get it all the way open, the way I've got it here. Okay, so then he has to bring his victims in one by one, but that's not hard if they're knocked out. I think they might all have been alive when they got here, but maybe he didn't want the kind of blood spatter he'd have on him if he chopped off their heads when they were alive. Okay, so—"

Voorhaven paused. "Say I'm the killer. I have one victim hoisted over my shoulder. I slip in. I probably have a light in here because I go straight to the deep end—way beneath the earth." He stared down at his drawing. "I'm guessing these murders were personal because it takes a lot of strength to strangle an adult man or woman—a lot of adrenaline, a lot of passion. Or desperation, if you're in a fight, but I don't think there was any fight. So, he drops off one victim, then goes back for the next. Of course, the kid's a different matter. Now, if our killer had balls, he did all this with the van parked out there. If he was worried, he moved it and came back."

"Or he or she had an accomplice," Aidan said. "We've been leaning that way."

"Right," Voorhaven agreed. "So, he slips through with one victim over his shoulder and then walks back to his van." The young detective thrust his crumpled sketch in his jacket pocket and mimed the action he described; Aidan and Van Camp followed.

"He throws the kid down. He's not really interested in the kid. He *is* interested in making it look like a psycho's busy in town. Okay, his victims are dead. He has a chopping block on the old altar and he left his weapons there in advance. He cuts off the heads—kind of a clumsy job, according to the coroner. He's never beheaded anyone before. But he gets the heads off. Now here's the thing. He had to know about the mausoleums here as well as the vaults."

"His next step would've been to get the bodies up

to the mausoleum," Aidan put in. "He would've been counting on the darkness."

"That's a little risky," Jimmy said, "because—over at Sleepy Hollow Cemetery—lantern tours could be going on as late as midnight. But, then again, I've taken that tour and if you're not close to the lantern light, it's still dark as all hell. Maybe he enjoys the risk. Anyway, the bodies first. Then he's practically across the street from the Headless Horseman restaurant. He makes sure he gets Richard Highsmith's head where he wants it. By then, everything is closed up. Who can see anything on these streets at night and at that hour? Who's even around to see anything? All he has to do next is move down the street about half a mile to the dry cleaner's display. Put Ms. Appleby's head in his little assembly of witches and spiders and ghastly things—including the headless horseman."

Aidan nodded. "I think your theory is right."

"Yeah?" Voorhaven asked.

"Yeah. Here's the next puzzle, though. Richard disappeared before his speech. It was still daylight. Wendy Appleby must've been grabbed about the same time. You're thinking a van or SUV as a vehicle—that sounds logical. I know most car trunks wouldn't fit two adults and a child. So, did he bring them here and kill them and go back—or did he hide them in plain sight, knocked out in the back of a van before coming here?"

"If Jillian Durfey, Taylor Branch and that security crew of Richard's was involved," Van Camp said, "they couldn't have been driving out here. They were all seen at the convention center."

"J.J. told us how he and his mother were taken. We know there had to be two people. I'm thinking someone in that bunch is guilty—whether it's Jillian Durfey or not—and that there was someone on the outside, as well. Someone who wanted Richard and Wendy Appleby dead," Aidan said.

"We need to find out why this person wanted to kill them *both,*" Voorhaven said.

Van Camp nodded.

"Anything else?"

"To summarize, it sounds like hoods or pieces of cloth soaked in chloroform were thrown over their heads," Van Camp said. "We're agreed that suggests two attackers. You think Wendy Appleby and the boy were taken first—and then Richard?"

"Getting Richard out would be harder, so, yes, probably," Aidan agreed. "Let me just do a walk-through," he said.

He left them and tried to focus on the task at hand. He returned to the entry of the tomb. By day, it was stark and dreary, with broken and chipped seals on either side. It had been abandoned by family and friends for a long time, perhaps a hundred years or so.

A rat ran over Aidan's foot. He found himself thinking about J. J. Appleby, waking in the dark, screaming until he was hoarse, crawling around, seeking a way out.

Being in the vault alone in the dark was bad enough. But shreds of clothing and bits of decaying humanity were visible through the broken seals. Maybe the kid hadn't seen how dismal and creepy his surroundings had been. Still, he might have accidentally touched some protruding bit of cloth or bone....

The outer area of the tomb had been ignored by the killer, who'd gone straight to the back. He'd known the altar was there; he had his knife and hatchet waiting. He'd strangled his victims—and, judging by the coroner's report, he wasn't experienced with cutting off a human head. Whether he'd wanted it to look like the work of a psycho or he was giddy with anticipation regarding his own efforts and their identification with the headless horseman, Aidan couldn't be sure. But the beheading part, after the murders, had been well planned.

He moved on to the back of the vault. The crime scene people had collected what they needed and moved carefully. Aidan could make out two places where it seemed that the dust of the ages had settled—and been disturbed.

That was where he'd left his victims while going about his preparations.

And it was where J. J. Appleby had been thrown. Luckily, he'd been unconscious when his mother was butchered.

"Anything?" Van Camp asked, approaching him a minute later, together with Voorhaven.

"I'm getting the same thing as the kid," Aidan replied, grinning at Jimmy.

"See, old man?" Jimmy teased.

"Never argued with your theory," Van Camp said. "We've got the *how* of it all. We just need a definite who and why." He looked at Aidan. "She's been charged, but the case was nearly dismissed," he said. "Durfey, I mean. And she swore up and down—with and without her attorney—that she's innocent. I guess letting her out on bail was the best the judge could do, seeing as it was circumstantial."

"Yeah, and, if you two don't mind, I'll need some help tonight," Aidan told them.

"I wasn't expecting a night off," Van Camp said.

"What is it?" Voorhaven asked.

"Surveillance duty." He explained what he was after.

"I like it," Van Camp said. "You tell us the time, and we'll be there."

Mo nearly jumped when Rollo started barking, she was so deeply engrossed in what she was reading.

He wagged his tail, which meant, she supposed, that Aidan had arrived.

She peered through the small window in the door and let him in. It was a cool day; he had a trench coat on over his suit. She stepped back, a little breathless. It really wasn't the time to be thinking about how much she liked his looks.

"Thanks for waiting," he said.

"No, I'm glad to go and see him with you," she said. She wrinkled her nose. "Most people, even hospital staff, love Rollo. We do hospital visits at Christmas and bring cards and games and— Well, never mind. But if there's a fierce nurse on, she'll see you and Rollo. You're both so official-looking, I won't have to explain that he's more of a cure than a menace."

He grinned. "Are you ready?"

"Yes, just let me close my computer. I've spent the day looking for your Lizzie."

"And?"

"I might have found her."

She walked him back to the computer, where she'd keyed in a "find a grave" search. "Elizabeth Hampton. I came across her in a history book about the area. The historical evidence is that Andre was in love with Peggy Shippen, who wound up marrying Benedict Arnold, instead. And, at some point, he had a broken engagement. But, as you know, he was a charming and well-liked man, and it's not hard to imagine that there might've been another woman he loved—who loved him in return. There are stories that, on his moves through the area, Major Andre met Elizabeth Hampton and it was love at first sight. It's hard to tell exactly when they managed to meet and fall so deeply in love, but apparently they did. Andre, of course, came to a sad finish at the end of a rope. But there were those who considered Elizabeth a traitor for having fallen in love with a traitor—and probably hiding him at times. No one knows how, but poor Elizabeth came to a bad end, as well. Less than a year after Andre's hanging on October 2, 1780, at Tappan, Elizabeth was found dead. A local merchant discovered her body by the river. Her throat had been slashed, her jewelry was stolen and the authorities at the time believed they were looking for a transient murderer and thief.

"Most people suspected, however, that she was killed by local toughs, executed for betraying her patriot family and friends...and the local boy who was in love with her. Andre's body wound up in Westminster Abbey. Elizabeth's is somewhere at the old Episcopal burying ground, not far from where we found Richard Highsmith and Wendy Appleby. But I haven't located any references that tell us the exact spot, whether she was buried in a family tomb or vault, or if she was just placed in the ground. The next step would be to search local records."

"Good work," he said. "We'll find her. I don't know what any of this means. But we'll find her."

She wanted to tell him she'd seen Richard High-smith. But she hadn't learned anything yet. She'd wait.

She sat in her computer chair and he bent to look at the screen. She fought the urge to touch him.

Or to reach out, drag him close and bury her face against his jacket just to breathe in his scent. She stood quickly—and managed to bump into him. "I'm so sorry! But I was thinking I should get Rollo and we should go. It's silly under the circumstances, but this is Halloween in Sleepy Hollow and I promised to help out, so I need to go be the Woman in White again." She was babbling. She wanted to touch him, but she was afraid to.

He seemed unaware and glanced at his watch. "Yes, let's get going." Rollo was already dressed in his service-dog vest. Mo attached his leash and they set out.

"I listened to the news today. They talked about J.J. and the woman who'd been arrested. Has anything else happened?"

"Anything new? Anything that's brought us closer?"

"Yes."

"It's a slow process. We do have some answers, thanks to forensics and J.J. We know that two people have to be involved. And Wendy Appleby wasn't randomly killed. She was targeted. We're questioning people, waiting for forensic reports—and we'll follow every clue until we get to the truth."

"He was a nice guy, wasn't he? Richard Highsmith?" she asked.

Aidan nodded. "He was the real deal."

"I'm sorry. And I'm sorry, too, about Wendy Appleby. She was a good mother. You could tell from the house and the way J.J. talks about her. I hope he'll be okay. At least, he seems to love Debbie, so I hope it'll work out for them."

"She's a friend of yours, right?"

"Yes. Not a really close friend, like Grace. Remember, I wasn't from here. I got to come for weekends and summer vacations. But you know Debbie. And you like her."

"She's sincere and very cooperative," he said.

"You met her at the strip club." She tried to speak casually. She and Aidan had been thrown together because of horrible events. So had Debbie Howell and Aidan. She couldn't help thinking about Debbie, her beauty and effervescent personality, her cooperativeness with the law. Mo felt an uncomfortable surge of jealousy and tried to shake it. She was creating a whole dreamworld with a man who was just a professional associate.

"Yes, I questioned her, but she didn't recognize the first image. Once Jane put some life into it, Debbie recognized her right away."

Long days, long nights, not enough sleep. Mo turned away because she was suddenly grinning.

"What?" he asked.

"Nothing," she said.

"No, really."

Her smile deepened. *What the hell.* "Sorry. I know you had to visit the strip club for work—and that made me picture you going undercover as a stripper. I bet you'd be good at it."

"Oh?" He slowly raised a brow in surprise, but she was glad to see the hint of a smile on his lips. "I'll remember that, the next time someone needs an undercover male stripper. May I return the compliment?"

"Pardon?"

"Well, if you get tired of the greeting card business, I'm sure you'd make a bundle as a stripper, too."

"Uh, thanks," she said.

And luckily, that conversation went no further. They reached the hospital, and within minutes J.J.—whose face still bore witness to hours of tears—was hugging Rollo and smiling as if the sun had managed to walk into the room.

10

Patience was everything with children. So Aidan had recently learned.

He'd also discovered that he really liked J. J. Appleby. It would still have been murder and he would've had to give it the same dedication, no matter who the victims were, but it seemed all the worse for the fact that Richard had been one of the few men to survive politics with a soul and Wendy Appleby had obviously been a kind, giving person and a wonderful mother.

And that J.J. was such a great kid and an orphan now.

Finally, however, Mo and Debbie—who had kept her word and stayed with the boy—finished talking. Rollo's giant head rested beside J.J. on the bed, and Aidan could ask the boy a few more questions.

"I know this is hard for you, J.J., but have you remembered anything else you could tell me?" J.J.'s face was strained, his forehead wrinkled in thought, but he didn't cry again. He looked at Aidan.

"Do you remember where your mom parked?"

J.J. nodded. "Kind of by the side. Mom said the easiest way out was when you parked at the side. You could get onto the highway from there."

"Thank you, J.J. Now, do you remember anything else—like a sound?" Aidan asked. "Or maybe a smell?"

J.J. thought again. "Not a sound. But I do remember a smell."

"Good smell, bad smell?" Aidan asked. "This was before the hood—or whatever it might've been—was dropped over your head, right? That was a different smell, wasn't it?"

"Yeah. That was awful—sicky sweet. This other smell, it was earlier. Maybe a couple seconds before... the other thing happened. It wasn't a *bad* smell," J.J. said. "It was like...heavy perfume."

"Would you recognize it if you smelled it again?"

J.J. nodded. "But it wasn't nice and light—like the perfume my mom wore." He paused and bit his lip. He had obviously decided he'd cried enough. "I loved the way she smelled. This was more like...I don't know. Not pretty or light."

"More like a man's cologne, maybe?" Aidan asked.

"Maybe."

"Thank you," Aidan said. "Okay, I'm just going to ask you one more question for now. Someone came up behind you. You didn't get a chance to turn or scream or fight because they put something over your head." He hadn't wanted to subject J.J. to a more intensive interrogation the day before and hoped to learn more now.

Again, J.J. gave Aidan his full attention and nodded.

"Did you get a chance to notice what it was? Like was it a rough cloth or was it smooth?"

"Really rough."

"Black, brown, green, blue?"

"No, no. It was light. Tan, maybe. But it happened so fast. I tried to scream. I wanted to scream—but then

I didn't feel anything at all. I was… I don't remember anything else. Except then the first smell was gone—and, like I said, there was that sicky sweet smell."

"You've been a tremendous help, J.J.," Aidan told him.

"Your mom would be so proud," Debbie said quietly.

J.J.'s face crumpled. But, once again, he kept from crying. As if on cue, Rollo whined and nudged J.J.'s hand.

"He's such a cool dog. I wish he could stay here," J.J. said.

Mo smiled at him. "He can visit every day."

"J.J. might be out of the hospital by tomorrow," Debbie said. "And so far…well, the social worker suggested I get a new job. I'll have to talk to a lawyer, but like I mentioned, Wendy told me she was putting me in her will as J.J.'s guardian. You know, if something happened to her… I don't want anything to go wrong, so I'll find a different line of work. I'll do *anything* to keep J.J. and me together."

"I may be able to help you," Mo told her.

"Yeah?"

"My friend Grace works for the tourist company that runs the Haunted Mausoleum. I'm sure you'd be a great tour guide. You've been here forever."

Aidan found himself watching Mo again—and liking everything he saw. "Speaking of which," she was saying, "I've got to get back home. I'm working tonight."

"Hey!" J.J. said hopefully. "Maybe Rollo could stay here while you're at work!"

Mo paused, obviously surprised.

"Um…"

"Please!" J.J. asked. "Debbie, it's okay, right?

"Honey, it's not up to me. It's up to the hospital," Debbie explained.

"He's decked out the way he's supposed to be," Aidan pointed out, waiting for Mo to make a decision.

"I...I suppose he could stay. It's a private room. I can come back and get him—if they'll let me—later, after the evening's over."

"I can run him down to you whenever you come by," Debbie said eagerly, "if you're worried about waking J.J. or the staff being disturbed because it's so late."

Mo raised her hands. "Well, I guess he can stay then." She went over to the dog and spoke to him. "Rollo, I'm going to leave you with J.J. for a bit—is that okay?"

Rollo let out a soft whine; he knew he was in a hospital.

Aidan stood. "All right, then, thank you, J.J., for all your help. And Debbie, thank *you*."

"I'm not doing anything. I wish I could do something," she said.

"Why don't you walk us down?" Aidan suggested. "J.J. has Rollo, so he'll be okay for a few minutes, and there's an officer in the hall."

"Is that's okay with you, J.J.?"

"I have Rollo," he assured them.

"Be right back," Debbie said.

As they headed down the hallway, Aidan told Debbie, "You can help by trying to remember if there's anything Wendy might have said about going to New York—and going to hear Richard Highsmith's talk."

"She was excited about their trip. She and J.J. were staying with a lovely gay couple she'd worked with once. I don't think they were all that close. They were just good people who offered her a place to stay whenever she wanted to visit."

"Do you know their names? We haven't heard from anyone in New York City."

"No, she just told me about them. She was careful with her money. And hotel rooms in New York are so expensive! She told me she and J.J. would be fine," Debbie said. "I didn't know she was stopping by the convention center. I did know that she admired Richard Highsmith."

"Did she ever mention meeting him?" Aidan asked.

"No. She just liked his politics. I'm not sure how she'd meet him."

"Well, they were both living in New York at the same time," Aidan said.

Debbie laughed. "Them—and eight to twenty million other people, depending on the time of day. If she knew him, she never mentioned it to me."

"Well, if you think of anything…"

"I'll call you."

They'd reached the ground floor. Debbie turned to Mo and hugged her. "Thank you!" she said.

"Me?" Mo asked, as if slightly embarrassed.

"Offering to help me with a new job. Always treating me like a real person."

Mo smiled. "You *are* a real person, Debbie. And a really good one. I'll see you later tonight." Aidan opened the door, and they both waved to Debbie as they walked out.

"It feels funny," Mo said.

"Leaving without Rollo?"

"Yes. But he's such an exceptional dog. He knows when people need him."

"You're pretty exceptional, too."

She looked at him, startled. "Me? Well, thanks."

"You don't think so?"

"Not particularly—but I'm mostly surprised by hearing that from you."

"Maybe I'm just jealous because you seem so comfortable with yourself and your life," he said. They were in a parking lot; he wasn't sure he wanted the conversation getting any deeper. "So, tell me, what exactly do you do at this Haunted Mausoleum?"

"I'm the Woman in White."

"Ah, yes—and no one's determined precisely who she was!" They'd reached the car. He opened the door for her and she slid in.

Aidan resumed the conversation. "There are so many tales around this place," he said.

"I imagine a lot of places have great tales. But what this area had was Washington Irving. The headless horseman was supposedly a Hessian soldier who'd fought for the British—and had his head blown off in the fighting. Irving turned it into a charming and scary tale that gained a loyal following from the time it first appeared. Since then it's been made into movies and even a TV series. There's so much history here, from the Native Americans on, but I still think there might not have been an actual Sleepy Hollow if it hadn't been for Washington Irving."

Aidan laughed. "And it's doubtful there would've been a town called Irving, either." His mood became grim as he drove. "I do believe, though, that regardless of the legends, there would've been a murder. The headless horseman simply provided the killer with a ghoulish way of displaying his victims." He glanced over at her. "You're with people all the time you're at that Haunted Mausoleum, right?"

"Oh, we're in excellent company, don't worry. I'm a family tomb away from Grace. It's a good crowd to work with. Our biggest fear is that one of us will get too close to someone we're spooking out and wind up socked in the jaw or something."

They'd arrived at her house. He hesitated because she wasn't with Rollo, but reminded himself that there was no reason to worry. Still, he'd been taught all his life that you walked your date to the door and made sure she was safely inside before you left.

He wasn't on a date. But he was beginning to feel... responsible.

Responsible wasn't really the word for what he was feeling.

"Mo, I'll see you in. And don't forget, if anything— or anyone—bothers you, call me right away."

"Of course."

As she spoke, another car came into her drive.

"Grace is here. We're back in the nick of time," she said.

"Do you have to go in and get anything?" he asked.

"No. That's the great thing about being a character at a haunted attraction—you get your clothing and makeup there. No prep work."

"Don't forget to pick up your dog on the way home," he said, then felt a little stupid.

She didn't have to reply, since Grace stepped up to the car just then. "Hello, Agent Mahoney, Mo. Is everything all right? Did you need Mo again, Agent? Where's

Rollo? I saw the news—and I'm so grateful you found that boy. I'm babbling. Sorry. Mo, can you still come with me tonight? Are you needed somewhere else?"

Getting out of Aidan's car, Mo laughed softly. "Grace, I don't even know where to begin. But I'm fine, and I guess we should go," she said.

"You're doing okay with the investigation?" she asked Aidan.

"It's moving along, Grace. And today, yes, we're just happy to have the boy back alive," Aidan said.

Grace seemed to want to linger by his window. Mo took her by the arm. "We're leaving *now,* Grace. Aidan, thank you for the ride."

As they walked away, Aidan could hear Grace whispering to Mo. He could guess what she was saying. He smiled. He wasn't sure what Mo wanted, but he *was* pretty sure he knew what Grace was after. She wanted Mo to get involved—with him.

It was a sweet moment.

He called the hotel and spoke with Logan. Van Camp and Voorhaven were already there, marveling at Will's multi-camera angles and the screens that showed them everything they needed to see to keep tabs on their suspects.

As soon as he returned to the hotel, they'd all meet up and, using everything they'd learned, try to recreate what had happened the night Richard Highsmith and Wendy Appleby had been kidnapped—and subsequently killed.

There was no way to avoid the fact that Mo was going to have to give a few explanations when she went in for costume and makeup.

She'd been with Ron and Phil and others when Aidan had come to the café looking for her. She played it down as best she could, telling them that, yes, Rollo had been helpful, and yes, she was thrilled and relieved that they'd found J. J. Appleby alive.

Then she had to deal with Grace's teasing. "What's the matter with you? I'd be jumping his bones."

"You don't jump an FBI agent's bones," Mo said primly.

"What? You think the man doesn't have sex? Just because *you* don't have sex—"

"I have plenty of sex."

Grace protested in the most embarrassing way possible. She laughed.

"I just think it should mean something," Mo said irritably.

"Sometimes it just means you have an opportunity— an intelligent, great-looking guy who happens to be available—and you take it!" Grace told her.

Mo didn't want to argue with Grace—or try to explain that she didn't want a man like Aidan just for a night. She wanted something more, something richer.

"People tend to think I'm…different. I've dated some guys who want to know all the gory details of personal cases that turned out to be homicides in New York City, and it scares the hell out of me that this is the kind of thing that turns them on. Other guys act like they're afraid of me because I work with Rollo on missing persons cases that become homicides. And don't laugh at me about sex, Grace. I have had it, know what it is and prefer that there be a relationship. That's my personal choice."

"I'm not suggesting you sleep with half of Manhattan or anything. But, Mo, that guy likes you."

"I think Rollo's the one he likes."

"At least Rollo's smart enough to like him back!"

She and Grace had that conversation in the makeup room. Before Mo had been completely transformed into the Woman in White for the evening, both Ron and Phil were agreeing that she should at least indulge in *something* with Agent Mahoney.

"Honey, trust me," Ron told her. "If he was gay, I'd be on him like white on rice!"

Finally, she was finished, and the crew of monsters and villains was ready. Mo hung back, hugging the wall of her mausoleum.

That was when she saw him again. The ghost of Major Andre.

He wasn't perched on a stone that night; he was standing, a handsome man in Revolutionary-era clothing, watching her pointedly.

She looked carefully around. The other characters were in their places waiting, most of them texting or playing games on their phones before the call came to turn off their devices.

Mo hurried out to the path between the mausoleums and the tombs and stones.

"Major Andre," she said softly.

He came toward her, real and yet not real in the moonlight. "You see me, yet you are living," he said. "You see me clearly, do you not? Do you hear me, too?"

She nodded. "You were watching me the other night."

"You reminded me of someone."

"Was her name Elizabeth Hampton?" Mo asked.

He bent his head to one side in surprise. "You know her?"

"No, but I've read about her."

He smiled poignantly. "She's not here," he said. "I look for her... But I in all my searching, all my watching, I have not found her. My dearest love..."

"I don't know her, but I've heard the legend of the Woman in White since I was a child. Elizabeth may be the Woman in White—and if she is, she's somewhere in the area," Mo said. "Do you know where Elizabeth Hampton's buried?" Mo asked.

He stiffened and seemed to be in pain. Not angry with her, just in pain.

"I know I am buried in Westminster Abbey, far from here. In the country to which I gave my loyalty and my all. It astonishes me to see that the country I fought and died for and this new nation are now the best of friends and allies. Of course, it has been..." He shook his head. "One does lose track of time." He stopped speaking to give her a slow smile. "I've seen many people look twice or shiver when I am near. But it's been a long, long time since I've spoken with the living."

She smiled back. "And I've heard about your being here, in spirit, all my life. I'm pleased to finally meet you. And I desperately need your help. People have been killed, cruelly killed. And the one man who died left a message that said *Lizzie grave*. Do you know what that could mean? Do you think it could refer to your Lizzie?"

"Perhaps it does. Although I cannot explain why. I need your help, too," he added. "If you can see the dead, will you look for my Lizzie...out there, somewhere?"

"I will. Can you tell me where to start?"

"Tappan," he said.

"Pardon?"

"Tappan, in this place, now the state of New York. It was where I was hanged. Perhaps she lingers there."

Mo nodded.

"And perhaps it is not my Lizzie's grave that your friend was seeking. Perhaps it was my daughter's."

"*What?* Major Andre—"

"My name is John, my dear. And among friends, that is how I am known. Neither patriot nor redcoat. Just John."

"According to the historical record, sir, you left neither children nor a wife."

"She was with child," he said. "I saw this, although she did not see me. I did not see her murder. I learned of her death. I watched our daughter grow in the home of gentle people who loved a child and saw her not as a rebel or a traitor, but as a child. When my Lizzie was killed and betrayed by those who should have loved her, my daughter was raised in gentle company."

"And she died here?" Mo asked.

He didn't answer her. There was a sudden commotion—the first group of visitors for the night was coming through.

"Wow! She's good!" A female voice whispered with fear and awe. "You'd swear that Woman in White was talking to another ghost!"

"It's okay," a masculine voice returned. "Just a special effect!"

Major John Andre faded. Mo put on her deadpan expression and made her first circle around "her" mausoleum.

It was a long night. She kept an eye out for Major Andre as it went on.

He did not reappear.

With Van Camp and Voorhaven at the hotel watching the cameras, Aidan felt free to make use of his entire Krewe. They drove out to the convention center.

Aidan walked them through what he knew of the events of the day, showing Will, Logan, Jane and Sloan where each person had claimed to be when Richard was last seen.

"Was Bari Macaby certain she heard someone answer her from the restroom?" Logan asked.

"She's convinced she heard someone, yes," Aidan said. "And assumed it was Richard."

"Let's play it out. I'll be Jillian. I was supposedly here—and then onstage with the sound people," Jane said.

"I'll take Taylor Branch," Sloan offered. "And, Aidan, you should be Richard Highsmith. You knew him. You can never tell when something you know about a person might kick in," Logan said.

"That means Will or Logan gets to be Bari Macaby," Jane told him, grinning.

"I'll be Bari," Logan said. "Will can supervise and make sure we'll all where we—or rather, they—claimed to be."

"We'll go through it once with the assumption that Jillian was involved, and once assuming it was Taylor Branch. We'll even do a version figuring that Bari Macaby might have been the one," Aidan said.

As planned, they began going through the scenario three times.

"All right," Aidan eventually said. "Let's see if this works. Richard, Taylor and Jillian are all in the green-room. Bari stops by to see what Richard would like to eat. As soon as she's gone, either Taylor or Jillian leaves the room. He's left with just one of them. Say the accomplice arrived by a delivery truck. Bari would be in the kitchen then, arranging for the snack Richard requested. That would leave one of them several minutes with Richard—either to knock him out and carry him, or trick him into accompanying him or her."

"Via Bari's emergency exit to her secret smoking nook," Jane said.

"I think he was tricked into going out with whomever," Aidan said thoughtfully. "It would be easier to get him out if he was moving under his own steam, voluntarily. He wasn't a small man. He was fit and well-muscled. So let's go with the scenario that he was tricked. But if the person in question knew everyone else's timing, he could conceivably knock him out, throw him over a shoulder and carry him out." He paused. "That does suggest a man rather than a woman."

"But there's an alarm on the door," Sloan pointed out.

"And the code number to bypass the alarm is 5421," Aidan said dryly. "Anyone could have gotten that code. I was with Bari Macaby when she used it. Not hard to watch someone and memorize a four-digit code."

"Maybe Richard was tricked into going outside. What would've made him do that?" Jane asked.

"The belief that he was needed," Aidan said decisively.

"Let's keep walking through this," Logan suggested.

"Okay. Will, watch everyone. We'll begin with the three of us in the greenroom," Aidan said.

"So here we are, the three of us. And I'm Bari," Logan murmured. "Mr. Highsmith, what would you like? Ah, yes, tea and some cheese and crackers. Okay, I'll be in the kitchen." They went through the motions twice. Both times it took Logan thirteen minutes to walk out of the room, make his way to the kitchen, wait three minutes for a tray to be set up, and return. In each simulation one or the other—Taylor or Jillian—had time to leave while the other urged 'Richard' out of the greenroom and down the hall to the emergency exit.

"Four minutes before Jillian had to be back in the stage area so she could be seen by everyone," Jane noted.

"So, the moment Richard is outside, a vehicle's ready to take him," Jane mused. "Probably some kind of delivery truck. Someone, an accomplice, is there and either knocks him out and whisks him away or grabs his unconscious body and whisks that away."

"And, of course," Aidan said, "the way we've figured it…there are a few minutes in there where *anyone* might've gotten into the greenroom. If, that is, Taylor Branch and Jillian Durfey both prove to be innocent."

"We'll look into the security men and the sound-system people, and check out records related to every name that was collected when Highsmith disappeared," Logan added.

Aidan nodded. "And we'll need to find out who delivered what on the day of the murders."

"I'll get on that research immediately," Jane said. "We'll send the info to the home office on everyone questioned when Richard first disappeared."

"We need more on Wendy Appleby, too. What was her real connection to Richard?" Aidan asked.

"That could be the key," Logan agreed.

"I'll trace her history. And as for other possible candidates who were in this building, I can cross-reference names with any possible political tie-ins," Will said.

"Concentrate on what you can learn about Bari Macaby," Logan told him. "Make sure she's exactly who she says she is." He turned to Aidan. "It would help, of course, if we had some contact with one of the deceased."

Aidan took a deep breath, trying not to feel the usual knot in his stomach that came up whenever the situation—or their discussion—had to do with the living seeing the dead.

"Okay," he began. "You're all part of this experienced special unit. And I'm not completely sure why I was called in. Apparently you all have what it takes to be Krewe, and I'm not convinced that I do. Not anymore. If I ever did."

Logan studied him. "You've got something. Jackson Crow wouldn't have asked you to join the New York office if he hadn't seen that skill in you. We'll do our best, but you knew Highsmith, and that makes a difference."

Aidan couldn't remember if he'd ever mentioned to any of the Krewe that he'd known Richard.

But they had so much reference material available to them…

Of course they knew. They knew everything about him. Maybe even the kind of shirts he bought or his favorite brand of toothpaste.

And hadn't he been asking Mo Deauville to do what *he knew* could be done?

"I haven't made contact with Richard in any way," he said quietly.

"Maybe, you will soon," Logan said, just as quietly.

Mo was surprised to find Aidan Mahoney outside the emergency room entrance when she and Grace arrived to pick up Rollo once they'd had finished for the night.

"He's here!" Grace said in a loud whisper. She looked at Mo. "He's here—for you. He's got the dog."

"No, he's not here for me. He's here because he checked on J.J. after doing…whatever he did tonight. And he was nice enough to bring Rollo down for us."

"You're pathetic," Grace muttered.

Maybe he did have an interest in her. He was ever hopeful that she'd contact Richard.

She *had* contacted him.

She was happy to oblige in any way she could; she'd do anything to help.

She and Grace got out of the car and walked over to the hospital. Grace was obviously amused, certain that someone was about to get lucky.

"Good evening, ladies," Aidan said. Rollo wagged his tail ecstatically.

"Good evening, Agent Mahoney!" Grace returned. "Nice to see you again."

"I wanted to check on things," Aidan said. "And… well, I figured it was so late, I'd bring Rollo down for a bathroom break and have him out here when you came by."

Rollo barked, apparently agreeing with that explanation.

"Thanks," Grace said. "And since you're here…" She

paused and smiled like some kind of matchmaker. "You can drop Rollo and Mo off. I'm much closer to the hospital and that way I won't have to double back. And you two can talk about…finding people and stuff like that."

Mo didn't protest, although she was horrified by Grace's broad grin and her unmistakable attempt to throw the two of them together. But Mo knew that if she said anything, she'd look like an idiot who didn't care about making her friend drive around all night.

"That's not a problem," Aidan said. "I can easily drive them home."

"Well, then, you two can see me safely to my car." She turned toward the parking lot. "Agent Mahoney, have you taken part in any of our haunted happenings yet? You should come through the Haunted Mausoleum sometime. We've gotten rid of our headless horseman for the season," she added somberly.

"Perhaps I will," Aidan said.

Grace got into her car, revved the engine and bade them both good-night, still smiling secretively.

Aidan and Mo were left there to stare at each other.

"How was J.J.?" Mo asked.

"Fine. Or as fine as possible under the circumstances. They were going to release him tomorrow, but I've asked that he be kept another day."

"Oh?"

"He's safe at the hospital. Once he and Debbie are out of there…he'll need round-the-clock protection."

"But the killer had his chance to kill J.J. He didn't."

"He chose not to strangle and behead a young boy," Aidan said. "He left him in a vault deep in the earth. If J.J. had been there much longer, he would've died."

"You think you can catch the killer overnight?"

"I wish. Well, let me drive you and Rollo home," he said.

They walked to his car and Aidan opened the door for Rollo, then for her. When they'd driven for a few minutes, she felt the silence between them had grown uncomfortable. Awkward. "Is the investigation getting anywhere?" she asked him.

"We're somewhere," he told her. "I still believe someone in Richard's retinue was involved, but it's possible—though not plausible—that it was someone else, someone at the convention center. We know there had to be a connection between Richard and Wendy, although we haven't established what it was. We strongly feel we're looking for two people." He glanced over at her as he drove. "And I still believe that *Lizzie grave* meant something, that it's important to the case."

Mo hesitated. "I think I may know a little more about that."

"Oh?" He glanced her way again.

She stared straight ahead, realizing that her words might sound ridiculous. "I saw Major Andre tonight."

"Major Andre?" he repeated. "You don't mean as one of your characters at the Haunted Mausoleum, right?"

"No. I play the Woman in White. I thought I saw him the night before. But tonight, I…spoke with him."

She waited for him to deny that was even possible. His wanting her to speak with Richard's ghost was one thing. Her speaking with a Revolutionary spy might be quite another.

"What did he say? How could he help?" he asked.

"From the way he looked at me, I could tell that he thought he was seeing another ghost. Dressed up, I must have resembled his Lizzie—or Elizabeth Hampton. He's been searching for her all these years. But, here's something I hadn't known. He told me Lizzie had a child—named Lizzie, or Elizabeth, too. He believes the words might refer to *her* grave."

"And did he know where it was?"

"No, but he wanted me to find his Lizzie, Elizabeth Hampton, for him."

Aidan didn't respond. He seemed disappointed. "I'm not sure how that'll get us closer to the truth," he finally said.

"I don't, either, but you're the one who was interested in Lizzie's grave. Maybe if we find the Woman in White, she could tell us more about it. And if we do find Lizzie's grave, the daughter's grave, I mean, that'll help."

"Did he give you any idea where to start?"

"Tappan, New York. It's not far from here."

"I know."

"It's where Andre was hanged."

He smiled. "I know," he said again.

They'd reached her house. He exited the car just as she did. When Rollo had bounded out, Aidan came around to walk her to her door.

"All right," he said. "I'll pick you up in the morning—a few hours from now—and we'll go to Tappan. You're willing to go?"

"Of course."

They were at her door by then. She opened it, her mind racing. She could've told him that she'd also seen Richard Highsmith. But Richard hadn't given her anything useful, not yet; she should wait. Wait until she did have something to say.

They stood at her door. She was shocked when he

touched her chin, raising it gently, his actions curious and almost tender, puzzlement in his eyes.

"What is it?" he asked her.

"Nothing," she murmured. "I, uh, just have to find my keys."

She fumbled in her purse, her eyes still on his.

She could imagine what Grace would be saying if she was there. Grace would be pushing her, prodding her. Grace would whisper, *Hey, go on in. Release a little tension. Come on, guys, get it on!*

"I saw Richard Highsmith," she said in a rush.

His hand seemed to freeze.

"You saw him? You didn't tell me?"

"Because he was gone before he could say anything. He's...he's new. To being a ghost. Sometimes the dead have a hard time retaining...form, I guess. But he knows he can come to me now. I'm hoping..."

She thought Aidan would pull away in frustration. Or anger.

But he didn't.

"You do have something really wonderful, you know?" he said softly.

Then his head lowered and his mouth touched hers. It was a slow kiss, as if his fascination with her had inevitably drawn him close.

His mouth lingered, but he finally lifted his head. "Sorry," he murmured, stepping away. He smiled ruefully. "I'll be back in a few hours. I can see you're all right here, or Rollo would be barking like Armageddon was upon us. Go on in. I'll see you in the morning."

She stood, frozen.

"Mo, go in. And don't wander out at night—even for Richard."

She managed to retrieve her keys and open the door. She stepped inside, locking it, and then, through the little window, saw him walk away.

Mo leaned against the door, feeling as if her knees had turned to rubber.

He'd kissed her. Better than crazy, wild sex.

No, crazy, wild sex would've been great, too.

Rollo barked; she snapped to her senses.

It was really late, and Aidan was coming back for her in just a few hours.

She went to bed, but couldn't sleep. In the dim light cast by the hall lamp, she stared at the bookshelves by her dresser.

Washington Irving's series on George Washington was on one row; his other works, including "The Legend of Sleepy Hollow," were on another.

She closed her eyes and tried once again to sleep. She wasn't sure if she did or not. In her mind's eye, she saw the forests of Tarrytown as Washington Irving had seen them in his day.

She saw the bridge that Ichabod Crane had needed to reach to escape the horseman.

A slow mist rose from the ground and swept around graves and she was running through it.

She had to get to the bridge, race over it....

There was someone ahead of her in the mist. She saw that it was Aidan. His arms were outstretched and he was waiting for her.

Then she heard the sound of hoof beats and the whinny of a horse—and some kind of thunder that made the earth tremble.

She turned back. There was a horseman. The Headless Horseman of Sleepy Hollow.

The horse reared in the passion of the hunt.

The headless horseman was hunting *her.*

She started to run, just as Ichabod Crane had run on his worn-out nag. The night seemed alive with the bright eyes of nocturnal creatures.

Owls hooted. The moon came out and hid again behind the clouds, and she realized the thunder she heard was her own heart.

Aidan was waiting....

She could see him just across the bridge, his arms outstretched.

But she could feel hot, fetid breath on the nape of her neck. The horseman was almost upon her.

She heard Aidan then, shouting to her, calling her name.

"Aidan!" She breathed in a desperate plea.

But the horseman was practically on top of her. She turned to scream but she couldn't face him. It would be too horrible. Because she was terrified that she would see her own head on his shoulders.

She began to hear Rollo as if in a fog, barking wildly.

And then she woke up abruptly; someone *was* calling her name.

Aidan.

It was morning—and he had come for her.

11

Mo sprang out of bed and went racing down the stairs. Rollo was already at the door, wagging his tail madly. Mo threw open the door and called Aidan's name. The sun was up, bright and high. She had evidently slept and slept deeply—and for several hours.

"Aidan!"

A moment later, he appeared from around the side of her cottage, relief clearly written on his face.

"I was about to break down the door," he told her.

"I'm sorry. I was sleeping so soundly." She supposed that was true enough; she didn't mention the half sleeping, half waking dream she'd had. She suddenly noticed that he was dressed in jeans and a warm sweater and she was…

Standing on bare feet with her hair tousled and wearing a T-shirt emblazoned with a children's cartoon character in a sleeping cap.

"You need to keep your phone with you. I was getting worried," he said.

"What time is it?" she asked.

"About ten-thirty," he told her.

"Wow! I slept longer than I realized. Come in. I can be ready in five minutes. I'm sorry."

"You don't have to be sorry. I'm just relieved you're all right. I'll make some coffee while you get ready."

Mo was upstairs, in the shower, dressed and back downstairs in the five minutes she'd promised. Aidan was in the kitchen, holding a cup of coffee. Judging by his expression, he was trying to work out some deep puzzle.

She headed to the coffeepot. "At least it's only about a twenty-minute drive from here." He nodded absently.

"What is it?" she asked.

"There's just something about this house," he said.

"What do you mean?"

"I felt like I was being watched. And when I turned to look down the hallway, I thought I saw a shadow. But I guess it's nothing. Rollo's been just fine."

Mo looked down the hallway herself. She saw a sweep of skirts and smiled. "Candy," she said.

"Candy?"

"She lives here. Exists here, I mean. She was a slave. This house wound up being used as a hospital during the Civil War, and they even cared for some Confederate prisoners. Candy was escaping the South and helping in the hospital. She fell in love with one of the Confederate officers who'd had been brought here— Colonel Daniel Parker. Daniel is around, too, but Candy is more curious."

He was staring at her again, just staring at her.

He'd *asked* her to try to speak with a dead man. And now they were about to go and look for a ghost—at his request. He *couldn't* think she was...

Weird. Different. Cursed. To be avoided.

"Oh," he said simply. "Should we go?"

"Rollo, come on," she called, finishing her coffee and collecting the dog's leash and service vest. "We're going on an outing."

Rollo bounded over to her. They were quickly on the road, and for a while, they drove in silence—but this time their silence wasn't awkward.

Mo gazed out as they crossed the Hudson over the Tappan Zee Bridge, which extended across one of the widest parts of the river. She'd always loved the view from the bridge. She saw the sign that told her it was officially the Governor Malcolm Wilson Tappan Zee Bridge. Tappan was the name of a Native American tribe. *Zee* was the Dutch word for *sea*.

"It's beautiful," Aidan said, smiling. "As often as I've come over this bridge, I still love the drive."

Was it just her? Or did the memory of his kiss seem to linger on the air, just as it lingered on her lips?

It had just been a kiss. Offered in gratitude—nothing more.

"Yeah, Tappan really is beautiful," Mo murmured. "There's such interesting history there, too. The first Orange County courthouse was built here in 1691. And Major Andre was held at Yoast Mabie's house—now a restaurant. Not only that, Washington had his headquarters here *four* times during the war," she said enthusiastically. She glanced at Aidan, who looked back at her with a wry grin.

He knew all that, of course. He was from the area.

"Yup. And I know exactly where the Andre memorial is. Are we going there?" he asked.

"Yes, let's do that."

They drove over to where the memorial to Major

John Andre had been erected—a stone that briefly described his deeds, his part in persuading Benedict Arnold to become a traitor to the American cause—and the plan to turn West Point over to the British.

The memorial, surrounded by a fence, was on a roundabout in a suburban area. Aidan pulled off the road to reach it. "I think the first time someone tried to create this memorial, there was an outcry over commemorating a British spy. Some people tried to destroy the first memorial to him. As I recall, there used to be a pedestal, but it was blown up one too many times. Now I suppose we remember him mainly for dying young," Aidan said as they stood in front of the memorial.

Mo read the inscription aloud. "'His death, though according to the stern rule of war, moved even his enemies to pity, and both armies mourned the fate of one so young and brave.'"

Aidan nodded.

"A lot of people desperately wanted to save him," Mo went on. "They wanted to have a prisoner exchange—but he'd been a prisoner and part of an exchange once before. And as much as Washington admired him, he decided he had to abide by the rules of war, just like it says here. Yet his death pleased no one."

"'He was more unfortunate than criminal. He was an accomplished man and gallant officer.' That's a quote from George Washington," Aidan said. "You're right, his death pleased no one. But the British hanged Nathan Hale. It was war. Still, a sad note in history."

Mo nodded, then looked around. It was another beautiful fall day, with the sun high overhead and a few white clouds coasting across a brilliant blue sky.

Cars drove around the monument.

"Do you…see anything?" Aidan asked Mo.

"No," she replied.

"This is about ten miles from the Sleepy Hollow–Tarrytown area," Aidan said. "It isn't much of a distance now, but it was quite a ride back in the seventeen hundreds. We believe that Lizzie, our Woman in White, lived on the other side of the bridge, yet she must've come here to see Andre. Maybe she had friends on this side. Maybe she was buried here."

"Ghosts seldom hang around their own graves. Who wants to think about their bodies rotting?"

"You have another idea?"

"What about where the Old Dutch Church is in Sleepy Hollow? Or the place that used to be the Mabie house, since that's where Andre was held," Mo said.

"I'm ready for some lunch, anyway," Aidan told her.

They went back to the car, Rollo trotting happily beside them.

Like a kid out with Mom and Dad for the day! Mo thought.

Since Rollo was wearing an official service-dog vest, they had no problem taking him into the old Mabie house, now the 76 Restaurant.

Mo had been there before, and she loved it. It was old and heavily timbered, and the decor had been influenced by history. Andre and Benedict Arnold were represented in likenesses on the wall, with the portrait of Benedict Arnold upside down.

A friendly hostess seated them. But as soon as she'd ordered, Mo got up and went to what was now a banquet hall. It was where Andre had been held.

She tried to feel the history here.

But she knew that Andre was back at Sleepy Hollow where he'd been seen through the centuries on dark and misty nights.

He was fond of the area, perhaps drawn there by the time when his life had been an adventure and he'd been on a quest—and in love.

And what about the Woman in White?

Did she mourn here, where her lover had died, for all eternity?

"Anything?" Aidan asked when she returned to the table.

She shook her head. "I'm sorry. I might have wasted your time today."

"Well, we have to eat. And the local police and the rest of my Krewe are working all the angles that have to do with the various leads we have."

"Did they get anything out of the vault?"

"They're still testing trace evidence, but of course, the killer wore gloves. He left his beheading tools in plain sight, but he wore gloves the entire time. They haven't got a decent fingerprint. All they found were prints that matched J.J.'s."

"How do you know you'll ever catch him?" Mo asked.

"Because I won't stop until I do," he answered. "And one of the killers will have made a mistake somewhere. Two people are involved, we're sure of that. And when two people are involved, it's actually easier for us. One of them is going to slip up. Or there'll be a falling-out."

"I do wonder, though, if there's really a connection between our Lizzie and this crime. Did you ask if there was a stripper named Lizzie Grave?"

"There's not."

Their waitress arrived with their food, and they enjoyed their meal then left, with Aidan asking her again, "Anything?"

"We can try the area where she was killed—the Old Dutch Church isn't there anymore but there's a new building. Well, middle-of-the-1800s new. Maybe..."

"We've come this far," he said. "We might as well."

As they drove, Mo was intensely aware of everything about him. The way his hands held the wheel. The texture of his sweater. The scent of his soap or aftershave. His snug jeans...

She looked out the window.

When they reached the Old Dutch Church and the relatively new church and its grounds, they took a leisurely walk with Rollo.

"Quite different from Manhattan," Aidan commented. "Although it's equally historic."

She nodded. "I love New York City, too. Wall Street, the churches, figuring out exactly where the old drained pond and the Five Points were..."

She let her voice trail off.

"You worked with the police there," he said. "Searching for missing people. You found a lot of them. Dead."

She drew in a breath. "Yes. I wish I could explain it to you. I can...hear the dead. Obviously not all the time. And I can hear—or figure out, using logic, which is half of it!—where the missing might be. It started when I was young. I had Rollo's mom then. She was a beautiful female wolfhound named Heidi. I heard a lost child crying one day—that was in Sleepy Hollow—and I told my mom what I heard. She thought she was humoring me. We found a little boy lost in the woods. I told the truth, I said it was Heidi who'd led me to the child. Anyway, it happened again. And that time the police came to me, and we found the girl who'd gone missing. A few years later, I offered my services and Heidi's when a woman disappeared in the city."

"And?" he asked when she didn't immediately continue. "You found her?"

She nodded. "Only we didn't find her alive. She'd been killed in the park. But after that...I was called fairly frequently. And, most of the time, I was finding the dead. But what I really wanted to do was help the living. There are so many wooded places that get so dark around here, and people, especially visitors, easily become lost. That made more sense to me. I decided to live in Tarrytown. Of course, it made a difference that I already loved the area. I got to know Purbeck when I was a kid, and now, if someone goes missing anywhere around here, he calls on me."

"You're very special," he said.

She flushed and turned away. "I just have...voices, I guess. And, yes, I see the dead. Sometimes. And talk to them. When they're willing to talk to me. When they *can* talk to me."

He didn't express his feelings on her ability. He asked, "Anything here?"

She shook her head. "One last try?" he suggested.

"Where?"

"The graveyard. I can't think of anything else."

Rollo barked, as if agreeing it was the right thing to do.

The Tappan cemetery was established in 1694, according to the inscription at the gates, and still accepting burials. The place offered a veritable time-traveler's tour of burial sites, with stones dating back to the founding of the area, markers from the Revolution, and soldiers' monuments from every war in U.S. history. The Victorian era had brought in the grandiose, and during the Great Depression, many had been buried with no markers at all; only the master plan stated where their remains could be found. Aidan wandered off to look at a historic stone that had been re-etched.

"'Sleep my child, rest in love's embrace; And know that I will join thee soon. In sweet earth together then, 'til judgment come with our Sweet Lord's grace,'" he read out loud.

Listening to him, Mo stopped abruptly.

She could see a woman. At times, especially Halloween, there were costumed interpreters at historic sites. But she knew she wasn't seeing the living.

The woman peered at Mo from around a tomb— much as Mo did to frighten visitors at the Haunted Mausoleum.

But this woman wasn't seeking to frighten anyone. She saw Mo looking at her and seemed surprised. She stood very still for a minute, then turned, as though she intended to hurry away.

Rollo made a whining sound and came to stand by Mo; she knew the dog saw the apparition just as clearly as she did.

"Please!" Mo whispered.

Aidan was busy reading another tomb. "'Death's hold shall not my spirit still, For I shall rise as is His will, I rest not here, nor should ye weep, For I live now in my Lord's gentle Keep.'"

Mo ignored him and moved quickly toward the woman. "Lizzie?" she said softly.

The woman paused. She had beautiful features and

a gentle smile and she was young—or had been young when she died.

"Lizzie?" Mo repeated.

"I am Lizzie, yes. I am Lizzie," the young woman said.

At first glance, Mo appeared to be talking to herself. The dog lay attentively beside her.

Aidan stood completely still, just watching her. But, as he did, he began to see something. A faint outline in the air, white and misty. He blinked, but the image remained.

He found himself looking around the cemetery.

Yes, that's right. He was looking around, he admitted to himself, to see if anyone else was watching. To see if he needed to be embarrassed because he and Mo probably looked as if they'd lost their minds. Talking to imaginary friends from childhood, perhaps.

He closed his eyes, fighting something inside him. Was that it? Had that been the problem his whole life? He'd been embarrassed? He'd become an agent because he believed in the law, in his country—and in helping victims. But he'd thrown away what might have been his biggest asset because, at heart, he'd been a coward. Afraid of what others would think. Afraid that he couldn't shrug it off and just go his own way. Still, as Logan had made clear, the Krewe had recognized in him what he hadn't wanted to recognize himself.

He focused on the wispy form and on Mo. He decided not to move forward; he was going to let her discover what she could. His stumbling half sight might ruin everything.

Mo spoke softly now and then. He wasn't sure what

she was saying. He noted, though, that when she wasn't speaking, she was listening. *Really* listening, as few people did anymore.

She turned suddenly, beckoning to him. He walked toward her, thinking that the cloudlike image would vanish completely when he came too close.

But it was still there.

"This is Lizzie—Elizabeth Hampton," Mo said.

Even though he felt a little stupid, he didn't allow himself to look around. Not this time.

He nodded politely. "How do you do?"

Mo, he realized, knew that he wasn't seeing the woman as distinctly as she did.

"She's going to ride back with us. I've told her where I've seen John Andre and that John has been searching for her. She's desperate to see him. And I saw him at the Haunted Mausoleum, so if you don't mind, we'll take her there."

A hitchhiking ghost! Aidan thought.

"We'll leave right away," he said aloud.

"She confirmed that she had a daughter, also named Elizabeth. Elizabeth—this Elizabeth, Lizzie—kept out of sight—stayed in, and no one ever knew she had a child. A second cousin, Lizzie's best friend, helped her, then took the child and raised her. Lizzie never let on that she'd had the baby. She was too afraid someone might figure out that her child had been John Andre's. Back then, she didn't dare admit the association."

"I understand," he said.

"Lizzie was killed by Ashley Gunter, her onetime suitor, and two of his *friends*. They claimed they executed her for being a traitor. Lizzie tells me they were cowards who weren't with an army themselves—either army—and she knows she was killed because Gunter was bitter that she'd rejected him. And," she added, "Lizzie says that the brief time she shared with Andre was sweeter than a lifetime with any other man. But if we could connect the two of them now...well, that would be wonderful."

"Of course," he agreed. "Shall we go, then?"

They walked to the car. He wondered if he should be opening the door for the ghost, but it wasn't really much of a question. He had to open the door for Rollo, anyway. The indistinct white shape seemed to move past him; he felt as though a hand rested on his for a brief moment. Mo was watching him and she smiled.

"That was a thank-you," she told him.

He nodded, let Mo in and got into the driver's seat.

"Tell her I'm sorry," he said. "I'm so sorry about what was done to her. I hope her killers were caught and punished."

He glanced in the rearview mirror. Lizzie was there, a gentle, wafting shape lingering beside Rollo.

"Lizzie said they weren't caught. Too many people still felt so bitter about the British army at the time. If they knew—or suspected—they didn't speak up. But Gunter didn't last long. He was killed in an accident with a wheat-grinding stone. Crushed to death. And his two accomplices drowned in the Hudson River. So perhaps they *were* judged. And punished. All Lizzie really cared about was her daughter—and the child was loved by her cousin and well raised."

"And she spent her days here? Happily?" Aidan asked.

"She did, and so did her children. And her children's children. But after that, they moved away. Our Lizzie had at least twenty great-grandchildren that she knew about. Then, around the time of the Civil War, they all scattered to various cities."

"I'm glad she got to see her family grow," Aidan said.

"That's always both good and bad," Mo said after a moment. "You see the triumphs, and you see the sadness. Children dying young of disease. Accidents striking down others. The pain of unrequited love. Just as you see the joy at the birth of a child or at a wedding."

Aidan excused himself to call Logan Raintree on his hands-free phone. "Anything on that end?" he asked.

"Jillian and Taylor Branch left the hotel to go to a movie and have dinner. She was wearing a wig. I suppose she doesn't want to be recognized in the area. The security guys went to a sports bar for lunch and to a gym. They're back now," Logan told him. "We've been pulling records on everyone. Haven't found anything yet. Will re-interviewed the men who were working with the sound system. Jane interviewed the receiving clerk and is doing thorough investigations on each of the food and delivery companies as we speak. Van Camp and Voorhaven have been out at Tommy Jensen's place, hoping they'll catch a customer or passerby who might've seen something. Moving along—but so far, getting nowhere. You?"

"I'm not sure yet," Aidan said. "We're heading back in. I'll let you know as soon as we have anything solid."

He ended the call and turned to Mo. "We're going to the Haunted Mausoleum, then?" he asked.

"Yes," she replied. They parked on the street. It was still early, so it was easy to do. During the major visitor season—this time of year—the mortuary didn't open for tours. It only opened at night for the "haunted" experience.

"We just walk in?"

"No, there are gates. I'll have to ask one of the bosses to let us in."

He followed Mo, Rollo and the wisp that was the ghost of Elizabeth Hampton to the mortuary door. It was opened by a pleasant older woman in a sweater and slacks who was happy to greet Mo and Rollo—and to meet *him*. She was Sondra Burke, vice president of the historic tour company that owned and operated many of the historic buildings and tours, including the Haunted Mausoleum.

"Terrible things have been happening, Agent Mahoney," she said, shaking his hand and patting Rollo. She was oblivious to the aura that followed them in. "It's good that everyone out there is trying to decipher the truth. How ghastly—and how well planned, or so it seems. But I imagine Mo has you here for a bit of a breather and a few minutes of fun."

"Aidan is an aficionado of old churchyards and cemeteries," Mo told her. "I thought I'd take him through the house and for a walk out back."

"Of course," Sondra said. Her eyes twinkled. "But don't be too late, if you don't mind, Mo. We'll need you back here fairly soon. You've become a real hit with our visitors."

"Sure," Mo promised.

She led the way through the mortuary with its now web-covered chandeliers and decorated hallways. The old viewing rooms had been staged in different ways for Halloween. In one, an animatronic mad doctor worked to reattach limbs to the wrong parts of a body. In another, a funeral was supposedly going on; the viewing was for an old Vaudeville star, who would be played by an actor. When people entered the room, he came back to life, jumped out of his coffin and began singing an Al Jolson tune.

"Down below, there's the murderers' gallery. You have to go through the streets of London and pass by Jack the Ripper and other infamous murderers. All are live actors, too. They're good."

"And where are you?" Aidan asked.

"Outside," she told him. "Follow me. We go through the rear basement door."

They exited to the graveyard that took up the rear and both sides of the immediate property. As they headed out, she explained which historical character or legend waited where.

The graveyard was fitted out with skeletons that looked around the corners of mausoleums. Rats and spiders lurked and lingered. Bits and pieces of bones were cast about here and there. The graveyard itself provided the rest—creepy old mausoleums and crooked stones—and there were three empty coffins that appeared to have fallen out of broken sarcophagi. When opening time rolled around and the actors were all in their places, it was truly creepy.

"Real actors will get into the coffins—and they'll sit up groaning or jump out."

"Nice."

"It's definitely spooky at night," Mo said.

She came to a small mausoleum off the side of a path. "This is, er, my haunting ground. And where I saw Andre."

He wasn't sure if she was speaking to him or the

ghost of Lizzie, but suddenly he heard something like a whoosh of air.

He thought maybe the spirit gasped.

Rollo barked.

Mo smiled.

"What is it?" Aidan asked.

"He's here—and they've seen each other," Mo whispered.

"Ah."

"Oh, Aidan, it's really lovely. Try to see."

He did see…something. Two indistinct shapes. The one shape he'd come to know—and another. It almost seemed as if light clouds circled each other—and finally came together.

He couldn't tell if he simply heard Mo's description of the two of them embracing—or if he actually saw them, a man and a woman meeting after a very long time.

He waited before he whispered to Mo, "Can she take us to her daughter's grave? I don't mean to be callous, but…time's slipping away."

She turned to him. "You can ask her, Aidan."

He shook his head. "I know they're there," he said. "But I can't see their faces. I just have what everyone has, Mo. The sense of someone else there."

She studied him for a minute and he found himself caught in the beauty of her eyes. He stood very still; something in her made him want to reach out, to touch her—hold her as he believed Andre held his precious Lizzie. But he had to keep his distance. He'd touched her once and it had been wrong. He was an agent, here for a short time, working a case. They seemed to share some kind of attraction—physical, yes, but more than that. She aroused his instincts *and* his feelings. He forced himself not to think about caressing her face or kissing her lips. The thought was enough to arouse all those male instincts and this definitely wasn't the time or place.

"You knew something when you came here, when you first came to Sleepy Hollow," she said.

He nodded. "I knew that Richard was dead."

"How?"

"I dreamed about him coming to tell me."

She nodded with a grim smile.

"Yeah. Too bad he didn't tell me who did it, right?" he asked, his tone harsher than he would have liked.

"He came to you because he knew you'd pursue his murderer. That you'd achieve justice," she told him. Then she stepped forward and spoke gently with the ghosts he couldn't quite see.

"We can go to the cemetery now," she said a minute or two later. They thanked Sondra for letting them in and left, with Mo promising she'd be back in plenty of time for costuming and makeup for the night's event.

He drove them toward the Old Dutch Church and turned onto the road by the graveyard, along the border of Sleepy Hollow Cemetery. He parked as close as he could to the site where St. Andrew's Church had once stood. Where they'd found the bodies of Richard Highsmith and Wendy Appleby and the vault where they'd been beheaded.

The killer's lair, Aidan thought.

When they were out of the car, Rollo barked and wagged his tail. But he wasn't following a scent; he followed in the wake of the ghosts.

They climbed uphill and came to the vaults. They

passed the tomb where Wendy Appleby's form had pointed the way to the inner sanctum.

They came to another vault deep in the recesses of a hill.

Aidan noted that the name in worn stone atop the vault was Bakker.

"That's Lizzie's cousin's married name," Mo said.

"And Lizzie's daughter is buried there?" Aidan asked.

"Yes," Mo told him after conferring with the ghost.

Aidan walked up to the heavy brass gate that guarded what appeared to be an old seal. To his surprise, when he set his hand on the lever to open the gate, it gave. He pushed at what should have been a two-hundred-year-old seal.

It, too, gave.

He pulled a penlight from his pocket and ran its beam over the inside of the tomb as he entered. He felt Rollo come up to him and knew that Mo was directly behind.

Inside was an altar. To either side were rows and rows of dead but the seals seemed to be mostly intact.

The vault was very dark, and his penlight did little to illuminate the space. He heard a squeal, but it was just a rat racing by. The dog barked his disapproval. Mo, however, didn't react.

Then he felt as if he'd been touched again. Someone urged him to turn, to follow. At the back of the tomb was a sarcophagus in heavy stone with a name deeply engraved in it. "Elizabeth Bakker Highsmith."

"Highsmith!" he said, his voice choked. He looked at Mo.

"What do you think it means?" she asked.

"I'm assuming it means that Richard was tracing his family tree. That he found out somehow that he'd had a relative he hadn't known about who'd lived back in the Revolutionary days. What I can't figure out is how it could be connected to his death."

"But he was from here, isn't that right?"

Aidan nodded. "But...time passes. And if he'd learned about this grave being here, he probably wouldn't have thought anything of it. Everyone from this area has ancestors buried in one or more of these cemeteries."

"It's still possible that Lizzie's grave doesn't really have anything to do with why he was killed," Mo said.

He was thoughtful. "I don't think so. The matchbook with *Lizzie grave* on it came from the Mystic Magic strip club. And Wendy Appleby, who worked there, was targeted when she came to hear Richard speak. They were killed together. It all has to mean *something*," he said. He turned around abruptly. In the near-total darkness of the mausoleum, he couldn't see the ghosts at all—they weren't even puffs of white in the air. But he said aloud, "Thank you, Miss Hampton. Thank you, Major Andre. Right now I don't know exactly what this means, but it may become very important."

A silence hung in the dank air of the tomb.

Then Mo spoke. "You're welcome, Aidan. If they've helped in any way, they're pleased."

"Come on," he said. "Let me get you home so you don't miss your call time." He paused. *Had Richard Highsmith been here?*

The gate and the seal had given easily. Someone had come here not long ago. Richard? Or someone else?

"Let's go," he said.

"I should get there soon. And I still have to take Rollo to the house. Grace is picking me up there, so if I'm late, she will be, too."

As he started to leave the tomb, he bumped into her and instinctively set his hands on her to steady them both. He felt as if the scent of her soap or perfume pushed away that of death and decay. The warmth of her body, so close to his, was vibrant, filled with life.

He wanted to pull her against him and hold her there and believe for just a minute that he'd found the answers. That they could step into the daylight together and...

"Sorry!" he murmured.

"It's okay. I must say, a *living* human touch in here is nice."

Rollo whined.

"Oh, yes, and so is a dog. A dog's always good!" she said.

He left the tomb, catching her hand so she could easily follow. Rollo had no problem; it seemed he could see in the dark.

Aidan didn't release her hand as he picked his way through the monuments and stones to go back down to the car. She didn't seem to mind keeping her hand in his.

As he neared the pathway that would hide the vault from their view, he looked back. For a moment, he at least imagined he could see them.

The handsome Andre—"more unlucky than criminal"—and the beautiful woman he had secretly loved before his death.

The woman who'd paid the ultimate price for loving him.

He walked on down the hill, Mo's hand in his, Rollo beside the two of them.

What the hell did it all mean?

If he could figure that out, he just might catch the killers.

12

Grace showed up just as they returned to Mo's house. She spoke with Aidan while Mo took Rollo inside, fed him and made sure his water bowl was filled before heading out for the night.

They said goodbye to Aidan and got into Grace's car to leave. Grace waved as she eased out of Mo's drive.

Then she turned to Mo, beaming. "So?"

"So?"

"Have you two done it yet?"

"Grace! He's an agent, working on the case."

"He's a man, honey. You mean to tell me you haven't…" She shook her head. "You're one asexual woman. If you don't do something pretty soon, what a waste! A total waste. Do you want me to offer myself up? You can't just let a divine hunk of masculinity like that go! What's the matter with you? I mean, what's available here? Tommy Jensen? Creepy Tommy?"

"Grace!" Mo protested.

Grace said, "Oh, we all like Tommy now. There's nothing wrong with him. Granted, he's more like a brother. And Phil's like another brother from a different mother! Or Ron…never mind, he's gay and in a good relationship. But what are *you* doing?"

"Grace!"

"Tell me you aren't fascinated with the guy."

"I am."

"Oh!" Grace said, clearly surprised. "Well, then?"

Mo sighed and swung around to look at her. "What do you want me to do, Grace? Just say, 'Agent Mahoney, the pickings here are slim, and you've got all the right parts, and they seem to be in working order. Should we have sex?'"

"No, that would be rude. Crude."

"Worse than rude or crude. Humiliating!" Mo groaned.

"It's the way you said it. Just, 'I'd love to have sex with you.' That would be the way to do it," Grace said.

Mo groaned again.

"If you don't see it, you're blind. Sparks seem to pop off both of you when you're together."

"I'm trying to help him find a killer!"

"And he *will* find the killer," Grace said with certainty. "That's his job. It's what he does. But he's still a man and he deserves a life beyond work!"

Mo couldn't argue with that. "Don't we all," she murmured. "I brought him by the Haunted Mausoleum today," she said, hoping to change the topic.

"That should've been fun—but I'm sure you turned it into work somehow."

Mo didn't answer. "We're just studying local legends, you know?"

"And only you could make that not fun!"

Mo didn't bother to respond; they'd reached the Haunted Mausoleum.

She went in to start her makeup right away. Grace joined Phil and some of the others and indulged in donuts.

Sondra stopped by the makeup chair to tell Mo she'd enjoyed meeting Aidan Mahoney. Ron pursed his lips as he worked on Mo's face.

Mo remembered guiltily that she'd promised to ask about a job for Debbie Howell. She told Sondra about her—and about how she'd be trying to keep the orphaned son of her murdered friend.

"You know this woman well?" Sondra asked her.

"Not that well," Mo replied honestly. "But I've seen the way J.J. looks at her and I believe she's good person and deserves a chance. She also knows everything about this area."

"Have your friend call me. We'll arrange an interview," Sondra assured her. "As you know, I love doing research on the area. My family goes back so far... I could use an assistant on that angle and someone from here who knows and loves the place would be perfect. I'm researching a story about Continental currency right now."

In the mirror, Mo could see Ron raise his brows as he worked on her hair. "Continental currency?" he asked. "What's that?"

"The paper currency issued by the Continental Congress. A lot of it supposedly disappeared from this area before the Civil War," Sondra said.

"Was it worth anything by that time?" he asked.

"Certainly. There were collectors then, just as there are now," Sandra explained. "And, of course, there were thieves then, too."

"Yeah? I'd imagine they used it for kindling!" Ron

said. "When the Revolution was over, wasn't it about useless?"

"Ron, we won the Revolution," Sondra said, smiling.

"Yeah, but—"

"New money was printed after that, yes, and quite quickly. That's why Continental currency became so valuable to collectors. Well, that's all just a bit of history, and as I said, I'd like to write an article on it. Anyway, back to tonight's work. Mo, bring your agent friend by anytime," Sondra said, and moved on through the dressing area and makeup room to return to the front office.

"Ooh," Ron teased Mo. "The plot thickens."

"Continental currency?" she asked.

"No! Dating the federal lawman!"

"We're just rehashing local legends," Mo said.

"That's all?"

Mo lowered her head and laughed. "No, Ron, I've had this weird fantasy all my life—and it's not about a knight in shining armor. It's about an FBI man—and fooling around naked on a cold fall day in the middle of a burial ground. Oh, the decay! Wow, what a turn-on!"

Ron laughed, too, and leaned closer to her. "You own a house, my love. Use it!"

When she was ready that night and at her post, Mo didn't expect to see Major Andre or his Lizzie. But they were both there for a moment, waving to her. Then, hand in hand, they wandered off.

She went through the motions, her mind racing.

What could *Lizzie grave* have had to do with Richard Highsmith's murder? It seemed more and more evident that there was no serial killer running amok. Just someone who'd wanted both Richard and Wendy Appleby dead.

Aidan didn't go back to the hotel. Instead, he called Logan.

The suspects they were watching were all in; they'd probably head out to dinner, but the members of the Krewe were ready to follow each one of them if necessary. Detective Van Camp had been interviewing more and more people on his own, while Detective Voorhaven had been working with the agents, ready to follow a suspect if needed or scrutinize the video screens if not.

Aidan told Logan what he'd learned. Logan promised to look into the Highsmith, Hampton and Bakker lineage to see if he could find any dark secrets—or get some facts about the murder of Lizzie herself—to decipher what it could mean. And whether it related to Richard's death…and Wendy's.

"The hospital's alerted me that J.J.'s being released," Logan said. "There's an officer with him, so he's fine, but I'm not sure he and Debbie should go back to Wendy Appleby's home. At least, not yet."

Aidan agreed. "Can we get another room on our floor?"

"I'm sure we can. I'll book something with a door that connects to one of us."

"Then I'll drive to the hospital now to pick them up."

Right after that, Aidan went to the hospital.

Even considering what they'd learned, he wasn't sure why the killer would want to kill J.J.—or, at any rate, leave him to die in the vault. What would Richard Highsmith's relationship with a long-dead woman have to do with Wendy or J.J.? But none of it made sense. What did make sense was to watch over J.J. and keep him safe.

When he arrived at the hospital, both Debbie and J.J. were pleased to see him. And Debbie was relieved about his plan to take them to the hotel where his unit was staying.

Because of his nature—which was both protective and suspicious—and perhaps because of his work, he found that he was keeping a close eye on Debbie, too. She'd been close to Wendy Appleby. But J.J. evidently loved and trusted her; she'd been his mother's best friend. And she appeared to be grateful that she was going to be at the hotel with the agents and the police. It made her feel safe, she said.

"I couldn't tell J.J., of course, but I've been worried about leaving the hospital, about being alone with him. We could've gone to my apartment instead of his house, but I'm still scared. The only thing is…I can't pay for the hotel. I haven't worked since it all happened, and if I want to keep J.J., I don't even have a job to go to anymore."

"We're taking care of it. J.J. is a material witness, so you don't need to worry," Aidan assured her.

They waited while the doctor came and signed the papers to release the boy. Then J.J. said goodbye to the medical staff who'd come to care about him. Finally, they walked down to Aidan's car.

"Where's Mo?" J.J. asked Aidan as they drove off.

"She's working at the Haunted Mausoleum tonight," Aidan told him.

"I wish you had Rollo," J.J. mumbled.

"I'm sure you can see him tomorrow," Aidan said.

He called Logan again and found out that he'd gotten the room for Debbie and J.J. It was attached to his room. Detective Voorhaven would meet them downstairs and take them up.

Voorhaven was in the parking lot to meet them with keys. He took the bag of clothing and toiletries Wendy had brought and led the way.

Before he let her go up to their room with J.J. and Voorhaven, Aidan stopped Debbie. "I need you to do me a favor."

"Yes?"

"I need you to think of any reason at all that someone would want Wendy dead. And what her connection with Richard might have been."

"I will. Oh, my God, yes, I will!" Debbie vowed.

He escorted her up to the room where Voorhaven waited with J.J. Once they'd settled in, Voorhaven met him at the door. "I want to apologize," he said in a low voice.

"For what?"

"For being an ass. You know, touchy over the federal-local thing. Your guys here—and Jane!—are great. I'm sorry. We never could have handled this without you. We just don't deal with this kind of situation very often. Thank God."

"It's okay, Voorhaven." Aidan smiled.

"James or Jimmy."

"Jimmy, it's okay," he said.

But when Aidan went to Logan's suite to catch up with the others and work on their future strategy, he was dismayed that Jimmy joined them. He wasn't ready to talk about the ghosts *he* didn't actually see—but

Mo did—in front of someone who wasn't a part of the Krewe.

But that was easily solved. J.J. wanted to go to the hotel's game room. Voorhaven volunteered for the duty of accompanying him and Debbie down to play games. "I don't show mercy, even to kids," Voorhaven warned J.J. "And I'm a kick-ass air hockey player."

"You're on!" J.J. told him.

When he was alone in the room with Logan, Sloan, Jane and Will, Aidan went over everything that had occurred that day.

"All the local legends coming to the fore," Jane said. "The headless horseman, Andre's ghost and the Woman in White. But why would anyone kill over any of them?"

"Revenge?" Will asked. "Yeah, I know, revenge for a two-hundred-year-old death may be crazy—but there are crazies out there. And as for Elizabeth Hampton and her family—Lizzie was a murder victim! If you were out to avenge her death, you wouldn't kill her descendant."

"There has to be an answer. I believe Richard did find out about *Lizzie grave*," Aidan said. "But even if a man found out he was related to a woman who had been killed for her association with a Revolutionary-era spy, what would that mean today? Half the population around here can trace their ancestry back to the founding days."

"Maybe this goes deeper," Sloan suggested.

"People kill for love, hate, jealousy and money. I don't see here where money enters into this. Richard poured his life's earnings into his work. And Wendy was barely getting by," Aidan said. "But, maybe that's an angle to look into."

Will stood up suddenly. "Doors opening on the Taylor Branch floor," he said. He pointed to the screens. "Yes, there's Branch, out in the hallway, and there's Jillian Durfey. They're meeting up to go out together."

"I'm on it," Sloan said. "I'll be out in the car, watching them, and I'll tail them when they leave."

"More movement," Jane noted. "The security guys are heading out, too. Looks like they're surprised to see Taylor and Jillian in the hall—like it's a coincidence that they're all out there now."

"Go down and be ready to leave, too," Logan told Will.

Sloan and Will hurried to the door, and Jane followed. "I'll take one of them if they split up."

"Let me know as soon as possible who leaves with whom," Logan said.

The others left. Aidan continued to watch the screens. Branch slipped an arm around Jillian Durfey's shoulders; she looked up at him gratefully.

They moved toward the elevator.

Aidan leaned forward, trying to see if he could make out any of the conversation.

"I think the big guy—Muscles, what's his real name? Cory Stile?—is telling Branch that they need to start looking for new jobs," Logan said. He glanced at Aidan. "I read lips—a little. I took some lessons in sign language and I worked with the deaf years ago in college."

"What's Branch doing? Looks like he's arguing with him," Aidan said.

"Branch is telling him they can't go yet, can't leave town, because the police need them."

"So there *is* trouble among the five of them," Aidan murmured.

"I don't know. Branch comes across as sincere," Logan said. "As if he wants the truth."

"Here's what I can't figure out. To my mind, it had to be someone close to one or both of our victims. Someone who knew that Wendy Appleby was on her way to see Richard. And if it wasn't someone close to Richard—then who? By all accounts, Wendy was a private person." He sighed. "We have to keep watching this group. See what they're up to at all times."

"I agree," Logan assured him.

As they studied the screen, Jillian smiled at something Magic said. They both seemed to enjoy each other.

Branch pulled Jillian closer to him.

"Hmm. We can learn a lot from body language," Aidan murmured.

"Yup. Trouble in paradise, all right. That's good for us," Logan said.

Aidan's phone rang. He didn't look away from the screen but hit Answer. It was Van Camp. "Aidan, that boy and Ms. Howell with you?" he asked.

"Yes. Detective Voorhaven took them to the games room."

"Good. The neighbors at the Appleby house reported a disturbance. There's a patrol car on its way. I'm going out there, too, and I'll meet you there."

Logan had heard their conversation, which had been on speakerphone. "I'll get Voorhaven back up here with Wendy and J.J. and I'll keep them in here for now. Go."

Aidan nodded and left.

In the lobby, he ran into Richard Highsmith's retinue. Taylor Branch called out to him. "Agent Mahoney, what's happening?" The man seemed to be grinning.

As if he knew something had happened.

"We just keep working," Aidan said. "We just keep working. Good evening," he told the others and hurried out. Maybe Branch was pleased about whatever was going on. Maybe he *knew* what was going on.

Well, Aidan was pleased, too. When the group left, their moves would be tracked.

The thing was...

He knew damned well that one of them had to be involved.

And that there had to be an accomplice on the outside.

But who could that second person be? Someone who knew both Richard and Wendy. Someone who'd had an agenda.

What was he missing? If he could just understand *why* they'd been killed, he'd be on his way to identifying the killers.

The night drew to an uneventful end. The last group of squealing visitors went out. They'd been a group of college-age kids, eight of them, and they'd been especially silly, screaming constantly.

Of course, "haunted" venues made their reputations on screaming and scaring, so she supposed that was good.

On the other hand, Mo was getting tired and the screaming had just seemed...

Annoying.

A voice boomed over the loudspeaker, informing them that the last group had gone through. A floodlight didn't brighten the entire graveyard, but it did a lot to dispel the shadows—and to show the actors for what they were.

Fading.

Makeup was beginning to crack or congeal, and they were all looking a little the worse for wear.

Grace came over to Mo's area and said with a sigh, "Another night down! At least we're doing really well. We've sold out for Halloween a week early, Sondra was telling me." She grimaced at Mo. "I'm so glad you've done this. You *are* the Woman in White, one of our most famous legends!"

Mo smiled. No, she wasn't *the* Woman in White.

Phil walked over to join them, rolling his shoulders to work out muscle kinks. "You're divine, ladies. Divine. Are we going to eat? I'm starved."

"Sure," Grace said. "Mo?"

Ron came out from the setup area. "Everyone accounted for?" he asked. "Me, Phil, Grace and Mo. Come on out, kiddies. I just don't know where Sondra went. I'm dying to get out of here—no pun intended. Starved. Too bad we get off so late that even Tommy's is closed. That means the café. Maybe Mr. FBI agent will show up at the café again, huh, Mo?"

"Let's hope not. I don't want anything else to be wrong anywhere," Mo said.

Phil frowned. "You said everyone's accounted for?" he asked Ron.

"Except Sondra, and we can't leave without her!" Ron said. "Have you seen her?"

"This afternoon, when I came by," Mo said. "And then when I was in makeup."

"That's odd," Phil muttered.

"What?" Grace demanded.

Phil pointed. One of the "cracked" coffins was leaning against a tomb. There still seemed to be someone in it.

"That's Joshua Kirbin's spot," Phil said. "And I said good-night to Joshua already. He lit out of here in a hurry, trying to catch up with some friends working the hayride."

Mo didn't know *how* she knew. She just knew it was bad. Really bad.

They all turned to look in the direction Phil had pointed.

There was definitely a body in the coffin. It was loosely covered in what appeared to be a black shroud. The coffin was a prop, of course, built to appear like an old Victorian coffin but with a glass window at the head area. The bottom half of the lid was broken off; the head area with the window remained.

The four of them looked at one another.

Mo didn't want to take a step toward the coffin. It was across a field of broken gravestones, scattered "bones" and thick webbing.

"We have to go and see," she said flatly.

She started across the center of the graveyard. She could hear Grace behind her, pushing Phil. "Get up there! Help her."

"I'm going, I'm going!" Phil said. "Why me? Why is the heterosexual male supposed to be the brave one all the time?"

"Oh, please, just get out of the way!" Ron told him.

Mo heard them, but she reached the coffin first.

She peered through the Victorian window....

And there was nothing.

For a moment she dared to breathe, dared to hope, that it was a prank—in extremely bad taste—being played on them.

But she reached out and opened the broken lid.

And she saw it.

The bloody stump of a neck.

She'd seen nothing through the window...

Because the corpse had no head.

When Aidan reached the Appleby house, Van Camp and police had already arrived.

"Crime scene units are on the way," Van Camp told him. "The place is trashed. What someone was looking for, I have no idea."

"The neighbors heard a commotion, but no one saw anything?" Aidan asked.

"Hey, you expected this to be easy?" Van Camp asked dryly.

"I wish to hell *something* would be easy," Aidan said. "Who called it in?"

"The guy in the sweater over there, talking to the woman in the cat slippers with the trench coat over her pajamas. I've talked to them both. You go give it a try." He glanced down at his notebook. "The guy is Marshall Long. The lady is Penelope Seaford. Like I said, he called it in. She came out once we got here. She lives right next door, and the house on the other side of Wendy's is empty. Long, who lives across the street, met the cops out here. He didn't see a car or anything, although he's pretty sure he heard someone burn out of here while he was on the phone."

Aidan walked over and introduced himself to the neighbors and fielded their questions. Marshall told

him he was a teacher. Penelope Seaford, an attractive woman of about fifty, told him she worked for the
chamber of commerce. She'd loved Wendy Appleby.
"Wendy was a great neighbor. She caught my escape-
cat for me several times," Penelope said. "Everyone
in the neighborhood was devastated to hear that she'd
died."

"And so horribly!" Marshall said, shaking his head.
"A lovely woman."

"Did she date much? Was she seeing anyone?" Aidan
asked. The police had been through that round of questions already, Aidan knew, but he'd yet to talk to anyone
other than Debbie who'd been close to her.

"Date? No. No boyfriend. She was devoted to her
child," Penelope said.

He asked them a few more questions, then went into
the house.

The least affected area was J.J.'s room. Wendy Appleby's bedroom, office and kitchen had been ripped
to smithereens. The intruder's first area of concentration had been the office, Aidan thought.

"There's no computer," he pointed out as Van Camp
came into the room with Gina Mason, the head of the
forensic unit, whom he'd met before.

"But there was evidently one here," Grace said. "You
can see the outline on the mat. Looks like it had a
seventeen-inch screen."

He nodded to Gina. "Thanks. I think I remember it
being here when we came and searched the house once
Debbie Howell gave us Wendy's identity."

"Someone was after something," Gina said. "Every
desk drawer has been dumped. It's the same in her bedroom. Clothing all over the floor. I just gather up the

evidence and I'm no rocket scientist, but I'd say, yeah—whoever came through here was looking for something. And if it's the same person—or persons—we've been dealing with on the murders, they're smart. I guarantee you we won't find a fingerprint. The best I'm going to come up with is some answers from the tire print out front. Someone did burn rubber. We'll know what kind of tire it was pretty quickly," she promised him.

Aidan paused. A framed picture had fallen over.

He picked it up.

The photo was of Wendy Appleby as she'd appeared in life, with her son, J.J. He studied the picture, and a sort of epiphany came over him. It was often hard to tell with kids, but...

He'd been friends with Richard when they were both J.J.'s age.

And there was something about J.J. that reminded him of Richard. He wondered why he hadn't noticed it before—but, of course, he hadn't been looking for it or expecting it.

The picture had been taken at one of the cemeteries. As he narrowed his eyes to study the shot, he saw the mausoleum with the name Bakker engraved in the stone.

They were both smiling for the camera. There were other children in the background and a woman who seemed to be trying to herd them.

A school trip?

Wendy and J.J. looked happy. As if they'd been having a great day. Maybe Wendy had volunteered to chaperone the outing.

He decided to take the picture out of the frame.

When he did, he was startled when he turned it around to study the back.

There were two words written there: *Lizzie grave.*

There it was again. Puzzle pieces would somehow fit together if he could just maneuver them properly.

He stared at the picture, wishing, hoping, that it could give him more.

Then his phone rang.

He saw that it was Mo. She should've gotten out of the Haunted Mausoleum a few minutes ago. She was probably heading out with her friends for their late-late dinner or very early breakfast.

"Mo?"

Her voice was controlled, but he could still hear the terror in it. "There's another one, Aidan. There's another. A body here. A real one, I mean. We think it's Sondra…but it—the body—has no head!"

Mo was pretty sure she'd acted as quickly and competently as possible under the circumstances.

Having discovered that they definitely had a dead body on their hands, she'd called Aidan immediately.

She'd told the others not to touch the body.

"Touch it? Are you crazy?" Phil demanded.

"We've got to get out of here," Grace said. "Whoever did this… Oh, my God! The actors have barely left. Someone was in here while we were…while we were scaring people! Oh, my God, they did this after Joshua Kirbin left. That means it was just a few minutes ago. That means—"

"Grace, they've done what they came to do. They're gone," Mo said. She was trying for courage; Aidan was on the way.

She'd found corpses before. But she'd been with cops—and Rollo. Or Heidi. She'd never been with just a few terrified friends in the middle of a cemetery.

"Let's go out front. Let's get the hell out of here!" Ron shouted.

"We can't just go. We have to watch this scene until the cops show up," Mo said.

"Watch it? For what? Are we worried about what can happen to this…this woman?"

"You're sure it's a woman?" Grace asked.

"That—or a man with boobs!" Ron said. "Oh, my God. It's Sondra. It has to be Sondra. That looks like of her little scoop neck tops. *This* is why we haven't been able to find her."

"Where's her head?" Phil asked.

They were all silent for a moment.

"I don't want to know!" Ron said softly.

They stood there, silent again. The weird lights and the fog machine had been turned off, but it felt as if they were very alone in a vast sea where the floodlight seemed useless against the darkness of the night.

"We gotta get out of here," Phil said. "We—"

"Wait!" Mo broke in. "I hear a siren."

They all paused. It was distant at first, but then the sound became stronger.

"I have to go let them in. I locked the front gates," Ron said.

He left, and the remaining three stood there as if frozen, waiting.

Then Mo saw Aidan. He was leading the way. Van Camp was right behind him, along with several men in uniform. Relief flooded through her and she abandoned her post by the coffin and raced to him. She didn't throw herself into his arms.

She plummeted into them.

"Hey, hey, it's all right!" he told her softly. "Well, it's not all right, but we're here. Your hands are frozen." He rubbed them for a moment before extricating himself from her hold. Walking over to the others, he moved past them to get to the coffin. Van Camp joined him; everyone else stepped back as the agent and the detective studied the body.

"Could we go in where it's warm?" Grace asked, shaking.

"Yes, yes," Aidan said, turning to them. "Go into the parlor and sit. We'll be there shortly. Officer Calloway, will you take them in, please?"

A young man in uniform escorted their group into the parlor of the mortuary. And now they sat among fake spiderwebs, by the piano with a bony hand atop the keys, red velvet draping and black all around them as well as a chandelier that seemed to hold centuries of dust.

Usually, it was just…where they worked. Where they knew what was fun and spooky, what was real and what wasn't.

They sat there, the four of them, not talking, the officer standing guard. Mo sat on a Duncan Phyfe sofa with Ron; Phil and Grace sat in wingback chairs, both so pale they'd never made better ghouls.

It felt as though time was never-ending—and yet Mo was fairly certain it wasn't that long before Aidan came in with Van Camp.

"We need you to tell us what happened and in what order," Aidan said.

"It was closing time, " Phil began.

"The others took off," Ron added.

"We were planning to go to the café," Grace said.

"Whoa, hold it!" Aidan said. "Ron, Grace, you two go over there with Detective Van Camp and tell him what you saw it. Mo, you and Mr. Ainsley stay with me."

She looked at Phil, who nodded and then turned to Aidan. "The last group for the night had gone through," he said. "We're out in the distant reaches of the property here—Mo, Grace and me. We meet on that path to go back in. Mo has so much makeup on, she likes to wash it off. Sondra usually closes up, locks everything for the night. Ron came out to check on us, see who was still here. He said everyone was accounted for—other than the four of us, they'd all left—but that he couldn't find Sondra. At some point, I was just looking around and I saw that fake coffin. It's where an actor named Joshua Kirbin is usually posted, but I knew Joshua had taken off the minute we got the last tour announcement."

"Who makes that announcement?" Aidan asked.

"Either the box office clerk, Sondra or Ron. Tonight it was Cindy Chessy, the box office clerk. She's the first to leave every night. All she has to do is put the strongbox and computer in Sondra's office, then she can head out," he said. "Joshua had plans with friends who worked at a different venue. They were meeting for an early break-fast. I saw him leave and then I went to the mausoleum."

"Mo?" he asked.

"I wouldn't have noticed the coffin," she said. "I was tired and ready to go home. Phil pointed out that there was…someone in it. It's across a field of graves from us."

"And none of you saw anything?" he demanded, incredulous.

"Define *anything,*" Phil said dryly. "The graveyard is full of ghouls, and at the end of the night we pick up some of the props because it could snow. Anyone could have walked around here with a body and no one would've noticed."

"Okay," Aidan said. "Let me go over this one more time. Last tour is announced—"

"And we finish wherever we are, just to make sure everyone in the tour group is really gone. There's often one jerk in the last group who wants to stay behind," Phil told him.

"So, last tour, finish up, people run out—with body parts, bodies and other props," Aidan said.

Phil nodded.

"So then, your friend Joshua Kirbin left."

"Yes."

"Is that when you noticed his coffin?" Aidan asked.

Phil shook his head with a grimace. "No. I've seen this place a million times. The others were out—like I said, they're closer to the building—and I was just waiting for Mo and Grace. I saw Mo come around her mausoleum and Grace walked over to her."

"Then Ron came out, worried about Sondra," Mo said.

"We were talking and the floodlight was on," Phil explained. "I was looking in that direction. And I saw there was something in the coffin—and I knew it couldn't be Josh."

Mo watched Aidan. He seemed weary; she had a feeling that something else had happened since she'd seen him.

"Oh, my God. Oh, my God," Phil said, shaking his head again. "They'll close us down now, won't they? They'll close it all down. They have to. I mean, Lord, you could leave corpses and heads everywhere here, and it would take a while for anyone to notice."

"That is a problem, yes," Aidan said. He looked at them both. "An officer is going to come and take all this down. Please stay here until he's done and check with me before you leave. Mo—you and Grace—wait for me, please. I'll see you home."

It had been so shocking, so horrible, they hadn't thought about the loss yet. But as she and Phil looked at each other, they both whispered, "Sondra."

"I'm really sorry. I just met her today. She seemed to be a fine person," Aidan said. He stood there for a moment, then turned and went out back.

A few minutes later an officer came in and took their statements. After that, Ron and Grace returned to the parlor.

"I don't think I want to be here for Halloween next year," Grace said dully. "I'm going to save up and go on vacation. I'm going to find a country where they don't celebrate Halloween at all."

"I can't stop," Ron said. "Makeup and fabrication. That's my whole life."

Eventually, Aidan came back in. "Ron, Phil, you two are free to go. Grace, I'll follow you to your house. Mo, come with me," Aidan told her. "We'll get Grace home first."

She nodded, feeling numb. When she left, she hoped she'd never have to come back here.

They stayed close behind Grace but Mo wondered if it even mattered.

The sun was already coming up. She didn't know if it was because she was so shocked that she had nothing to say—or because she was just so worn-out.

When they reached Grace's home, Aidan got out of the car and went to the door with her. Grace had an alarm system; Aidan waited for her to key in the numbers and lock herself in.

When he came back to the car, he spoke to her a little sharply. "Mo."

"Yes?"

"Are you all right?"

She nodded. "Was it…was it Sondra?" she asked.

"It was. I'm sorry." His voice was as sincere, as sorrowful, as it had been when he'd said those words earlier.

"Me, too." She took a deep breath. "Aidan, does this mean there's some kind of psychopath on the loose? Sondra… I doubt she even knew Richard Highsmith or Wendy Appleby. This *can't* be connected to them."

He was quiet. Then he told her, "The Appleby house was broken into tonight—and trashed."

"Thieves who knew she was dead and that the house was empty?"

"Thieves take things. The only thing missing was Wendy Appleby's computer," he said.

"What are you thinking?"

"The Krewe's working on it now, but…I don't think Wendy Appleby had a husband who was killed in an automobile accident. I think that was just her story."

"What do you mean? And, anyway, why would that matter, whether she'd had a husband or not?" Mo asked. "Do you think she and Richard were having an affair? Is that what you're saying?"

"I don't know if they were having an affair now, but I think they did nine years ago. I think Richard was J.J.'s father."

"What...what led you to that conclusion?"

"I could be way off, but it's a theory worth exploring. We found the Woman in White—who had an affair with Major Andre. And then a daughter, who married a Highsmith. As for *Lizzie grave*—there was a picture at the Appleby house with Wendy and J.J. at the cemetery. It looked like a school outing. And on the back of it she'd written, 'Lizzie's grave.' It's too much of a coincidence that they both wrote those exact words. They might have met there—or planned to meet there. To discuss J.J. or the future? Maybe she'd hidden the truth from Richard all these years."

"And maybe you're wrong. Maybe they were both history buffs. Or else Wendy did know Richard, discovered the grave and just wanted to tell him about it. Wendy wasn't from here, you know."

"Yes, I know. Wendy Appleby was dancing on the Broadway stage nine years ago—and Richard always loved theater."

Mo shook her head. "From everything I hear, they were both decent people. Why wouldn't Wendy have told Richard? Why wouldn't they have at least let their child know the truth?"

"People have reasons—bad ones, sometimes—for doing things. It's possible that, at the time, Wendy didn't want to trap him into marriage but didn't want to give up her baby, either."

"That's just conjecture," she said.

"Yes," he agreed, but before he could continue, his hands-free phone rang. Mo heard his part of the conversation and wasn't surprised when he told her, "There's no Mr. Appleby. No father listed on J.J.'s birth certificate."

She nodded. "I could tell from what you were saying. But why kill people for that? And why kill Sondra? Like I said, I don't believe she knew either of them."

"Could be smoke and mirrors," Aidan said.

"Pardon?"

"Make sure someone else dies in the same gruesome manner. To create a diversion, send us in the wrong direction," he explained. When they reached her house, he got out of the car and walked her to the door. "Mo, I'm sorry to ask, but can you get Rollo and can we keep going tonight?"

"Keep going?"

"We have another head to find," he said. "And I'm sure you know the location of just about every headless horseman in the city."

Her heart sank.

She didn't want to find Sondra's head. She hadn't known Sondra the way Phil and Ron and Grace had. But she'd met her through the years—and Sondra had been wonderful to Mo for the few days she'd worked there.

But she also didn't want to think of Sondra's head set up as a ghoulish mockery to be discovered by someone else, a child, perhaps.

"I'll get Rollo," she said.

13

"Where should we go?" Aidan asked Mo as she returned to the car with Rollo.

"There's the large metal headless horseman by the bridge," Mo said. "But that one's huge. You'd need several people to get a head on top of it. And there's one at the entrance to the village set up specifically for Halloween. Other than that…at this time of year, they're everywhere."

"Yes, but you and Rollo can locate the one we need." He paused. "How did you find Richard Highsmith's head the day we met?"

"I had a piece of Richard's clothing and I let Rollo get his scent."

Aidan didn't want to sound ridiculous, but asked his next question, anyway.

"Did you get a feel for Richard then—or see him?" Mo looked out the front window of the car. He hadn't started the engine yet.

"Let's go back to the Haunted Mausoleum first," she said. "I may get a sense of where to go from there— and we can find one of Sondra's sweaters or something she wore for Rollo."

As he drove, he glanced over at Mo. She'd been up all night again.

So had he.

But he'd had more experience with nights like this.

Today, the announcement that another murder had taken place, *at* a haunted attraction, would mean the events would be closed again. Mo wouldn't be expected at work tonight.

"Are you all right?" he murmured. "Tired?"

She turned to him. "I'll survive."

When they reached the Haunted Mausoleum, the police and crime scene experts were still busy. While Mo went to retrieve something of the dead woman's from her office, Aidan took the time to check in with Gina Mason, who was supervising her crew. She stood with Detective Lee Van Camp out in the graveyard.

"Anything here?" he asked the two of them.

"Anything?" Gina repeated. "This place was *full* of people last night. The people in costume who were at work—and the hundreds walking through. There are cigarette butts everywhere, even though smoking's not permitted in the graveyard. Kids will sneak off. There are footprints all over the place, not to mention fibers and hair."

"What about the body?" Aidan asked. "Any results from that? Any witnesses?" he added.

Van Camp answered him. "We can hope, but we don't know yet. The M.E. came for the body, and his people will examine it. But as far as witnesses go, this is almost like a magic trick. You know, it's all about distraction. An event was going on here, and the problem is, everyone was looking at that and screaming. They're *supposed* to get scared and scream. The killer could've carried that body in front of dozens of people—and they'd all have thought it was part of the show."

"We're going to have to speak to every one of the employees. *Somebody* must've seen something," Aidan insisted.

"I've got police messengers heading to every address," Van Camp said wearily. "We'll get to all of them."

"So we believe she was in her office when she was taken—right here, right on the property. We can assume she was knocked out with chloroform first, but there's not a drop of blood in the mortuary itself. Or have you found something?" Aidan said.

"Nothing that remotely resembles a trail," Gina Mason told him. "And, I swear, Agent Mahoney, my people are good."

"I don't doubt it. But we found the killer's lair at the old cemetery, which would've been too far for him in this time frame. However, it's where we found his tools for cutting off the heads."

"A hatchet and knife, available in any hardware store in the nation," Gina told him.

"Okay, she was knocked out in her office, carried out by the killer masquerading as an actor and then…then beheaded somewhere else, maybe at his previous lair, and brought back here to the graveyard," Aidan said.

"That's what we've got so far," Van Camp agreed.

He heard a ruckus from somewhere in the building. Turning, he saw that Rollo seemed to be leading Mo out. One of the techs yelled, "Hey, what the hell? Get that monster away from my crime scene."

Van Camp moved forward quickly. "Hey, that's Rollo. Leave him be!"

Mo tugged on the dog's leash and got control of him, then skirted around the scene, but Rollo was barking furiously.

"Let him go," Aidan said.

She did.

Rollo raced straight to the mausoleum, the one Mo had walked around all evening as the Woman in White.

She shook her head. "I don't know what he's after. That mausoleum hasn't been touched, other than by an outside cleaning or painting crew, in well over a hundred years."   •

Aidan walked to the front of the mausoleum. As Mo had implied, it was tightly closed. The iron gate was locked, and beyond that was a seal. He pushed and shoved and prodded at the seal, it appeared to be, as she'd said, untouched for a very long time.

Aidan stepped back and spoke to Van Camp. "The dog wants us to go in."

"I'll get the sledgehammers and crowbars," Van Camp said.

Aidan stood next to Mo. He wanted to put an arm around her shoulders, but right here and now that would be entirely inappropriate.

"Did Rollo find the head?" he asked her. "Is that what he's signaling?"

"I don't think that's where the head is," she replied. "How could anyone possibly even get in there? How do you hack up a body without being heard?"

"Easily enough. There's a sound system, which was playing funeral music and creepy noises while the killer was doing whatever he was doing, wasn't there?"

"Yes…" She turned to look at him, a confused expression on her face. "Aidan, I didn't leave my post all night. I did nothing but walk around and around that mausoleum."

"But I doubt you would have heard anything even if the killer passed right by you," he told her. "As I understand it, there's constant commotion during one of these events."

Van Camp's officers began to work with their sledgehammers. In ten minutes, they'd broken through the seal.

"After you," Van Camp said to Aidan with a little mock bow.

Aidan took one of the massive flashlights from an officer, then stepped inside and flooded the tomb with light.

It had been built for a family, allowing for about twenty-five bodies to be entombed. There was an altar at the rear. A cross that was encrusted with tomb dust and spiderwebs had been set aside. The altar was covered in blood.

A hatchet and knife had been left beside it.

Aidan damned himself a thousand times over for not finding the killer more quickly.

Whoever was doing this was doing it under their noses and certainly getting a thrill from knowing that he was killing people—and cutting their heads off— virtually in plain sight.

But how had the killer gotten into the tomb?

This one really seemed to be a locked-room mystery.

"Van Camp, we need more lights!" he called.

He reminded himself that there was really no such thing as a locked-room mystery. There was always an answer.

Van Camp came in with two officers, directing them to stay near the entrance and hold the lights high.

"How the hell?" Van Camp asked.

"This is a mortuary. Maybe there are tunnels to bring the dead straight out from the embalming rooms," Aidan suggested. "Also," he said, "the last interments here took place shortly after the Civil War. God knows, it might have been part of the Underground Railroad, too. This might even have been a way to hide runaway slaves."

"But where would those tunnels be?" Van Camp demanded, looking around.

Aidan stepped back out and saw Mo watching him silently.

"Do you know anything about tunnels from the embalming room to the mausoleums?" he asked her.

She shrugged. "Sondra would have known." She brightened just a little. "Grace might know, too. She's worked out here often enough."

"Can you call her?" She nodded, fumbling as she pulled her cell phone from her pocket. They'd taken Grace home a while ago; she might have fallen asleep.

No. Her boss had just been murdered. Grace answered on the first ring.

Mo spoke to her for several minutes then put her phone away. "She said there might have been tunnels. My house became a hospital during the Civil War, and she said this place was where many of the dead were brought because the mortician was one of the best embalmers of his day. Embalming became popular during the Civil War when soldiers died far away. Anyway, along with the dead, sometimes people were smuggled—alive—in coffins. She knows of one area where there really was an extension of the basement. It was kept shut because they were doing secret things here. They were hiding people who were running, sometimes slaves—and sometimes soldiers deserting the Southern cause. It's behind the room where the actor who plays a mad doctor has his, uh, chop shop."

"Thanks," Aidan said, and hurried back to the mortuary, Van Camp in tow. Mo and Rollo were close behind. He headed straight down to the basement. The tour groups went from the basement—the embalming area—out to the graveyard, after going by the creepy displays and actors.

Mo was almost touching his back. "Over there," she said. "You can see the gurney and the plastic bloodied body parts. You can just see the outline of a door there." She pointed at it as she spoke. "The door's painted the same white as the wall, and you can barely see the latch. It's painted, too."

Aidan walked behind the display and felt around until he found the almost-invisible latch. It was really just an outer ring. He twisted it and pushed the door open. The tunnel beyond was empty, stretching into darkness.

He turned on the light the officer had given him and walked through the tunnel. He didn't protest when the others followed. Eventually he came to a wall and began looking around.

He glanced up at the ceiling—and saw a hatch. "Hey, anybody up there now? Gina!" he shouted. "Hey!"

He heard Gina Mason's voice as if from the bottom of a well. "Yeah, yeah, I'm in here!" Gina called down.

"Watch out!" he warned her.

He reached up and pulled on the clasp that held the

hatch door closed. It gave easily. All he had to do was figure out how the killer had hiked himself up into the tomb. Carrying a body…

A moment later, Gina's face appeared above him. "You've found it, Aidan," she said excitedly. "We couldn't see it from up here. The entry's kind of a stone square, just like the other ones on the floor."

Aidan turned to Van Camp. "The killer went to Sondra's office, knocked her out and…" He paused, looking at Mo. "He strangled her there. Well, the M.E. hasn't said so yet, but I'm willing to bet he will. Then the murderer carried the corpse right through the mortuary and down to the basement without being stopped or questioned. The guests, the tour groups, would've thought it was part of the show, and I'm assuming the actors were so busy with their own parts they didn't notice. He came through the tunnel with her and somehow got her body up there. But then how did he get the body out of there to put it in the coffin—just after the real actor who'd stepped out of the coffin had left?"

"He must've come back through here, with, um, both body parts," Mo said.

"We'll be talking to every performer who works here," Aidan muttered, "in case anyone was aware of an extra 'actor.'"

"There are a few employees who wear black with Haunted Mausoleum insignias on their shirts. They direct people and keep them moving, and they know where the exits are if there's an emergency," Mo explained.

"We'll be talking to them, too," he said. "We're reaching out to every single employee."

When they'd exited the basement, he hunkered down

beside Rollo, petting him and praising him. "Rollo, you are the best. You're a·very smart dog."

Rollo woofed his appreciation.

Aidan stood up and saw that Mo was almost as pale as the Woman in White she'd played.

"Mo? What's the matter?" *Besides the obvious,* he could have added.

"I was there. I was right there while it was happening," she said. "I should've known something. I should've *heard* something. Sondra was killed, and I was there and did nothing," Mo said.

"She was killed in the office, Mo. You couldn't have done anything."

She turned to him with glazed eyes. "You don't know that, Aidan. He knocks them out—but we aren't sure yet where he kills them."

"The evidence is that he kills them right away, Mo. She was knocked out and strangled, and then brought here. You couldn't have done a thing."

Aidan was reasonably certain of that, but there was room for doubt. Still, it was important now for Mo to believe it—true or not.

"I'll get you home," he said.

She shook her head stubbornly. "No. We're going to find…the rest of Sondra. She was a friend, and she was Grace's boss for years. We're not to let her head be a bizarre spectacle on the street somewhere."

Van Camp had been listening. "I have officers out looking at all the horsemen we know about," he said.

She nodded. "It might not be a headless horseman that's always up, always visible. It could be like part of someone's Halloween display."

"Do you have any ideas?" Aidan asked.

She stood for a minute, unmoving, her eyes closed. He started to fear that she might pass out. Van Camp placed a hand on Aidan's shoulder as they waited.

"There's one near the dry cleaners where we found Wendy Appleby's head, which is down the street from Tommy Jensen's. This horseman is part of a display in front of a big local retailer with a massive parking lot. They also have witches and goblins and pumpkins and other stuff. The headless horseman is the centerpiece," Mo said, opening her eyes.

"Let's go. Let's get there quickly before someone else discovers it," Aidan said.

"It's just my...theory. I may be wrong."

"But it is a logical conclusion," Aidan told her.

He didn't really think it was simply a logical conclusion. Mo had a gift, an ability he'd never seen before. She could close her eyes, it seemed, and somehow *watch* what had happened, watch it in her mind. She could envision what they were looking for.

She and Rollo made one heck of a team.

"I'll follow you," Van Camp said. He walked over to Gina Mason. "Have your team ready to go when I call you."

"My team only stretches so far," Gina responded in a tired voice.

"Get the county to send out another team," Van Camp said.

"Okay, I'll get in touch with them now."

Aidan took Mo's hand. Her eyes met his, and for a moment, he felt as if his heart had stopped. She was so stricken by what had happened. And he realized, looking into her eyes, that he was *involved* with her.

He'd hardly touched her yet—but he was involved with her as he'd never been with anyone else in his life.

Because he'd never dared so much before. He hadn't let women get close. He'd preferred one-night stands and affairs that he could easily escape. He'd believed that he deserved nothing but a life alone, a life with his own fears and...unusual abilities.

But Mo understood those fears, understood those abilities, and she'd shown him that loneliness didn't have to be his future. "We *will* get to the truth," he vowed.

She nodded. With Rollo at their heels, they left the graveyard and the mausoleum and made their way to his car. They were silent as they drove. He found that he didn't like the silence, that he suddenly wanted them both to be honest.

"How do you do it?" he asked her, looking for more than a partial or evasive answer this time.

"I wish I knew," she told him. "I...I think of the person. I see his or her face. Then I build something around the face. And then...well, as you saw, Rollo really does have his own talents."

"Do the dead speak to you, call to you?"

She winced. "Sometimes. At least, I *think* I hear a voice." She turned to him and said almost desperately, "But it's not always the dead. I find the living, too."

He reached for her hand and squeezed it. "That's a true gift, and if you don't believe me, ask someone you've been able to find. Ask J. J. Appleby," he added softly.

He hoped he'd helped her.

She directed him down the street past Tommy's place

and the little strip mall with the dry cleaners. "There," Mo said, pointing.

The store had a very large parking lot, convenient for shoppers. The Halloween display had been created beneath a giant sign advertising wholesale prices, claiming they bought surplus stock of the best brands.

The parking lot was empty except for a few cars near the door. It was very early morning. The first of the employees were probably coming in. Later, mothers or fathers might bring their children to enjoy the Halloween display. It was well designed, with a witch stirring a cauldron as bats on wires flew over her head. There was a smiling vampire on the other side, one that resembled the friendly count from a kids' TV show. And there were little leprechauns peering around the skirt of a fairy-tale princess. Dead center in the display was the headless horseman.

And, as Mo had seen in her mind's eye, he now had a head.

Van Camp and a number of police officers hurried up to them. Aidan slipped an arm around Mo's shoulder. "I can take you home now," he whispered.

He glanced at Van Camp, who nodded. "I've got this," he said. As Aidan started to turn, Van Camp said, "We'll have the employees assembled at the station in a matter of hours."

"Can you call me when they're in? And keep them separated as much as you can."

Van Camp offered him a grim smile. "We're actually pretty good cops, you know?"

"I do know," Aidan assured him with a conciliatory grin. "Sorry."

He left with Mo and Rollo; it was time to get away from murder and death.

Full daylight had broken by the time they arrived at her house. When she opened the front door, she said, "I know you have a million things to do. You should probably sleep. But…could you stay a little while? I'm sorry, I don't mean to be an annoyance, it's just that…"

"I'm here," he told her. Mo headed into the kitchen with Rollo. "Yes, you deserve a big treat, young man."

Aidan called Logan at the hotel, describing events as he'd seen them the night before.

Logan filled him in, too. "We followed Richard Highsmith's assistants and security force all night. Someone had an eye on them at all times. I'm assuming the charges against Jillian Durfey will be dropped by Monday morning, since she was nowhere near the latest murder scene."

"Oh, I'm sure. Listen, I'm going to catch a few hours' sleep on Mo's couch," he told Logan. "She's shaky, and I don't blame her." He sighed. "Except that I should be going to the M.E.'s office—"

"That's why we have a Krewe," Logan said. "One of us will get over to the M.E.'s. Probably Sloan. And then I'll head over to the station to start questioning employees. You'll be useless without some sleep."

"Yeah, I know. Thanks, Logan. And whether they dismiss the charges against Jillian Durfey or not, I *know* one of them is involved."

"I don't disagree. But whoever that person is, he or she is working with someone on the outside. Someone who knows Sleepy Hollow. It almost sounds as if we're looking for a historian."

"If you grow up around here, you grow up with

the history of the area. We're proud of our role in the Revolution—and very proud of our literary hero, Washington Irving. Most kids go to the various historic venues with their schools quite a few times. But I believe you're right—it *has* to be someone who knows Sleepy Hollow backward and forward."

"Yeah, but for now, just get some sleep, Aidan. We'll reassess when we see you."

"All right, I'll sleep for a few hours. My phone is on and it'll be next to me. Call if you need anything at all."

Mo was there, her eyes dull. She was obviously exhausted. And feeling guilty and in pain. In a way, she saw this as her fault.

"Mo," he said sternly, "like I told you before, you couldn't have done anything to save her."

"But...I was right there."

"Get some sleep," he ordered. "I'm going to."

She nodded. "Use the guest room."

"I'll take the sofa in the parlor."

"It's an antique, horribly uncomfortable."

Shaking his head, he smiled at her. "I'll be fine down here."

"Don't leave, please, without waking me."

"I won't."

She trudged up the stairs, Rollo trailing dutifully behind. The dog stopped to look at Aidan and whined.

"Hey, sleep down here with Aidan if you want. I'm way too tired to be offended," Mo told him, patting his head.

But Rollo was loyal to his mistress and followed her up.

Aidan leaned back on the sofa. He believed that

Richard had been betrayed by someone he considered a close confidant.

Somehow, it all had to do with the Woman in White, either Lizzie Hampton or her daughter, and the fact that Richard Highsmith could legitimately claim to be a descendant of Major John Andre.

Aidan wondered whether he was right about J. J. Appleby being Richard Highsmith's son.

He felt a moment of doubt, afraid that his theories were nonsense, and that he was focusing on the wrong direction.

But it was more than possible that at some point in his life, Richard had indulged in an affair.

And it was possible that he'd fathered a child with Wendy Appleby. They could have met in New York. Maybe Richard had talked about his home in Sleepy Hollow and that might've made Wendy think of this area when she left New York City. By all accounts, her life in recent years had been wrapped up in her son, and she'd shown little interest in dating. Of course, working at Mystic Magic had given her a reason to dislike men in general, since she'd usually seen them only when they had one thing on their minds.

But now...

Another murder. And while Sondra was being killed and Wendy Appleby's house ransacked, all five of their major suspects had been under surveillance.

He was just too tired. He let his eyes close and drifted off to sleep.

It felt good to lie down. Mo hadn't realized how physically exhausted she was until then. And when she lay there, listening to Rollo settle on the floor by her side, she reveled in the comfort of her bed. And the security of having an agent sleeping downstairs with a gun nearby. She could sleep in peace. Except that she couldn't really feel a sense of peace. What had happened tonight was so horrible, she couldn't even grasp it.

Sondra was dead. The thought struck like a dull thud in her temples.

How? Why?

Had she been killed just to divert suspicion from the woman who'd been arrested and arraigned and those who were with her? She didn't know that much about the law, but she assumed they'd dismiss the charges against Jillian Durfey now.

Had Sondra been nothing but a token kill? No, killing her had been too complex for that. Just as someone had known the convention hall and the graveyards, he or she knew the Haunted Mausoleum.

Mo tossed and turned and finally punched her pillows and told herself she was all right. Aidan was down in her parlor; Rollo was at her side.

She finally fell asleep. And when she did, she was in the dark forest again, the forest where Ichabod Crane had traveled and feared the headless horseman. She could smell the damp earth, feel the breeze and listen while the leaves rustled in the trees. Night creatures scampered; the light of the moon made skeletons of tree limbs.

And there was someone behind her.

She remembered the story. All she had to do was cross the bridge.

There was some kind of light before her on that bridge. In that light, she could see Aidan. He wasn't standing on the new bridge, not the modern structure that existed today. This one was wooden. It was old, and there was nothing else around it, nothing but the light and Aidan—waiting for her.

She could hear a rustling behind her...

Feel a pounding against the earth.

The horseman was coming, coming for her.

Aidan seemed to be trying to cross the bridge. But each time he tried, something seemed to throw him back.

Then she could feel hot breath on the back of her neck.

The hot breath of the horseman's stallion. He was so close.

"Aidan!" She called his name. He could reach her, she knew he could reach her, if only he'd let himself. Yet his eyes touched hers with misery and desperation and...

"Mo!"

She woke. Not instantly, she felt groggy. She was no longer in the forest. She was in her own bed, safe in her own house.

She blinked into the darkness, which was relieved only by a glimmer of light from the hallway. The whisper that had awakened her was soft.

She saw Candy there, accompanied by Colonel Daniel Parker. Rollo had gotten to his feet, wagging his tail as if he recognized that they had trusted visitors.

"What is it?" Mo asked.

"He's here!" Candy announced.

"Oh, you mean Aidan," Mo said. "He— Oh, it's a long story. There was another murder. He stayed at the house for me. I was kind of a wreck last night. Candy, the victim was someone I knew."

"She's not referring to your agent, Mo," Daniel told her. "His friend is here, the man who was killed. Richard Highsmith."

Mo stared at them both, threw off her covers and climbed out of bed. She ran to the landing but then paused. She didn't want to race downstairs like a crazy woman.

She started down quietly on her bare feet.

He was there, indeed. Richard Highsmith. He stood by the fireplace, looking at Aidan with the smile an old friend might give another.

He was speaking in a soft voice.

Mo continued down. At the first sound of a board creaking, Aidan was wide-awake, his hand instantly reaching for his gun.

He saw her and smiled. "Morning, Mo. Did you get some sleep?"

She nodded. "Aidan, Richard is here."

He was immediately alert, sitting straight up—and yet he didn't move.

Richard Highsmith turned to her. "He doesn't see me."

"He wants to. Richard, we need your help."

"Ask him what happened," Aidan said.

Aidan might not hear or see Richard, but Richard heard and saw him. "I was in the greenroom alone. Jilli had just gone out to the stage, and Taylor was talking to our security people. The convention woman—Bari, Bari Macaby—had gone to get me something. I went to wash my hands. I was scrubbing them when…darkness.

And then…I saw myself. Saw myself dead in a cavern and I was—in pieces."

"He never saw who killed him," Mo interpreted. "They came from behind when he was washing his hands. He doesn't know who did it."

"Ask him," Aidan said quietly, "if he knows *why*."

"He can hear you. He's standing by the fireplace," Mo pointed out.

Aidan turned in that direction. "Why? And why Wendy, too?"

Mo thought she saw tears in the ghost's eyes. He lowered his head, obviously finding it difficult to talk.

"For the love of God, I don't know," he said. "Wendy was…wonderful."

Mo didn't wait for Aidan to ask the next question. "Is J.J. your son?" she blurted out.

Richard raised his head to look at her. "I hope so. I believe so. But Wendy…she didn't want to trap me. Not when she first found out she was pregnant—and then… I don't know. We'd seen each other in the city many times…so long ago. We lost contact, and I hadn't heard from her in years.

"Then, one night last May, we ran into each other, believe it or not, on the street. In the city. We met and talked and I…I was in love all over again. We agreed to spend time together after I came here. I believe she was going to tell me that her child was my child. She said she had some special news that involved me and her child, and she had to give me the opportunity to choose. I think she didn't want me to face a political scandal. But, yes. She and J.J. were going to come to the convention center. She'd told everyone she was spending a few days in the city—but when the speech was over I was going to be free for the next few days. We were planning to stay at a motel on the highway, talk…"

Mo paraphrased his words for Aidan.

"Ask him why they both had notations about *Lizzie grave,*" Aidan said.

"I didn't know about it," Richard Highsmith replied. "Wendy said she'd been on a field trip with J.J.'s class and that she'd gotten interested in local history. She told me she'd found a reference to a woman who was murdered, a woman who had loved Major Andre." He paused. "She was aware that the major was an ancestor of mine. We were both going to look into it."

Again, Mo repeated his words.

Aidan was staring in the right direction. She thought he'd actually seen something of Lizzie and John Andre the other day.

If he would just let himself…

She remembered her dream, the nightmare in which he couldn't reach her.

Because he couldn't cross the bridge.

"Ask him—" Aidan began.

"Aidan," she said. "You ask him. Richard is your friend. He came to you for help. Please, let him talk to you."

"I can't…I can't see anymore."

"Yes, you can. I know you can—if you let yourself."

Aidan closed his eyes for a moment and sighed, his head bowed.

Then he looked up, directly at Richard.

Richard looked back at him, a crooked grin on his lips. "They got me, my old friend. They got me," he said quietly.

Somehow, the words made it through.

Aidan stood. "Richard," he breathed.

"I came to you because I know you're the only one who would understand—and the only man who'd believe that a dead man could help."

14

Aidan could see him.

He could see his old friend, almost as if he were there in the flesh.

For a moment, he was so shocked that his entire body seemed to go weak; luckily, the sofa was behind him, and when his knees buckled he simply sat down.

Richard moved away from the fireplace. He faded somewhat, but came and sat by Aidan on the sofa. The man looked at him with trust—trust Aidan wasn't sure he deserved.

"I'm not that good yet at...at keeping form, I guess," Richard said. "These people here, these very nice people, Candy and Daniel, have tried to advise me. It's in the concentration, they tell me. I'm learning. But you'll know I'm not being rude if I disappear."

Richard seemed to find the wry humor in his situation.

"I swear, we'll get to the truth," Aidan told him. He tried to regain his senses.

He'd always known that there was something more, that the dead could reveal themselves, that they could talk.

He had just denied it for so long. Denied his ability to see and to hear.

He tried to make his voice stop shaking. "It would've helped a lot if you'd told me more in my dream that night. Or if you'd shown up here—before we had to go tearing vaults and mausoleums apart."

"Sorry! I've been, er, coming to terms," Richard said. "But it seems you've had a good companion in Mo."

"Thank you." Mo nodded politely. "Let's get down to it, shall we? While we still have you, Richard."

"I don't know how much more I can tell you," Richard said. "It's true that I believe J.J. might be mine. But Wendy wasn't seeing anyone, hadn't seen anyone in years. So there was no jealous boyfriend—or ex-boyfriend—in the picture. And why would anyone kill over that, anyway? If anything, my political enemies would be pleased. There'd certainly be talk, whether it turned into a scandal or not. At the very least I'd be the no-good bastard who walked out on a pregnant woman."

"Did you receive any threats?" Aidan asked him.

Richard shook his head. "No, I've never gotten anything that sounded even slightly like a death threat."

"So," Aidan said, "you came here and you'd planned a romantic reunion with Wendy. Do you think the fact that she'd been working as a stripper had anything to do with…your deaths?"

"Why would it? Again, that would only please my enemies," he replied. "To the best of my knowledge, my life was moving forward. My personal life was about to be good again. I was coming home in the ways that really matter."

"Had you ever been out to the Haunted Mausoleum?" Mo asked. "Either when you lived here or more recently?"

"Oh, the old mortuary out on the farmland? Yes, once as a kid, on a class excursion. It was all about history at that time. We didn't call it haunted, although we all thought it was cool. We wanted to see the gruesome parts, but our teachers wanted to discuss history."

"That would have been when?"

"Almost thirty years ago. An old lady owned it back then—she sold it to the tour company soon after."

"Did you know Sondra Burke?" Mo asked.

"I never met her when I was alive," Richard answered. "Nor have I seen her…now."

"We may need to start looking at people who are obsessed with the old legends," Aidan said to Mo.

She smiled. "That's half of Tarrytown and Sleepy Hollow."

"Some people here don't care in the least," Richard told her. "My mom hadn't even read 'The Legend of Sleepy Hollow.' She just loved that the place was so beautiful." As he spoke, Aidan could gradually see the sofa through Richard.

The specter was fading.

"You'll come back?" Aidan asked.

"I will," Richard promised. "And thank you, old friend," he said quietly.

Then he vanished.

Aidan looked over at Mo. She was adorable and sensually beautiful at the same time. She wore one of her long T-shirt nightgowns. Her feet were bare and her hair tousled. She looked like someone who had just been rousted from bed.

He stood up and walked over to her, coming so close he was only an inch away.

"Thank you," he said gently.

Warmth emanated from her. Her eyes were on his, and a smile curved her lips. "You're welcome," she said.

Neither of them moved. He wondered if they were both hesitant, each waiting for other to make the next move.

Be a man, he told himself.

He stroked her cheek and felt the silky smoothness of it. She moved toward him, drawing even closer. She rose up and touched his lips with hers. He pulled her into his arms. She smelled as sweet as a spring day in the woods, with a hint of the earth about her. Desire came instinctively to life in him and he could have sworn his own body temperature spiked a thousand degrees as their lips met and melted, as he tasted her mouth. He felt the pressure of her hips against him, the crush of her breasts.

He took his mouth from hers and looked down into her eyes. He had no real idea what he was going to say. Probably something that would give her an out.

But he didn't.

Instead, the words that fell from his lips were, "I think I'm falling in love with you."

She smiled. "According to Grace, I was supposed to ask you to have sex with me several days ago."

He almost laughed. "Sex? Just sex?"

"I wasn't supposed to ask rudely or crudely, of course. Grace was firm about that. And Ron believed I should've told you that you had a great body and you shouldn't let it go to waste."

"And what did you think?"

"I didn't know what to say."

He kissed her again. Kissed her slow and long and deep, and allowed his hands to run down the contours of her back and splay over her buttocks, drawing her even harder against him. He felt her touch, her fingers over his back, felt the passion in the kiss she returned. Their path was charted; he wanted to taste her forever, and he wanted her clothes off and both of them naked together. While he savored the one sensation, he imagined the next and then...

His phone rang.

No.

He had to answer it. Mo knew that. She'd already backed away from him and was straightening her nightgown, watching him.

It was Logan, calling to say that they'd gotten the workforce from the Haunted Mausoleum down to the station. He didn't know how long they could keep them there.

"I'm on my way."

Aidan ended the call and looked at Mo.

"I have to go," he said huskily, and he was sure he'd never regretted anything so much in his whole life.

She smiled—and he knew he *was* falling in love with her.

"You're not going without me," she told him. "You shouldn't drive without coffee, anyway! If you make some, I'll be down in five, I swear it."

She took off for the stairs and paused just once. "Um, can we hold on to that thought—the one we were just having?

"Yes," Aidan promised. "Oh, yes."

Rollo barked.

"Okay, Rollo. You can come to the station with us," he said.

He was glad that he felt so comfortable walking into her kitchen. He knew how to make coffee there. This was— What? The third time? He thought about what Richard had said.

It was like coming home—when he hadn't even realized he'd been away.

Logan Raintree was at the station when Mo and Aidan arrived; he was the first to meet them at reception. He didn't seem surprised to see Mo and he greeted her cordially—and Rollo, too.

"Everyone who was working last night is here," Logan told Aidan. "And so far not one has complained about being called in. A number of them have been crying. They lost an employer they all cared about."

Lieutenant Purbeck came out to the reception area. "Mahoney." He nodded at Aidan. "Glad you're here. Van Camp's been talking to people, but I'm down one officer. Agent Raintree here assigned Voorhaven to do guard duty with the little boy, J. J. Appleby," he said, glancing at Logan.

"J.J. really likes Jimmy," Logan explained. "And we feel J.J. and Debbie need to be protected until we get to the bottom of this."

If they got to the bottom of it.

The unspoken words seemed to linger in the air. No one said them.

No one here would accept them or would even willingly acknowledge that possibility. Mo knew that without a doubt.

Purbeck smiled at her. "You doing okay, Mo?"

She nodded.

"Thank you again. You and Rollo. You were there last night, too, right?"

"I was," Mo said. It still bothered her terribly.

Why hadn't she heard—or sensed—anything wrong?

"And you saw nothing?"

"Nothing at all," she said with disgust. "I thought the night was so routine, it was almost ridiculous. I walked around and around."

"Too bad Rollo wasn't playing a ghost dog," Purbeck noted. "Anyway, Aidan, I'm stepping out of my office. You can do your interviews there. Mo? You want to hang with me? I'll get you some typically bad coffee."

She started to tell him that, sure, that would be nice.

But Aidan said, "I'd prefer to have her sit in with me. She knows all the players, and she knows the place. She'll be able to tell if what she hears is the truth. It might make a difference. We're not interrogating these people, we're hoping to get something from them."

"As you like," Purbeck agreed.

"I'll start sending them through," Logan said.

"Great. But, Lieutenant Purbeck, can we begin in the conference room? I'd like to throw them all together first," Aidan said.

Within ten minutes, everyone had gathered in the conference room. Those who hadn't yet greeted one another with hugs of commiseration did so. Everyone crowded around to pet Rollo, too. Hug him, actually. The dog must have seemed like a bastion of strength and normalcy to them. Grace, Ron and Phil came over to Mo and hugged her especially tight. Then they all found places to sit.

"So," Aidan said, from his position at the head of the table. "We all know what happened last night. And I am so very sorry for your loss. I met Sondra Burke briefly, and she was lovely."

Heads bowed.

He looked over at a young woman whose white-blond hair contrasted dramatically with her tanned skin. "Ms. Chessy, right? You were at the hostess stand, taking money?"

Cindy Chessy, a nice enough girl Mo barely knew, nodded vigorously.

"Did you see anyone who looked out of place?" Aidan asked.

"No. No one weirder than usual," she replied. "People aren't allowed to wear costumes when they come here. Only the actors can wear costumes. That way, no guests can try to freak people out or get into anything."

"Makes sense. What did you do after you sold the last ticket?"

"Closed the entry gate and took the lockbox to the office. Sondra wasn't there, but I didn't think anything of it. She slips out to observe sometimes."

"And then you left?"

"Yes." Tears welled in her eyes. "Then I left. I'm always first out of there. I'm not an actor—and I'm not paid as much as the actors. They know I leave early and no one cares."

"I'm sure they don't." He had a group of folders in front of him, folders containing each person's work file.

"Let's see. Phil and Ron, we talked last night. So let me start with Joshua Kirbin," Aidan said.

"Me?" Joshua squeaked. He was sagging against the wall. There were only about twelve chairs at the conference table and the people who weren't in them either leaned against the wall or sat on the floor.

"You were in the coffin," Aidan said.

"Whatever happened, it happened after I was gone," Joshua insisted. "I had plans last night, so I got out of there as fast as I could. The Ripper—Jack the Ripper." He pointed at Phil. "You saw me."

"I told them I saw you leave, yes," Phil said, "and that was maybe…ten minutes before I saw the body. Or rather, that there was something in the coffin." Aidan swiveled in his chair to look across the table. He gestured at a tall boy, a senior at the local college, Mo thought. His name was Harry Pickford.

"Harry, you were playing the mad doctor. Do you remember somebody going by to get to the doorway behind you?"

Harry stood up, opened his mouth and then sank back in his chair. "Yes," he said. He glanced over at Phil. "I thought it was you— Someone in a sweeping black cloak like yours but with a hat lowered over his face. I thought…I thought it was a new gimmick."

"Me!" Phil protested. His voice sounded like a squeak, too. "I never left my place. I was outside all night."

"Weren't the historical characters inside, and outside it was the legendary characters and well-known ghosts?"

"Mostly, yes, but…Jack the Ripper was supposed to skulk through the cemetery and show up unexpectedly. So I did my little walk around one of the tombs. Like Mo," Phil said.

"Anyone else see this Jack the Ripper character slipping past?" Aidan asked.

"I'm pretty sure I saw him go by," another young man, Perry Lichtman, said. He raised his hand as he spoke, as if they were in school. "I'm the one being operated on by the mad doctor. I saw *something*—but I'm in this boxlike thing, poking my head out, screaming most of the time. I saw someone out of the corner of my eye. He seemed to be bent over."

"No one would think anything of it," a girl, Mindy Myers, who played Countess Bathory, told Aidan. "The Grim Reaper—Tony over there—flits around the place all the time."

"Did any of you see anyone go to the office last night?" Aidan asked next.

The room was silent as they looked at one another, shaking their heads.

"No, but I thought that the person moving around like a hunchback and carrying a big sack was Tony," Ron said. "The Grim Reaper."

"So, you saw it, too?"

"Yeah, I usually sit in the dressing room and read magazines or whatever, waiting to clean up at the end. I leave with Sondra. Or, if she's already gone, I make sure everyone else is out before we close up. Sometimes during the show I wander through to see how people look in their makeup and do costume checks. I saw the figure moving—and I thought Tony was doing a hell of a job," he added dryly.

Mo had been standing by the back wall, Rollo obediently crouched beside her. She suddenly felt weak and decided to sit on the floor. They'd all been there, at the mausoleum; they'd all been there while a killer had snuck in on Sondra and killed her. Then that killer had come through the place, carrying Sondra, to behead her in the mausoleum. After that, he'd crept back through the whole site with the head and the body. He'd left the body—and gone on to display the head. And no one had noticed him, seen what he was doing, even when he'd been right in front of them.

"So, the killer slipped into the office, killed Sondra and came out among you, without anyone thinking he was anything but part of the show?" Aidan asked.

They all stared back at him. Then someone started to cry.

"I'm not trying to upset you. I'm trying to find her killer," he said. "If anyone remembers anything else, please get hold of us as quickly as you can." He stood and handed out his cards, then turned to introduce Lee Van Camp. "If you don't reach me or someone at the main number on that card, call the station—or you can call Detective Van Camp directly."

Lee nodded and walked around the room, also handing out cards.

"Thank you all for coming in," Aidan said.

"We're free to go?" someone asked.

"You're free to go." Purbeck had been just outside, by the door. When the last of the Haunted Mausoleum employees had filed out, he came in to speak to Aidan.

"I heard from the M.E.," he said quietly. "Same everything. Chloroform to knock out his victim. Manual strangulation—and then beheading. There's one thing that's a little bit different. He's cleaner with his hatchet. He's learning how to remove the head with greater ease."

Aidan was silent for a minute. "They say that the horror of the French Revolution went on as long as it did because the guillotine was so swift and sure. We have to stop this guy before he gets any better."

"Well, in a way, we're further behind than we were. The charges against Jillian Durfey have been dismissed. No judge was going to hold her to a court date with this new killing that's taken place," Purbeck said.

"We need another task force meeting," Aidan told him. "We're moving in the right direction. What we need is a lot more research. The killer is organized, knowledgeable and intelligent—and he's thumbing his nose at us. Can we get everyone together?"

"Van Camp?"

"Thirty minutes, sir."

"What about your people, Mahoney?"

"Logan is here. Sloan is at the morgue. Jane and Will are watching Richard Highsmith's people."

"Highsmith's bunch is free to leave at any time," Purbeck reminded Aidan.

"We're still following them," Aidan said. He smiled at Mo and inclined his head. "I think a few of your co-workers are hanging around out in the hall, waiting for you."

"Oh," she said. "I'm not sure—"

"We have thirty minutes," he said. "Want some coffee?"

"Some? I'd take a gallon."

She walked to the door with Rollo on a short leash. When she turned, Aidan and Logan were behind her. Logan was friendly and courteous; he had an air of easy confidence about him and a polite concern for those around him. She thought he was a good match for Aidan. They seemed to work well together, as equals.

They dealt with some horrible cases, she thought.

So did she. But sometimes, she found the living. And that made it all worthwhile. Sometimes…

Maybe it even helped the dead, appeased them and brought them peace, when the truth was uncovered and justice was served.

Logan opened the door for her, so she and Rollo stepped out into the hallway.

"We waited for you," Grace said.

"Yeah, we wanted to say goodbye," Phil added.

"We couldn't leave without saying goodbye," Ron told her. He frowned at Aidan. "I saw him. I saw him and didn't even know it."

"Could you speak with a colleague of ours, so she can do a sketch?" Aidan asked. He then introduced Logan to the group.

Purbeck came out. "This is a police station, not a social club!" he said. Then he smiled, belying the harshness of his words. "There's a coffee shop next door. Get out of here for now, get yourselves something to eat or drink. See what comes up when you relax a bit. That can work, you know. And take Detective Van Camp with you. Van Camp, that's an order. Grab something to eat. Everyone's been on this around the clock, and we're going to have to stay on it around the clock until the killer's caught, so we're in it for the long haul. Now go."

He made a shooing motion. "And be back in thirty!" he said as he turned and walked toward his office.

Van Camp seemed a little uncomfortable.

Grace hooked her arm through his. "Please, Detective, join us. We're all scared. It's good to have another cop with us."

She marched toward the elevators, and Van Camp looked back at them with a hint of panic on his face.

Aidan grinned at Mo. "He's a good guy," he said in a low voice.

They were lucky in their timing at the café. It was late for lunch and too early for dinner. They were seated immediately and their waitress promised she'd have their food out quickly.

Mo had been keeping Rollo in his service-dog vest, so there was no problem with having him there. He lay quietly under the table.

Better yet, their waitress was a dog lover. She brought him a huge bowl of water before she even produced menus.

Watching Aidan, Logan and Van Camp, Mo thought Purbeck was no fool. Yes, it was a social setting, but no one there could stop talking about what had happened.

They all scanned the menu and ordered. When the waitress left the table there was silence for a minute. "Where did you get your costumes for the Haunted Mausoleum?" Aidan asked, bringing the conversation back to what was on everyone's mind. "You said that you thought the killer was one of your actors, Ron, but wouldn't you know which costumes were yours? I'm assuming you have a count?"

"We do, but we have several cloaks for a grim reaper, and a number of men's trench coats and frock coats. People have to substitute for one another sometimes, or we have to bring in a new actor to replace someone we've lost, and not everyone takes the same size. The attraction has existed for over a decade now, so we've accumulated a pretty decent wardrobe selection," Ron told him.

"But you'd know something was missing if you went in there and counted?"

"Well, of course. We keep an inventory list," Ron said.

"Most people get out of their costumes before they leave," Phil put in. "But some people wear them home. They're trusted to bring them back."

"You still know who does and doesn't change on the premises, right?" Aidan persisted.

"I know exactly who wears what. And if you take it home, you're responsible for getting it back," Ron said.

Their food arrived.

"What about that tunnel?" Van Camp had been quiet. After the waitress delivered their food, he suddenly spoke up. "Who knew it was there?"

Mo shook her head. "I didn't."

"I never thought about it," Grace said. "We hear so much, we learn so much—as guides, I mean—but we never used the tunnel, we never took people there. Technically, the business could do what it wanted with the property, but…it's historical. It's maintained with integrity. Okay, maybe the Haunted Mausoleum doesn't seem like it has a lot of integrity, but that's for fun."

"Yeah, and it helps support a lot of the 'integrity' through the rest of the year," Phil pointed out. "There's not always a lot of tourism here. Some months are lean."

Van Camp turned to Aidan. "I'll go with Ron and find out if anything's missing from their costume supply. I don't need to be at the task force meeting. You can bring the officers up to date."

"I'll head out with Lee and Ron, take a look around the site. I haven't seen it yet," Logan told him.

"Ah…can we go, too?" Phil asked, gesturing at Grace and Mo. "Maybe you'll need us for something."

"Mo and Rollo should stick with me," Aidan said.

"Rollo will be a real asset. The officers sometimes trust a dog more than they do a federal agent."

"Feds! They're suspicious people. I mean, we all love the FBI —and we're all suspicious of it!" Phil said, and nodded knowingly, bringing a laugh from everyone around the table. It felt good to laugh.

"It might help more if we have Mo and Rollo with us. Let's meet back at the Haunted Mausoleum when you've finished with the task force meeting. I doubt you'll be that long."

Mo studied Aidan, waiting for his reaction. She almost smiled—but managed not to.

He didn't like her being away from him now, she thought. Was he worried about her?

Whatever the reason, it was nice.

"Okay," he agreed with obvious reluctance. "I'll go over the facts and tell the officers what they need to be looking for out there."

"I think it is smarter if I go with Logan and Detective Van Camp," Mo said. "I was there last night, walking around the mausoleum where Sondra was beheaded." She paused for a minute. "Ron, do you think she could have been killed because of something she knew? Something she'd discovered?"

"Like what?" Ron asked her.

"When you were doing my makeup, remember? She came by and talked about how she'd like a research assistant. She mentioned the Continental currency that had disappeared before the Civil War. She thought it made for interesting history—and that it would be worth a fortune."

"But she didn't know where it was. If she'd found it, yes, that might have been a motive. But she hadn't..."

"Interesting," Aidan murmured.

"Continental currency?" Ron asked, still skeptical. "I really doubt it."

"People kill for money often enough," Aidan said with a shrug. "Mo, that's something you could research."

"I can try. It's a story I haven't heard before."

"But you have a good library, with lots of old books. Maybe we should follow up on that."

She nodded. "I will," she said. "But for now, I'll go with Detective Van Camp and Logan and the others."

"I'll keep an eye on everyone, and we'll be surrounded by cops," Logan said.

Aidan got to his feet. "Fine. Let's go, then. I'll meet up with you there." He hesitated. "We're already losing daylight."

"I can get all the houselights and the floodlights up," Ron assured him.

"All right. I'll see you there," Aidan said.

When they left the restaurant, Mo found that she was going to be driving out with Logan. It seemed to be a natural assumption. Phil, Ron and Grace had come to the station together.

Rollo sat in the back. As they turned onto the street, Logan asked her quietly, "How long have you been seeing the dead?"

She turned to him, surprised. He flashed her a smile. "I think you have a great dog—but I think you have a lot more. Aidan is new to us, but he has it, too. He doesn't want to *think* he does. He prefers to believe that he doesn't really belong with the Krewe."

"He may feel differently now," Mo said. "You all don't...know each other very well?"

"He just transferred into our unit. Our director, Adam Harrison, is an elderly gentleman who never went through the academy. He was sought out. Adam just had a talent for hiring the right people. He lost a son who had real precognition and after that...well, he recognized it in others.

"He started with Jackson Crow, who's basically commander in chief of our field agents. Adam has a way of watching people. He'd been watching Aidan for a while, and he liked what he saw. Adam can home in on particular and sometimes unusual skills, even when people don't see it or admit it themselves. So, how long have you been seeing the dead?"

"Since I was a kid. I was lucky because I had a dog then, too. Rollo's mom, Heidi. I just let everyone think the dog did it all— Oh, and trust me! Rollo is a great scent hound, although wolfhounds are supposed to be sight hounds. Anyway, it works for us." Mo frowned. "You see the dead, too?"

He nodded, watching the traffic. "When they want to be seen—and can be seen. With everything we've done and everything I've seen, I've still never figured out why some just go on and others stay behind. However, it makes sense to me that a man like Richard Highsmith would linger. He'd want the truth—and he'd want justice." He glanced at her. "Has he stayed on?"

"Yes, but it was just today that he managed to talk to us. And actually, what he told us, Aidan had already surmised."

"Ah, but knowing that you're not wasting time developing a theory that's taking you in the wrong direction can be important!"

When they reached the Haunted Mausoleum they

found an officer on duty overseeing the crime scene. Van Camp identified himself, and Ron hurried up to the porch and passed the massive columns, stopping in front of the crime scene tape at the door.

"Don't worry," Van Camp said with a wry grin. "We have more tape."

Rollo hung obediently at Mo's side.

The killer wasn't here anymore, Mo thought. There was nothing for Rollo to find, and Rollo knew that, just as she did.

At the task force meeting, Gina Mason gave a frustrated report on the forensics findings. The blood discovered on the tools at the beheading sites belonged to the victims. The tools had been wiped clean of fingerprints at both locations.

"One thing we did get last night—tire tracks. By the cemetery. We've narrowed down the tires to a new make and model by a specialty company—Horsepower. They've become popular in this region, though, because they're excellent on snow. But the make and model suggest that the vehicle we're looking for is a medium-size SUV or van. So keep your eyes open and make traffic stops on those vehicles when you can. Remember, serial killer Ted Bundy was caught because of a broken taillight."

Dr. Mortenson told them that, fortunately, the beheading appeared to have once again been postmortem.

What Aidan had to say took longer.

"Years ago—years and years ago—the Hudson Valley was a hotbed of activity for the Revolutionary War. As we all know, one of our most talented American generals defected to the British, and he did so with the assistance of a brilliant and charming British officer, Major John Andre," he began. He realized that the officers, detectives and technicians in the room were looking at him as if he'd lost his mind.

"Bear with me," he told them. "I believe it's all related. Major Andre fell in love with a local girl, a patriot. He was hanged, and she went on to bear a child. An old suitor and several of his friends murdered her, either because they thought she'd betrayed the Americans, or possibly her suitor urged it on because he was enraged by what he saw as a personal betrayal. But the lady had expected something like that might happen. She'd given the little girl over to the care of a cousin, whose name was Bakker. The family had a mausoleum at the old graveyard by Sleepy Hollow Cemetery. And the child is entombed there under what became her maiden name, Bakker—and the name she married into. Highsmith."

No one protested or said anything. They just stared at him blankly.

"History repeats itself. Years later, in New York City, a man meets a woman. He's a politician, she's a Broadway dancer. When she becomes pregnant, she hides the fact from him because she doesn't want to put a rising political star in a compromising position. The man was Richard Highsmith, and the woman was Wendy Appleby.

"We know that Wendy was not killed accidentally. She was targeted. But I believe she and Richard were targeted for some reason having to do with the distant past. Exactly what or why, I don't know yet.

"Now, here's what we *do* know, or what we feel we're safe to assume. The killer is not just familiar

with Sleepy Hollow history, he's immersed in it. He—
or an accomplice?—studied it, or at least specific aspects of it. He grew up going on field trips to every
historic building and venue here. I say *he* because we
suspect it's a man. Dr. Mortenson says the strength
needed to strangle a person to death is considerable,
and the bruises on the victim's necks suggest power-
ful hands.

"We could, of course, be looking for a very strong
woman. I'm referring to the person who physically carried out the killings. But I believe that someone in Richard Highsmith's life was the orchestrator."

"What about Sondra Burke?" an officer asked.
"What do you think is the reason for her death?"

"Three possibilities. She was killed to make it look
like the killings were random. Or there's a connection
between her and Highsmith and Appleby. Or...I recently learned that she was checking into a story about
Continental currency—worth a fortune in today's col-
lectibles market. Except that she hadn't found it.

"Maybe someone thought she was close. Whatever
the reason, and we'll be examining every possibility,
her killer carried out her murder, dragging her dead
body around the Haunted Mausoleum as if she were
nothing but a prop. We need to research any connection. But during your workday, be on the alert for those
who know the area and seem fixated on the history,
especially pertaining to the graveyards. Watch for the
kind of vehicle Gina described. And we'll continue to
keep an eye on the Highsmith retinue."

There were a few questions and he did his best to
answer them. No, he didn't believe any of the mausoleum employees were involved. Yes, they'd be canvass-

ing local hardware stores to find out whether anyone on staff recalled selling the tools the killer had left behind. And, yes, an officer had been detailed to go through DMV records.

When the meeting broke up, Aidan called Jane. "I'd like to pull phone records. I don't want a wiretap on anyone, just records from the past couple of months."

"Who do you want?" she asked.

"Highsmith's party."

"I'll get them. What am I looking for specifically?"

"Conversations among the five in Richard's retinue—Taylor Branch, Jillian Durfey and the security trio."

"Consider it done."

He put a call through to Logan; the group was still at the mausoleum, so he left the station and drove out to join them.

He wondered idly if it made him a bad person—or just a bad agent—to want the day to end so he could be alone with Mo.

15

Van Camp and Logan Raintree watched as Ron described the various setups and themes at the Haunted Mausoleum. Following that, Grace, Phil and Mo went through the different actions, showing them where everyone was and when. Mo was standing by "her" mausoleum—where a woman, *a friend* had been beheaded—when it occurred to her to walk around the massive iron fence that surrounded the property.

"The police have already done that," Van Camp told her.

"I figured as much," she said. "But we worked out how the killer murdered Sondra and carried her past probably hundreds of people. Then he went into to the tomb to behead her. After that, he must have come out the same way…with both body parts. He had to wait until Joshua Kirbin was gone for the night to get the body into the coffin and then he had to leave. That means he just walked out of here—carrying a human head."

Van Camp nodded, his mouth tight.

"So, he left with a head, which had to be wrapped

in something, and he walked right out among everyone else?" Mo asked incredulously.

"So it appears."

"*Someone* must've seen him leave. One of us, I mean."

Van Camp looked like a weary bulldog when he said, "All right. We'll make calls again to try and find someone who did see something. I guess it's a different question now. Did you see any coworkers in costume leaving with a bundle?"

Rollo suddenly began to bark excitedly, and Mo saw that Aidan had arrived.

She realized that just seeing him brought color to her cheeks. She lowered her head as she gave Rollo permission to rush off and greet him. When he joined the group, Logan filled him in on their latest thoughts.

They walked out of the graveyard and went to the costume and makeup area. Mo felt Aidan behind her, his hand on her back, and knew that she was enraptured by him. She didn't want to dwell on what had happened—on death or murder or Sleepy Hollow. She didn't want to think about the future.

She just wanted the night to come.

"The costume was ours," Ron announced. "Unless someone else took home a grim reaper outfit last night. Whoever did this knew how to sneak in here when I was out among the guests, and he knew how to slip out with what he wanted. There's a slouch hat missing, too. He wasn't just familiar with this place, but with everyone's schedule and habits and exactly how the show ran."

Van Camp had been on the phone, but now he approached them. "It's an SUV we're looking for. A dark SUV. Harry Pickford—the kid who plays the mad doctor—was one of the last people out. He was waving to some friends in the parking lot and saw an actor in a grim reaper getup leave in a dark SUV."

"And he didn't mention that at the meeting?" Aidan asked, aggravated.

"He didn't think about it, he says. And that's because he was sure whoever waved back at him was one of his friends," Van Camp said. "So we'll get our people searching the county DMV records for registered dark SUVs. That's a whole lot more specific than just any van or SUV. It could be our first real break."

"Gina finished with one of their forensic searches," Aidan said. "The tire track they got was for a new brand—Horsepower. The problem is, it's become popular, and hundreds, maybe thousands, have been sold in this area. Harry Pickford didn't happen to get a make or model, did he?"

"No," Van Camp said. "No such luck. We'll keep talking to other employees and try to get it narrowed down."

"Let's call it a night," Logan suggested. "We'll start fresh in the morning. Will Chan can find just about anything as far as a record goes. We'll let his computer do the walking for a while."

"What about us?" Grace asked. "Are we...safe?"

"I'll follow you all home," Logan said.

"Just follow us to Grace's house." Ron shivered. "We'll stay together."

"I'm going to the hotel. I'll relieve Jimmy for a while," Van Camp said. "He's been sitting with Debbie Howell and the kid for a long time. I'll take over. I know they're on the same floor as you FBI guys, but it's scary for the poor kid. His mother murdered—and the father he didn't even know killed at the same time. There's some serious therapy ahead for that kid."

"The detective is watching Debbie Howell?" Phil said. "No hardship in that!"

"Hey, when did *you* last see Debbie Howell?" Grace asked him.

Phil flushed. "Some of us go to strip clubs. So what?"

"She was kind of a dorky kid—but she sure turned out pretty. And she has a great body," Grace said.

"Debbie is okay." Mo immediately defended her. "There's nothing wrong with what she's doing, either. She's a wonderful dancer and she was making an honest living. Anyway," she added, "Debbie quit that job."

Grace laughed. "I didn't say there was anything wrong with it. But Debbie Howell's always been kind of on the outside. You know, the kind who tries too hard. She was never really popular and always hung around on the edges. Sort of pathetic."

"Grace, don't judge," Mo snapped.

"And let's not stand around talking about her," Aidan said. "Sleep has been sadly lacking in our circles lately. Let's lock this place up and get some rest."

Mo was eager to leave. She was sure that Aidan was just as eager to get to the house as she was.

No one commented on the fact that she and Rollo got into his car. It had come to be expected by his Krewe that they'd be together, she thought.

And yet, as soon as they were on their way, he said, "There has to be a connection."

"A connection?"

"Between Sondra and Richard and Wendy," he said.

"You don't think Sondra was killed just to get suspicion off Jillian Durfey?"

"No. I considered it but I've ruled it out. Because I don't think Jillian was guilty. I tend to think it was Branch—and yet Richard was his whole career." Aidan sighed tiredly. "Maybe I'm completely wrong. I don't know. I'm just frustrated. By all accounts, Wendy Appleby was a very private person. But I believe that someone knew she was going to see Richard. Maybe that person even knew the codes to get into the center." He looked at her. "Tell me if you can think of any possible connections between Sondra and Richard and Wendy. Any idea at all would be great."

She nodded, despite a surge of disappointment. She'd felt so certain that he'd been obsessively anticipating the two of them being alone—as she had. Apparently not, since his mind was still churning with the case. Yet she understood how difficult it was to stop trying to solve the kinds of puzzles it created.

When they reached the house, she went straight to her office and started scanning the books.

And that was when he came up behind her. He turned her into his arms.

"I didn't mean this second!" he whispered.

His lips touched hers as she slipped her hands beneath his coat and sweater, sliding them along his bare skin. She felt him tremble as they deepened the kiss. He continued to kiss her while struggling out of his coat, then helped her out of hers until both coats lay on the floor. His mouth lifted from hers as she moved her hands along his back.

"Gun," he whispered.

"What?"

"Gun...I need it by me...." He pulled away for a minute and his eyes met hers filled with humor, a bit of awkwardness and a hunger that made her heart and all her senses soar. "Bedroom?"

"Yes. I have one," she said, and laughed.

He caught her hand and headed for the stairs. When they entered her room, she turned into his arms again. He found her lips, then drew back.

"What?" she asked.

"Dog?"

"Oh, Rollo, I'm sorry. You're in the hallway tonight!"

She ushered the dog out, then stepped back into the room and closed the door. It was dark, but she'd left the drapes open, and moonlight shone in on them. He removed his holster and the gun he carried and set them on the bedside table. Then he was back with her. She helped him take off his sweater; he took off hers. They kissed again. And kissed. And each insinuation of his tongue seemed to hint at things to come and increase the sweet arousal that was coursing through her veins.

She slid her fingers under his waistband and felt him tense at her touch. She found his belt and loosened the buckle, then let her hands move along his hips, pulling down his jeans and briefs, and reveling in the sensation of need and desire...and Aidan. His hands were on her naked flesh and she felt each touch like a burst of flame.

His arms swept around her and they fell on the bed together, where he kicked off his shoes and finished stripping off his jeans and briefs. He turned to her, this time encircling her in his arms as he brought her down with him. His finger moved around to her bra strap and he freed her breasts, lowering his mouth to each nipple, teasing and stroking with his mouth and tongue. She writhed, coming closer and closer to him.

But he was a smooth and practiced lover, sliding his hands along her arms to catch hold of her hands, raising them high above her head as he kissed her lips, then her collarbone, and her breasts again, then slipping to her midriff and below. The weight of his body was vibrant and hot, and she threaded her fingers through his hair. He moved ever lower, teasing, kissing, caressing. Her inner thighs received his kisses until she burned like wildfire at the place between them.

He made love to her in a way that left her gasping and straining and arching until a delicious climax broke over her. There were moments during which she felt she wasn't even there anymore as she drifted to some higher place of ecstasy. Then he shifted on top of her, his eyes like the deep blue sea, gazing into hers. Their mouths met again and she skimmed her hands between them, down the length of him, and touched his arousal. Her slightest touch had him adjusting his weight.

Then he pulled away, groaning as if he was being tortured.

"What?"

"I dreamed of this all day, and…my pockets. I have to look in my pockets."

"Birth control?" she whispered.

"Yes."

"I'm prepared."

"Oh," he said. "There isn't someone… Is there a reason we shouldn't—"

She smiled. "No. I've just been ever hopeful that… that someone like you would come along in my life."

He smiled, too, and stroked her cheek with the utmost tenderness.

Then he muttered, "Thank God!"

And he moved into her with a smooth thrust, overwhelming her with sensations and emotions she'd never known.

She hadn't thought she could so quickly soar again, but she did. As he moved inside her, she was achingly aware of her own raw need and desire, and she was deliriously glad she'd never settled, that she had waited—for someone like him.

They'd both shut themselves off, she thought. She emotionally and physically, Aidan emotionally. She was sure he was far more experienced than she, and yet she sensed that this experience was still somehow different.

She forgot the world and was glad that only the moonlight drifted in, riding over his bare shoulders and the muscles that gleamed, sleek with sweat, as they moved together. The things he could do, the way he touched her, kissed her, arched against the feel of her fingers on his back…it all seemed to heighten the driving climax between them. And when it happened, she cried out, the feeling so wonderfully erotic and explosive she couldn't contain the sound.

From the hallway, Rollo barked, afraid she was being hurt.

She and Aidan both froze with him looking down at her, smiling as he breathed hard and his heart thundered.

"Dog," he muttered. "I guess I have to let him know I didn't hurt you."

"I will!" Mo said.

She leaped up, dragging the sheet with her, and

opened the door to the hallway. Rollo looked at her, barking.

"Not used to me having a life, eh, boy?" she asked. "I'm okay. Go back to sleep!" Rollo evidently believed her. He barked again, walked in a circle, then found a place on the floor.

She walked back into the bedroom and laughed, looking at Aidan.

"I beg your pardon?"

He was simply worn-out, but his physical perfection, the way his head rested on the pillows and his body reclined on the bed, reminded her of a classic sculpture.

"No, no, not laughing *at* you. I'm happy, that's all," she said, running over to join him. She slid in next to him, curling up against his side, and he kissed her again. A moment later, she became fascinated with his shoulders. "What's this scar?" she asked.

"I took a bullet."

"And you do that often?"

"Not as often as you might think. An awful lot of what we do in the FBI is research."

She frowned, finding another scar. "Bullet, too?" she asked.

He shook his head. "I fell climbing a fence when I was ten," he told her. His eyes glittered teasingly. "Did you want to make a thorough inspection?" he asked.

She smiled and crawled on top of him. "I intend to. *Very* thorough," she said, and leaned down to press her lips to his chest.

And then she heard his phone ring. Another inopportune call, she thought. Another interruption. It was in the pocket of his jeans, down at the foot of the bed.

Their eyes met. Neither of them wanted to answer it. And yet they both moved to do so at the same time.

Mo reached his jeans first and handed them to him. He dug in the pocket and pulled out his cell. She watched his face. "I'll be there as soon as possible," he was saying. "And, yes, I'll have Mo and Rollo."

He hung up and looked at Mo. "Jimmy Voorhaven, Debbie Howell and J.J. have disappeared."

"*What?* How is that possible?"

He let out a breath. "Voorhaven took the two of them to a restaurant near the hotel to get something to eat. They didn't come back."

Aidan was glad he was with his Krewe. By the time they got to the hotel, everyone there had already rolled into action. Will and Sloan had taken off to check out Jimmy's home, Debbie's place and the Appleby residence. Jane was staying put, scanning the cameras. Logan had gone to speak with Jillian Durfey, Taylor Branch and the security trio. None of the five had left the hotel; the Krewe was aware of that because Will Chan's cameras had been monitoring the halls and doorways.

When Van Camp had arrived to relieve Jimmy, the detective and his charges had apparently just left. So he'd waited. But then Jimmy, Debbie and J.J. hadn't come back.

Jillian was in the hallway. Taylor was there, too. He had an arm around Jillian's shoulders.

"I told you I was set up!" Jillian insisted. "And now... where are they?"

"They're probably fine," Taylor said. "You didn't see the two of them together, did you?" he asked, turning to Aidan. "Debbie seemed to idolize that detective, and I'm sure he noticed. They might have headed out to spend some time together without being watched."

"With a young boy?" Logan didn't hide his skepticism. "Hardly."

Rollo was given pieces of clothing that belonged to Jimmy Voorhaven, Debbie Howell and J.J. They started behind the restaurant, where Rollo barked and paced in circles, then tugged at his leash, urging them back to the hotel. At the parking lot, he made his way to the rear—a shaded spot away from the security cameras near the restaurant.

"They got into a car here," Mo said. "Rollo can't take us much farther unless we have a place to begin."

"A tomb or a vault," Aidan said. "A cemetery."

Mo looked at him, her eyes wide.

"Which one?" he asked her. "I'd thought the killer would stick to one area, but we found his first lair— and we found the second."

"They must've been taken by surprise," Van Camp said. "Jimmy's a good cop. He loves kids, too. He'd have died for that boy in a heartbeat."

"Unless…" Aidan said.

"What?" Van Camp demanded.

"Unless Jimmy is in on it somehow."

"No. No way," Van Camp said firmly. "You don't know Jimmy."

"And," Logan pointed out, "Jimmy was here—at the hotel—when Sondra was killed last night. Debbie, too."

Aidan hesitated uncomfortably. "Granted, it's not likely but it *could* be one of them," he said. "We haven't really considered Debbie, but we know that two people were involved. At least two people."

"That makes it even more imperative to find them. One thing for damned sure—J.J. isn't in on it. He could easily be a victim."

Mo had been waiting for them to finish before she spoke. "Someone could go back out to the cemetery where we found Richard and Wendy. And someone else should head back to the Haunted Mausoleum. Cover both old haunts."

Van Camp nodded. "All right, I'll take officers out to the mausoleum. I have a pretty firm grasp of the place now. And we already have an all-points bulletin out on a dark SUV with Horsepower tires. Oh, and by the way, Jimmy doesn't own an SUV. He drives a Chevy."

"Good." Aidan nodded, feeling a sense of relief. "We'll take the old cemetery that borders Sleepy Hollow Cemetery," Aidan said. He glanced at Mo as they began walking toward his car. "I just have a feeling...."

"What?"

"It all goes back to *Lizzie grave.*"

They reached his car and got in, Rollo clambering into the backseat. Logan was preparing to follow them. "Can you have Jane trace Sondra Burke's lineage?" Mo asked.

"Sondra was from here?"

"Her family goes back a long way, but...I'm thinking she might have been related to the Highsmith family. Which would have meant—"

"That *she* went back to Lizzie—Major Andre's daughter—as well."

Mo nodded. "Lizzie grave, Highsmith, Continental currency. Do you think—"

"That the Continental currency could be in Lizzie's

grave?" Aidan finished. He pulled out his phone and asked Jane to get on it immediately.

"Aidan, what if it has something to do with the grave itself?" Mo asked. "Wouldn't the killers have gotten to it by now?"

"They might have been missing the last piece of the puzzle. Or…it could've been too much of a risk. But maybe they were getting rid of any and all Highsmith descendants," he said.

"J.J.!" she whispered.

He turned to her, a concerned expression on his face. "Well, we're headed there now," he said. He called Logan and conveyed their thoughts. Logan was calling Adam Harrison; he'd get the proper clearance to tear the old graveyard apart and exhume a few bodies.

Aidan glanced at Mo again.

He was definitely falling in love. She was beautiful, engaging, honest.

And they could be together and even work together. True, he worked in the city. She'd left the city for a little peace.

But this life was what she'd found. Maybe she needed to realize she'd come here trying to ease her turmoil. She'd tried to escape a particular place. Whereas he'd tried to run away from the strange talent that could allow him to be the most helpful—and even save lives.

Maybe he could make her see that they'd both been running.

And perhaps they could both stop running. Together.

She looked at him. "What?" she asked.

He shook his head. "I'm just thinking."

"About the graveyard?"

"About you—but I *am* going to think about the graveyard and the mausoleums now."

He drove down the side street.

"There's no SUV," Mo noted.

"Someone could have gotten them here, knocked out with chloroform and then moved the vehicle."

"Do you really think he always kills them when he first takes them?" Mo asked quietly. "That would mean— Well, maybe no hope. You told me last night that you were certain Sondra was killed before she was taken to the tomb and...beheaded."

Aidan inhaled. "Yes, I said that. But I don't know for sure when they were killed—how long after they were kidnapped. I'm not certain even the M.E. would be able to determine the timing exactly."

Logan parked his car behind them, and as he got out, he handed Aidan two extralarge flashlights, one for him and one for Mo. "It's a big place. I'll go left. If I hear Rollo, I'll know you're on to something."

"We'll take the wall of vaults over here," Aidan said.

Aidan and Mo walked along the vaults together, casting light in all directions. Rollo sniffed and sniffed as Aidan ripped away vines.

"The whole situation doesn't make sense," he mused. "The crew around Richard was definitely in the hotel. We know there are two people, so that means nothing. But since all five were in the hotel at the time, how the hell did one person sneak up on two adults and a child and knock them out?"

"You think Detective Van Camp is wrong—and that Jimmy *is* involved?" Mo asked, sounding a little shocked.

"I'm not sure what I think." His phone rang and he answered it quickly.

"Bingo," Jane said. "Going back to the Civil War. Sondra Burke's great-great-grandfather, Albert Highsmith, was a Union colonel. He left behind a son, Richard Highsmith's however-many-greats grandfather, and two daughters. One didn't marry. The other married Augustus T. Burke. I've got a search going for other descendants, but it seems that the line died out. Other than Richard Highsmith—and Sondra Burke."

"Thanks, Jane," he told her. "I'm not sure how it's going to help tonight—but I suspect it means something. I think it confirms that Andre's descendants are being targeted. Keep checking. See if you can find any connection with anyone else."

"How about Debbie Howell?" she asked.

"Maybe. Can't hurt to look," Aidan said. "But tonight…I'm afraid the killer was after J.J."

"How's it going there?"

"Nothing yet."

"I'll keep in touch," she said, and the ended the call.

"Rollo isn't interested in these vaults," Mo told him. "Should we go up?"

"There's a manageable slope we can get up right there," Aidan said.

They trudged up the hill. Even with his flashlight and the golden cast of the moon, it was dark. Trees surrounded them. And, as if on cue, as if they were in some bizarre B-grade horror movie, a ground fog was rising, swirling around graves and headstones, cherubs and angels.

"There are more vaults in that area, against the next hill," Aidan said. "Let's walk Rollo around there."

"The Bakker mausoleum is here," Mo said. "Where Lizzie's buried."

He nodded. But he doubted Voorhaven and Debbie had been brought here; that would've been too obvious. It was also too easily accessible.

"We're going to have Lizzie exhumed?" Mo asked.

"Yes. I think we have to," he said.

"You don't suppose it was just a place Wendy wanted to bring Richard? Where, perhaps, she meant to give him the gift of his past?"

"I had thought that, but...it's too much of a coincidence that both Richard and Sondra are descendants of the same man—through an illegitimate birth. The child Lizzie had by Andre. And what scares me the most is that J. J. Appleby is now the last of the descendants."

"But someone would have to *know* that. And how would they know—unless Richard or Wendy told them?"

"That's why it had to be someone close," he said.

His phone rang again and he paused to answer it. As he did, he called to Mo, asking her to wait; she and Rollo had walked on to a little hill farther into the graveyard. He watched her for a moment. She seemed to be a beautiful vision in the moonlight, her hair flowing behind her, whirling in the slight breeze that stirred the fog. Graves were all around her, and she stood by a large angel with folded wings that looked down at the earth and wept.

"It's Jane," Jane told him unnecessarily, since he knew the sound of her voice and had recognized her caller ID.

"I found something. Not sure if it means anything."

"What?"

"Tommy Jensen—the owner of the Headless Horse-man Hideaway Restaurant and Bar—has a black SUV. Will is on his way to Jensen's residence now. He'll check it out."

Tommy Jensen?

Well, he'd lived in the area forever. And it would've been damned easy for him to get to the convention center, whisk away his victims and take them into a vault—a vault that was right across the street from his workplace.

He heard Rollo let out a bark, and he looked up; Mo and the dog were still standing on the little hillock that led toward more graves and more cliffs and vaults.

"Aidan, you there?"

"Yes, yes, I'm here. Jane, I know it's late, but find someone who works there, at Tommy Jensen's restau-rant. Find out if he was at work last night or if he was out for any appreciable length of time."

"I'm on it," she said.

He put his cell away. "Mo?"

She wasn't on the rise.

Panic instantly clouded his mind and swept through him.

"Mo!" he shouted. But she'd just been there. Seconds ago she'd been there!

He ran up the hill. "Rollo, Rollo! Here, boy!" No re-sponse from the dog.

He climbed to the top of the hill, certain that he'd see her there. Mo might've thought she'd discovered something. She might have walked a few steps ahead.

But she wasn't there.

Fog puffed and twisted and turned at his feet.

The winged angel monument seemed to weep real tears.

And there was nothing else. No sight of Mo or the dog among the broken stones and crypts before him.

"Mo!" he shouted, and he began to run.

16

Mo opened her eyes. Her head hurt like hell.

For a moment, she was completely disoriented. She was in the dark, pitch-black dark. It took her time to remember. She'd been in the graveyard with Aidan and Rollo. They were looking for J.J., Debbie and Jimmy. Mo was sure that she'd screamed. She must have screamed!

Because one minute she'd been walking, following Rollo, and the next she was falling. It was as if the earth itself gave way beneath her feet.

Maybe she didn't actually scream. Maybe it was just a gasp as the air was sucked out of her lungs.

She tried to move, hopeful that all the places that hurt didn't mean she'd broken any bones. She was sore everywhere, but her limbs seemed to be working. There was dirt all over her. When she looked up, she could see nothing—no moonlight. It was as if she'd been part of a cave-in.

Perhaps she had. *A grave-in,* she thought, and realized her mind was running toward the hysterical.

Alarm seized her then. Rollo! If she'd fallen, he should

have been barking, He should have been going crazy, leading Aidan to her. Unless he'd plunged down, too.

Dread that she fought to dispel seized her.

"Rollo, Rollo, where are you boy?" she called, creeping around in the dark pit. She stared up again—and still saw nothing except the merest glimmer of light from above, where she'd fallen through. But if Rollo was above her, he'd be barking! She eased to her knees.

"Rollo!"

She crawled through dirt and broken stones, pieces of wood—and what she feared was a pile of bones.

But she kept going.

And then she came upon the dog. He had fallen, too. "Rollo, Rollo!"

He didn't respond. She ran her fingers over him to see if he was alive. She found his neck and tried to ascertain any damage. He was still warm.

He can't be dead. He can't be dead! He's knocked out—like I was. He was too good, too loyal, too wonderful a companion to lose!

She had to find out where she was and get help for both of them. She tried shouting. Nothing, not even an echo. She didn't know where she'd fallen and whether she'd rolled when she hit the ground.

She'd had a flashlight.

"I'm here, Rollo, I'm here," she whispered to the dog. "I will never leave you. Except to go for help so I can get you out of here." There were tears forming in her eyes. She had no idea how badly the dog had been hurt. She couldn't feel any blood or obvious broken bones but he wasn't responding to her, either.

She began running her fingers over the ground, looking for the flashlight. She nearly shrieked as something crawled over her hand.

Rat, she told herself.

She'd fallen into a vault. She was surrounded by the dead. In the dark.

She closed her eyes—although she could see nothing. She wasn't afraid of the dead, she reminded herself.

No, but you are *terrified of this kind of darkness!* a voice inside her mocked.

"I could use the dead right now, Rollo. Someone I know—or don't know!—who could help us get out of here."

She kept groping around for the flashlight. As she did, she paused. She heard a sound—like something being dragged along the ground.

She almost cried out but stopped herself.

Jimmy and Debbie and J. J. Appleby were missing. *And the killer might have brought them here.*

She crept forward, still feeling for her flashlight— and then she found it. As she clutched it, she looked behind her, blinking. She could see a faint light in the distance.

Coming from where she'd heard the dragging sound.

Her fingers tightened around her own light. She didn't turn it on. In the darkness she inched closer to the source of the light, which was somewhat downhill.

She hit a crumbling wall of earth, but there was a fairly large ill-defined hole that let her look through.

And when she did, she caught her breath. She could see by pale light into the vault just below her and to the right. There was no altar, but there was a low-lying tomb with a large stone slab.

Beside it rested a hatchet and a knife.

And slumped over by the altar was J. J. Appleby. They'd come to find J.J.

And she had.

"She's gone. Vanished. Disappeared!" Aidan said into the phone. "She was here—and now she's not. I'm going over every inch and I can't find her. It's impossible! She and Rollo. Just gone, as if the earth swallowed them up. Which means the earth *did* swallow them up. I need a search party here, Logan. I need everyone. We have to find her!"

"On the way," Logan assured him. "I'll get Van Camp and half the force up here, too."

"Get the whole force!" Aidan knew he had to get control of himself. If he didn't, his lack of competence, of composure, could get her killed.

He called Jane on a hunch.

"I was about to phone you. I reached one of the cooks. Tommy Jensen was there last night to open, but then she didn't see him again. He left the bar in Abby's hands. She's his main bartender."

"Yes, I know. Did Will and Sloan get him at his house?"

"No. He wasn't there, Aidan. They're on their way to the cemetery now. Don't worry, we'll find Mo."

He wished he could believe her. As he slipped his phone back into his pocket, he noticed that he was standing on the highest point of the hill; he could see across to Tommy Jensen's. There was a light on inside.

He called Logan. "Get everyone looking over here—right by the giant weeping angel with the folded wings. I'm trying a different route."

"Aidan?"

"I'll just be a few minutes," Aidan said.

"What—"

"Trust me. That's what Krewe members do, right?"

Digging at the hole with her bare hands wasn't easy but Mo was persistent. Of course, it would've been *somewhat* easier if she hadn't been trying to avoid any noise. She knew that the crypt extended farther in a direction she couldn't see from where she crouched. That was where the light came from—someone had left a lantern there. It illuminated the place where J.J. lay on the floor.

She didn't see Debbie Howell or Jimmy Voorhaven. And, she didn't see blood on the axe or the knife or the tomb.

She kept clawing away at the hole in the earth, making it larger and larger.

There was movement below her. She could see that someone or something was creating shadows in the vault—a vault like any other. Shelves of coffins on both sides, old, decaying and chipped.

She and Rollo had gone by every vault on the lower level! Rollo would have known J.J.'s scent; he would have barked furiously to tell them J.J. was there.

And then she understood. The killer had come here *after* that. Maybe, since he'd been bold enough to walk through the Haunted Mausoleum with a body and a severed head, he'd been bold enough to come here when he knew they were searching the graveyard.

She continued to claw at the earth. Eventually, she'd get through.

Then what? Attack with a killer flashlight?

She leaned forward to see more of the vault. She saw a leg extended toward her, an adult leg.

Debbie or Jimmy?

She couldn't tell.

Suddenly, her excavating worked—far better than she'd intended. A massive block of earth wrenched free and, to her horror, she slipped through the opening and fell several feet, landing on the hard ground again. She gasped for breath, then raised her head.

There was Debbie, lying on the floor, Jimmy a few yards away.

She'd found the missing.

Were they still alive?

Or was she too late? And too close, with no weapon, alone and about to join them? Because the killer was either there...or about to come back.

Aidan ran down the hills to the lower level, then tripped and slid down the last one, landing on his ass. He scrambled to his feet and cut around the little group of trees that led to the main road. It was past midnight, so there was almost no traffic. He ran across the road and headed straight to the restaurant.

Halloween greeted him. Spiders and skeletons and silly grinning cats.

Yes, the place had been set up well.

He slammed his fists against the glass door. There'd been light in the restaurant, and he was sure that, as he approached, he'd seen movement.

But of course, a killer wasn't going to politely open the door to a cop banging on it like a madman.

"Aidan, do you hear someone screaming for help in

there?" he asked himself out loud. "Why, yes, Aidan, I think I do!"

He ripped off his coat and wrapped it around his arm, then made use of his Glock, too, slamming the glass so hard it broke on his first try. Knocking the splintered glass aside, he found the two door bolts, turned them and burst into the restaurant.

It was dark, except for that glimmer of light, the one he'd noticed earlier. Macabre images in plastic and paper hung everywhere. Skeletons seemed to dance on the bar. He moved through the bar and seating area, and hurried to the kitchen in back, hoping he hadn't taken so long that Tommy Jensen had managed to escape.

He ran into the kitchen, the source of the light. Where the outer area had been dark and filled with creepy-crawlies to celebrate the season, the kitchen was bright and seemed even brighter because the light was reflected by all the steel and chrome. He didn't see anyone. Swearing, he tore around two workstations.

The back door stood open.

But then, something made him turn. It was as if he'd felt a hand on his shoulder.

He saw the walk-in refrigerator.

Striding toward it, he grabbed the massive handle and yanked it open.

And there was Tommy Jensen, facing him with a frying pan. In a furious burst of rage, Tommy charged him.

He rammed into Aidan; Aidan threw him off and before Tommy could charge again, Aidan lifted his Glock in both hands and aimed it at him. "Where are they?" he raged.

"I don't know what the hell you're talking about!"

Tommy shouted back. "I'm just working in my restaurant that you're destroying!"

Aidan moved slowly and steadily toward him.

"I intend to put this gun down your throat and hold it there—after I shoot both of your kneecaps and your groin."

"You won't! You can't! They'll fire your ass. They'll put you in jail. And you know what happens to cops in jail— Hell, you won't be worth flypaper when they're done!" Tommy mocked him. "You don't have anything on me, you—"

"When they open your SUV, Tommy, they're going to find a costume stolen from the Haunted Mausoleum. And there'll be blood all over it. I don't know if you or your partner killed Richard and Wendy, but you sure as hell killed Sondra!"

"You're full of it!"

His denial was firm. Aidan's mind raced as he took another step toward Tommy.

"Tell him, Tommy. Tell him."

Aidan realized that the ghost of Richard Highsmith was standing behind him. But Tommy didn't see him, couldn't see him.

"You know, the man you killed is here, Tommy. And he's going to make your life a living hell if you don't tell the truth."

"Bull!" Tommy scoffed.

But then a pork loin went flying off a shelf. Followed by a leg of lamb.

And a cut of roast beef. It flew into Tommy's face. Richard was learning to be an effective ghost—one with good aim, at that.

Tommy fell onto his knees. He ducked and screamed when a pound of bacon came his way.

"Stop, stop, stop!" he cried. "The…Anderson vault… it's hard to find. That's where… I think… It's for the boy. You should hurry."

Aidan stared at him. "Hurry? God, tell me you didn't kill them yet!"

"I didn't even know they were there yet, I swear it!"

"What?"

Tommy laughed, a sickly sound. "Did you think *I* was behind all this? Really? Hell, the things a man will do for what he wants in life!" He laughed again, a laugh filled with self-mockery. "The things a desperate man will do for a woman. I don't even believe it myself."

Aidan barely took the time to close and lock the refrigerator door.

In a strange way, it almost made sense.

Mo rolled; she hit Detective Voorhaven's leg and reached out to touch his throat. He was alive. She crawled over to Debbie. Placing her fingers on Debbie's throat, she heard her make a noise, a sort of moan.

"Debbie, wake up! We have to get out of here," she said. "Debbie! You're in a vault."

"A vault," Debbie said, opening her eyes. "Jimmy… J.J.?"

"Debbie, come on! The killer—he's coming back!"

"What about Jimmy?" she asked.

"He's alive."

"He is?"

"Yes, but he can't help us. He's out cold, Debbie. Let's start moving. We have to get J.J. out of here first."

She pulled Debbie to her feet.

And only then did she see that Debbie was holding something in her hand. A big white table napkin. Labeled Mystic Magic.

And it was drenched with something. *Chloroform.*

Debbie had not been knocked out herself. She'd been *faking it,* aware that someone was coming close. She'd lured Mo down here, just like a fly to a spider's web.

But Debbie couldn't have been the one to kill Sondra. She'd been at the hotel last night with Jimmy—and under surveillance.

"What are you doing?" Mo asked her.

"Securing my future," Debbie said. "Would you please stand still? I don't really want to hurt you—and it won't hurt with the chloroform. You'll just go to sleep. And you're such a good person, Mo. You'll wind up with the angels, I'm sure.

"Decent, beautiful Mo! Back when we were all kids, you whisked in and out from the city, and whenever you deigned to come here, the world stopped—everyone always wanted to see you! Well, I'm sorry. I didn't really wish you ill, but you're here, which leaves me no choice. Here's how it's going to work. Jimmy has to kill you and the boy—and leave me crying and hysterical, because, of course, I managed to wake up and kill him before he could kill me."

Mo stared at her incredulously. "How stupid do you think the police are?"

Debbie laughed. "Pretty stupid. My partner carried out part of my plan last night, right in front of you all. You idiots—you and Grace and everyone—just watched him go by. And the cops? Hopeless. They still don't have a clue."

"Your partner?"

"You really have no idea, do you? Well, I won't let you die in the dark— That's funny, huh? Tommy. Tommy Jensen. That man would do anything for me. The rest of you girls ignored him all his life. Tommy wasn't sexy. Tommy wasn't cool. Well, he wanted someone to love. He got me. And when I told him what we'd achieve in the end…he knew he'd get me *and* everything he could possibly want."

Mo hunkered down and carefully lifted J.J. from the stone tomb as she spoke. "Listen, Debbie, if you haven't actually killed anyone yet—if Tommy did the killing— then you can work out a deal. You can still have a life."

"Oh, I intend to have a life." Debbie chuckled. "I'll be so far away from here they'll never find me."

"Wendy was your friend," Mo said. "And you love J.J."

"I used Wendy. Well, actually, the plan came from Wendy, although she didn't realize it. After she told me what she'd discovered, all I had to do was get rid of anyone with a connection to the Highsmith name. And when J.J.'s gone, they're all gone."

"Debbie, you went to the convention center and helped kidnap Wendy and J.J. How did you know they were going to be there?"

"Oh, Wendy confided in me, of course! She told me everything she'd researched and found out—and she told me she was going to see Richard and give it all to him. They'd been talking over the past few months. She'd been in New York and she'd run into him on the street and he told her he'd been thinking about her and…well, there's nothing as nauseating as rekindled love."

"How did you get into the greenroom at the conference center?"

"Through the back, of course. Tommy had arranged to make some food deliveries—for friends of his in the business. He didn't have a contract to supply food himself. That could've been traced. We both know the center well enough, and it's actually pretty easy to get in if you're doing food delivery. All that security didn't make a bit of difference," she gloated. "But that's the thing. People think they're secure—and as soon as they trust in the technology of a place like that, they forget that other people might know about codes and security, too. Or be able to figure them out..." She chuckled. "I dropped by to see Bari Macaby a few weeks ago and went out for a smoke with her—and I don't even smoke!"

"Even if you planned this to the nth degree, you're not getting away with it. The cops are going to find you here," Mo said.

"I'm planning on it. Remember? After Jimmy killed you and J.J., and I had to kill him? Oh, and I guess your dumb mutt will be collateral damage. I heard some screeching a while ago—sounded like a dying dog to me," Debbie taunted.

The words were like a sucker punch, but Mo knew she was being baited and she refused to fall for it. Debbie had a hatchet within easy reach, and she already had the knife. But Mo had her flashlight—and a desperate will to survive.

"I still don't understand. Why?" Mo asked.

"Why? Because of Lizzie's grave, of course. And the fact that if there's a living descendant, what's inside the grave would go to him or her."

"It's the Continental currency, isn't it?" Mo asked, the certainty rushing in. "You're not psychotic or jealous or in any way mentally impaired, are you, Debbie? It was about money. By the way, Aidan knows all this."

"About the Continental currency? No one does. At least not as much as I know."

"Yes, they do," Mo said. Except that she wasn't sure exactly *what* Debbie knew.

"You're lying!"

"I'm telling you the truth. Sondra Burke was researching the story."

"Yes, she was, wasn't she? I heard her speaking once—and she was telling her audience about the currency disappearing. I didn't know she'd mentioned it to you."

Mo laughed. "She was going to give you a job, to help her work on the story. But you'd already guessed some of it, hadn't you? When Lizzie—the daughter— was buried, someone buried the money with her. The family had it all along, and it was buried with Lizzie for safekeeping until the war was over. But it was never dug back up. I'm presuming that a family member— killed in the Civil War—put it in Lizzie's grave. And afterward, only rumors of it existed. I think, however, that reading soldiers' letters and memoirs, Sondra figured it out."

"Well, well, how ironic. But not only did Sondra know about the currency, she would've had a claim on it. Yes, I'd heard about the Highsmith connection, distant though it was, because she was quite proud of it. I heard her discuss her revered great-great-grandfather, the colonel, in an interview, and eventually I put two and two together—with Wendy's help."

Debbie shook her head. "You look skeptical, Mo, but I suppose you thought you knew everything about local history. According to Sondra, the currency was buried with Lizzie. We're all about Sleepy Hollow and the Revolution here—seems like we forget that the years went on and there was more history." She shook her head in mock dismay. "I first read about it when I found an article in some obscure journal about a Bakker who'd been killed during the fighting at Gettysburg. It was said that he told his friends about a 'buried treasure' for his family back home. Do enough research, and you just never know what you'll discover. Too bad I can't dig up the whole place, really."

"News flash, Debbie. Continental currency isn't good these days."

"I can tell you what it's worth on the collectors' market," Debbie said. "I looked into it."

"But you don't have it yet, do you? And if you were to put it on the market, you'd be picked up in seconds flat. Things like that don't go unnoticed."

"Oh, trust me, there's an underground market. Money makes the world go 'round, Mo. I learned that the hard way. You all had nice parents. I had assholes. I've made my own way in this town forever and I'm ready to shake off the dust of this place. But I had to make sure the Highsmith heirs were all gone first. And Wendy, because she figured it out. Plus, she was getting back together with Richard."

"And then there's J.J.," Mo breathed.

Debbie nodded. "I would've had a couple of options. J.J. loves me. I could've kept him around and used him—you know, in case something went wrong and people thought the money belonged to the kid. I'd be in control of it!"

"Not if you kill him!" Mo pointed out.

"Well, another option is that I can make myself look like a hero by saving J.J.—and making Van Camp look like a homicidal cop!"

"And you involved Tommy."

"Easy as pie. I guess you never paid much attention to Tommy. Growing up, no one ever did. He was a loser. He had acne and he was clueless and awkward. Poor Tommy. He was so willing to get into this scheme with me. So helpful. He even broke into Wendy's for me to steal her computer, and he trashed the place so it wouldn't look obvious. Mo, he thinks he hit pay dirt with me. I haven't decided what I'll do about Tommy. But for now...I convinced him we'd put one over on the cop—and then just walk away."

"I doubt it. They probably have Tommy by now— and he's probably telling them everything."

"He would never betray me. He *wanted* to do all this. He wanted to help me. Mo, he swore he'd do anything for me! I told him I could handle this and that when they found me, I'd convince them it was the detective. Then Aidan could go on thinking that yes, Highsmith's people were involved. Which is exactly what he thinks, you know. I realized that whenever I overheard him talking about what happened—and I made a point of overhearing him. Now it'll all fit together. Aidan will figure they were in on it with the detective. He'll spend the rest of his life wondering, but he'll never prove anything!"

"But Tommy—"

"When they find me here and they know this has all

taken place when Tommy wasn't anywhere nearby—
well, he'll be in the clear."

"So Tommy did what he did out of…love. Some
screwed-up, twisted kind of love."

"You could say that. But I can tell you he started to
like it. Killing—even just hearing a killing that you or-
chestrated—is exhilarating! And maybe we'll share the
treasure. That's what I promised him, anyway. But…
we'll see."

"You said Wendy helped you put it all together…."
Mo decided to keep her talking. It worked in mystery
novels and suspense movies—and at this point she had
nothing to lose.

"Yeah, it was just a matter of sorting out all the
pieces. See, Sondra knew about the currency and she
knew the tale about Lizzie, but like I told you, she didn't
know who Lizzie had become. The little girl, Lizzie, I
mean, who married into the Highsmith family. I did—
because of Wendy! Sweet Wendy, who loved to con-
fide in me! Anyway, I'm probably running out of time.
They'll come here, and they have to find you and the
kid and the detective dead—and me bleeding."

"You've not only betrayed Wendy, you're an idiot,"
Mo said flatly. "Aidan's figured all of this out."

Debbie lifted the knife. "No. He thinks I'm beautiful and kind. Ask him! You know, I wanted to be nice
to you, Mo. You were always decent—at least before.
But I guess you're as big a jerk as the others." Debbie
started to move her arm; Mo eluded her, dashing to the
other side of the low flat tomb.

In her flurry of movement, she kicked Jimmy Voorhaven's arm.

She thought he stirred.

Debbie made another lunge for Mo, and Mo jumped back against the tomb again.

Then Jimmy started to move in earnest. Debbie swore—and raised the knife to bring it down on him. Mo started to fly at her, but she didn't have to. She heard a roar as Rollo came running out of the darkness and shadows. He leaped at Debbie, knocking her off her feet. But Debbie still had the knife and Rollo's throat was vulnerable.

"Here! Rollo, here!" Mo commanded. She wouldn't risk a human life for her dog, but neither would she let him die needlessly.

He scrambled back to her—just in time to miss the blade of the knife.

Debbie staggered to her feet at the same moment Jimmy did. He reached for his gun, but it was gone. She'd apparently had the sense to disarm him. He was weaving as he stood, still drugged, barely conscious.

"What...what..." he muttered.

The hatchet remained by the tomb. Mo jumped for it just as another sound caused the earth to shudder; it was the iron door of the vault being shoved in.

For a second, Mo saw nothing but the silhouette of a man, larger than life, standing in the doorway.

"It's him! He's the killer!" Debbie cried, pointing at Jimmy.

"No, no. Don't...don't shoot me," Jimmy said, still confused.

"It was him. He forced me here, he—"

"Oh, get over it!" Aidan snapped. "Debbie Holloway, you're under arrest for the murders of Richard Highsmith, Wendy Appleby and Sondra Burke. And for the kidnapping of—"

He didn't finish. Debbie had apparently decided that suicide by cop was going to be better than the life she would encounter in prison.

Shrieking, she rushed Aidan with the knife high in her hands.

He didn't intend to let her die so easily. He stooped down just as she reached him, letting her fly over his head onto the dirt path beyond. Then he hurried toward her, knocked the knife away with his foot and thrust her hands back to cuff her.

She began spouting all kinds of furious and vindictive words at him. He ignored her, walking back into the tomb, seeking Mo. She saw that he hadn't come alone; Van Camp, Logan, the rest of Aidan's Krewe and other cops were out there, too.

Aidan paused in front of Jimmy Voorhaven.

"You going to be okay?" he asked.

"Yeah." Jimmy sagged against the tomb behind him.

Then Aidan knelt by J.J., and Mo heard his sigh of relief.

After that, he walked over to Mo. He took her by her shoulders and looked into her eyes. "Mo?"

"I'm okay!" she said. "Really dirty, sore, but... Tommy. Aidan, she did this with Tommy."

"I know. He and I had a little talk." He smiled at her and dusted dirt from her face. "A lot has happened since you went down your rabbit hole," he told her.

Rollo barked. Mo began shaking.

She was alive. Her dog was alive.

And Aidan was standing there, holding her as if she were the most precious thing in the world. She threw her arms around him and held him close for a minute. Then she drew back. "We need help in here. J.J. and

Jimmy— Well, Jimmy's up now, but J.J.'s still out, and if he wakes up in a tomb again—"

Aidan turned and went straight to the fallen boy. He picked him up gently and walked out of the tomb. Mo followed.

Van Camp had Debbie's arm in a tight grip. She was still cursing, but he ignored her, calmly chanting her rights.

As Mo went with Aidan to take J.J. to a waiting ambulance, she saw something beautiful.

A man and a woman. Richard and Wendy.

They were ahead of Van Camp and Debbie on the path, holding hands and gazing at each other. The man seemed to smile.

When Debbie passed, he extended a spectral foot.

Debbie sprawled onto the gravel path, literally eating dirt.

The pair turned toward them. Mo could just hear Richard. "Thank you, my old friend," he called to Aidan.

Aidan lifted a hand. "No, thank *you*," he said softly.

"I'll be going to the hospital with J.J.," Mo told him.

"I'll be right with you," he said. "Always."

Epilogue

Mo ran down the stairs, followed by Rollo. She was, Aidan had decided, more than attractive. She was beautiful, not just in her face and form, but in her voice, her movements—in her life and her vibrancy.

"People will be over soon," she told him. "And I still have so much to do—" She broke off when the doorbell rang. She ran over, looked through the little window and opened the door. Grace had arrived with Jimmy Voorhaven and J.J.

Aidan was still astonished that it had all worked out so quickly. Mo had been spending a lot of time at the hospital, which meant that Grace kept going there, too. Jimmy was also in the hospital, and Grace had begun splitting her visits between Jimmy and J.J.

Mo had told Aidan that Grace—being Grace—hadn't messed around. She'd gone straight after Jimmy and had sex a lot faster than Mo had managed. Grace and Jimmy were already engaged. Mo was creating the invitations for their wedding, which would take place that summer—only four months away.

It was amusing and a little worrisome. They were head over heels within a week. Grace had J.J. living with her and was working with social services to be his foster parent and, hopefully, adopt him one day.

It was great for J.J., who needed plenty of love and care. Grace turned out to be the perfect guardian for him—patient, relaxed, honest.

In fact, that was part of why Mo was so excited about today. She had a present for J.J., one that Grace—and Jimmy—would love, too.

But right now they were waiting for everyone. Purbeck was coming with Van Camp, Jillian Durfey, Taylor Branch and the security trio. Logan, Sloan, Will and Jane were, too. And they hadn't forgotten Phil and Ron, who'd actually invited themselves when they'd learned Mo was having a last-day-in-town-for-a-while dinner.

Mo needn't have worried about getting everything ready. Once Jane was there, she organized everyone, assigning tasks, and in another hour, they were all seated in the huge, old-fashioned dining room, the chairs around the table a little close, but that was fine. Mo had prepared a roast and all kinds of vegetables and side dishes, and everyone who'd been involved with the case was there.

Once dinner was over, talk turned to the case that had brought them all together.

"I really have no hard feelings," Jillian assured Aidan, not for the first time.

"You were on the right track all along," Logan noted. "It had to have been someone close. We were just looking at Richard, not Wendy."

Will was off with J.J. in another room, teaching him card tricks, so it seemed safe to speak about the events. No one wanted to distress him by bringing up what had happened to his mother—or Debbie, of whom he'd been so fond.

"Wait!" Jillian said. "I still don't understand. How did the chloroform get in my drawer?"

Logan stepped in to explain. "Debbie actually bragged about that. We—all of us in law enforcement—were so stupid. Anyone could have done it. She just went to the hotel and pretended to be a guest. Ironically, she did become a guest later on. But that day she took the elevator up to your floor and got a passkey off a maid's cart. You have to remember that until Will set up his cameras, there was no surveillance there."

"I hope she rots in hell!" Jillian spat.

"For someone like her, prison will be hell on earth," Aidan assured her.

"And what about creepy Tommy?" Grace asked. She shivered, and Jimmy placed an arm around her shoulders.

"Tommy. Who knows the real truth about Tommy, except that he'll be locked away for the rest of his life?" Logan said. "I can understand that a man like him could be taken in by a woman like Debbie, but still…he went into the whole scheme, ready for blood and death and whatever she called for."

"Did you get the treasure from Lizzie's grave?" Jillian asked. She lowered her voice. "Did you get the money—the Continental money or whatever it was—for J.J.?"

Aidan nodded. "We had the body exhumed within a few days. The notes were tucked into the coffin. They'll be offered to various historical societies, but wherever they go, they'll sell for a pretty price, and the money will be set aside for J.J. in a trust."

"I'm sure he'd rather have had his parents," Jillian said sadly.

"I'm sure," Aidan agreed. "We'd all rather have had them alive."

The doorbell rang. Grace started to rise. "I'll get it, Mo."

"No, I will," Mo said, grinning at Aidan. "I'm expecting someone special!"

She hurried out with Rollo at her heels, and came back in again carrying a puppy. It was a floppy-looking thing, almost ugly. Aidan smiled.

"J.J., this is Brian Boru, and he's yours. His mom is one of Rollo's cousins, so our dogs are related. How's that?" Mo asked.

J.J.'s face was bright enough to light up the room. He stared at Mo wide-eyed. "For me, really?" he asked breathlessly.

Grace groaned. "Oh, my God. It's a good thing we're getting married. We'll need two incomes to keep him in food!" She looked at Mo, breaking into a huge grin, and whispered, "Wow, thank you!"

J.J. was excused to play with his new puppy. Rollo, naturally, joined them.

"So, you're really leaving us," Ron said, turning to Mo.

She smiled, raising her glass to him. "Ah, Ron, do any of us ever really leave Sleepy Hollow? I'll just be in the city. Rollo and I are moving in with Aidan, but I'll still own this place and we'll be back all the time."

Ron stood up and nodded at Phil and Grace. "Well, we have a present for you, too," he told her.

He produced a box. She carefully unwrapped and then opened it. "This is so beautiful! Aidan, look, it's

'The Legend of Sleepy Hollow' and 'Rip Van Winkle' and other tales by Washington Irving—with gold-trimmed pages. Oh, guys, this is gorgeous!"

"We were afraid you'd forget us," Phil said. "We wanted to remind you of everything that was good here, too." He gave her an awkward smile. "I know there was a lot of...ugliness, but we don't want you to associate us with all of that."

"Of course not! Friends are one of the best parts of life and I couldn't possibly forget any of you."

Dinner went on until it was time for goodbyes. Aidan didn't have to report in to the New York office tomorrow, but he had to be there early the next day. He'd figured if they left by the afternoon it would be fine.

But when the others left, the second set of arrivals began. Candy and Daniel, of course, who were always at the house or nearby. And then Richard and Wendy showed up. And they began talking to each other in the dining room. The four of them were going deep into history and creating their own party.

"It's a little busy in there," Aidan noted, putting a dish away.

"Not quite our private haven, is it?" she asked. She came over to him, pressing him against the counter and touching his lips in a brief kiss. "You know," she said, slipping her arms around him, "there's an incredible hotel near us, here in Tarrytown. It's the Castle Hotel and Spa and it really looks like a castle. The rooms are gorgeous. And there's room service with things like champagne and chocolate-covered strawberries. We could slip away, and then just come back here in the morning. I'm pretty much packed. There are suites at this place, so Rollo can even have his own little room."

"Sounds...private," he murmured.

She smiled. In another ten minutes, they were leaving, but their guests didn't even notice them.

As he stood by the driver's door, ready to open it, Aidan found himself looking down the river toward Sunnyside, the home Washington Irving had loved so much.

The sun was setting, and the light seemed to be doing strange things.

But he thought he saw Irving standing there, straight and regal, supported by his walking stick, as if he were out for a constitutional.

A train went rumbling by. The vision of Washington Irving lifted his stick at the metal monster, shaking it.

Then he saw Aidan. He smiled and doffed his hat.

Aidan smiled back and waved, then slid into the driver's seat and started the car.

He'd come home. He'd found home.

Sleepy Hollow would remain part of him.

But with Mo...

He would always be home.

* * * * *